PRIVATE L.A.

Jack Morgan is having a bad week. His twin brother is up on a murder charge and determined to frame him for the crime, and one of Jack's clients has just called to report the burnt bodies of four surfers on his beach. But what seems like a random mugging gone wrong soon reveals something far worse – a killer going by the name of No Prisoners is holding the city to ransom. And there's more bad news: Hollywood's golden couple, Thom and Jennifer Harlow, have been kidnapped, along with their adopted children.

PRIVATE L.A.

PRIVATE L.A.

by

James Patterson and Mark Sullivan

Magna Large Print Books
Long Preston, North Yorkshire,
BD23 4ND, England.

British Library Cataloguing in Publication Data.

Patterson, James and Sullivan, Mark
    Private L.A.

      A catalogue record of this book is
      available from the British Library

      ISBN   978-0-7505-4004-9

First published in Great Britain by Century, 2014

Published in Large Print 2015 by arrangement with
Random House Group Ltd.

Magna Large Print is an imprint of Library Magna Books Ltd.

Printed and bound in Great Britain by
T.J. (International) Ltd., Cornwall, PL28 8RW

For Betty Jane
–M. S.

PROLOGUE

NO PRISONERS

One

It was nearing midnight that late-October evening on a dark stretch of beach in Malibu. Five men, lifelong surfers, lost souls, sat around a fire blazing in a portable steel pit set into the sand.

The multimillion-dollar homes up on the fragile cliffs showed no lights save security bulbs. Waves crashed in the blackness beyond the firelight. The wind was picking up, temperature dropping. A storm built offshore.

Facing the fire, four of them with their backs to surfboards stuck in the sand, the men sipped Coronas, passed and sucked on a spliff of Humboldt County's finest.

'Bomber weed, N.P,' choked Wilson, who'd done two tours in Iraq and had come home at twenty-six incapable of love and responsibility, good only for getting high, riding big waves, and thinking profound thoughts. 'With that hit I most assuredly have achieved total clarity of mind. I can see it all, dog. The whole cosmic thing.'

Sitting in the sand across the fire from Wilson, hands stuffed in the pouch pocket of his red L.A. Lakers hoodie, N.P. wore reflector sunglasses despite the late hour. He smiled at Wilson from behind his glasses and scruffy beard, his nostrils flaring, his longish, straw-blond hair fluttering in the wind.

'I second that emotion, Wilson,' N.P. said, and flicked the underside of his cap so it made a snapping sound. His voice was hoarse and hinted at a southern accent.

'Wish I coulda scored weed that righteous in the go-go days before the crash,' said Sandy dreamily as he passed along the joint. 'I would have seen all, slayed the markets, and lived a life of wine, women, song, and that beautiful herb you so graciously brought into our lives, N.P.'

Sandy had lost it all in the Great Recession: Brentwood house, trophy wife, big job running money. These days he tended day bar at the Malibu Beach Inn.

'Those days are frickin' long gone,' said Grinder, barrel-chested, dark tan, dreads. 'Like ancient history, bro. No amount of pissin' and moanin' 'bout it gonna bring back your stack of Benny Franklins, or my board shop.'

Hunter, the fourth surfer, was stubble haired and swarthy. He scowled, hit the spliff, said, 'Ass-backward wrong as usual, Grinder. You wanna bring back that stack a Benjamins, Sandy?'

Sandy stared into the fire. 'Who doesn't?'

Hunter nodded toward N.P. before handing him the roach. 'Like Wilson was saying, N.P., this weed brings perfect vision.'

N.P. smiled again, took the roach and ate it, said, 'What do you see?'

Hunter said, 'Okay, so like we rise up and storm Congress, take 'em all hostage, and hole up in there, you know, the House chamber. We do it the night of the State of the Union Address so they're all in there to begin with, president, generals, frick-

14

in' Supreme Court too. Then we make the whole sorry bunch of 'em hit this weed hard enough and long enough they start talking to each other. Getting stuff done. Tending to business 'stead of bitchin' and cryin' and blamin' about who spent the biggest stack and for what.'

'Speaker of the House hitting it?' Wilson said, laughed.

Grinder chuckled, 'Yeah, on the bong with that sourpuss senator's always trying to shove his morals up your ass. That man would be in touch with his inner freak straight up then.'

'Not a bad idea,' Sandy said, brightening a bit. 'A stoned Congress just might get the country going again.'

'See there, total clarity,' Wilson said, pointing at N.P. before getting a puzzled expression on his face. 'Hey, dog, where you come from, anyway?'

N.P. had showed up about an hour ago, said he'd take a beer or two if they wanted to partake of the best in the state, Cannabis Cup winner for sure.

Smiling now, N.P. turned his sunglasses at Wilson, said, 'I walked down here from the Malibu Shores Sober Living facility.'

They all looked at him a long moment and then started to laugh so hard they cried. 'Frickin' sober living!' Wilson chortled. 'Oh, dog, you got your priorities straight.'

Joining in their laughter, N.P. glanced around beyond and behind the fire, saw that the beach remained deserted, and still no lights in the houses above. He took his chance.

15

He got to his feet. His new friends were still howling.

Nice guys. Harmless, actually.

But N.P. felt not a lick of pity for them.

Two

'N.P.?' Sandy said, wiping his eyes. 'Whazzat stand for, anyway? N.P.?'

'No Prisoners,' N.P. said, hands back in the hoodie's pouch again.

'No Prisoners?' Grinder snorted. 'That some kind of M.C. rap star tag? You famous or what behind them glasses?'

N.P smiled again. 'It's my war name. Sorry, dogs and bros, but a few people have to take it the hard way for people to start listening to us.'

He drew two suppressed Glock 9mms from the pouch of his hoodie.

Wilson saw them first. Soldier instinct took over. The Iraq vet rolled, scrambled, tried to get out of Dodge.

N.P. had figured Wilson would be the one. So he shot him first, at ten yards, a double whack to the base of the head where it met the spine. The vet buckled to the sand, quivered in his own blood.

'*What the...?*' Sandy screamed before the next round caught him in the throat, flattening him.

'Frick, bro,' Grinder moaned as N.P. turned the guns on him. The surfer's hands turned to prayer. 'Don't blaze me, bro.'

The killer's expression revealed nothing as he pulled the trigger of each gun once, punching holes in Grinder's chest.

'You mother-loving son of a...!'

Hunter lunged to tackle him. N.P. stepped off the line of his attack, shot him in the left temple from less than eight inches away. Hunter crashed into the fire, began to burn.

The killer glanced up at the closest homes. Still dark. He pocketed the guns. The wind blew north-west, hard off the Pacific, swirled the beach sand, stung his cheeks as he dragged the other three corpses to the fire and threw them in, facedown. The smell was like when you singe hair, only much, much worse. But that would do it, a nice touch, increase the panic.

N.P got a plastic sandwich bag from his pocket. He crouched, opened it, and shook out what looked like a business card. It landed facedown in the sand. He kicked it under Sandy's leg, picked up six empty 9mm shells, and pocketed them. His beer bottle he took to the ocean, wiped it down, and hurled it out into the water.

Satisfied, he snapped the underside of his Lakers cap, waded into the surf up to his knees. He walked parallel to the beach, toward Pacific Coast Highway, head down into the wind, the salt spray, and the gathering storm.

PART ONE

A VANISHING ACT

Chapter 1

Shortly after midnight, as the first real storm of the season intensified outside, the lovely Guin Scott-Evans and I were sitting on the couch at my place, watching a gas fire, drinking a first-class bottle of Cabernet, and good-naturedly bantering over our nominees for sexiest movie scene ever.

For the record, Guin brought the subject up.

'*The Postman Always Rings Twice*,' she announced. 'Remake.'

'Of all the movies ever made?' I asked.

'Certainly,' she said, all seriousness. 'Hands down.'

'Care to defend your nomination?'

She crossed her arms, nodded, smiled. 'With great pleasure, Mr. Morgan.'

I liked Guin. The last time I'd seen her, back in January, the actress had been in trouble, and I had served as her escort and guard at the Golden Globes the night she won Best Performance by an Actress in a Supporting Role. Despite the danger she was in, or perhaps because of it, a nice chemistry had developed between us. But at the time, relationships were not clear-cut in her life or mine, and nothing beyond mutual admiration had developed.

Earlier that evening, however, I had run into her leaving Patina, a first-class restaurant inside the Walt Disney Concert Hall complex, where she'd been attending a birthday party for her agent. We had a glass of wine at the bar and laughed as if the Golden Globes had been just last week, not ten months before.

She was leaving the next day, going on location in London, with much too much to do. But somehow we ended up back at my place, with a new bottle of wine open, and debating the sexiest movie scene ever.

'*The Postman Always Rings Twice?*' I said skeptically.

'I'm serious, it's amazing, Jack,' Guin insisted. 'It's that scene where they're in the kitchen alone, Jessica Lange and Jack Nicholson, the old Greek's young wife and the drifter. At first you think Nicholson's forcing himself on her. They wrestle. He throws her up on the butcher block covered with flour and all her baking things. And she's saying, "No! No!"'

'But then Nicholson comes to his senses, figures he misread her, backs off. And Lange's lying there panting, flour on her flushed cheeks. There's this moment when your understanding of the situation seems certain.

'Then Lange says, "Wait. Just wait a second," before she pushes the baking stuff off the butcher block, giving herself enough room to give in to all her pent-up desires.'

'Okay,' I allowed, remembering it. 'That was sexy, really sexy, but I don't know if it's the best of all time.'

'Oh, no?' Guin replied. 'Beat it. Be honest, now. Give me a window into your soul, Jack Morgan.'

I gave a mock shiver. 'What? Trying to expose

22

me already?'

'In due time,' she said, grinned, poured herself another glass. 'Go ahead. Spill it. Name that scene.'

'I don't think I can pick just one,' I replied honestly.

'Name several, then.'

'How about *Body Heat,* the entire movie? I saw it over in Afghanistan. As I remember it, William Hurt and Kathleen Turner are, well, scorching, but maybe that was because I'd been in the desert far too long by that point.'

Guin laughed, deep, unabashed. 'You're right. They were scorching, and humid too. Remember how their skin was always damp and shiny?'

Nodding, I poured the rest of the wine into my glass, said, *'The English Patient* would be up there too. That scene where Ralph Fiennes and Kristin Scott Thomas are in that room in the heat with the slats of light, and they're bathing together?'

She raised her glass. 'Certainly a contender. How about *Shampoo?'*

I shot her a look of arch amusement, said, 'Warren Beatty in his prime.'

'So was Julie Christie.'

There was a moment between us. Then my cell phone rang.

Guin shook her head. I glanced at the ID: Sherman Wilkerson.

'Damn,' I said. 'Big client. Big, big client. I ... I've got to take this, Guin.'

She protested, 'But I was just going to nominate the masquerade ball in *Eyes Wide Shut.'*

Shooting Guin an expression of genuine shared

23

sympathy and remorse, I clicked ANSWER, turned from her, said, 'Sherman. How are you?'

'Not very damned well, Jack,' Wilkerson shot back. 'There are sheriff's deputies crawling the beach in front of my house, and at least four dead bodies that I can see.'

I looked at Guin, flashed ruefully on what might have been, said, 'I'm on my way right now, Sherman. Ten minutes tops.'

Chapter 2

Speeding north into Malibu on the Pacific Coast Highway, driving the VW Touareg I use when the weather turns sloppy, I could still smell Guin, still hear her words to me before the cab took her away: 'No more dress rehearsals, Jack.'

Pulling up to Sherman Wilkerson's gate, I felt like the village idiot for leaving Guin, wanted to spin around and head for her place in Westwood.

Wilkerson, however, had recently hired my firm, Private Investigations, to help reorganize security at Wilkerson Data Systems offices around the world. I parked in an empty spot in front of the screen of bougainvillea that covered the wall above the dream home Wilkerson had bought the year before for his wife, Elaine. Tragically, she'd died in a car wreck a month after they moved in.

Head ducked in the driving rain, I rang the bell at the gate, heard it buzz, went down steep wet stairs onto a terrace that overlooked the turbulent beach. Waves thundered against the squalling wind that buffeted various L.A. Sheriff's vehicles converged on a crime scene lit by spotlights.

'They're in the fire, four dead men, Jack,' said Wilkerson, who'd come out a sliding glass door in a raincoat, hood up. 'You can't see them now because of the tarps, but they're there. I saw them through my binoculars when the first cop showed up with a flashlight.'

'Anyone come talk to you?'

'They will,' he said, close enough that I could see his bushy gray brows beneath the hood. 'Crime scene abuts my property.'

'But you have nothing to worry about, right?'

'You mean did *I* kill them?'

'Crime scene abuts your property.'

'I was at work with several people on my management team until after midnight, got here around one, looked down on the beach, saw the flashlight, used the binoculars, called you,' Wilkerson said.

'I'll take a look,' I said.

'Unless it's dire, tell me about it all in the morning, would you? I'm exhausted.'

'Absolutely, Sherman,' I said, shook his hand. 'And one of my people is coming in behind me, in case you have the driveway alert on.'

He nodded. I headed to the staircase to the beach, watched Wilkerson go into his house and turn on a light, saw moving boxes piled everywhere.

Either poor Sherman was leaving soon, or he'd never really arrived.

Chapter 3

My cell rang when I was just shy of the yellow tape.

It was Carl Mentone. Also known as the Kid, a twenty-something hipster, tech geek, and surveillance specialist I hired last year in one of my smarter moves.

'You here already?' I asked.

'Up on Wilkerson's terrace,' the Kid replied. 'Eagle's perspective.'

'Shoot what you can in this slop. Record what I'm transmitting.'

'Smooth on both counts, Jacky-boy. I've got a lens hood, no need for infrared with the lights, and I'm already getting a feed from your camera to the hard drive.'

'Don't call me Jacky-boy,' I said, clicked the phone, saw a sheriff's deputy coming to the tape, and shifted the pen clipped to my breast pocket. The Kid and I now saw the same things.

'We're asking people to stay away,' the deputy said.

I showed him my badge. 'Jack Morgan. Who's commanding?'

The deputy got lippy. 'You may have clout over at LAPD, but...'

I spotted an old friend moving out from under the tarps, called, 'Harry?'

Captain Harry Thomas ran the sheriff's homicide unit. I'd known him since I was a young teenager. Sixty-two now, the homicide commander had been a friend of my father's, back before my dear old dad crossed the line, bilked clients, and ended up dying in prison. There was a time, when the old man was going downhill, and before I joined the marines, when Harry Thomas was one of the few people who seemed to care what happened to me.

Harry's craggy face broke into a grin when he saw me. 'Jack? What the hell brings Private out here in the middle of a storm?'

Ducking the rope past the miffed deputy, I said, 'Four dead bodies burning in a fire, and my client owns the house right above us.'

'Public beach,' Harry said, glanced at Wilkerson's home. 'Thin reason to be inside my crime scene, unless your client wants to confess?'

'He's clean. But now that I've had to leave my incredibly lovely date in the lurch and I'm all the way here, I'm curious. Can I take a look?'

Harry hesitated, said, 'No funny business, Jack.'

'Me?'

'Uh-huh,' the homicide captain said, not buying it. 'Boots and gloves.'

A few moments later, wearing protective blue paper booties and latex gloves, I ducked under the tarp system that had been erected over the crime scene. The space stank of burned flesh. The victims, four men in après-surf wear, lay facedown in the wet ashes of a fire pit. Forensics techs were documenting the scene. I got out a tissue and pretended to blow my nose before passing it over the camera pen on my lapel to remove any raindrops.

Harry said, 'Dog walker found them. Crazy to be out in this storm. Lucky for us, though. We managed to protect it within an hour of when we think the shootings went down. Illegal to have a fire here with or without a portable pit. It was like they were begging for trouble. People are very touchy around here about the rules.'

'C'mon, Harry,' I said. 'You think someone double-tapped each of these guys over fire pit rules? This looks professional. A planned hit.'

'Yeah,' he admitted, distaste on his lips. 'Looks that way to me too.'

'IDs?'

'All locals. All die-hard surfers. One's a former investment guy, tends bar now down the highway. Another's a young vet who came back from Iraq with some issues. The other two: still waiting. They weren't carrying wallets like the first two.'

'Armed robbery gone bad?'

'If one of them was carrying something valuable enough, I suppose.'

'Or they all shared something in common, a secret, maybe, and this was revenge,' I replied, squatting to look at the sand around the corpses' feet. 'Rain and wind must have hammered this place. No tracks, no drag marks.'

'That's all she wrote until the lab work tells me more,' the homicide captain said. 'But about that, Jack: I won't be keeping you in the loop.'

In an easy manner, Harry was telling me that, old friend or not, my time was up. I was about to rise from my crouch when I noticed a mustard-yellow card sticking out from beneath the dead bartender's leg.

Before anyone could tell me not to, I scuttled forward and snatched it up.

'Hey, what the hell are you doing?' Harry demanded.

Back of the card was empty. I flipped it to face my camera pen, paused, handed it to a scowling Harry Thomas, and saw what was written in eighteen-point letters:

NO PRISONERS

Chapter 4

The killer who called himself No Prisoners drove an Enterprise rent-a-car toward a set of automatic doors in the City of Commerce in southeast Los Angeles. He pressed an app on his iPhone and the doors began to rise, revealing a large, high-ceilinged, cement-floored work space that had once housed a diesel truck repair shop, with three additional roll-up doors at the far end.

He took the place in at a glance: two white delivery vans, six cots, a makeshift kitchen, four metal folding tables pushed together to create one large surface covered with computer equipment, and several tool and die machines, including a lathe, a grinder, and a welding torch with two tanks of acetylene.

Five ruggedly built men turned from their work to watch him pull in out of the rain, park, get out, and draw the two Glocks from the pouch of his

Lakers hoodie. None of the men looked remotely concerned. Not even a blink.

The killer expected no less of them.

'How'd it go, Mr. Cobb?' called one of the men, late twenties, with a gymnast's muscles and the attitude of an alley dog that has fought for every scrap life has grudgingly yielded to him.

'Outstanding, as expected, Mr. Nickerson,' the killer replied before setting the guns in front of a bald, lean Latino man who sported tattoos of the Grim Reaper on both bulging biceps. They were new tattoos, livid. 'Break these down, Mr. Hernandez.'

'Straightaway,' Hernandez said, accepting the pistols. He laid them on a heavy-duty folding table set up as a gunsmith's bench. A sniper's rifle sat in a vise awaiting adjustment.

A slighter man, early thirties, with a bleached goat's beard, got up from behind a row of iPads, all cabled to a large server beneath the tables. 'Did the rain screw up the feed?'

Cobb removed the sunglasses. 'You tell me, Mr. Watson.'

Watson took the sunglasses from Cobb, cracked open a hidden compartment in the frame, removed a tiny SIM card. While he fitted the card into a reader attached to one of the iPads, Cobb tugged off the baggy sweatshirt, revealing a ripped, muscular physique beneath a black Under Armour shirt. He reached beneath the collar of the shirt. An edge came up. He pulled.

The beard, the latex, the blond wig, the entire No Prisoners disguise came off, revealing a man in his late thirties, with a gaunt, weathered face that time and misfortune had chiseled into something remarkable. Scars ran like strands in a spider's web out from the round of his left jawline toward a cauliflower ear barely hidden by iron-gray hair.

It was the kind of face people never forgot.

Cobb knew that about himself, and he'd suffered for it in the past. He wasn't going to make that mistake twice. He laid out the pieces of the disguise on a third folding table before looking to a wiry African-American man holding another iPad connected to a set of earphones hung around his neck.

'Where are we, Mr. Johnson?' Cobb asked.

Johnson stabbed a finger at the iPad. 'From the traffic we've been monitoring, L.A. sheriff's got their big guns on the beach.'

'Better than we hoped for,' Cobb remarked before glancing to the fifth man, the largest of them all, curly red hair, ice-blue eyes, and a rust-colored, out-of-control beard that made him look like some crazed Viking. 'Mr. Kelleher?'

Kelleher nodded. 'Associated Press brief ran fifteen minutes ago, four dead males on Malibu Beach shot gangland style and set afire.' He looked up. Puzzled. 'That wasn't the plan, Mr. Cobb.'

Cobb regarded him evenly. 'Burning them amplifies things, moves events along quicker, Mr. Kelleher. Other coverage?'

Kelleher took that in stride, said, 'All-news radio picked up the AP story.'

'Outstanding,' Cobb said. 'Start the social media component.'

The big man nodded and went to sit next to Watson, who stroked his goat's beard and looked

31

at Cobb, smiling. 'You caught just about everything. I edited it down to the pertinent sequence. Got sporty there, didn't it?'

Watson was by far the smartest man in the room, a genius as far as Cobb was concerned. He'd never known anyone like Watson: a man who could handle tasks of extreme physical endurance while digesting vast amounts of data and information at a baffling rate. When Watson worked with computers, it was like he was attached to them, his own brain melding with the processors, able to analyze, compute, and code with the same mind-boggling speed.

'Let me see,' Cobb said, moved behind Watson. So did the other men.

Watson gave his iPad a command and the slayings from Cobb's perspective played out on the screen. Hernandez chuckled when Grinder, the barrel-chested surfer, pleaded for his life.

'It's like he's saying "Don't Tase me, bro,"' Hernandez said.

The others weren't listening. They were engrossed in the blinding-quick move Cobb had used to avoid being tackled by the final man to die.

'Damn brilliant, Mr. Cobb,' said Nickerson. 'You lost none of it.'

Johnson scowled. 'I still say you should have sent one of us. We're expendable.'

Cobb stiffened, felt angry. 'No one here is expendable. Ever. Besides, why would I ask you to do something I wouldn't do myself?'

'You wouldn't,' Kelleher said admiringly. 'First in.'

'Last out,' Cobb said. 'We are in this together.'

Watson said, 'Upload to YouTube now, Mr. Cobb?'

Cobb shook his head. 'Let's wait, let them make the connection to the letter before we hit them with total shock and awe.'

Chapter 5

The Kid met me up on Wilkerson's rain-soaked terrace around one thirty that morning, about the same time the first news of the killings was reaching the Los Angeles airwaves.

'You get it all?' I asked.

'Everything you shot,' the Kid replied, tugging his hood down over hair he slicked back crooner style. 'I didn't get squat from my perspective. Smell bad?'

'Horrible. Have Sci review the footage, then attach the files to Wilkerson's personal stuff.'

'Reason?'

'Case someone says he did it and we need to prove he didn't,' I replied, headed toward the Touareg, suddenly tired and wanting to sleep.

On the drive home, as my headlights reflected off the water sheeting Highway 1, I considered calling Guin, but knew she had to be up in five hours, getting ready to head to London. Then, for reasons I can't explain, my thoughts slipped to the only person I know who has never minded me calling at odd hours.

I reached over to the touch screen on the

dashboard, called up Justine's number, which appeared with a photograph of her I'd taken a couple of years ago. She was standing in an avocado orchard above the ocean in Santa Barbara. It was late in the day. Golden light. A breeze was blowing. Justine was brushing her hair from her eyes and smiling at me.

As I glanced at the photo, the full memory of that day came in all around me, as if I were there with Justine again in the orchard and the warm breeze blowing off the Pacific, back when it had all seemed perfect and inevitable between us.

But then we ran into the same problem again – I couldn't open up to her the way she wanted me to. The way she needed me to. So we decided we had to keep our relationship strictly professional. Whatever the hell that will mean.

Blowing out a rueful breath, I wondered if I was ever going to get over a woman I still love but just can't seem to be with, at least on her terms. And maybe mine. It's complicated. Justine is a psychologist, a fine one. She also works for me, and–

My cell phone rang so loudly I jerked the wheel and skidded before righting the Touareg. The touch screen was flashing caller ID. I stabbed the answer button, said, 'David Sanders, how are you?'

'Not good, Jack,' Sanders croaked. 'Not fucking good at all.'

Sanders was a powerful entertainment lawyer who'd been a discreet client of Private's several times in the recent past. And every time Sanders had called, it had been like this, in the middle of the night, with some mess to be cleaned up.

'You ever sleep, Dave?' I asked.

'Not when I'm dealing with a shitfest of potentially titanic proportions,' Sanders growled. 'I want to hire Private. You personally. I'd like you leading.'

'I'm...'

'Hired,' Sanders insisted. 'Be at LAX at seven thirty. The heliport. Bring a forensics team with you and someone who knows kids.'

'Kids? Where are we going?'

'Ojai,' Sanders said. 'Thom and Jennifer Harlow's place.'

'Uh-oh,' I said.

'A very scary uh-oh,' Sanders said before hanging up.

Chapter 6

The streets in Santa Monica were still slick and blustery around five fifteen that morning as Justine Smith climbed out of her car in shorts and a sweatshirt, drinking water and groaning. Her muscles hurt in places she hadn't known she had muscles. And yet here she was, back for more punishment.

Am I a masochist at some level? Is that why I work too much, my love life is a zero, and my body feels like someone whacked it with two-by-fours?

Unable to formulate a coherent answer, Justine stiffly crossed the street toward a light-industrial building with a garage door that bore a sign reading 'Pacific Crossfit.' Justine had a hate-love relationship with Crossfit, which was tougher than any other exercise program she'd ever followed. No high-tech machines. No mirrors. No fashion statements. Just Olympic free weights, gymnastics equipment, and the guts to perform brief, insanely intense workouts that often left her soaking wet, gasping on the floor, and sore for days.

Justine came from academics, not law enforcement, but her current job at Private required her to be kick-ass strong. So when she'd discovered that many US Special Forces operators, firefighters, and cops were switching to Crossfit for their physical training, she'd signed up at the gym, or 'box,' closest to her.

The first few weeks she honestly thought she was going to die during the workouts. Rather than let the new regime defeat her, however, she had embraced it with her typical zeal. No matter what, she'd been first at the door on Monday, Tuesday, Thursday, and Friday mornings, even before the ex-SEALs and LAPD SWAT team cops who usually showed up for this early class.

Six months, she thought, then admitted that she still feared Crossfit. But she absolutely loved the fact that she could now do twenty dead-hang pull-ups, deadlift two hundred and twenty-five pounds. And her abs were ripped. There was no other way to describe them.

The coach opened the door to the box from inside. A blue Toyota Camry rolled up to the curb and a guy Justine had never seen before climbed out stiffly.

She crossed through a small lobby, past a changing room, and out into the box itself. She glanced at the whiteboard on the wall before starting her warm-up. When she saw the workout of the day written there, her stomach fluttered with anxiety.

'"Grace: thirty clean and jerks for time"?' a man's voice groaned behind her. 'That's crazy. I can't move from the box jumps yesterday.'

Justine looked over her shoulder and saw the new guy, midthirties, curly brown hair, trimmed beard and really, really nice hazel eyes.

'Soreness is a way of life here,' Justine said.

He smiled at her. A really nice smile. 'Paul,' he said, holding out his hand. 'It's my fifth class.'

She smiled back, shook his hand, and said, 'Justine. A little over six months.'

'Does it get better?'

'Nope,' she said. 'Not one bit.'

Chapter 7

It only gets worse, Justine thought, fighting the queasy feeling building in her stomach as people all around her grunted, moaned, and dropped bars loaded with rubberized weights that boomed and bounced off the rubber floor.

Justine was twenty clean and jerks into the workout, with the prescribed ninety-five pounds on her bar. The big timing clock on the wall was running. Four minutes had passed since she'd started. Impossibly, one of the ex-SEALs had called, 'Time,' at one minute forty seconds before collapsing to the floor.

A big part of Justine wanted to lie down there with him and beg for mercy. But a better part of her got angry. She was not giving up. This was a fight to the finish. And she was finishing.

Ten more, little sister, Justine thought before leaning over to grab the bar with both hands. She gripped it, squeezed her core tight, and rose slowly, keeping the weight snug to her legs until the bar crossed her knees. Then she exploded upward, shrugging her shoulders, raising her elbows, creating a moment of inertia when the bar felt weightless. Quick as she could, she dropped beneath the weight, caught it in a racked position, and then exploded again, driving the bar overhead, where she balanced it a second before letting the weight crash to the floor with all sorts of satisfying fury.

Sweat gushed off Justine's forehead. Almost every muscle in her body burned, but she was grinning. She liked the grunting, the weights crashing, the feeling like you were in a race against time. It was primal, physical in a way she'd never known before.

Nine more, little sister.

'You, lady, are an animal,' Paul gasped minutes later as Justine struggled to get off the floor and to her feet. She'd finished 'Grace' in personal record time.

'Thanks,' she panted. 'I think.'

'No, seriously,' Paul said. 'You just kicked my ass with a heavier weight.'

Justine smiled. 'Welcome to Crossfit, where strong is the new thin.'

Paul laughed. 'I guess I need to learn to check

38

my ego at the door.'

'That's what they say.'

Still smiling, she turned away and headed toward the locker room and the showers, thinking how funny it was that she was able to go from Justine the warrior goddess to Justine a little boy crazy in a matter of moments. But he was nice, and self-deprecating. *And did you notice? No wedding ring?*

'Justine?'

She startled, looked into the lobby. The giddiness faded, replaced by a vague sense of loss. Jack was standing there, looking like he hadn't slept.

'Jack?' she said. 'What are you doing here?'

'We caught a case that feels epic. And I need you with me on it. Now.'

Paul passed by. Justine's eyes flickered to him and then back to Jack. She shook her head. 'I'm already swamped. It's not fair to our other clients, expecting me to–'

Jack took a step closer, murmured, 'Thom and Jennifer Harlow.'

Justine blinked. 'Give me ten minutes.'

Chapter 8

Forty minutes later we were harnessed into jump seats bolted to the interior walls of a helicopter that Dave Sanders had chartered for some ungodly sum of money. The lawyer, a bear of a man in a linen blazer, an orange Hawaiian shirt, khakis,

39

and sandals, sat beside me.

Next to Sanders was Dr. Seymour Kloppenberg, or Sci, the hip polymath criminologist who runs Private's lab in Los Angeles, and Maureen Roth, also known as Mo-bot. Roth works with Sci as a technical jack of all trades, is even quirkier than he is, and at fifty retains one of the sharpest and best-educated minds I know. Opposite us were Justine and Rick Del Rio, my oldest friend, a fellow ex-marine with a pit bull's heart. Next to Del Rio were two people I'd heard of but never met before. Camilla Bronson, a very put-together blonde in her forties, was the Harlows' full-time publicist. Originally from Georgia, she spoke with a soft, genial twang. The tall, ripped, and red-haired man in his midforties beside her was Terry Graves, the president of Harlow-Quinn Productions.

'What we're about to tell you goes nowhere without our permission,' Sanders announced as we lifted off and he handed me a folder. 'I expect all of your people to sign these nondisclosure forms before we get to the ranch, Jack.'

'Not necessary, Dave, you're covered under client privilege,' I said, fighting off a general un-ease that had been growing since we'd boarded the helicopter.

I flew choppers in Afghanistan. I got shot down in a Chinook and a lot of men died. I've never been truly comfortable in a helicopter since. I glanced at Justine, who was watching me. Dealing with the memories of the crash was how I'd come to meet Justine, one of the few people I've ever let get a glimpse of what goes on inside my head. I glanced at Del Rio, who'd been on the bird with me when it went down, the only other survivor of the crash. I guess I expected him to be agitated, or at least tense, but true to form, Del Rio was stone cold.

'Just the same, we'd like them signed,' sniffed Camilla Bronson.

'A lot at stake here,' Terry Graves agreed, removing sunglasses to reveal bloodshot eyes.

'Suit yourself,' I said, taking the folder. 'Tell us what's going on.'

Sanders hesitated, said, 'Thom and Jennifer, and their three kids, disappeared from their ranch in Ojai. They've vanished.'

'What?' Justine said. 'How's *that* possible?'

Del Rio snorted, said, 'Yeah, people like *that* can't just disappear.'

Mo-bot and Sci were nodding too.

I understood and shared their skepticism. Thom and Jennifer Harlow were arguably the most powerful and glamorous couple in Hollywood these days, megacelebrities who had won multiple Academy Awards, written bestselling books, and given their time and names to causes worldwide, including a foundation they'd set up themselves called Sharing Hands that raised millions for orphanages across the Third World.

During the twenty minutes it took us to fly north to the rolling hills of Ojai, Sanders, Camilla Bronson, and Terry Graves laid out what they thought we should know.

For the past nine months, the Harlow family had been living in Vietnam, where they had been making a film, *Saigon Falls,* an epic and tragic story of love and intrigue that unfolds in the last

41

doomed years of the American war. Thom Harlow was writer, director, and lead actor. Jennifer Quinn Harlow was starring opposite her husband. Through their company – Harlow-Quinn – they were also producing the film.

'It's the project of their lives,' Sanders said.

'The one that will immortalize them,' Camilla Bronson agreed.

'You should see the rushes,' said Terry Graves. 'Just brilliant stuff.'

The Harlows had come back from Vietnam on their private jet four days before. To avoid the paparazzi, they'd kept the details of their return secret and landed at Burbank. The lawyer, the publicist, and their head producer were there to greet them. The Harlows were blitzed from the long flight and the longer shoot on location. But they were also determined to complete the principal filming on a soundstage on the Warner lot starting the following month.

'So *Saigon Falls* is a Warner project?' Justine asked.

Terry Graves shook his head. 'They're a minor player. No other studio in town wanted to touch the project. They all thought it was too risky, more art than commerce. Warner is involved in a nominal way, kind of a nod to Thom and Jennifer for how much money they've made for that studio over the years.'

Camilla Bronson said, 'Thom and Jennifer raised money for the film privately to supplement what they decided to fund themselves.'

'Which was how much?' Mo-bot asked.

The publicist and the producer looked at Sanders. The attorney shifted in his seat, glanced at Justine, who was signing the nondisclosure form, said, 'Sixty of the ninety-three total at last count.'

'Personally?' Dr. Sci said, as shocked as I was.

'The vast majority of their fortune,' Sanders affirmed.

'But they were passionate about *Saigon Falls,* zealots, in fact,' Terry Graves explained.

Camilla Bronson nodded, said, 'Thom and Jennifer were either going to make a masterpiece and a bigger fortune, or they were going to lose everything they had.'

Sanders said, 'In all honesty, I met them at the airport because I desperately needed to explain that costs associated with *Saigon Falls* had overwhelmed their ability to maintain their current lifestyle.'

'You mean they were broke?' I asked.

'Not quite. But they were teetering right on the razor's edge of it.'

Chapter 9

As the Southern California landscape blurred below us, Sanders went on: 'At the airport, I explained their dire financial situation, held nothing back, told Thom and Jennifer they were going to have to take draconian measures or face bankruptcy.'

'What did they say to that?' Justine asked.

Terry Graves said, 'Thom acted unconcerned

and said he had it covered, that a new investor had appeared who was underwriting the completion of *Saigon Falls.*'

'He say who that investor was?' I asked.

The producer shook his head, looking highly irritated. 'Thom is like that. Likes being mysterious for no reason at all.'

'Creative tension,' Camilla Bronson explained. 'Thom – and this is off the record – believes in withholding information. He does it with everyone. So does Jen, for that matter. They believe it keeps people on their toes.'

'Okay,' I said. 'So then what happens?'

Sanders replied, 'They pleaded exhaustion and left along with Cynthia Maines, their personal assistant, in two rented Suburbans, bound for the ranch for six days of R&R.'

Terry Graves looked like he'd bitten into something sour. 'Typical of them. They knew we had a week of endless meetings set up – they'd been out of the country nine months, for God's sake – but they just announced that it would all have to wait, and away they drove, leaving us in the lurch.'

'Jen thought the kids deserved it,' said Camilla Bronson. 'Six days to help them reacclimate.'

'Anyway, that's the last we've heard of any of them,' Sanders said.

'So how do you know they've disappeared?' Justine asked. 'They've got two days left, right?'

The Harlows' publicist said, 'True, but they just stopped answering their phones, texts, and e-mails.'

'When?'

'Night before last,' the producer said. 'I called all

44

day yesterday on their private cell numbers, and Cynthia's cell, and got no response from any of them.'

The Harlows' attorney said, 'Finally, around midnight last night, the housekeeper at the ranch, Anita, answered the house phone.'

The housekeeper claimed to have just returned to the ranch with two other members of the staff. The Harlows had given them all nine months off with partial pay while a caretaker maintained the place in their absence.

'Anita said the ranch was empty,' Sanders said. 'She said there were signs that the Harlows had been there, but that there was no one there now. No one. I told her not to touch anything, that she and the others were to go to their quarters and wait for me. Then I hung up and called you, Jack.'

'So let me get this straight,' I said, trying to wrap my head around the situation, looking for fact, not conjecture. 'Not only are the Harlows and their children missing, but the Harlows' assistant–'

'Cynthia Maines,' said Camilla Bronson. 'Yes, she's missing too.'

'And the caretaker?'

'As I understand it,' the attorney said.

'No one else?' Justine asked.

Sanders hesitated, replied, 'Not that we know of.'

'How do you know they haven't just gone off somewhere on vacation?' Mo-bot asked.

'Because TMZ or one of the other gossip sites would have found them,' Terry Graves said.

'Okay,' I said, skeptical. 'Ransom notes?'

The attorney said, 'Maybe there's one at the

ranch. We don't know yet.'

'I'm not questioning your judgment here, Dave,' I replied. 'But why not call the FBI in? They're the missing persons experts.'

'We can't do that,' Camilla Bronson said. 'At least not until we find out what's going on.'

Sanders nodded. 'We don't know what's happened, and until we do, we're not going anywhere near law enforcement.'

I said, 'It's also a question of business, isn't it? If the people already invested in *Saigon Falls* were to find out the Harlows were missing, all hell would break loose.'

Terry Graves stiffened but said, 'Understandably, we don't want that.'

I wondered how far we could push a missing persons investigation before the Feds found out, took over, and tried to hit us with obstruction charges. That likelihood would be amped by the celebrity factor. The FBI loves celeb cases.

'Fair enough,' I said at last. 'But any evidence of violence and we're notifying the cops and the Feds.'

Before any of them could respond, the helicopter swung on the wind and dropped suddenly. I had a moment of flashback to the Chinook, right after we were hit by ground fire and the rotor disintegrated above us. I glanced quickly to Del Rio, who looked unaffected as he said, 'Maybe you're wrong. Maybe the Harlows did take off to some unlikely place, wore disguises, managed to avoid the paparazzi.'

'Not a chance,' Sanders replied. 'I checked the Harlows' Visa and AmEx records. They haven't

46

spent a dime since they bought gas down in Ojai the night they arrived.'

'Which is an absolute impossibility,' added Camilla Bronson.

'Why is that?' Kloppenberg asked.

The publicist said, 'Because Jennifer Harlow is a certifiable, world-class shopaholic.'

Chapter 10

'It's true,' Sanders said. 'The Harlows, and Jen in particular, rack up a lot of credit card charges every day. But since the night before last, nothing.'

Out the helicopter window the Harlows' Ojai ranch came into view, a beautiful, otherworldly place with a sprawling white ranch house, gardens, fountains, barns, and other outbuildings flanked by horse pastures and groves of almond, orange, and pecan trees.

I spotted the two Suburbans in the driveway before we landed. As the rotors died down, I finally released the tension in my fists, and all sorts of ideas bounced around in my mind. Were we on some kind of wild-goose chase? Would the Harlows just be sitting inside having breakfast?

Climbing from the helicopter after Sanders, Camilla Bronson, and Terry Graves, I spotted three middle-aged Latina women in maroon uniforms trotting toward us from one of the outbuildings.

The publicist, the producer, and the attorney

immediately veered off course and went straight to the women, with my team in tow.

'Have you spoken to anyone?' Camilla Bronson demanded.

The three wrung their hands, shook their heads. The tallest, whose blouse was monogrammed 'Anita,' said, 'No. I swear to you. We do exactly what Mr. Sanders say. We go to our rooms, say nothing to nobody. Just wait for you. We no sleep.'

'Let's continue to keep it quiet,' Sanders replied.

The publicist glanced at me, said, 'The press jackals will be all over this if we let them.'

'Besides, we really don't know anything yet, do we?' Terry Graves said.

We followed him. Behind me, I heard Sci whisper to Mo-bot, 'Well, I was thinking alien abduction, little green men looking to perform experiments on the most beautiful beings on Earth. What about you, Maureen?'

'Specters? Ectoplasmic transport?' she said.

I had to suppress a grin.

'Who ya gonna call?' Kloppenberg whispered. 'Private Ghostbusters!'

I glanced over my shoulder to find the two of them beaming at their wit, and Del Rio and Justine hiding their smiles.

Sanders turned from the three Mexican women. 'Is there something funny in all this?'

'No, Dave,' I said, covering. 'Not at all.' Looking to Justine, I said, 'You interview the help.' To Del Rio, I said, 'Take the outbuildings and the security system. Sci, Mo-bot, you're inside with me.'

'We're coming inside too,' Camilla Bronson said.

48

'I'd rather you didn't,' I said. 'At least until we've done our initial sweep.'

'Not a chance,' the publicist replied icily, and followed Sci and Mo-bot toward the veranda. Terry Graves and Sanders followed her.

Before I could argue with them, Justine squealed with delight. A female Old English bulldog had appeared out of nowhere, panting, nervous, her white fur and paws soiled as if she'd been digging in the dirt.

'That's Miss Stella Kowalski,' Anita choked, tears welling in her eyes as Justine went to pet the bulldog. 'She's the children's. Miguel's. You see? The dog goes everywhere with them. Even Vietnam. This no good. She's therapy dog. Miguel ... he loves her.'

At that the bulldog began to whimper and cry.

Chapter 11

It took us several hours to make an initial inspection of the Harlows' ranch house. Most rooms remained in mothballs, the furniture still wrapped in plastic. But the core area of the sprawling home spoke of a family wearily trying to resettle after a long journey, and, yes, of a life interrupted.

Littering the kitchen counters were dirty dishes, half-eaten meals, and glasses crusted with dried red wine. The fridge was filled with vegetables, fruit, cartons of soy milk, and the pantry was stocked with a multitude of gluten-free items. The trash in the compactor stank of chicken blood. A cold mug of coffee sat in the microwave, which flashed 'Finished.'

The telephone answering machine was filled with multiple messages from Camilla Bronson, Terry Graves, and Sanders, as well as several production assistants, film editors, and fashion designers, all of them apologizing for intruding but desperate for a few minutes of the Harlows' time. The television in the den off the kitchen was on, muted, showing the Cartoon Network and Scooby-Doo facing down yet another monstrous imposter. Lining a hall that led out to the garage was evidence of Jen Harlow's legendary consumerism: stacks upon stacks of unopened boxes, recent and past shipments from various catalog merchandisers. In the garage, we found five wheelless cars set up on blocks under custom covers that identified them as a Bugatti, a Maserati, a classic Corvette, and two Land Rovers.

'That's not right,' Terry Graves said, openly worried now. 'Thom told me he was looking forward to driving the 'Vette.'

There were pictures of the celebrity couple all over the house. Most of them were what I call power shots, photographs with politicians, say, or with various Hollywood moguls, at awards ceremonies and the like, images designed to boost an insecure creative soul.

A few candid photos showed the couple with their three children: Malia, thirteen, adopted in Ethiopia; Jin, eleven, adopted in China; and Miguel, eight, adopted in Honduras, and born with a severe cleft palate. More images depicted

Thom or Jennifer or both in some far-flung and impoverished land, posing with gangs of smiling children, or holding a withered infant in their arms.

Camilla Bronson's lower lip trembled as she saw the photos, and she said, 'Oh, God, what's happened to them? They're such good people.'

I left her and went to the west wing of the ranch house, which held guest quarters, a state-of-the-art gym, an indoor pool, and a twenty-seat screening room. The pool was empty. The gym and the screening room appeared unused.

Lights burned in the hallway that led to the east wing and five bedrooms laid out like a dormitory, with two bedrooms on either side of the hall and the Harlows' master suite at the far end. The bedroom on the right-hand side, closest to the living area, was Malia's. Her suitcases were half empty on the floor. An iPhone 4S with a dead battery lay hidden between the bed and the end table. The sheets were rumpled and cast lazily aside, as if the teen had gotten up for a drink of water, or to go pee, or maybe had just left the bed unmade for the day.

Jin's room across the hall was more chaotic, with clothes in piles on the carpet and strewn on the furniture, a canopy bed covered in stuffed animals, and another menagerie on the dresser.

The bedroom of the boy, Miguel, however, was different, neat-freak different, the bed made with almost military precision. But when I walked past the bed I smelled something acrid in the air. Sniffing around, I soon found its source. Someone had wet the bed.

The room across the hall from Miguel's was empty, the mattress stripped, the blankets folded and put into clear plastic protectors. I wondered if it had been set aside for some future fourth orphan the Harlows planned to adopt.

I reached the master suite, a simple yet elegant space with a Steinway grand in the corner, shelves bulging with books, and a huge teak bed, crisply made with fresh white sheets and a folded duvet. A bay window overlooked the orchards. Paintings and several mirrors, including one narrow mirror six or seven feet long, hung horizontally, high on the interior wall of the bedroom, all feng shui remedies, no doubt.

'Found the Oscars,' Mo-bot called to me as she exited a massive walk-in closet to my right, hands behind her back. 'They were all wrapped in newspaper and stuck at the bottom of one of Jennifer's drawers. Can you imagine doing that to an Academy Award, Jack?'

'The Harlows are unimpressed with themselves,' Sanders said, coming in behind us with Camilla Bronson and Terry Graves.

'They don't judge themselves on the basis of public accolades,' Terry Graves said. 'Deep down it's always about the work.'

'If you say so,' Mo-bot replied with little conviction. 'Know what else I found piled on top of the Oscars?'

'I couldn't imagine,' the publicist sniffed. 'As I said, Jennifer has one of everything.'

Mo-bot smirked as she brought out from behind her back a rather large and anatomically realistic dildo with a suction cup jutting out the back end.

52

Chapter 12

'You know why they'll go for it?' Cobb asked Nickerson as he steeled a knife with a short, wicked-looking obsidian blade. 'They'll go for it because big-city hot shots or not, deep down they're just like some limp-dick chieftain in the Old Country: small-minded, predictable, and therefore susceptible to fear. Ignorance breeds it, fear, which is useful, as you know.'

'Damn straight, Mr. Cobb,' Nickerson replied, turning the blade. 'Justifiable in a state of war.'

They were in the garage in the City of Commerce. Johnson was sacked out on the cots. Kelleher and Watson worked at computers. Hernandez watched coffee drip and worked more salve into his new tattoos.

Cobb made a pistol with his fingers, aimed it at Nickerson, and said, 'Perfectly justifiable in dire times such as these. People who get power have to be worms in order to get power. What we're doing is just electrifying the soil they live in, getting it so hot and shocking they'll be forced to surface and squirm in the light of day. Then we'll have them.'

Hernandez came over, set a mug in front of Cobb, said, 'With all due respect: the pharmacy? Is that the place to maximize our efforts?'

Cobb ran two fingers over the spiderweb of scars on the left side of his face and considered Hernandez with cold intent. Hernandez was brave to the point of being impetuous, which made him one of Cobb's best men and also his worst man. Hernandez had amazing physical skills and would fight to the death if provoked, but he tended to ad lib on plans when it was unnecessary. And he couldn't see the big picture, a general weakness of character and intellect, at least as far as Cobb was concerned.

'For this to work, Mr. Hernandez, we don't want anything that could be construed as political,' Cobb said at last. 'Nothing symbolic, if you will. No statements. Nothing to suggest this is anything other than a single maniac at work. So why the pharmacy? It's mundane. It's everyday, and because of that more people will relate to it, and the fear and the panic and the pressure will grow. We want every citizen of L.A. to feel like their daily lives are jeopardized.'

End of discussion. He turned from Hernandez, glanced at the atomic clock on the wall – fourteen hundred hours – and said, 'Okay, Mr. Watson, upload it.'

'Straightaway, Mr. Cobb,' Watson said, and began giving orders to his iPad. 'I'm taking it through scrubbing sites in India, Pakistan, and Hong Kong. Zero chance they'll pull an IPN on us.'

Cobb understood. 'Make sure you mix up the paths you take online. It's just like being on the job. No routine routes. Change it up, all the time.'

'Got the Facebook page up,' Kelleher said, pivoted in his chair, stroked his red beard. 'You like?'

Cobb glanced at the iPad in front of the big

54

man. A Facebook page filled the screen, topped with the headline NO PRISONERS: FACES OF WAR L.A.

'Outstanding,' Cobb said. 'Show them their ignorance, sow fear through them virtually. I'm going to catch a nap before things really ramp up.'

'Sixteen hundred?' Hernandez asked.

'Yes,' Cobb said before going to a cot and lying on it with one arm flung over his eyes. As a matter of survival, he had long ago taught his mind and body to shut down on command. When they did so this time, he plunged into a deep, dark void that after an hour gave way to dreams.

It was night. The chill wind smelled of wood smoke, tobacco smoke, coffee brewing, horse sweat, and the high desert. Boots crunched on sand and rock. Dogs began to bark before gunfire threw jagged flares through the night.

Women and children began to scream. In his dreams, Cobb heard men begging for mercy. He felt nothing but satisfaction at the screaming, at their pleas, and with that grew a sense of righteousness that surged when the first explosion hyperlit his mind, shook his body so hard he thought for a moment he'd been hit by the rocket-propelled grenade.

Then Cobb bolted upright, instinctually grabbing the throat of the man shaking his shoulder. Watson choked and looked down at him bug-eyed.

'No, Mr. Cobb!' Kelleher yelled, grabbing his wrist. 'It's a good thing.'

Cobb came free of the dream, fully awake, and slowly let go of Watson's throat.

'We've gone viral,' Kelleher said as Watson

choked and coughed.

'Already?' Cobb said, sitting up, shedding the grogginess. Johnson and Nickerson were standing there too.

Watson crowed in a hoarse voice, 'One hour twenty in, we've got seventy-five hundred hits on YouTube.'

Kelleher grinned. 'And two thousand thumbs down on Facebook.'

'Those numbers will grow,' Cobb remarked.

'Definitely,' Hernandez said behind him. 'Frickin' exponential.'

Cobb twisted to see not bald Hernandez but blond-locked and bearded No Prisoners slipping the mirror sunglasses on to complete his disguise.

Cobb smiled, said, 'Outstanding in every goddamned way, Mr. Hernandez.'

Chapter 13

'Put that thing away,' Sanders snapped, reddening after the initial shock of seeing the dildo in Mo-bot's hand. 'Jennifer Harlow's private, uh, needs are not at issue here.'

'Maybe, maybe not,' Mo-bot shot back. 'There are drawers full of sex toys and gear in her closet. His too.'

Camilla Bronson blanched. 'You cannot mention this to anyone!'

She must have said that six times over the next fifteen minutes as we discovered all manner and size of dildo, butt plug, suction tube, cock ring, and artificial vagina in the Harlows' closets. There was also a sex swing and a device that resembled a gymnast's vaulting horse equipped with a powerful motor inside and a mechanical penis jutting out of the top.

'Never seen one of those before,' I commented.

'It's called a Sybian,' said Sci, who'd just come in. 'The penis attachment not only goes up and down, it can be set to rotate or corkscrew.'

'And you know that how?' Terry Graves asked.

'Kit-Kat's got one,' Kloppenberg replied matter-of-factly.

Sanders frowned. 'Who the hell is Kit-Kat?'

'Sci's virtual girlfriend,' Mo-bot said.

Not really wanting it discussed that my chief criminologist's private life consisted of online video sex with a woman in our Stockholm office, I quickly changed the subject, asked, 'Find anything in the kitchen, Seymour?'

Sci nodded. 'Enough mold and bacteria to say those dishes and glasses are from thirty-six to forty hours ago at the outside. I'll be able to give you a more definitive answer once we get back to the lab.'

Thirty-six to forty hours. Which meant the Harlows had left the house voluntarily or involuntarily roughly two days after they returned home from Vietnam. What had happened in those two days?

I left the others and again walked around the house, trying to see something I'd missed on the first pass, trying to imagine the things that might have unfolded in the time before the family disappeared. Had they left on their own, or at gunpoint?

In what vehicle? And what about the caretaker, and the personal assistant, Cynthia Maines?

I had more questions than answers, and the growing feeling that I was indeed missing something, something that was staring me right in the face. Then again, little of the scene made sense to me. There were no signs of violence that I could find, no indication that they'd been forcibly taken, no blood, no broken furniture, certainly no ransom note or demand of any kind.

So what had happened here?

I discovered an editing room in the basement below the east wing of the house, with five big screens all linked to a mainframe server and a state-of-the-art editing and mixing console. I tried a door beyond the console. It was locked.

I turned, my eyes drifting across the electronics in the editing room, and it hit me. There were no computers anywhere. No desktops. No laptops. No tablets. No handhelds except for the dead iPhone in Malia's room.

This was a wealthy family in a home equipped with the highest-end techno-gadgets. No computers beyond that phone? Impossible. So they were gone too. But there had to be some kind of backup system, right? A cloud connection, at least.

I was about to go find Mo-bot and the trio I'd come to call the Harlow team to dig into that issue when Del Rio found me.

'Went through the caretaker, Hector Ramon's, place, Jack,' he said. 'It's like the main house, used, but abandoned. There's a cat down there, walking around meowing.'

'No signs of struggle?'

58

'None,' Del Rio said.

'Maybe Sci's not that far off, then. Maybe that's what scared the bulldog and made the computers all disappear. It *is* an alien abduction.'

'Yeah, maybe, except for the fact that for two hours the night before last, either the electricity blacked out and the backup to the security system suffered a complete failure, or the system was disarmed and fucked with by total pros.'

Chapter 14

Me, Del Rio, Sci, Mo-bot, Sanders, Camilla Bronson, and Terry Graves were all crowded into a small room off the garage watching a big screen split into ten frames. Each frame displayed a different feed from security cameras arrayed around the ranch, at the gate, near the barns, above every exterior door, and at intervals on the roof, panning the near grounds.

'Fairly sophisticated system,' said Del Rio, who on the whole is largely unimpressed with security he didn't himself design. 'Redundant controllers. Satellite link. Cable link. Pressure sensors inside the fences. Lasers in the hallways. Fiber optics in the windows. Panic room off the master suite.'

'I didn't see any panic room,' Sci said.

Del Rio tapped a feed that showed a room equipped with couches, a refrigerator, and two sets of bunk beds. 'Entrance is off Jennifer's closet. Looks like a frickin' fortress. But obviously

59

they never made it in there.'

'Which means something happened to the security system?' Mo-bot asked. 'They were never alerted?'

'Something did happen,' Del Rio agreed. 'I reviewed the logs in the two computers that run the show. At seven twenty-seven p.m. two nights ago, the entire system went down, the backups failed, and no alerts were issued to police or the folks who installed this.'

'And who was that?' I asked.

Del Rio got a sour look. 'You're not going to like it.'

I cocked my head in disbelief. 'Tommy?'

'His people, anyway.'

'Who's Tommy?' Camilla Bronson asked.

'My brother.'

'The guy in the papers?' Sanders asked in a groan. 'The one implicated in that murder?'

'One and the same,' I said.

What was the likelihood of that? My brother designed and installed the system, a system that failed?

'You think he could be involved here?' Terry Graves asked.

I considered the producer's question but then shook my head. 'Tommy's a wack job, but his specialty *is* security systems. How exactly did it fail?'

Del Rio ran a paw over his stubbled chin. 'Logs say the computers ran diagnostic software upon rebooting at nine twenty-seven p.m. two nights ago. It detected a failure in the trip connection to the backup generators four seconds before the ranch's main power line died.'

'You call Southern Cal Edison?' Sci asked.

Del Rio nodded. 'A transformer blew about that time, cut power all over Ojai. Took three hours to bring electricity back online.'

'But you said the computer logs show the system was only down for two hours, not three,' I said.

'That's right,' Del Rio said. 'The logs say the generators kicked back to life at nine twenty-seven, main power came on about an hour later.'

'So someone *inside* cut the generator, and then what, reconnected it?'

He nodded again. 'I figure coordinated attack, inside, outside. Takes a few minutes for the system to reboot. Enough time to vanish when you're done.'

My mind raced through the people who were supposed to have been on the ranch that night. The Harlows. Their kids. The caretaker. The Harlows' personal assistant.

'Cynthia Maines,' I said.

'What?' Camilla Bronson asked.

'Unless I'm out to lunch here, the only beds in the house I've seen used were the family's. If Maines was here, where did she sleep?'

'Maybe she didn't,' Terry Graves said.

'Or maybe she cleaned up after herself, made it look as if she hadn't slept here,' Mo-bot said. 'I mean, the Harlows' bed was made, right?'

'Or Jennifer and Thom just hadn't gone to bed yet,' I said, gesturing at the screen. 'You find tapes from these feeds?'

Del Rio nodded, gave the keyboard several

61

commands. The screen images jumped and now carried a time stamp four days prior.

Del Rio said, 'The cameras are set up with motion detectors. They only record when there's movement. Lights too. You can see the two days of activity leading up to the system failure in like five minutes.'

He speeded up the tapes. My focus jumped all over the split screen, seeing the Harlows arriving four nights ago, hauling gear from the Suburbans into the house, greeting a man wearing a straw cowboy hat, who I assumed was the caretaker, Héctor Ramón; and the three kids going in and out of the house multiple times during the days and into the evenings with the bulldog rambling behind them. The dog seemed never to leave their side.

Thom Harlow appeared infrequently. His wife was everywhere, a frenetic personality. On the second evening, however, Thom came to the back door to watch Jennifer leave on her run, which Sanders said was a daily ritual, along with yoga. The last recording took place moments before the system failed, roughly thirty-six hours after the Harlows had returned to the ranch. The back-door and deck view again, looking down at a steep angle: Jennifer returned from her run in the dark, sweating, chest heaving, and climbed onto the lit deck.

Del Rio typed, turned that frame full-screen. Jennifer slowed, stopped, turned to look behind her. The light beyond the deck was dim, shadowy, so I caught only a flicker of movement in the shadows, the hint of a human form before the screen blinked black.

'What–' Mo-bot began.

Del Rio held up his hand. 'Wait, you're gonna see the first thing the cameras picked up after the system rebooted two hours later.'

The screen jumped back to life.

Stella, the Harlows' bulldog, was on the deck in much the same place where Jennifer had been when the screen went blank. The dog was frantic, howling and ripping at the screen door as if she'd seen something worse than a ghost.

Chapter 15

At the same time, one hundred miles to the south, in her Civic hybrid parked down the block from a CVS pharmacy on La Cienega Boulevard, Sheila Vicente was a woman on the verge of a nervous breakdown.

An assistant district attorney juggling a monstrous caseload, including the upcoming prosecution of a capital murder case, she was also a divorcing mother of two, and on the line with her soon-to-be ex-husband.

'Do you think I'm a doormat you can just walk on?' Vicente demanded.

Silence. Then her husband, cold, said, 'No, just the same old inflexible–'

'Bitch?' she said, struggling for control. 'I'm a bitch because you have the gall to call me at the eleventh hour and ask for a different weekend

63

with the boys so you and your plastic-boob girl-friend can jet down to Cabo for a quick forty-eight in the sack?'

'Pat's got two days off from rotation,' her husband shot back. 'It's rare.'

'Not as rare as a day off is for me!' Sheila shrieked. 'I haven't had one in three weeks.' She threw down her cell.

Sheila shook from head to toe, trembled against every bit of will she had left, staring into the distance at what had once been a dream life, barely aware of the blond man with the scruffy beard, the mirror sunglasses, the baggy pants, and the Lakers hoodie pimp-strolling confidently by her car, up the sidewalk, and into the pharmacy.

'Mommy?' a thin little voice came from the backseat. 'Mommy sad?'

She looked in the mirror, saw her two-year-old son so worried, and knew now she had no choice. She had to go through with it.

As much as she hated the idea, she was going to fill a prescription for antidepressants. Serious antidepressants.

Chapter 16

Hernandez checked his disguise in a mirror in the cosmetics section. Not even his own not-so-dear and dead mother would recognize him like this. *Gringo to the max, man. I could be one chubby boy under all these clothes, right?*

64

'How many?' Cobb's voice muttered through the earpiece hidden beneath the locks of the blond wig, breaking Hernandez from his thoughts.

'Nine total,' Hernandez replied.

Silence, then a comment from Watson: 'Video and audio feeds are crisp and strong.'

Cobb said, 'Take five, Mr. Hernandez, drop the card, and leave.'

'Going mundane,' Hernandez said, feeling a familiar thrilling sense of descent, of regressing to the primitive, of tasting bloodlust.

He angled through the store, sniffed the perfumed air, plucked a king-size Reese's Peanut Butter Cup, and tore it open. He dropped the candy into his mouth, savoring the melt as he walked to the prescription window, noticing that the pharmacist was on break. An old black woman stood to one side, hands on her wooden cane, waiting for her medicine, looking at him suspiciously.

A pimply redheaded woman, the only one behind the counter, said brightly, 'Here to pick up, sir?'

'More like a drop-off,' Hernandez said, drawing the suppressed weapons.

He shot her at point-blank range with the right-hand gun and then whirled, looking for the old woman. The crazy bitch was already swinging at him with her cane. It broke across his arm, right across the new tattoo, setting it afire, shocking him, but only for a moment before he realized she was moving to stab him with the splintered end of her cane.

Hernandez's left hand swung instinctively, aimed at the old woman's chin, and shot her there. She crumpled to the tile floor.

'Weak, Mr. Hernandez,' Cobb said. 'You should have taken her first.'

Hernandez ignored the criticism, stalked through the aisles, his arm screaming in pain, but believing that no one else in the store, what with the Muzak braying, had heard the suppressed shots or the bodies falling.

Guns back in his hoodie's pocket, he walked past a teenage girl shopping for nail polish in aisle three. He skirted a plump guy looking at razors in aisle five but killed an older man checking out incontinence pads in aisle seven.

He considered the middle-aged woman perusing the paperback racks, a mystery novel in one hand, but then shifted his focus to the two clerks manning the front desk, man, woman, both in their late twenties.

The male clerk died stocking cigarettes, shot in the back.

'You got company coming,' Cobb said. 'Move.'

The female clerk died screaming, the first to be aware of her impending death, trying to crouch and hide beneath the cash register.

Hernandez turned, surging on adrenaline. He began to hum a favorite tune. It never got old, this feeling, better than any video game ever. Nothing came close to the real thing. Difference between porn and...

Ten feet away, an anxious Latina woman in a blue business skirt and pink blouse and her thumb-sucking toddler in the seat of her shopping cart were staring at him, frozen with terror.

'No,' Sheila Vicente sobbed. 'Please, I'm just

here for the Xanax.'

Every nerve fiber, every cell in Hernandez told him to wax her, right now. The kid too. It would make a statement. No quarter would be given.

He took two steps toward the young mother as she wrenched her child to her breast and sank to her knees, begging incoherently. He stood over her, the guns aimed at her crying eyes and the back of her little boy's head, savoring the power, smelling the torrents of fear pouring off her. His fingers sought the triggers.

'Stop,' Cobb said, and then told Hernandez exactly what to do. Hernandez didn't like it, but for once he followed orders to a T.

'Cell phone,' Hernandez barked at her. 'Give it to me.'

Shaking, crying, Sheila Vicente got her cell and threw it down. Hernandez crushed it with his heel, slid the guns into his hoodie. He crouched before her, handed her a Baggie with a lime-green card in it, said, 'I want you to personally give the mayor this. Don't show the cops. Just tell them that you have a personal message for the mayor from me. Tell that bitch that unless she complies with my demands there will be no mercy after this. None.'

Then Hernandez stood, turned, chuckled, and walked out the door of the pharmacy, humming that favorite melody of his, as if he had not a care in this world.

PART TWO

SQUEEZE PLAY

Chapter 17

Stella the bulldog sprawled on her side, panting hard, as if she had run for miles in a torrid heat. Justine lay on the veranda floor, stroking the poor beast's head and laying wet towels over her body. Justine has a thing for dogs. And they have a thing for her. She owns two, spoils them silly.

'She's been getting progressively worse,' said Justine when I exited the main house with Sanders and Del Rio. 'We're going to have to take her to a vet.'

'No vets,' Camilla Bronson snapped. 'I know for a fact that Thom and Jennifer put a chip under her skin. They'll ask questions.'

'So what? The dog's sick,' Justine said firmly.

'She probably got into some bad meat and now she's suffering for it,' Sanders said.

'Yes, just keep her out here so she doesn't dump or puke in the house,' Terry Graves said.

Justine set her eyes on the attorney, the publicist, and the producer in a way I'd seen before. She no longer liked the Harlow team. They were clients. She'd do the work, but she wouldn't like them. She stated flatly, 'This pup gets any sicker, I'm taking one of the Suburbans and going to–'

Trying to defuse the situation, I said, 'Tell me about the house staff.'

'What about them?' Sanders asked.

'I need to know their story.'

'I just spent two hours with them, Jack,' Justine said, then looked at Sanders, Camilla Bronson, and Terry Graves. 'Correct me if I'm wrong.'

Anita Fontana, thirty-four, the head housekeeper, had been with the Harlows for twelve years, ever since the actors bought the ranch. She appeared the most upset, kept looking at a picture of the family she had by her bed and weeping. She said she loved the Harlows, especially Miguel. The Harlows were demanding but fair, generous at times, surprisingly cheap at others, and somewhat aloof from their children.

'Aloof!' Camilla Bronson cried. 'That goes nowhere. Do you understand?'

'How couldn't they be aloof at some level?' Justine shot back. 'Busy careers and philanthropic work chew up vast amounts of time.'

'Jen and Thom are excellent parents,' the publicist retorted. 'Anyone who says otherwise is either a fool or a liar.'

'Then all three of them must be fools or liars,' Justine replied.

The cook – Maria Toro – agreed in large part with the housekeeper's take on their bosses. She'd been with the Harlows eight years; said Jennifer was always trying to keep Thom on a vegan diet, but that he loved meat. Jacinta Feliz, the maid, had been at the ranch two years before the furlough they'd been given during the Harlows' sojourn in Vietnam.

'She said Malia suffered nightmares and was a lonely girl,' Justine said.

'That's not–' Camilla Bronson began.

Terry Graves cut her off, said, 'Listen to the

woman and quit trying to spin things.'

The publicist was indignant. 'I'm not spinning–'

'Yes, you are, Camilla, and it's not helping,' Sanders said. 'Go ahead, Ms. Smith.'

'The boy wets the bed regularly,' Justine went on. 'Jin has several imaginary friends and believes her stuffed animals come to life at night.'

I said, 'What about the Harlows? When was the last time they were in contact?'

Justine replied that Anita said she'd been in touch with the Harlows several times in the last month, trying to coordinate their arrival with the house staff's. The original plan called for the three women to return to the ranch two days before the Harlows, but then, Anita said, she'd gotten a call from Cynthia Maines. A change of plans. The women were to return three days *after* the Harlows' return.

'First I've heard of that,' Sanders said.

Camilla Bronson threw up her hands. 'Which means what?'

Justine said, 'Changing the arrival date makes it possible for the Harlows to disappear. That way the caretaker is the only other person to deal with, which makes me think that Cynthia Maines is of interest to us, perhaps our insider.'

'My God,' Terry Graves protested. 'I can't believe that.'

Sanders shook his head. 'Cynthia was devoted to the Harlows.'

The publicist, for once, said nothing.

I said, 'I think there's sufficient cause to bring in the FBI.'

That soured the Harlow team.

'Do you know the shitstorm you'll cause?' Camilla Bronson demanded.

'For me? Or for you?'

Her jaw clamped shut, but she was staring bullets at me.

'I agree with Camilla,' Terry Graves said.

'I do too,' Sanders said. 'At this moment, there's insufficient evidence to bring in the FBI.'

'Dave, you called us in,' I began. 'I think the missing two hours and the dog's reaction are enough.'

'I don't, and you work for us, and for the Harlows, Jack,' the attorney said firmly. 'I, we, want Private to find them.'

'Yes,' Camilla Bronson said, more sure of herself. 'We don't want this getting out unless it absolutely has to.'

'Anything you need to do, you do, Jack,' said Terry Graves. 'Just keep this quiet for a few days to see if they show up or we get a ransom note. In the meantime, you keep your people working.'

'What's this about?' I asked. 'Money?'

'Damn right,' the producer retorted. 'We have a lot riding on *Saigon Falls*. All of us have sacrificed for this project, and word of the Harlows' disappearance could cause the entire project to collapse, taking tens of millions of dollars and our futures with it.'

Sanders and Camilla Bronson nodded.

I glanced at Justine, whose expression was hard. I could feel it too. These three had some other angle on this that we weren't seeing. But they were paying, and I had to agree that other than the traumatized bulldog there was no sign of violent struggle anywhere inside the compound. Except for the power and security system issues, they could have just walked away. Hell, for all we knew, maybe Thom and Jennifer had screwed with the security system, wanting to disappear for one reason or another. Thom liked keeping secrets. It would not be entirely out of the question.

'I'll give you two days,' I said.

'Three,' Sanders said.

Camilla Bronson said, 'Where are Anita, the others?'

'In their quarters,' Justine said.

'I'm getting them out of here,' she said, turning. 'They're coming with me to L.A. I don't want any of them talking to anyone.'

My cell phone rang. I glanced at the caller ID: LAPD Chief Mickey Fescoe.

I squinted, trying to think of what my fairweather friend might want this time. I flashed for a second on my brother, Tommy, who was being investigated in the murder of Clay Harris, a surveillance expert who once worked for me. I'd been in the next room when the shooting went down, heard the shots but saw nothing. My brother told me it was self-defense. I'd left him at the crime scene to deal with his own mess. Had Tommy implicated me? It was all I could think of, unless Fescoe had gotten wind of the Harlows' disappearance?

I turned away from the others, walked off the veranda out onto the lawn beneath the live oaks.

'Mickey,' I said, trying to sound even, nonchalant.

'Jack, how soon can you and Del Rio be in the

mayor's office?'

'What's going on?'

'How long, Jack?'

I looked over at the helicopter parked on the Harlows' front lawn. 'Give me clearance to use the helipad?'

'Done.'

'Forty minutes, tops,' I said.

'We'll be waiting,' Fescoe said.

'No clue, Mickey?'

'Turn on the radio, Jack. Turn on the TV. It's on every goddamned station in L.A., and they don't know the half of it.'

Chapter 18

'Well done, Mr. Hernandez,' Cobb said to the killer as he stripped off the No Prisoners disguise inside the rear of one of the white panel vans.

'Why didn't I take her?' Hernandez grunted.

'Because by our letting her live, the terror will rise. It has a face now, a voice.'

'Could have been her and the kid lying there and not talking,' agreed Johnson, who was up front, driving them east toward the City of Commerce.

'Could have been anyone,' Hernandez said, humming again.

'People don't like change, gentlemen,' Cobb observed. 'I don't care if you're a Taliban in East-Jesus-Stan or a mom in Litchfield, Connecticut.

76

People like their routines, their habits. When you threaten their habits and routines, they get upset, lash out, and do all sorts of things they would not normally do.'

'Like take sharp terms in a negotiation, Mr. Cobb?' Johnson asked, grinning in the rearview mirror.

'That too, Mr. Johnson,' Cobb agreed, allowing a rare smile that only deepened the lines of the spiderweb scar on the left side of his face.

'And now?' Hernandez asked.

Cobb's smile disappeared. 'We let Mr. Kelleher and Mr. Watson continue to execute their end of the plan. And we wait for contact.'

'You sure they'll try now?' Johnson asked.

'Dead sure,' Cobb said. 'Worms just can't help themselves when they feel the soil all around them getting prickly and hot.'

Chapter 19

On a screen in the private office of the Honorable Diane Wills, mayor of Los Angeles, the killer rose from a squatting position in front of Sheila Vicente, his back to the camera as he exited the pharmacy.

In a voice oddly composed given the traumatic experience she'd suffered not two and a half hours before, Sheila Vicente said, 'He was humming that old Doors song before he saw me and Enrique. He was humming it as he left.' She shifted in her chair, started to weep.

Mayor Wills went to console her while a handful of L.A.'s other high-and-mighty looked on. L.A. Police Chief Mickey Fescoe, L.A. County Sheriff Lou Cammarata, L.A. District Attorney Billy Blaze.

Del Rio and I had come off the helicopter twenty minutes before. We'd flown down from Ojai with the Harlows' management team and the help, leaving Justine, Sci, and Mo-bot to continue the search, at least until dark.

For the life of me I couldn't figure out what their angle was, calling us in on a missing persons case, then not taking our advice to bring in the FBI. But I had had little chance to think about that.

The entire flight down we'd watched the news coverage of the shootings at the pharmacy on La Cienega. Local news interviewed a teenager who'd been inside during the killings, shopping for nail polish.

'It was creepy,' the teen said, beginning to choke. 'I never heard a thing until one of the clerks started screaming bloody murder, like *Cabin in the Woods* or something.'

But that and the body count was about all we knew until we got to the mayor's office, watched the raw footage of the killing spree, and heard Sheila Vicente describe the killer humming as he left.

'"Peace Frog,"' Del Rio said. 'That was the song?'

Vicente had composed herself again. She nodded at Del Rio. 'You know – "Blood in the streets, it's up to my ankles"?'

78

'"Bloody red sun of Phantastic L.A.,"' Del Rio replied.

'You were supposed to give a message to the mayor, is that right?' Chief Fescoe said.

Ruddy coarse skin, early fifties, Fescoe is as smart as any man I know, also one of the most cunning. He's a good cop. He's a better politician. Which was what had puzzled me about the killings. Why were we here? Why had Del Rio and I been allowed to see the raw footage?

'Yes, and only to the mayor,' Vicente said, looking to Wills, a tall, formidable, red-haired woman who long ago played volleyball at UCLA and graduated first in her class at Stanford Law.

'What is it, dear?' Mayor Wills asked.

Sheila Vicente reached into her purse and with trembling hands drew out a Baggie. I could see there was something inside it but couldn't tell much more. The assistant district attorney started to hand the Baggie to the mayor, but Chief Fescoe was quicker and blocked the transfer.

'Lay it on the desk,' he said. 'No more fingerprints.'

'He wore gloves, flesh-colored thin gloves,' Vicente said.

I crossed the room to the desk, saw the lime-green card in the Baggie, and saw the printing: NO PRISONERS.

Four yesterday. Five today. He's on an escalating spree. Those were my first thoughts. I said, 'Captain Harry Thomas with sheriff's homicide has a card just like this, taken in evidence at the Malibu Beach killings last night.'

79

Sheriff Cammarata scowled but said, 'That's true.'

Sheila Vicente said, 'Mayor, he told me to tell you that unless you comply with his demands there will be no mercy after this. None.'

'What demands?' Mayor Wills said. 'I haven't heard any demands.'

There was a silence for a beat, broken by Chief Fescoe, who paled considerably before saying, 'I have. In letters yesterday and today, and then again on video two hours ago.'

'What?' cried Blaze, the district attorney.

'And you told no one?' demanded Sheriff Cammarata.

Fescoe bristled. 'At first we thought it was just some nut job writing crazy letters. We had no word that you found that calling card at Malibu last night. Until the killings at the CVS, we had nothing to say the threats were real.'

'What threats and what video?' Del Rio asked.

Fescoe nodded to his assistant. 'The ones we got two hours ago.'

The assistant tapped an order into a laptop computer. YouTube appeared on the big screen. The featured video on the page was entitled NO PRISONERS: FACES OF WAR L.A.

'Play it,' Fescoe said.

The slayings on the beach were ruthless, precise, and shot from the killer's perspective. The camera work seemed remarkably smooth given the brutality of the action. The only parts of the killer you saw, however, were the gloves and the guns.

After the last man fell dead, a warning appeared:

IF YOU DO NOT COMPLY
MANY MORE WILL DIE.
NO ONE IS SAFE. NO ONE

'Hundred and twenty-five thousand hits,' Del Rio said, tearing me from thoughts of being under the tarps the night before, looking at the burned bodies of the four men I'd just seen executed on video.

'Comply?' the mayor said. 'Comply with what?'

Fescoe paled again, swallowed, and said, 'He wants money to stop the killings. Lots of money.'

Chapter 20

'Let me get this straight,' Mayor Wills said, sinking into her desk chair. 'He's killing people to extort the city?'

'This explains it,' Fescoe said, nodding to his assistant again. YouTube disappeared, replaced by high-res photographs of two typed letters. 'We got the letter on the left yesterday morning, the one on the right this morning. Both through snail mail.'

I scanned the two letters. Both talked about 'senseless killings that could easily be avoided' and suggested that failure to accede to the demands would result in mass terror and damage to the Los Angeles economy. 'After all,' the letters read, 'who wants to be a tourist in Murder Central, USA?'

The first letter demanded a million dollars to prevent further killings. The second asked for two

81

million and threatened that the price would rise again if No Prisoners was not contacted by ten the following morning. The letters gave instructions for Fescoe to initiate contact by posting a specific term – 'tribute' – in an update on the LAPD's Facebook page.

In turn, the chief would get information about where and how to transfer the money. The letters also warned that failure to make contact and payment within twenty-four hours would cause the daily death toll to increase by one.

'Using social media as one of the levers,' Del Rio commented. 'You're dealing with someone young, educated, a planner.'

I nodded, 'And ex-military, I'd expect.'

Cammarata, a former US Army Ranger, snorted. 'Why? Just because he uses the handle No Prisoners? He could have played football, as in 'Take no prisoners.' Or soccer, for Christ's sake. Who is this amateur?'

I ignored the barb, said, 'Could very well be, Sheriff. That's just the way it feels to me.'

He nodded coldly. 'We pros don't go on feelings.'

'Well, there you go,' I replied. 'But honestly, I'm as confused as you are, Sheriff, as to why Rick and I were asked here.'

All eyes traveled to Chief Fescoe, who cleared his throat. 'In my opinion, what we have here is the makings of a first-class career Armageddon, a worse spree killer than the DC Sniper. How we handle this will pretty much determine our political fates, especially if the death count continues to rise. So what I'm about to suggest does not leave this room. Are we agreed?'

Slowly, reluctantly, all those gathered nodded, including me. 'I think Jack's right in his reaction and so is Del Rio, and that's part of why I asked them to join us,' Fescoe began. 'This "pay to stop the killing" angle. I've never seen it before. And there's something about the way this is being done, call it a feeling if you want, Lou, but this guy is not going to stop. He's highly trained. And he's going to kill until we either catch him or we buckle and pay him off.'

'We are not buckling,' Mayor Wills said emphatically. 'The City of Los Angeles will not be paying any murderous extortionist on my watch.'

'Exactly my thoughts, Your Honor,' the chief replied with a slow bow of his head. 'I never for a moment considered advising you to pay. But we are faced with a double-edged sword. If we don't pay, we must ask ourselves whether we are also dooming six innocent people to die tomorrow.'

'You don't know that,' Sheriff Cammarata snapped.

'You want to take the chance?' Fescoe shot back, reddening.

'No,' the mayor said. 'What are you suggesting, Mickey?'

Fescoe took a breath, glanced at me. 'We could call in the FBI and their profilers and let them take control of this, but then the extortion campaign would leak everywhere, any way you look at it a PR nightmare for us.'

'I sense an "or" coming,' Mayor Wills said.

'*Or* we can bring in Private on a hush-hush basis, as, say, consultants.'

'Why in God's name would we do that?' Sheriff

Cammarata demanded.

I was wondering the same thing. And I could tell Del Rio was too.

'Because they're not tied to the goddamned Constitution,' Fescoe said. 'They can simply do things we can't legally. They can take risks that we can't.'

'You mean they can cut corners and break laws?' the mayor said coldly.

'I didn't say that, Your Honor,' Fescoe soothed. 'But consider that six lives are at stake tomorrow, and seven the day after that. Wouldn't you cut a few corners to save those lives?'

I held up both hands. 'Whoa, whoa, whoa. Where am I legally here? Where is Private? My firm isn't going to do your dirty work and then have you turn around and slap us with some Bill of Rights violation.'

'That won't happen,' Fescoe said.

'How are you going to ensure that?' I demanded.

'The mayor is going to grant you blanket immunity beforehand, Jack. And the district attorney's going to sign the guarantee of that. And so are the state's attorney general and the governor.'

Chapter 21

In the garage in the City of Commerce, Watson clapped, pointed at the iPad in front of him, and roared, 'Thar she blows! "Tribute" on the LAPD Facebook page!'

Cobb set down a cup of hot coffee and hurried to see. There it was: 'Tribute to the fallen at CVS.'

'You were right on the money, Mr. Cobb,' Johnson said admiringly.

Cobb glanced at his watch. It was eight thirty in the evening. 'An hour before I'd predicted, but we'll take it.'

He turned to Kelleher, said, 'Your ball from here.'

The big man smoothed his red beard and began typing on his keyboard.

'Use the New Delhi and Panama crisscrosses,' Watson said.

Kelleher's left eye screwed up. 'Who taught you about the New Delhi and Panama crisscrosses?'

'Just saying,' Watson said.

'No chance they're paying us two million tomorrow,' Nickerson said.

'Of course not,' Cobb agreed. 'They'll try some sort of scam. Why?'

Watson muttered, 'Because the whole world's a scam, Mr. Cobb.'

'Damn right it is,' Cobb said, feeling in the groove of a familiar rant. 'Everybody's in a scam or being worked by a scammer. Look at Wall Street. Scam. Medicine? Scam. Politics? Scam. Religion? Bigger scam. Military?'

'Biggest scam,' said Hernandez and Johnson in unison.

'Plunderers,' Nickerson said.

Cobb cracked his knuckles, gestured with his scarred chin to Kelleher. 'Time to work them a little harder now. Turn up the voltage.'

85

Chapter 22

I got back to my house around ten. I'd been up for forty-two straight hours, running on fumes, desperately in need of rest. The following day was shaping up to be a brute and I wanted to have my wits about me, rather than stumbling around foggy, maybe making a mistake that might cost six innocent people their lives.

Justine called while I was brushing my teeth after a well-deserved shower.

'I just got home,' she said.

'Join the club,' I said, and yawned.

'What was the emergency meeting about?'

'Can't say. Anything new up at the Harlows'?'

'Not at the ranch, no. Or at least nothing until Sci and Mo-bot can run tests on the samples they brought back. I don't like Sanders and the other two.'

'I could tell. They're playing us somehow.'

In the background I could hear dogs barking. 'How's the bulldog?'

'Better,' Justine said. 'Settling in.'

'You took her with you?'

'You think I was going to let the dog be taken hostage by Camilla Bronson and locked in some hideaway along with the Harlows' help?'

'Locked? That's a little strong.'

'Is it?'

I knew better than to argue any further. 'Listen,

I've got to sleep.'

'One more thing,' she said. 'When I went on-line, I saw a story the AP picked up from a newspaper in Guadalajara.'

I rubbed my head, which was pounding. 'Okay?'

'It says that Thom and Jennifer Harlow were spotted stumbling around one of the more notorious sections of that city last night,' she said. 'Witnesses claimed they looked past the point of drunkenness.'

'Guadalajara?'

'Yes.'

I rubbed my temples. 'Looks like you're going to Mexico in the morning. Take Cruz with you.'

'But the dogs...' she began.

A beep sounded. Call waiting. I looked, closed my eyes, and swore my head was being split in two. My dear brother, Tommy, was calling.

'You're one of the most competent people I know,' I said to Justine. 'Figure it out. Get to Guadalajara. Find the Harlows.'

I hit ANSWER, said, 'Tommy?'

'Heh,' Tommy said, laughed.

He'd been drinking. My brother always laughs with a 'heh' when he's been drinking, another shitty trait Junior picked up from our late father. 'Didn't think you were gonna answer there, bro,' he said. 'Long time no see.'

'What do you want?'

We hadn't spoken in months, certainly not since Clay Harris died.

'My mouthpiece called a couple of hours ago,' Tommy said. 'That son of a bitch Billy Blaze *is* indicting me.'

I flashed on District Attorney Blaze during the meeting in the mayor's office. He hadn't said a word to me about my brother. But then, why would he?

Tommy kept grumbling drunkenly. 'Fucking murder one on circumstantial evidence. Can you believe that, Jack? They got no gun. No forensic evidence.'

'Other than the fact that you were picked up drunk and driving the dead man's car.'

'No powder blast on my coat or hands,' Tommy said.

'You've always been clever,' I replied. 'But anyway, sorry to hear you're going to trial. I'm beat-up tired, heading to bed.'

'Heh,' Tommy said, laughed with more bitterness. 'My liar says Billy Blaze will be there for the arraignment. Up for reelection next month, you know.'

'Tommy,' I began before my brother's voice changed, became arch and knowing.

'I get to speak, Jack,' he said. 'Did you know that? At the arraignment? I have the right to speak my piece, even against the advice of counsel and all. You should be there to hear what I have to say, brother. You really, really should.'

And then the line clicked dead.

A few minutes later, I lay in bed in the darkness, thinking, *What is there to stop Tommy from bringing me down with him? Implicating me in a murder I was in no way part of just to see me fall into the void after him? Just to see me ruined at last?*

Nothing, I thought as I plunged into sleep. *Nothing at all.*

Chapter 23

At five minutes to six the next morning, Justine sipped the last of her espresso and then groaned as she got out of her car and shuffled across the street toward the Crossfit box. She'd had barely four hours' sleep. Stella, the Harlows' bulldog, had whimpered until Justine had let her up on the bed. The dog had proceeded to snore and fart all night long.

But she really is a sweetheart, Justine thought as she entered the gym. What had happened to frighten her so badly? What had happened to the–?

'Justine? Hi.'

Justine startled and looked over to see Paul, the guy with the nice smile, nice eyes, and no wedding ring. He was stretching his hip flexors against the wall.

'Hi,' she said, realizing that she must look like hell. She hadn't even had time to run a brush through her hair before she'd run out the door.

But Paul didn't seem to mind. He just grinned, said, 'Trying to keep up with you yesterday put me in a coma at work.'

She flashed to the grueling workout they'd endured the day before. 'Sorry,' she said, moving to get a jump rope to warm up. 'What do you do?'

'I teach English.'

'UCLA?' she asked. It was the closest university

89

she could think of.

'No,' Paul said, his face falling slightly. 'Bonaventure. Charter school.'

Justine felt like she'd slighted him somehow. Instead of starting to skip rope, she said, 'Teaching is a noble calling. A way to change lives.'

Paul brightened again. 'I like to think so. My students. They're everything.'

'That's really nice,' Justine said, smiling as she started skipping. 'You make a difference.'

'I like to think so,' he said. 'What do you–?'

Before he could finish, the coach called the class into the group warm-up, three rounds of Russian kettle bell swings, lunges, and inchworm push-ups.

Ten minutes later, sweating, feeling her muscles burning to life, Justine prepared to start the actual workout, a twenty-minute AMRAP, or As Many Rounds As Possible in twenty minutes, of five handstand push-ups, ten wall balls, and fifteen box jumps.

'Handstand push-ups?' Paul moaned. 'Is that even possible?'

'Took me five months,' Justine said, kneeling on the floor, getting ready to kip herself up against the wall.

'You're bionic,' Paul said, and moved off to another part of the gym.

Justine watched him go, thinking how nice it was that he really seemed to love his job, saw it as a calling. It was rare these days to meet a guy who wasn't chasing money or power or whatever, a guy who–

'Go!'

90

She threw her feet overhead, balanced against the wall, and started to grind out the workout. *One, little sister. Four more now.*

When it was over, she'd done twelve rounds in the allotted twenty minutes. Not the best in the gym, but a perfectly respectable showing given the lack of sleep. She peeled herself off the floor as Paul staggered up and said, 'This is bad. I'm supposed to give a lecture on *Moby-Dick* in my AP class, and I feel like the harpooned whale.'

Justine laughed. It was an absurd line, but she liked it. A funny guy too.

'So,' Paul said. 'That guy who picked you up yesterday?'

Justine hesitated, then said, 'My boss.'

'Oh,' Paul said, looking relieved. 'What do you do?'

As a rule Justine didn't like talking about what she did, especially with single men. When they found out she worked for Private, many of them were intimidated. One guy had recently told her he couldn't date a woman who was capable of discovering his deepest secrets.

'Actuarial,' she said. 'Boring.'

'Sounds fascinating, actually,' Paul said, glanced at his watch. 'Feel like grabbing a cup of coffee before work? It's only seven.'

For a second Justine was tempted, but then she shook her head. 'Can't. Sorry, I have to be on a flight to Mexico at eight.'

'For actuarial work?'

'As a matter of fact,' Justine said. 'Rain check?'

'You bet,' he said, beaming. 'I'd like that.'

'Good,' Justine said, and left.

She ran across to her car, thinking that maybe the romantic part of her life was not such a mess after all. She had opportunities on the horizon.

Chapter 24

I don't think I moved a muscle all night. I opened my eyes around seven thirty, rolled over, and put a pillow over my head to block out the sunlight.

Dozing dreams are the most real, don't you think? I do. On the edge of consciousness, my mind conjured a scene from my childhood. I lay on the grass, screaming in agony while Tommy laughed because I'd broken my wrist trying to skateboard as well as he did. I played college football, but that had more to do with my tenacity; my brother was always the gifted one athletically.

My dreams mutated and I found myself lost in some kind of Rube Goldberg contraption populated by the people who'd gathered in the mayor's office in response to the No Prisoners killings.

'Find him, Jack,' Mayor Wills said, sounding like the Queen of Hearts in *Alice in Wonderland*. 'Stop him.'

'By any means necessary,' Chief Fescoe said.

'We'll work with and parallel to you,' said District Attorney Billy Blaze, who strangely wore a button with Tommy's ten-year-old face on it.

'But we don't want to know a thing about your tactics,' added Sheriff Cammarata. 'Are we clear on that, Morgan?'

In my dreams, it had all seemed perfectly clear. Find and capture No Prisoners, then turn him over, Private's role a complete secret to everyone but a select inner circle. But when my cell rang, waking me up for good, things quickly became murkier.

'I don't like this, Jack,' said Del Rio by way of hello. 'I've been up half the night because I feel like we're being set up to take a fall somehow.'

'They're granting us blanket immunity in advance. I'm supposed to see a copy of the document by nine.'

'What do they expect us to do that they can't?'

'I'm not sure they know,' I admitted. 'Whatever it takes to get No Prisoners behind bars.'

'They should be forming a task force or something. Put a hundred men on it. Bring in Cal Justice investigators. Bring in the FBI.'

'City, county, and state are all cash strapped. I guess they see Private as the cheaper alternative. And they don't want to cede authority to the bureau.'

'I still don't like it.'

'I don't either, but I gave my word, said we'd do it.'

Silence.

Another call came in. Mo-bot. I told Del Rio I'd call him the minute I heard anything from Chief Fescoe, hit ACCEPT, said, 'Maureen.'

'Cynthia Maines just showed up in our lobby,' Mo-bot said. 'She's demanding to know why we've been calling her cell phone nonstop and screwing up the first vacation she's had with her boyfriend in almost a year.'

Chapter 25

At twenty-eight and five-foot four in a pale-gray dress with pearls and black pumps, Cynthia Maines was a hyper, articulate, and forceful woman who'd attended the University of Southern California's famous film school and been hired almost immediately upon graduation as the Harlows' personal assistant and eventually coproducer.

'So you must have been intimately involved in the details of *Saigon Falls*,' I said early in the conversation, setting a steaming coffee cup before her. She and I and Mo-bot were in my office.

'Is this why you've been calling me?' Maines asked in disbelief. 'Look, I had a firm deal with Jen and Thom. I was to get three full weeks off, and it's only been like four days and they've got you calling me nonstop? I'd like to know what's going on. I've tried their cells, the ranch, and the apartment lines, and no answer.'

'Because they've disappeared,' I said.

Her head snapped back as if she'd been popped in the nose.

'What?'

'They're gone,' I said. 'Somewhere between the hours of six and eight p.m. three days ago, all of them disappeared except the dog, who we found terrorized in the help's quarters. Where have you been the last few days?'

Maines seemed more than dazed, suddenly lost, groping to find her way through what I was telling her.

'Mammoth Lakes,' she said in a dull voice. 'I was up there with Philip, my boyfriend. We rented a house and ... what are the police telling you? Why isn't it all over the news? Facebook?'

'Because no one knows, outside of the help; Private; and Sanders, Camilla Bronson, and Terry Graves, all of whom hired us to find you and the Harlows.'

Maines stared off for several seconds, then looked at us. 'This is for real? I'm not being punked here?'

'It's for real,' Mo-bot said. 'Got any idea where they might be?'

'I know where they were supposed to be,' she replied. 'They'd scheduled six days at home alone on the ranch. They wanted family time. And Thom was going to begin editing everything shot in Vietnam. Jennifer was going to work the logistics of the last scenes to be filmed at Warner in a couple of weeks.'

'That doesn't answer my question,' I said.

'I don't know,' she insisted. 'They could be anywhere. Where's the jet?'

'In its hangar at Burbank,' Mo-bot replied.

Maines shook her head. 'Then I have no idea. They could be anywhere, but that's not really true. I mean, someone would see them.'

'Exactly,' I replied. 'There is someone who claims to have seen Jennifer and Thom in Mexico the day before yesterday, very, very drunk.'

She shook her head again. 'They don't drink.

95

They made that pact when they got married. Neither of them has had a drop in fifteen years.'

'Okay,' I said. 'Any reason for them to be in Guadalajara, drunk or not?'

The Harlows' personal assistant sat there a long moment, blinking, then slowly rocked her chin right and slightly up before twisting it sharply left. 'No idea.'

'No business concerns there?' Mo-bot asked. 'No plans for an orphanage?'

'Not that I can remember. You could check with Camilla. She handles the schedule when it comes to Sharing Hands projects.'

'You don't have working knowledge of the foundation?' I asked.

She shook her head. 'Camilla and Sanders took most of that load. My involvement was limited to arranging up-to-the-minute itineraries for visits, photo shoots, that kind of thing. Why haven't the police or the FBI been notified?'

I shrugged. 'The three amigos asked us to keep it quiet. To wait and see if your employers turned up or if we heard from any kidnappers. I told him I'd wait until tomorrow latest before contacting the FBI.'

'Well,' Maines huffed, and made to get out of her seat. 'I'm not waiting, I'm going to–'

'Before you do anything, could you answer a few more of my questions?' I asked.

'Like what?' she said impatiently.

'Oh, I don't know, like do you stand to benefit personally in any way from the Harlows' vanishing?'

Chapter 26

Maines's manicured fingers rolled to form fists, and her words came out hot. 'There is absolutely no benefit to me. What are you, crazy? What possible benefit could there be to me in that situation? Look, I hitched my wagon to Thom and Jen six years ago when I had a lot of other compelling offers.

'It's been the best experience of my life,' she went on. 'Demanding and maniacal at times. But magical more often than not. And fulfilling. And lucrative. In no way whatsoever would I jeopardize that. No way. Ever.'

I believed her. 'Had to ask.'

'Any more questions?' she asked coldly.

'As a matter of fact.'

'What if I don't wish to answer? I mean, it's not like you're cops.'

Mo-bot said, 'We both have the same goal, Cynthia, to find the Harlows and find them alive, right? I mean, the more people working the better, no matter who's paying the bill, Harlow-Quinn Productions or Uncle Sam.'

Maines remained stiff but nodded. 'What do you want to know?'

'Give me thumbnails on Sanders, Bronson, and Terry Graves and their relationships with the Harlows.'

Maines thought about that.

'Dave's a typical attorney-agent, all business, with almost all his business coming from the Harlows,' she said. 'Camilla's a bitch but very good at what she does. She and Jen are friends. They enjoy plotting.'

'Graves?'

'I like Terry,' Maines said. 'He's also very good at what he does, which allows Jen and Thom to do what they do best: be creative.'

'No beefs between any of them and the Harlows?' I asked.

She shrugged. 'No more than the normal give-and-take. Their wagons are hitched to the Harlows too. Why would they upset the golden cart?'

'Tell us about life with the Harlows leading up to their arrival back in the States,' Mo-bot said.

Over the course of the next twenty minutes, Maines went on to describe the Harlows' whirlwind existence in the last year and what it took for her to help steer their personal and professional lives. She worked for them but considered Thom and Jennifer friends, people she admired and trusted. The time spent in Vietnam had been exhausting but exhilarating. And she'd been stunned at the breadth and depth of the saga the Harlows were depicting in *Saigon Falls*.

'It was like every day you knew something brilliant was being created,' she said. 'I felt like it was an honor to work on such a project.'

'Sanders said the Harlows were about out of money when they got home,' I said. 'Personal assets were going to have to be sold.'

That seemed to puzzle Maines. 'Is that true? If it is, that's the first I've heard of it.'

'Sanders said he told the Harlows about the situation shortly after they arrived back in the United States.'

'Well, there you go,' Maines said. 'I left as soon as I got off the plane. My boyfriend was there at the jetport waiting, and I was in no mood to stick around.'

'So you *didn't* accompany them to the ranch?'

'I did not,' she said. 'I was done once I got off the plane, and everyone knew it. Things had been intense for so long, I needed to breathe. I still do.'

'Did Thom talk about a mysterious new investor in the film?' I asked.

She half laughed. '"There are always mysterious new investors on the horizon." That's one of Thom's lines.'

'What about their sex life?' Mo-bot asked.

The assistant reddened. 'I ... I'm their personal assistant, but I'm not privy to their life behind closed doors.'

I said, 'There were lots of sex toys in their closets.'

Maines reddened again, looked at her lap. 'Look, that's way outside my pay grade. All I know is that Thom and Jennifer were devoted to each other and to their children, and that they led an exemplary life. And I've had just about enough of this. I'm going to the FBI, get them involved.'

'I think it's a good idea, but I don't know what standing you'll have,' I said as she got to her feet. 'Legally, I mean. You're not family.'

She hesitated, glanced at the door. 'So what should I do?'

'Let me make the call first,' I said. 'I'll tell the

FBI what we know, try to work with them from here on out. You can call afterwards, back me up with your concerns.'

Maines nodded, put a card on my desk, took mine. Then she thumped a finger on the edge of the desk, said, 'Remember that movie *All the President's Men*, about Watergate? That guy kept saying "Follow the money". It's always about the money, isn't it?'

'Point taken,' I said. 'Definitely point taken.'

Chapter 27

Twenty minutes later I was looking at copies of Cynthia Maines's financials courtesy of Sci.

'Maines receives a base salary of four hundred K a year,' Kloppenberg said. 'But she is underwater on six different investments she made before the crash, three of them in Vegas real estate. Her cash flow is strong, but she's got no savings to speak of. I'd describe her lifestyle as self-indulgent and her investment philosophy as incoherent. Other than a total lack of use of credit or debit cards over the last four days, Maines has a long and wide history of extravagant purchases. Luxury goods. *Robb Report* baubles.'

'No bangles?' I asked.

'Plenty of those too,' Sci said. 'Tiffany's most recently.'

'What else?' I asked.

'I think she was lying about the Harlows' sex

life,' Mo-bot said.

'Either that or she's a prude,' I said.

'But what are the chances of that in Holly-wood?' Mo-bot asked. 'And there was another thing she was being evasive about.'

'What's that?' I asked.

'Guadalajara,' Mo-bot said. 'I got the impression that she was conflicted, less than forthright.'

I thought back and felt she was right. 'Good thing Justine and Cruz are on their way there right now.'

Sci frowned. 'They took the jet?'

'Yeah, so?' I asked.

'I never get to take the jet,' Kloppenberg said, openly pouting.

'Report it to a human rights commission,' I said. 'And I want this same sort of report drawn up on Sanders, Bronson, and Graves.'

'Give us a couple of hours,' Mo-bot said.

My cell phone rang. Mickey Fescoe.

'Chief?' I said.

'Get down to the Huntington Pier ASAP,' Fescoe said. 'I want you and Del Rio to see what we're up against.'

Chapter 28

Wearing black polarized sunglasses despite the iron-gray sky, a floppy olive-drab fishing hat, flip-flops, shorts, and a T-shirt that read 'Bass Pro Shops,' Nickerson picked up a bait bucket, salt-water rod, and tackle box and shuffled out onto the Huntington Beach Pier, where a breeze was building.

With the possible exception of the earbuds he wore and the fiber-optic camera hidden among the various lures stuck along the band of his hat, Nickerson looked no different from thirty or forty other men trying their fishing luck out on the pier.

At its far end, more than a quarter mile out into the Pacific, the pier widened into a large diamond shape dominated by a red-roofed diner called Ruby's. Nickerson skirted left of the diner and took up a position along the rail where he could monitor the pier's west end.

'That'll do,' Cobb said in Nickerson's ear.

'How long you figure?' Nickerson muttered as he squatted over his tackle box and bait bucket.

'Any time now,' Cobb said. 'Get to work while you can.'

Nickerson settled in like a man certain of his craft, which he was. He removed lures that looked like pale-gray six-inch squid, with trailing tentacles. When he was positive no one was watching, he reached through the lower rails of the pier and pressed the lures up against a steel girder. The hooks had been magnetized, and soon the lures, six of them in all, were tucked up under the flange of the walkway. They were very close to the color of the girders and visible only from the sea, which meant only by surfers, lifeguards, or shore patrol, and only if they were studying the girders carefully with binoculars.

After rigging up a real lure and dropping his

line over the side, Nickerson braced his pole, then crouched over his tackle box. This time he picked up what appeared to be a lead weight painted dull gray. It was about the size and shape of a matchbook, as thick as a cell phone. Hoops like the eyes of fishhooks stuck out at either end of the weight. He used brass snaps to attach steel leaders to each eye. He got two large fishhooks from the tackle box and fixed them to the unattached end of each steel leader.

'Mr. Hernandez just spotted Fescoe coming onto the pier,' Cobb said.

'He alone?' Nickerson asked, glancing around.

An old Vietnamese guy stood at the rail about twenty feet to his left, jigging his pole, looking down into the sea. To his right some fifteen feet, a dad and young son rigged poles.

'So far as I can tell.'

The old Vietnamese guy gave a cry. Nickerson's attention shot to him. The second he realized the old man's pole was bent hard, he swiveled his back to the windows of Ruby's Diner and faced the sea, knowing that all eyes would be on the fight and the catch. Nickerson twisted the hoops at either end of the metal weight, one toward him, one away. Then he stuck the entire rig under the railing, pressing the hooks into the plastic bellies of two of the squid lures, thus completing a circuit.

He stood up immediately and turned to see the old angler bring up a stout bottom fish, a fantail sole that wriggled and flapped, provoking murmurs and soft cries of appreciation from the other fishermen.

'Nice fish,' Nickerson said.

'Good eating, this one,' the old man said, grinning. His teeth were brown.

Nickerson nodded. But behind the polarized lenses, he was watching Chief Fescoe moving toward the westernmost tip of the pier and two men he hadn't noticed before, one rangy and good-looking, the other shorter, stockier.

'Fescoe's got friends,' Nickerson murmured, and adjusted his hat so the camera better faced the trio.

'I see them,' Cobb said.

Watson said, 'Hold still for a capture.'

Nickerson froze, stopped breathing for a count of four.

'Got them,' Watson said.

'You done, Mr. Nickerson?' Cobb said.

'I am,' Nickerson said. 'You should be picking up a signal.'

Silence, then, 'That's an affirmative,' Cobb said. 'Leave them to their scamming. Move your fishing gear in toward shore. Fish for an hour. Chat with a few of the locals, then get the hell out of there.'

'On it,' Nickerson said, and got his pole, tackle box, and bait bucket, only once glancing over toward Fescoe and the two men with him, all of whom were looking westward toward the breaking waves.

Serves them right, Nickerson thought. *Like Mr Cobb always says, this is what you get for scamming.*

Chapter 29

'The pickup's gonna be here, nine tonight,' Chief Fescoe said as the breeze stiffened, throwing his hair into his eyes.

'Here?' I said, squinting at the wind, glancing around at the diner and the deck that surrounded it. 'Why would he do that? He'll be cornered out here.'

'No, we drop the money. It lands in the water. In the darkness.'

Del Rio cast a jaundiced eye toward the waves and the surfers and kiteboarders plying the water below us. He said, 'Still a tough pickup. No Prisoners has gotta be thinking police boats, helicopters, scuba.'

The chief stiffened. 'He is thinking that, and more. His letter says any sign of a police presence beyond me making the drop, and six civilians die.'

'We're not cops,' Del Rio said.

Fescoe breathed a sigh of relief. 'Exactly my thinking, and the mayor's. You're not cops, so your presence is safer. In effect.'

I squinted at him, then down at the waves crashing off the pier's stanchions far below me. 'So what's our goal?'

'Hunt the bastard, Jack,' Fescoe said. 'Set up an ambush. Capture him. Turn him over to us.'

I thought it through for several beats. 'So he claims that any sign of a police presence, he's a no-show and kills six, correct?'

'That's the threat,' Fescoe agreed.

'There's more than one guy, then,' I said.

Del Rio understood. 'He's got a watcher, or he's the watcher, and someone else is making the pickup.'

'That's how it looks to me,' I said. 'Which makes the situation more complicated. More demanding.'

'But doable?' Fescoe asked.

'Yes,' I said. 'Terms?'

'The immunity document's on its way,' Fescoe said. 'And the mayor's offering you three hundred grand in exchange for No Prisoners' capture or...'

I raised my eyebrow when his voice trailed off. 'You're suggesting?'

'I'm suggesting nothing,' Fescoe said, flustered. 'You're covered in any case, Jack. We simply can't afford to have some lunatic, or group of lunatics, killing increasing numbers of people in Los Angeles every day. He, they, must be stopped. Tonight.'

Looking to Del Rio, I said, 'What do you think?'

'You already know what I think,' Del Rio said. He gestured over the rail. 'Long fall from here, Jack.'

Still, the situation intrigued me. My mind was already coming up with possible ways we could set and spring the trap without triggering more murders.

'Okay,' I said at last. 'We're in. But we're going to need every bit of support you can give us. No matter what we ask for, Mickey.'

'Done,' he said. 'Whatever you need, Jack.'

Chapter 30

Private's jet, a Gulfstream G550, began its descent into Guadalajara around eleven thirty that morning. It had taken Justine and Emilio Cruz just shy of three hours and twenty minutes to make the journey.

Twenty-nine, with a dark, sleek ponytail and a clean-shaven face, Cruz was a former California Golden Gloves middleweight champion and special investigator with the state's Department of Justice. He'd joined Private two years prior, and had proved an exceptional detective.

Justine felt as if she couldn't have had any better partner on this trip. She spoke Spanish well, but not fluently. Cruz was fluent. More, he was the kind of guy who saw things that others did not. In some ways, he was almost as good at spotting clues and irregularities as Jack was.

Indeed, for the past ten minutes Jack had been the subject of conversation, as he often was when two or more members of Private were together out of their boss's presence.

'I know you got problems with him, but the dude's inspiring, all there is to it,' Cruz said. 'Jack gets his teeth into something, never lets go.'

'True,' Justine said. 'It's his greatest gift. He's got all these walls up around him, never letting you know exactly what he's feeling. What's with that?'

Justine was trained as a psychologist, and Jack's

unwillingness to reveal his inner emotions had played a critical role in the end of their short-lived intimate relationship. She figured Cruz, as a male, might shed light on this aspect of Jack's personality.

But Cruz shifted uncomfortably, said, 'Follow the Dodgers much?'

'Rarely, and only when it's necessary.'

'Right, which is exactly how I am with all this inner navel stuff,' Cruz said. 'I know you're brilliant at what you do, and I'm not criticizing your profession. Well, maybe a little. But after a while, you know, I find it better to face in one direction, in front of you, just let the past lay and get on with it, right?'

'But some people don't know how to get on with it,' Justine protested.

'Like a lot of Dodgers fans,' Cruz said.

Before she could reply, the pilot came on, told them to bring their seats upright for landing.

Inside the terminal, an immigration officer noted they'd arrived on a jet owned by Private.

'That's right,' Cruz said. 'We're here to look for several missing persons.'

'Who are these peoples?' the officer asked.

'We're not free to say,' Justine said. 'It's confusing. We don't even really know if they are missing, just that we got a report that two of them were seen here in Guadalajara recently.'

The officer had stared at them stone-faced for several moments, and then asked, 'How long you stay?'

'Long as it takes to convince ourselves whether they're here or not.'

'How many peoples are missing?'

'Five,' Justine said. 'A family. Americans.'

'And you think they was kidnapped here?'

'Or came here without telling anyone. We don't know,' Justine said. 'We're here to try and find out.'

The officer gave them that stone-faced expression again, then stamped their passports and said, 'Enjoy your stay in Mexico, *señor, señora*.'

Chapter 31

After checking in, Justine and Cruz left the Hotel Francis in the city's Zona Central. The temperature hovered in the low eighties. The breeze smelled of simmering chicken, probably a mole, Justine thought. In the distance, she could hear music playing. Brass horns.

'We should make contact with the local police,' Cruz said. 'See if any reports were made regarding the Harlows.'

'Why not go right to the horse's mouth?' Justine replied. She'd changed into a light summer shift, blue and conservative, covering her knees.

'And whose mouth would that be?' Cruz asked.

Justine fished in her pocketbook, found her iPhone, opened the notes app, said, 'Leona Casa Madre, the blogger who made the claim on her site.'

'She never saw them personally, right?' Cruz said.

'No, but she claimed to have interviewed two people who saw them.'

'Drunk.'

'That's what she wrote,' Justine said.

'No, I meant her, the blogger,' Cruz said. 'I looked her up as well. Two years ago, she got fired from *La Prensa* in Mexico City when her love of tequila overcame her ability to perform her job as one of the newspaper's court reporters. So she's hardly an unimpeachable source. We really should go to—'

'No,' Justine said, standing her ground. 'I have a gut feeling about this. I mean, if she can lead us to the people who actually saw the Harlows, it doesn't matter what her past is.'

Cruz hesitated, then said, 'Jack said you lead. I follow.'

'I like that,' Justine said.

'Figured you would. You have an address for her?'

'As a matter of fact,' Justine replied.

A short cab ride later, they pulled up in front of an apartment building on the Rio Panuco, east of González Gallo Park. 'Number eight,' Justine said when Cruz went to the security phone by a locked steel front gate.

He buzzed, got nothing. He buzzed again. Nothing. A woman pushing two children in a stroller came to the gate. She opened it, looked at them suspiciously, spoke to Cruz in blisteringly fast Spanish.

Cruz smiled, flashed his Private badge, and replied. Justine got most of it. The woman had asked who they were looking for, and Cruz had

110

given her the blogger's name, which the woman obviously recognized because her head lagged to one side in a gesture of *What are you going to do?*

'Leona always sleeps in late, two, three in the afternoon, then up all night, that one, writing her book, she says,' the woman said. 'She's up there. Just pound on her door. She'll hear you eventually. Maybe she'll even answer.'

Chapter 32

They found number eight on the second floor on the other side of a surprisingly well-tended garden where flowers were still blooming. Somewhere a cat was meowing, long and loud, as if in heat.

Cruz knocked on the oak door. 'Señora Casa Madre?' he called. 'Leona?'

After a minute of no response, Justine said, 'I think the lady said pounding was in order.'

Cruz shrugged, pounded with his fist, and they waited another minute. 'That should have woken the dead,' he said in frustration. 'Maybe there's a back door. Or a window or something.'

Justine was about to agree when something told her to try the doorknob. It twisted. She heard a click. The door sagged on its hinges and swung slightly inward. She pushed it open with her fingers, calling, *'Señora?'*

The cat was louder now, and Justine realized it was inside the blogger's apartment. She took a step into the doorway, finding a room dimly lit by the sun sneaking through the slats of closed blinds to reveal slices of a pack rat's nest. The apartment smelled of cat urine, rotting food, and the hint of things fouler.

Newspapers, magazines, and books were stacked on every inch of every piece of furniture save a simple, largely bare wooden desk, which displayed the greatest sense of order in the place. The cat meowed again, louder this time.

'Leona?' Cruz called.

Justine pointed beyond a kitchen that looked as if it hadn't been cleaned thoroughly in months. Dishes were stacked in the sink. There had to have been at least ten empty bottles of tequila, rotgut stuff, sitting amid other trash on the counters. The garbage reeked so badly she stopped breathing through her nose.

It was the lair of an alcoholic, one well down the road in the disease, far beyond caring about personal hygiene. Justine had been in these kinds of hovels before as part of interventions by concerned relatives. She'd never had the heart to explain to them that this sort of existence pointed to little or no hope.

'*Señora?*' she called, then continued in Spanish. 'We're with Private Investigations Worldwide. We wanted to talk about the story you put up on your blog, about the Harlows?'

But there was no reply.

'Let's check the bedroom and get out of here,' Cruz said. 'Place makes me want to take a shower. Make that several showers.'

Justine nodded, went to the hallway beyond the kitchen, turned on the light. The hallway had

112

been turned into a pantry of sorts, with canned food, human and feline, stacked on shelves beside several full bottles of tequila.

The bedroom was a shambles – clothes commingled with books and paper and trash – and Justine found herself wondering about the bizarre reaches of the human mind, how it could drift into a realm where living in a garbage dump felt like the exact right thing to do.

The cat meowed even more loudly and then hissed as if it were facing off with a dog. The noises came from behind a closed door in the corner.

'*Señora?*' Justine called, and knocked gently at the door.

When she got no answer, she looked at Cruz, who nodded. She twisted the knob and pushed the door open. The cat, an orange tabby with mangy fur, leaped off a counter and blew by Justine before she could fully digest what she was seeing inside the bathroom.

Leona Casa Madre was naked, bloated, sprawled between the toilet and the bath, a broken bottle of tequila beside her. Her head was turned toward the door as if she'd been listening for something or someone before she died.

Whether or not she'd seen Death come for her, or had talked to Death, was unclear. Her eyes were gone, eaten out of their sockets. Her lips were chewed off as well.

'Now do you think we should contact the cops?' Cruz asked.

But Justine was rushing from the room, wanting to throw up everything she'd eaten in the last five days.

113

Chapter 33

'All rise,' the bailiff cried at two that afternoon. 'The Honorable Sharon Greer presiding.'

Judge Greer, a handsome woman in her late forties, strode up onto the bench inside the Bauchet Street Superior Courthouse east of L.A.'s Chinatown. She sat, donned reading glasses, and asked her clerk, 'How many more?'

'Ten, Your Honor,' the clerk replied.

'Let's move...' The judge stopped her order in midstream, spotting the district attorney as he entered. 'Mr. Blaze,' she said, cocking her head. 'A surprise to find you in my courtroom. I didn't think you did arraignments anymore.'

'It's an honor, Your Honor,' Billy Blaze replied, running a hand down the front of his suit jacket as if to make sure it was buttoned correctly, swiveling his head, taking in the surprisingly empty courtroom and me.

I'd feared a media horde for Tommy's arraignment. Billy Blaze acted like he *longed* for a media horde. But I imagined that almost every journalist in L.A. was working some angle of the No Prisoners shootings by now.

In any case, the district attorney nodded stiffly at me, went through the swinging gates, set his briefcase on the state's table. A harried, mousy woman clutching a stack of manila files hurried after him and I groaned. Alice Dunphy was defending

Tommy? Dunphy was a public defender, and not the most organized person in the world.

Then again, maybe she'd just been asked to rep him for arraignment. I prayed that was the case. If Dunphy planned to defend Tommy through the criminal phase, he might as well call ahead to San Quentin to reserve a cell.

I noticed something else. Neither Tommy's wife, Annie, nor his nine-year-old son, Ned, was in the room. I had no time to consider what their absence meant because a door behind the bailiff opened. A sheriff's deputy led my brother in. He'd surrendered himself earlier in the day and now wore an orange jumpsuit, wrist and ankle shackles.

True to form, Tommy appeared not to care, as if he were wearing his latest suit from Hermès and had come to the room for a high-level meeting among equals. He spotted me, winked, then turned, sat, and began whispering to his attorney.

The wink. I kept seeing it. Was this it? Was he going to implicate me in a killing that I absolutely had not committed? Clay Harris might have killed my ex-girlfriend, but I still suspected that Tommy was behind it somehow. And that would explain why he had gotten rid of Clay – to tie up any loose ends. Now he was trying to pin Clay's murder on me. Was my brother going to destroy me for spite?

'The State of California versus Thomas Morgan, Jr.,' the clerk announced.

Alice Dunphy nudged Tommy. My brother stood, looking at ease, in control, unshaken by the gravity of the proceedings.

'Charge?' the judge asked.

'Murder in the first degree,' Billy Blaze said, paused for dramatic effect. 'Your Honor, the state plans to seek special circumstances in this case.'

Special circumstances. Blaze was seeking the death penalty for my brother. The charge and the potential penalty shook me. They seemed to mildly amuse Tommy, however, because he looked back over his shoulder at me and winked again, as if to say, 'Care to join me in the gas chamber, brother?'

'Ms. Dunphy?' the judge said.

Before the public defender could speak, Tommy put his hand on her forearm. 'I'd like to speak on my own behalf, Your Honor.'

'Only a fool acts as his own attorney, Mr. Morgan.'

'Yes, Your Honor,' Tommy said, turning on the Irish charm. 'I've been called a fool and worse many times before.'

Judge Greer sighed. 'Your choice, Mr. Morgan. How do you plead?'

'Not guilty.'

'Why doesn't that surprise me?' the judge replied, then looked at the district attorney. 'Bail, Mr. Blaze?'

'The state seeks remand,' Billy Blaze said. 'Mr. Morgan is a flight risk.'

'I'll surrender my passport,' Tommy offered. 'And, Judge, just so you know, we, I, am going to mount a vigorous defense. I know who the real killer is. I have compelling evidence, overwhelming evidence that the real killer is...'

His voice faded. The next moment was as long as any I have ever experienced, as long as the

116

moment after a Taliban rocket hit the rotor of my helicopter in Afghanistan, my life once again hanging in the balance.

Chapter 34

'You're arresting *us?*' Justine cried at Commandant Raoúl Gomez of the Jalisco State Police, and Arturo Fox, the chief of municipal police in Guadalajara.

Bizarrely, or at least it seemed so to Justine, the two high-level law enforcement officials had arrived at virtually the same time in the courtyard below Leona Casa Madre's apartment, roughly a half hour after Emilio Cruz had called the body in and not ten minutes after the first uniformed officers had arrived. The two men had gone cold, hard, and sardonic when Justine and Cruz presented their Private badges and identifications.

'You are in this country conducting an investigation without declaring yourself to law enforcement, without working through proper channels?' Commandant Gomez asked. He was a small, imperious man who believed nearly everything he said in a scornful tone.

'We told Immigration who we were,' Cruz said.

'It is customary to notify the police,' Commandant Gomez said.

'There's a body upstairs,' Justine said. 'We thought you'd like to know.'

'Yes, you did want us to know,' Chief Fox

replied. He tapped his temple with a thick finger. 'But I think the two of you are clever. I think you tell us this to cover your tracks.'

Fox was as big as Gomez was small, with a broad belly and cheek wattles that shook with indignation as he delivered the accusation. Gomez watched, flicking the nails of his index fingers against his thumb pads.

'Don't be a couple of corrupt jackasses trying to show off your penises to each other,' Justine retorted. 'The woman's been dead at least a day or two. We only just arrived in Guadalajara. Check the facts. Look at the time stamp on our passports.'

Justine had moved to dig out her passport, but Chief Fox and Commandant Gomez seemed only to have heard her calling them corrupt jackasses trying to show off their penises, because that was when Justine and Cruz had been told to put their hands behind their backs and she'd demanded to know if they were under arrest.

'Of course you're under arrest,' Gomez snarled. 'You broke into an apartment. You may have murdered someone. And have you not heard? In Mexico, we have Napoleonic law. Here you are guilty until proven innocent, and that has not a thing to do with jackasses or penises or corruption.'

'Look,' Cruz said, trying to remain calm. 'I'm sorry. She's sorry. We're here looking for five missing persons. We believed Señora Casa Madre might have some knowledge of their whereabouts. We found her dead. End of story.'

'Yes?' Chief Fox said, not buying it. 'Who is this

118

missing people?'

Justine and Cruz exchanged glances. Then Cruz said, 'Thom and Jennifer Harlow, the actors, and their three children.'

At that Gomez's head jerked back as if he'd sniffed something fouler than the decomposing body of Leona Casa Madre. But then Chief Fox chortled disdainfully, 'You really do think we are corrupt jackasses.'

'Take them away,' Commandant Gomez barked at one of the uniformed officers standing guard. 'We'll see if this story of much nonsense changes after a night in the cells.'

Chapter 35

Everyone in that courtroom was staring at my brother, including me and District Attorney Blaze, who filled the silence before Tommy could finish his thought and implicate someone else, probably me, in a cold-blooded killing.

'Objection, Your Honor!' Billy Blaze shouted. 'This man can't just go around accusing people of murder, slandering them in a public venue without cause. If Mr. Morgan has such evidence, he should have brought it to my office, which he has not.'

'Sustained,' Judge Greer said, glanced at Tommy while my insides churned. Even from my angle, I could see that my brother was enraged that his little drama had been interrupted; and I half expected him to start shouting that I was to blame, that I had gotten him drunk, committed the murder myself, put Tommy in the victim's car, fled the scene, or some diabolical nonsense like that.

'Mr. Morgan,' the judge went on. 'The matter is bail, not your countertheory regarding the manner of Mr. Harris's death.'

'I am not a flight risk, Judge,' Tommy insisted. 'I have a business here, a wife, a son. And these charges are not true. I plan to fight. I plan to win.'

Greer hesitated, but only for a moment. 'Mr. Morgan, you are to surrender your passport to my bailiff. And your bail is set at five million dollars.'

She rapped her gavel.

Five million? That number sank in, along with the general weakness I suddenly felt as the adrenaline that had seized my body began to ooze away. Tommy did not have five million. He was a recovering gambling addict. He didn't even have the five hundred grand he'd have to come up with to get a bondsman to cover his bail.

But my brother looked unruffled at the figure, said, 'I can live with that.'

Judge Greer rapped her gavel, looked at her clerk. 'Next.'

A sheriff's deputy came for Tommy, while a new inmate appeared from the door to the holding cells. Tommy looked at me, said, 'Help me, brother.'

I watched him disappear as if he'd gone overboard in the darkness, leaving me the only one capable of throwing him a lifeline.

'Morgan,' Billy Blaze said in a harsh whisper, and pointed toward the door.

I startled, got up, and followed the DA into the outer hall, where in that same harsh whisper, Blaze demanded, 'Who's he gonna implicate?'

'I have no idea. Tommy and I aren't close.'

He squinted. 'And yet you come to your brother's arraignment?'

'Blood's thick,' I replied coolly. 'Haven't you heard?'

Billy Blaze studied me. 'I think the chief and the mayor have grossly overestimated you, Morgan.'

'Think whatever you want, Billy,' I said.

The district attorney clucked his disapproval and said, 'I'm watching you, Jack. Your brother's a killer. It wouldn't surprise me if you turn out to be one too.'

As Billy Blaze walked off toward the elevators, I wasn't thinking about what he'd just said to me. I was wondering instead if the strange tattered bond that still existed between my brother and me was strong enough to warrant my posting his bail on a murder charge that he might try to implicate me in as part of his defense.

In all honesty, the thought of Tommy sitting in a jail, stewing, forced to ponder a life behind bars, or worse, a death by lethal injection, definitely had its appeal. But in the next moment I thought of my late mother, who'd told us often that as toddlers we'd spoken our own language, and that the blood of twins was thicker than any other bond, and that by our shared DNA we were committed to each other for life.

Enslaved to each other is more like it, I thought, unsuccessfully fighting the idea that I could just walk away. Keep your enemies closer, wasn't that the old saying? In any case, it was the argument I relied on as I took the elevator to the clerk's office, where I planned to find out what I needed to do to post the bail and get my brother back where he belonged for the time being: at home with my sister-in-law and nephew, not sitting in a cell, resentful and plotting ways to destroy me. Or at least that was how my illogic was evolving when the elevator doors opened. I went to the clerk's office, where a plump, cheerful woman at the front desk said, 'How can I help you, handsome?'

I smiled, saw her name tag, said, 'You made my day, Judy.'

Judy tittered, 'Just doing my job, sir.'

I pulled out a checkbook. 'I'm here to make bail for Thomas Morgan, Jr.'

Her face fell into confusion. 'Well, someone's just done that.'

Shocked, I said, 'Who?'

'Me,' said an all-too-familiar voice.

I looked to my left and saw an overeducated, impeccably dressed, and utterly ruthless gangster named Carmine Noccia leaning against the counter, holding a BlackBerry.

Chapter 36

Rick Del Rio was born into a family of hunters who lived in southern Arizona. His grandfather often took him out into the desert and taught him how to track deer, javelina, and quail. One of the most important things Del Rio learned from his grandfather was to move swiftly through country where there were no new tracks or old ones; and to slow to a crawl when he found fresh sign, as it usually indicated the animal was about to bed.

Standing close to where Chief Fescoe would drop the money at the far end of the pier, Del Rio felt like he was in his prey's bedroom somehow, but he couldn't understand exactly why it had intentionally cornered itself, or at least exposed itself so blatantly to capture.

At the same time, there was no doubt in Del Rio's mind that the killer or killers felt comfortable, confident, even, that a pickup of two million dollars could be made as well as a daring escape. But were they actually going to have Fescoe make the drop at the end of the pier, or did they plan to take him on some kind of long runaround like in those old Dirty Harry movies he loved so much?

Since Jack had left for his brother's arraignment, Del Rio had walked all around the drop zone from above, studied it from the beach, both north and south aspects, imagining a boat, a jet Ski, a scuba man. He realized that in a few hours the underside of the pier would be black and shadowed. No Prisoners might approach underwater, but someone smart enough would spot the bubble lines, right? But what about a rebreathing apparatus? And what about the issue of a watcher, someone looking for signs of police presence?

Del Rio picked up his cell and hit a number he'd called almost an hour ago. 'Mentone,' came the reply.

'Anything, Kid?'

'No one I can peg yet,' said the Kid.

Del Rio then called Bud Rankin, a former LAPD cop Jack had hired the year before. Rankin was sixty-two, a virtual chameleon and an expert at surveillance. He was working the pier.

'Maybe they're not on site yet,' said Rankin, who'd also come up with nothing.

'No way,' Del Rio said. 'If it was me extorting that kind of money, I'd definitely have someone making damn sure the cops weren't all over the place.'

'I'd best keep looking, then,' Rankin said, and hung up.

Del Rio's attention returned over the rail, down to the water and the pickup spot. The ocean was turning grayer and white-capped. It could be dangerous to be down there, so close to the pier's pylons, if the wind really got roaring. But Del Rio couldn't see any other way to handle it. This time he called Jack.

Chapter 37

I felt my cell phone vibrate in my pocket but ignored it, every bit of me focused on Carmine Noccia the way a mongoose might focus on a particularly mesmerizing cobra. In too many ways, Carmine was the epitome of the New Age mobster. He came from a long line of organized criminals, stretching back generations through Vegas to Chicago to New York to Palermo.

But he personally exhibited none of the old Mob's more stereotypical traits, the 'deze and doze' accent, the cultured attire of a die-hard strip club fan, the spontaneous and ruthless acts of violence against all debtors and perceived traitors. Carmine had gone to Dartmouth, had done a stint in the marines as a commissioned officer, mustered out as a captain, and had even attended Harvard Business School for a semester. He'd studied the ways of the elite and wore their fashions, manners, dialect, and affectations as an almost flawless persona.

'It's been a long time, Jack,' Carmine said, his dark agate eyes betraying nothing, the muscles in his exfoliated cheeks betraying nothing. His hand reached for mine. 'Always a genuine pleasure.'

'Why would you post bail for Tommy, Carmine?' I asked, shaking his hand with zero enthusiasm.

His grip firmed as he smiled. 'Tommy and I go way back, remember?'

'I remember you wanting his legs and arms broken for welshing on bets.'

'You always buy into such dramatic nonsense, Jack,' Carmine replied, releasing his grip and making a dismissive gesture. 'Be that as it may, regarding Tommy, stuff happens, and allegiances change when circumstances warrant it. That's the mark of a pragmatic leader. And I very much consider myself a pragmatic leader, able to deal with changing circumstances.'

I made every effort to show no reaction, but I got the subtext of his reply as if he'd tattooed it on my skin. Earlier that year, Carmine had used leverage that I resented to force me and Private

125

to track down a hijacked truck full of contraband prescription painkillers with a street value of thirty million dollars. We found the oxycodone shipment but used a remote third party to report its whereabouts to the local DEA office. They'd seized the stash before Carmine's men could get to it. I knew Carmine suspected me of a double cross, but I also knew he had no proof of it. Or at least, that was what I believed.

I'd regrettably come to know the mobster when Tommy was mainlining his gambling addiction and into Carmine for six large. I'd gone to Vegas and paid my brother's debt, doing it for the benefit of my long-suffering sister-in-law and nephew, not Tommy. I hadn't been free of Carmine since.

And now he had coughed up Tommy's bail. Why? The mobster was all about leverage, so that was what this was at some level. But designed to lift what? Or move whom? And for what reason? Revenge? Against me?

'You honestly think you're getting that bail money back?' I asked.

Carmine adjusted the French cuff of his custom shirt. 'The difference between you and me, Jack, is that *I* rarely bet unless I know what horse is going to win. Emotion plays no part in it. Anyway, I have to be going, give Tommy a ride home. Great seeing you. Let's catch up real soon, shall we?'

Before I could reply, my cell phone vibrated again in my pocket and Carmine moved by me as if I were now some stranger on the street. I checked caller ID, hit ANSWER, and watched Carmine disappear toward the elevators.

'What do you know?' I asked.

Del Rio said, 'Come to the pier. I want to run my plan by you.'

'I'm on my way.'

'You might want to pick up a five-millimeter neoprene wet suit with hood and booties on your way.'

'I suppose a swim is unavoidable in this case.'

'I'm hoping less of a swim and more of a skim, Jack.'

Chapter 38

Inside the garage in the City of Commerce, Cobb listened intently to Hernandez, who had been keeping track of one of the two men Chief Fescoe had met with, the one who had remained behind, the one who had been all over the pier, studying it from every angle.

'He's not a cop,' said Hernandez. 'At least he doesn't act like one.'

'What's he acting like, then?' Cobb demanded.

'Like a scout,' Hernandez replied. 'He's making it damn tough for me to stay clean. And I think he's brought in a second guy, older, maybe sixty. He's been scanning the beaches and restaurants with views of the pier.'

'And you're sure you haven't been made?'

'One hundred percent,' Hernandez said.

'The squid?'

'Still in place.'

'Police presence?'

'Nothing beyond the ordinary patrols. Beach is quiet. Too quiet. It would be easier to stay hidden if it was hot and wall-to-wall bodies.'

'Fall back, then, Mr. Hernandez. Thousand meters if you can.'

'Straightaway, Mr. Cobb,' Hernandez said, clicked off.

Scouts, thought Cobb. But before he could ponder that, Watson got up from his desk with an iPad in one hand. 'I've got positive ID on the two men on the pier with Fescoe. The big guy with the surfer's build was Jack Morgan, owner of Private Investigations Worldwide, fastest-growing security firm in the world. Cutting edge, and known to cut corners to achieve his objectives. The other one's Rick Del Rio, also works for Morgan. Both of them are Afghan vets. Marines.' Watson handed Cobb the iPad. 'It's all there.'

Cobb scanned the documents pulled up on the screen, military records, evaluations, various articles about Morgan and the company he'd inherited and reimagined after his father was convicted and sent behind bars.

'Chopper pilots,' Cobb grunted, then gave a dismissive flick of his sinewy hand. 'Stellar safety records until they got shot down. Both have courage, tried to get back in the bird to save the other men, but neither man has any special-forces training that I can see.'

'Unless the training was obtained privately,' Watson offered.

'That kind's no good. It's never tested in the crucible,' Cobb said, handing the iPad back. 'We

128

are tested in the crucible, Mr. Watson. Hard tested. They have no chance. We're twenty moves ahead of them in this game.'

Chapter 39

At a quarter to nine that evening, the wind was coming hard out of the northwest, gusting to twenty knots, churning the Pacific off the Huntington Beach Pier into a roiling charcoal-colored beast that kept trying to rise up and snatch Del Rio and me.

We hung from linemen's belts on opposing pylons, twelve feet above the crashing sea and two pylon rows back from the western edge of the pier. Below us, two Sea-Doo water sleds strained and pitched at ropes that moored them to the pylons. The Sea-Doos were the fastest, nimblest sea vessels money could buy. Del Rio had found them at a dealer a few miles from the pier. We'd launched them right at dusk and had been up on the pylons in the deep shadows ever since, wiping the spray from our goggles, peering out toward the electric halos of light shining down from the pier. No fishing lines dropped to the sea. The weather was just too rough.

We counted down the minutes listening to the minimal chatter on the channel used by the law enforcement lurking at the perimeters of the operation. Two sheriff's helicopters were bucking the wind, moving in arcs two miles offshore, running

with no lights, ready to respond. Two police helicopters were cruising at high altitude two miles
inland.

Three high-speed boats, two from the sheriff's
detail at Marina Del Rey and one from the
county's Baywatch lifeguard unit, lurched in the
swells about a mile out, ready to intercept any
vessel trying to head to sea or run the coast.

'Chief's on his way,' the Kid said in my earpiece. He was posted on the roof of a building
across Highway 1 from the pier entrance.

'Nothing within five hundred yards,' said Bud
Rankin, who was up on top of Ruby's Diner,
using an infrared scope to scan the surroundings.

My right leg was starting to cramp when I
heard the chief say, 'Almost to the diner.'

In my mind I could see Fescoe, head down into
the wind, walking toward Rankin and Ruby's
Diner carrying two black dry bags, one on each
shoulder.

Chapter 40

Cobb wore a convincing fake beard, dark this
time, to hide his scars. With the hood of his green
rain jacket up, he left a pizza joint a mile north of
the Huntington Beach Pier. For a moment he was
back in those desert mountains hearing the children and women cry, hearing their husbands
begging for mercy when pity was long dead and
gone. What had they wanted from him? What had

130

they expected?

They expected us *to die,* Cobb thought coldly. *They all expected us to die and crumble to dust.*

That thought turned to blazing anger. *They abandoned us. They tried to bury us. Well, guess what, we're not dead, and we're taking what we're due.*

In a blind rage now, he punched in a number on a throwaway cell phone, said, 'You ready, Mr. Stern?'

'We're going to rip this,' Stern promised.

'We're counting on it,' Cobb said. 'And tell Mr. Allen, go big or go home. We'll find someone else.'

Stern's voice cooled. 'You just make sure you hit the record button.'

'Oh, we will,' Cobb assured him. 'Twenty-five seconds.'

'Synced, ready to launch.'

Cobb hung up, checked the time. It was eight fifty-eight.

He punched in a second number, poised his thumb above SEND.

We go big here, he thought. *Or we all go home the hardest way possible.*

Chapter 41

'Chief's by me, moving along the rail north side of Ruby's,' said Bud Rankin in the earbud tucked beneath the hood of my wet suit. 'It is eight fifty-nine and forty seconds. He's preparing to drop.'

I said nothing, just swept my attention out and

131

along the perimeter of that electric halo of light, looking for an intruder.

'Bags are gone,' Rankin said.

I saw the bags fall. I saw them hit the churning water forty yards in front of me. The dry bags slapped and spun on the writhing ocean surface. My attention darted away, back along that perimeter of light.

'Anything, Chief?' I asked. Fescoe was supposed to remain on the rail, advise us of any effort to retrieve the dry bags from below the surface.

That was going to be difficult in the extreme in any case. Inside the bags, Sci had placed two small pressurized CO_2 tanks hitched to a switch activated by a pressure gauge. Deeper than six feet and the tanks would expel their charges, inflate the bags, and drag anyone holding them to the surface. If the pressure-gauge trigger failed, Sci could activate the tanks by radio.

Fescoe cleared his throat, said, 'Not a god-damned—'

The explosion came without warning, a brilliant flash, crack, and roar that threw a ballooning plume of flame that witnesses later described as flat blue with a central core that burned as bright as mercury.

Del Rio was on the pylon almost directly below the explosion.

For a split instant I saw my friend backlit, jerked, and bent backward against the waistband of his lineman's belt before the force of the blast struck and body-slammed me. The hit tore my feet from the pylon, caused my rope to lose purchase. I was aware of falling.

Chapter 42

In retrospect, I was lucky to have dropped off the pylon and plunged into the Pacific. The cold water stung my face while currents and eddies swung me at the length of the lineman's rope. I fought to free myself, unclipped the carabiner that held the rope to the belt, kicked toward the surface.

The pier lights were still on. Dark smoke boiled thick in the air to the south, billowing out toward the darkness. Police sirens were gathering from multiple directions. There was enough light for me to see Del Rio hanging from his belt twelve feet up the scorched pylon.

'Rick!' I shouted.

Del Rio rolled his head toward me. 'Burned, Jack,' he grunted through the earbud. 'Back's broken, I think. Can't move my–'

'Don't move anything!' I screamed. 'Don't move at all!'

My instinct was to swim straight to him, to get him down and in the water. But I held on to my reeling sea sled and shouted into the microphone, 'Del Rio burned and injured on pylon below explosion. Probable spinal injury. Rankin, report. Do you see anyone coming from your position? Chief Fescoe?'

But there was no answer, only the soaring chatter of the L.A. sheriff, police, and fire departments being summoned to the scene. Then the

Kid came on, choked up. 'It's Bud, Jack. I saw him thrown off the roof. I think he's–'

In my peripheral vision, I caught a large, swift, dark blur, like some huge bird swooping out of the night just northwest of the pier. He rode a short, stubby black surfboard. He'd kicked his feet into bindings of some sort and was dressed much as I was, head to toe in a black wet suit.

But instead of a lineman's belt, he wore a full harness that connected him to a taut black sail about six feet by four that bellied out like a spinnaker in front of him. I figured he was traveling forty, maybe fifty miles an hour, some kind of kite-boarding genius; he knifed into the light surrounding the pier, spotted the dry bags, tacked hard toward them, leaned into his harness, and snatched the first bag up. He blew south into the smoke before I could utter a word.

'Pickup!' I shouted at last, scrambling to get aboard the SeaDoo.

I was straddling the sled, hitting the start, when the second kiteboarder appeared from the northwest and snagged the second dry bag in a move as brilliant as the first rider's.

The Sea-Doo roared to life. I tugged a knife from a calf sheath, cut the mooring line, drifted, and then hit the throttle. In a split second the sled gathered power, blew seawater through its turbine, and leaped from beneath the pylons like a bucking horse freed of a chute.

Chapter 43

The Sea-Doo launched off the first roller at an odd angle, which caused it to cant hard left and down, the turbine whining against the air. Throwing my weight the exact opposite way, I managed to level it before skipping up the face of the coming wave and out into the air again.

I'd ridden a similar sled chasing the three sisters who'd gone on a killing spree at the London Olympics four months before. But then I'd been out on the Thames, a tidal river, not in this chaos of waves that surrounded the pier.

The kiteboarders had danced across swells. I crashed through them past the pier, glancing at the scorched, smoking breach on its southern flank and the blown-out windows at Ruby's Diner. 'This is Morgan,' I shouted. 'Two of them riding black kiteboards, bearing southwest of the pier. In pursuit. Need support.'

'We are one minute out, Morgan,' came the voice of one of the sheriff's helicopter pilots.

'Baywatch vessels converging on your position,' came a second voice. 'Time of intercept two minutes ten.'

Del Rio had had powerful search lamps mounted on the handlebars of the Sea-Doo. I flipped them on the second I broke free of the halo of light surrounding the pier. *Rick's back's broken,* I thought as I disappeared into the darkness.

135

I'd called in Del Rio's condition and position. But there was nothing more I could do for him other than make sure the people behind the killings, the extortion, and now this bombing were made to pay.

I kept the throttle wide open, peering along the brilliant beam of light that shot almost a quarter mile out in front of me. Had they stayed on this same bearing? Or had they tacked? And if they had tacked, were they heading inland, or farther out to sea? Was there a boat waiting for them? A vehicle? Where...?

The beam picked up a shadow ahead of me in the waves. It was moving to my left, heading east for shore about two hundred and fifty yards out. I arced after the shadow, found the waves at my back, and surfed down them so fast that it felt like flight.

At one hundred and fifty yards I caught one of the kiteboarders fully in my beam, his back to me. He was cutting across the face of the swells. I could see the dry bag lashed there beside him on the board.

He looked over his shoulder, back at my light, and for a second I was sure he was going to draw a weapon and open fire. Instead, he tacked hard, came about, came right at me as fast as I was bearing down on him. It was a game of chicken I felt sure I'd win. The Sea-Doo weighed more than four hundred and fifty pounds. I doubted the board and kite weighed more than thirty.

I could hear intensifying chatter on the radio inside my wet suit hood. There were fatalities back on the pier. I also could hear the choppers closing now. Their searchlights joined mine, throwing a near-blinding glare on the kite-boarder, who never hesitated and never slowed.

At thirty-five yards, I ducked down, preparing myself for impact.

At twenty-five yards, a wave came between us. I lost him for a second.

At ten yards, he reappeared, launched off the crest, soared up and over me at least three stories, dangling below the kite, as calm as a bird.

Chapter 44

The move floored me. I'd seen kiteboarders in action before, but this guy was a superstar.

I down-throttled, drifted the Sea-Doo one hundred and eighty degrees, and accelerated, following the beams of the helicopters playing on the boarder. He'd landed and was speeding out to sea.

'This is the L.A. Sheriff's Department!' one of the pilots barked out of a loudspeaker. 'Drop your kite.'

The boarder never slowed, but I was gaining ground again.

Fifty yards separated us when the other kite-boarder appeared out of nowhere, launching from a wave to my left, and tried to take my head off with the steel fin that jutted from the bottom of his board. I ducked and almost dumped the sled but managed to keep it upright, right there on the verge of disaster.

I'd had enough by that point, and I had immunity, so I tore open the shoulder holster, freed the Glock, and went back after the first boarder, mindful that the second might reappear at any moment. These people had caused mass death. I would not hesitate to shoot one of them, aim for the legs, break them down for capture. But then I remembered what else was in the dry bags.

'This is Morgan,' I shouted. 'Tell Kloppenberg to blow the tanks. Repeat, tell Sci to blow the tanks.'

Before there was any response, the second kiteboarder flew through the air and landed in front of me, skimmed up beside his partner, both heading straight up the face of the oncoming, cresting wave, a ten-footer easy.

I instantly realized I'd probably be thrown into a backflip if I stayed on their course, and I cut the sled left where the shoulder of the wave wasn't breaking yet, watching the two kiteboarders reach the crest. The helicopter search lamps were on them when they exploded off the wave and out into space, sailing on their kites, thirty, maybe forty feet in the air.

Right at the apex of their flight, Sci triggered the CO_2 tanks.

They released with such force that the dry bags instantly inflated, straining against the cords that held them to the boards. The sudden change in aerodynamics threw both kiteboarders out of control.

The gusting wind caught the kites at the same time the dry bags burst, throwing a small amount of currency and a large amount of cut newspaper out into the sky like so much confetti. The boarders went flipping through the night, board over kite, somersaulting until the blade wash of one of the helicopters caught and hurled them like rag dolls straight down, twenty feet, through the swirling paper bills.

They crashed hard against the sea.

I sped up, sure now that I was looking for bodies, injured or dead. I spotted the first one facedown, partially covered by his kite. One of the Baywatch boats was on the scene now, heading for the other kiteboarder.

I grabbed mine by the back of his harness and yanked him up out of the water alongside the Sea-Doo. He hung there a second, then started choking and hacking. After several moments, he looked up at me in a daze.

'What the fuck, dude?' he moaned. 'Blowing us out of the sky was definitely not part of the script.'

PART THREE

A TIME FOR TRAUMA

Chapter 45

At ten o'clock that evening, forty minutes after I'd pulled one of the kiteboarders from the sea, county lifeguards and firefighters began to hoist the backboard and litter bearing Rick Del Rio up over the south railing of the Huntington Beach Pier, twenty yards east of where the bomb had detonated.

The smoke was gone, doused by the rain and fire hoses, but a harsh, charred chemical stench hung in the air as investigators worked to cordon off the area and document the carnage the explosion had wrought. Media helicopters circled the pier, filming the aftermath for the eleven o'clock news.

Six people were dead, including my surveillance specialist Bud Rankin, who'd been nearly decapitated by flying chunks of cement. The other five were an entire young family from Oxnard, the Deloits, husband, wife, and three kids under the age of ten. They'd been inside the diner at a table by the window having ice cream sundaes.

Another ten were injured, including Chief Mickey Fescoe, who'd been briefly knocked unconscious and had suffered cheek and arm lacerations. But he'd refused to be taken to the hospital and had just started toward me with a stone-faced Sheriff Lou Cammarata when Del Rio's litter appeared at the railing.

'Morgan,' Cammarata growled at me.

I held up a finger and went to Del Rio's side.

His face was burned, contused. He was in a lot of pain but alert. He focused on me immediately.

'You good?' I asked, feeling the enormity of the moment now. Del Rio was more a brother to me than my own brother. We'd been through hell together many times and had always survived and recovered. But he'd had a feeling about this gig. He'd tried to stop me from taking it on. The idea that now he might be paralyzed was almost more than I could take.

He shook his head stoically. 'Nothing from the waist down, Jack.'

I felt my stomach drop forty stories. 'Nothing yet,' I said. 'Stay positive.'

'Kind of hard when you've been on the wrong end of a yo-yo,' he replied. 'You get them?'

'Yes and no. I'll explain later. I'll see you at the hospital. Semper Fi.'

He nodded, said with little conviction, 'Hoorah, Jack.'

Two EMTs lifted Del Rio onto a gurney and slid him into the rear of the latest ambulance to back down the pier. The doors closed and he was gone.

'Morgan, you've ruined us,' Sheriff Cammarata said in my ear.

I pivoted to find him glaring at me. 'And how have I done that?'

He gestured angrily back toward shore. 'The other end of this pier is lousy with media. They're everywhere overhead. They're going to find out what happened and...' He looked like he wanted to throttle me. I understood why.

144

Cammarata was up for reelection in less than week. And Fescoe worked at the whim of the mayor. The chief was studying me as if trying to decide whether I was somebody to be saved or tossed to the wolves.

Struggling to keep my own anger under control, I said, 'I don't have immunity from the fact that I lost a man and may have seen the crippling of another. But no one, including you, Sheriff, or you, Chief, anticipated a bomb. Why would we have? This was supposed to be an extortion pickup, and No Prisoners turned it into an attack. Up front, he decided that the money was not going to be in those bags. Up front, he planned to kill as many as he could.'

'How the hell do you know that, Jack?' Fescoe demanded.

Chapter 46

'One of the kiteboarders stayed conscious aboard the Baywatch boat that brought us in,' I said. 'I questioned him until he was put in an ambulance.'

'What's the story?' the sheriff demanded.

I told them what I knew. Danny Stern and Willis Allen were boyhood friends, originally from Hood River, Oregon, and now lived on the Big Island of Hawaii. They'd each won major kite-boarding competitions in the past two years and had appeared in several extreme-sport films.

Two months ago a man named Richard North

had called Stern. North said he was a producer of action films who'd seen footage of Stern and Allen kiteboarding off Oahu. He said he wanted them to perform a stunt for a movie he was making. The fee was fifty thousand dollars apiece.

'North directed them to a website that seemed legit, so they accepted,' I told Fescoe and Cammarata. 'Stern said North bought airline tickets, flew them over five days ago, met them at LAX. He described North as a big man with long blond hair, beard, and sunglasses.'

'No Prisoners,' Fescoe said.

I nodded. 'He was driving a late-model BMW. He brought them here and gave them three pages of a script for a film called *Take No Prisoners*. In the script, dry bags containing money are dropped off the pier as part of a ransom deal. Then there's a diversionary explosion. In come the two kiteboarders. North told them to snag the bags and then improvise from there.'

Cammarata's scowl deepened. 'What do you mean, improvise?'

'North said he wanted their moves to unfold instinctively and raw after the pickup, like on a reality-television show,' I replied. 'Stern said he and Allen both knew they'd be chased after grabbing the bags. Their job was to evade capture as long as possible.'

'Which means you're right, Jack,' Fescoe said. 'No Prisoners, or North, or whatever he calls himself, had no intention of accepting the extortion payment.'

'I suspect he thought you'd do just what you did: pack the bags with a lot more newspaper

146

than hundred-dollar bills.'

'But he couldn't have *known* that,' Cammarata protested.

'Does it matter? He obviously believed it and acted accordingly.'

Both men fell silent, brooding on what I'd told them.

'In any case, it's all out of our hands now. FBI and ATF agents will be taking control,' I said. 'The scenario has gone beyond what any of us could be expected to handle.'

'Bullshit,' Cammarata said. 'The Feds may come in. They may offer expertise. But this is my county.'

'And my city,' Fescoe said. 'Yours too, Jack.'

'I'll think on that,' I said. 'Right now, I'm heading to UCLA Medical Center to find out if my best friend will ever walk again.'

As I left the men, I felt disoriented by the events of the evening, especially the loss. Had it been worth it? No, it hadn't. Rankin and Del Rio were not officers sworn to uphold the law. They worked for me. They did my bidding, and they had suffered for it.

Satellite television vans surrounded the police barriers at the east end of the pier, up against Highway 1. Reporters were badgering anyone who moved their way. I thought I'd jump the railing and avoid them, but several of them recognized me and started shouting.

'Jack Morgan? What's your role in this investigation? What's Private got to do with the explosion?'

One of them, to my surprise, was Bobbie Newton, a particularly vicious gossip columnist and

147

television reporter who lived up the beach from me.

'Jack!' she called. 'Jack, it's Bobbie!'

I ignored her and all of them, tried to move on. But then klieg lights blazed in my face. I looked at the cameras dead-on and said, 'I'm a consultant here, nothing more.'

'Consultant to whom?' Bobbie and ten others shouted.

I didn't answer, pushed my way by them before they could hound me further, and jogged across the highway, wishing I could talk to Justine. She has the rare ability to slice apart emotions like pain or confusion and expose the underlying fear or meaning. Ordinarily, navel gazing is not something I'm fond of. That night I felt in desperate need of a session.

But I had not heard from her or Cruz all day. I was at my car, about to call Mo-bot to see if either of them had checked in, when my cell phone rang.

'We've been contacted, Jack,' said Dave Sanders. 'They're letting the children go.'

Chapter 47

In the dim light after midnight Justine crouched in the corner of the holding cell, watching a woman named Carla. Early thirties, Carla was big, muscular, and heavily tattooed. She'd looked high when she was put in the cell not fifteen minutes before, and had taken an instant dislike to Justine. At the moment, Carla was stalking Justine, carrying the handle of a broken and sharpened plastic spoon as if it were a dagger.

After she'd joined Private, Jack had insisted that Justine take a course in basic self-defense. She'd chosen aikido, a Japanese art, and had pursued it until she felt confident enough to quit and take up Crossfit to build her strength. But had it been enough?

Justine adopted a triangle pose, held up her hands, prepared to fight.

In Spanish, she asked, 'Why are you doing this?'

Carla said nothing, just grinned, showing a missing upper-right incisor.

'What is your name, American?' called Rosa, the only other woman in the cell. Smaller, ratty, she watched with a worried expression.

Before Justine could answer, Carla said in English, 'Her name Bitch.'

Then the big woman lunged and slashed at Justine with the knife, just missing her belly.

'Guard!' Rosa screamed.

Carla grinned again, licked her lips through the gap in her teeth.

'Now you know I mean it,' she said to Justine, and lunged again.

Justine was quicker this time. She swept her right hand in a circle, chopping at the wrist of Carla's knife hand. The move deflected the blade down and away from her belly. It also knocked the big woman slightly off-balance. Justine encouraged that momentum, pivoted, and slammed Carla into the cement wall.

'Uhhhn,' Carla said, wobbled, but then spun and slashed at Justine.

The blade caught fabric and then skin above Justine's left breast. She began to bleed.

Carla slashed again, cutting Justine's forearm.

My God! Was she going to die here in this stinking cell?

All those aikido classes, all those Crossfit workouts, all those times when she'd wanted to give up or puke came back to her, made her remember to fight. When Carla moved to cut at her again, Justine's right foot shot out, connected with the woman's shin.

Carla grimaced in pain, tried to stab Justine. But Justine hammered down on the forearm behind Carla's knife hand, hit muscles and nerves, causing the woman's grip to evaporate.

The knife fell. Both women dove for it. Justine elbowed the woman in the face, snatched it up, and stepped away. 'You must have had a tough childhood,' she said to the stunned woman, who was slowly getting back to her feet. 'But that's no excuse for bad—'

Carla shrieked like a lunatic and charged Justine, put her shoulder into Justine's chest, almost knocking her off her feet. They slammed into the bars facing the hallway. Justine did the only thing she could think of and stabbed the woman in the thick muscles of her upper back.

Instead of crumpling, Carla went berserk. She head-butted Justine under the chin. Justine saw stars and felt herself weaken.

Carla grabbed Justine's neck with both hands and started choking her.

Fight, little sister!

Justine rammed her bloody forearm against the big woman's throat. Nothing. She reached over, grabbed the handle of the makeshift knife sticking out of Carla's back, and worked it like a gearshift. Carla's face turned demonic then, her strength grew exponentially, and Justine knew she would not be able to hold the woman off.

Chapter 48

Just when the stars became dots and began to gather before Justine's eyes and she felt herself losing consciousness, she heard boots running. Jail guards with batons appeared behind Justine, clubbed her, and then clubbed Carla.

'She attacked me,' Justine coughed. 'She tried to kill me.'

Her blouse was stained with blood. It dripped from her forearm.

'No way,' Carla spat back. 'Bitch tried to kill me. Put a shiv in my back, so I came after her.' She looked over at Rosa, the smaller woman. 'Ain't that right?'

Rosa seemed not to know what to say. One guard said, 'Don't matter. She's coming with us now.'

One set of guards grabbed Carla. The other two snapped handcuffs on Justine and roughly led her down the hallway past a row of other holding cells where women hung on the bars and looked at her like she was part of a sideshow, making kissy-kissing noises, or telling her what a bitch she was, or asking her to carry messages for them. Her legs were shaky from adrenaline, and she thought she might heave for the second time in less than twelve hours. What was happening to Carla? Where were they taking the woman who'd tried to kill her?

After an elevator ride, Justine was led down another hallway that had an antiseptic smell. Commandant Gomez stood outside the jail clinic. If he felt surprise at her condition, he wasn't showing it. Instead, he stared at her with an annoyed expression. 'You and Private Investigations have powerful friends in Mexico City, Ms. Smith. You and Señor Cruz are to be freed and taken directly to your jet, where you will leave the country and not return.'

'A woman just tried to kill me in the cell,' Justine said in a shaky voice. 'What the hell's going on here, Commandant? Where are the Harlows? Do you know? Are you part of a conspiracy? Covering up Leona Casa Madre's murder too? Trying to have me killed?'

Gomez turned nasty. 'I am part of no conspiracy, *señora*, and I most certainly did not try to have you killed. The cells are the cells. We cannot control what happens in them. Leona Casa Madre, for your information, let notorious members of a drug cartel use her apartment from time to time. It's the only reason she could afford the place, pigsty that it was, drunk that she was.

'And I have personally checked out these lies about the Harlows. Both supposed "witnesses" told me they made their stories up, trying to get some US publication to pay them to describe things that did not happen. Now, you have a phone call waiting inside. And I will personally investigate this attack on you. I assure you.'

'I'll bet you will,' Justine said. 'Where is Carla? The woman who attacked me?'

'You have a phone call waiting inside, *señora*,' Gomez said again, stoic, gesturing toward the clinic, where Justine saw Arturo Fox coming in another door. A nurse was holding a cell phone toward her.

Justine felt disgusted, degraded. 'What cartel?' she asked the commandant. 'What drug cartel was Leona in with?'

Gomez hesitated, said, 'De la Vega. Beyond that I have no answers.'

Justine glared at him, then held out her cuffs. The commandant thrust his chin at one of her guards, who unlocked them. She walked into the clinic, ignored the blood all over her, and snatched the cell phone from the nurse without another glance at Gomez.

'Justine,' she said.

Jack said, 'You don't know how happy I am to hear your voice.'

Given the weight of all that had happened to her in the last twenty minutes, Justine burst into tears. 'Some crazy woman tried to kill me in here.'

Stunned silence. 'You're not hurt, are you?'

Justine could hear pain and guilt in Jack's voice as plain as day, did not understand it, said, 'I'm okay. Cut a few places and my jaw doesn't feel right. But I'm okay. How did you find us?'

'Long story,' Jack said. 'Took a few calls to our

153

office in Mexico City. Calderón pulled some levers and we popped you.'

'We're not backing off this, I hope you know,' she said.

'I'm not,' Jack said. 'But I need you here ASAP.'

'No, Jack, this has gotten personal–'

Jack cut her off. 'Last night Dave Sanders was contacted by the kidnappers. They say they're letting the Harlow children go. I need you here to examine and evaluate them. We'll be getting instructions in six hours.'

'I'll be there in four, maybe five,' she promised. 'Where are you?'

'UCLA Medical Center,' he said, the pain palpable now.

'What's happened?' she demanded.

'It's Rick, Justine,' Jack said. 'He's hurt real bad. Can't feel his legs. He's in surgery right now.'

Chapter 49

I sat up all night on a couch outside the surgical facility. Mo-bot joined me around one, Sci an hour later.

Del Rio had gone under the knife at eleven p.m., two hours before I got to the hospital after a short visit to Sanders's Beverly Hills offices, where a simple e-mail message from a blind source declared, 'The children will be released tomorrow. Time to be determined. We contact. Justice has been served. They are innocents.'

154

As hour upon hour ticked by on the clock with no word from the doctors trying to treat Del Rio's burns and back, I felt unable to think or talk about the Harlows, or No Prisoners, or Tommy, or Carmine Noccia, for that matter. For the first time in a long time, probably since my mother's death, I prayed, confessing my belief that I had caused Bud Rankin's death as surely as No Prisoners had. I was also the reason my best friend was five hours into surgery, and now six. I begged God for mercy, for Rankin's soul, for Del Rio's spine.

I didn't know whom to contact about Rankin. The man had no family and was a real loner. I vowed, however, to honor his passing in some way.

Overriding those thoughts was the fact that I'd always considered Del Rio virtually indestructible – a force fused to me in battle, a fellow marine, a blood brother who would never desert me, a man whom I would never desert. As dawn broke over Los Angeles, the idea of that man in a wheelchair for the rest of his life nearly broke my heart.

I sipped a coffee Sci had gotten me and gazed up, numb, at the television blaring coverage of the bombing and the deaths on the Huntington Beach Pier. The media had much of the story now and was blaring every aspect except, it seemed, Private's involvement. The mayor was even shown admitting that the explosion had taken place during a phony drop of–

'Jack?' Justine said, shaking me from the screen.

Cruz was there too, but I could only look at her. She looked exhausted. Her right forearm was wrapped in bandages. Her lower face was slightly swollen. And yet she was beautiful as always. But

155

I could see that something had been taken from her in Mexico, or cracked in her in Mexico, and that only served to bewilder me more.

A tiny woman in surgical scrubs exited the operating room. She introduced herself as Dr. Phyllis Oates, chief neurosurgeon at the medical center.

'Who is Mr. Del Rio's next of kin?' she asked.

I swallowed hard, instantly feared the worst, and said, 'I'm closest.'

For a moment, Dr. Oates just looked at me, and I felt like I was being pushed over a cliff. Then the surgeon managed a tired smile and put her hand on my arm. 'I wanted you to know what a lucky, lucky man Mr. Del Rio is. By all rights, he should have been paralyzed from the waist down, but the lineman's belt and the wet suit held the broken vertebrae in place, prevented them from severing his spinal cord. There's considerable swelling, and it might take several months, but I believe he'll walk again. And run.'

I looked at Justine, and Sci, and Mo-Bot and Cruz, and we all began to cry and hug. I don't remember being happier or more grateful in my entire life.

Chapter 50

'We've got their attention now, Mr. Cobb,' Watson said, looking away from several computer screens streaming early-morning coverage of the Huntington Beach Pier explosion, as well as clips from the killings at Malibu and at the CVS.

'We do indeed, Mr. Watson,' Cobb said. 'Two more cycles and we'll have a clear shot at the prize.'

They were inside the garage in the City of Commerce. Cobb was stuffing the Lakers hoodie, the blond wig, the sunglasses, and the cap into a trash bag. There would be no further need for the disguise. It had served its purpose and more. For the time being, law enforcement would be focused on a man answering No Prisoners' description, which was how Cobb wanted it.

'Today?' Kelleher asked.

'Today we rest and regroup, Mr. Kelleher,' Cobb said. 'In the meantime we let the media do its job, get the drumbeat of threat going, build the panic exponentially, get the government worms all squirming like they've been plugged into a socket. We let them assure the people that they are safe, and then we wait until we start hearing them speculate that we might be finished, that we've left Los Angeles alone. That could be twelve hours after the assurance of safety. Could be thirty-six, or forty-eight.'

'And then we go again?' Johnson said. The wiry black man was sitting on the foot of his cot, cleaning a pistol.

'Yes, Mr. Johnson,' Cobb said. 'When that happens we go again. Meantime, anybody up for breakfast at Robby Eden's? I could go for three eggs over easy, two sides of bacon, and an order of sourdough toast.'

157

Chapter 51

By noon I was running on fumes, riding shotgun with Cruz driving the company Suburban. Justine was in the backseat. So were Sci and Mo-bot. Behind them were stacked boxes of forensics gear.

'I don't believe the Mexicans,' Justine said for the fourth or fifth time. 'The Harlows are down there, Jack. Or were.'

'I'm not saying they aren't, or weren't,' I replied. 'But the kids can tell us more. And then we'll decide if we need to go back to Mexico.'

Cruz barreled us into the Beverly Center parking lot ten minutes after Sanders called to say that we would find the children on level six of the luxury shopping mall, near the top of the Macy's escalator and the Apple Store.

I caught up with Dave Sanders, Camilla Bronson, and Cynthia Maines on the escalator between levels four and five two minutes later. The Harlows' lawyer was talking on his cell phone, head down, intent. The personal assistant looked like she'd been crying. The publicist wore dark sunglasses and scanned everywhere around her.

'Ms. Maines,' I said. 'Surprised to see you here.'

'Camilla called last night,' Maines replied. 'She thought I should be here.'

'Familiar faces,' Camilla Bronson said, still looking all around.

We rode the escalator to level six in a pack.

Sanders spotted the children first. All three were sitting in wheelchairs, backed up against the wall beside the bustling Apple Store, directly across from the Traffic boutique. They had iPhones in their hands and stared at them like zombies.

'Malia!' Maines cried. 'Jin! Miguel!'

But of the three, only Malia, the Harlows' oldest adopted daughter, raised her head toward her parents' personal assistant. Malia had high cheekbones and almond-shaped eyes, which were bleary, red, cried out. She blinked at Maines a second, then said in a little girl's voice, 'Why are we here, Cynthia?'

'Oh, dear God,' Maines said, rushing to her, tears boiling down her cheeks. She embraced the girl. 'You're safe, Malia. You're going to be okay. You're all going to be okay. Jin? Miguel? I'm here. Cynthia's here now.'

The other two children just continued to stare at the phones in their laps.

'They've been drugged,' Justine said.

'I agree,' said Mo-bot, and moved forward, carrying a medical kit. Over the years, she had somehow found the time to earn her EMT's license, handy at moments like this. 'We're going to want blood samples.'

'Here?' Camilla Bronson said, horrified. 'No. Get them out of–'

'Mamá?' Miguel said suddenly. The boy's head had come up. Over the years he'd had several operations on his cleft palate, which made him look different from pictures I'd seen. He gazed around in bewilderment. *'¿Dónde está mi mamá?'* He began to whine, and shook his arm violently free when Mo-bot tried to touch him. 'Where's Mommy?'

Jin began to cry as well.

Up until this point, Sanders had stood off to one side, unnerved by the children's stupor. But now he saw that patrons leaving the Apple Store were looking at the upset children in the wheel-chairs.

'Camilla's right,' he said to me through gritted teeth. 'We've got to get them out of here before–'

'Is that them?' cried a familiar skewer-sharp voice I'd heard just the night before. 'The Harlow brats?'

I turned in shock. Bobbie Newton was leading the charge off the Macy's escalator. She had two cameramen in tight tow.

Chapter 52

'It *is* them!' cried Bobbie Newton. 'Wheelchairs? Wheelchairs! What's happened to them? Where are Thom and Jennifer?'

'Downstairs!' Camilla Bronson cried, moving into the gossip reporter's way. 'Thom's buying her a huge diamond at Cartier. The kids are just playing a game, that's all.'

Bobbie Newton was having none of it. 'I've got Cartier's wired. They alert me when anyone of that stature comes in. Where are they? What's happened to those kids? Tim, you getting this?'

Seeing the cameraman aiming tight on the

children, Justine stepped up beside the publicist. 'They're minors. They have the right to privacy.'

'They're Thom and Jen Harlow's kids,' the reporter shot back. 'Which means they are de facto celebrities, whoever *you* are. I have every right to ... what's wrong with them? Where are the Harlows?'

In a soothing tone, Camilla Bronson said, 'Bobbie, we'll have a statement later in the—'

'They're missing,' Cynthia Maines called out loudly. 'Someone kidnapped the entire family and only just released the children.'

Bobbie Newton's trembling free hand shot to her mouth, unable to disguise her blossoming joy. 'Oh, my God!' she said in a drawl that ended in a squeal. 'Is that true? It's the story of the year! It's the story of the century!'

'Bobbie!' Camilla Bronson said. 'Bobbie, calm down. It's nothing—'

But the gossip reporter spun around gleefully, microphone in hand, ignoring the publicist. 'Three, two, one,' she snapped at the second cameraman. The other focused on the Harlow children, who were still dazed, unsure where they were.

Part of me wanted to lunge for the cameras and hurl them over the railing, but a crowd was gathering, and I have always hated seeing other people grabbing cameras and destroying them. It smacks of thugs and book burning, and I despise both. So like everyone else, I had to just stand there and listen to her.

'This is Bobbie Newton, your best friend forever,' she brayed. 'I'm at the scene of a shocking, shocking story that's about to rock Hollywood to

161

its core. Jennifer and Thom Harlow, the most powerful couple in all of film land, have been kidnapped. You heard it here first. And in a dramatic update, their children have only just been released, drugged out of their loving little minds, and they're right behind me. Look, just look at the poor darlings!'

'You're fired,' Camilla Bronson snarled out of the corner of her mouth at Maines.

'You can't fire me,' the Harlows' personal assistant shot back. 'I work for Thom and Jen.'

'But *I* can,' Sanders said.

'I don't work for you either,' Maines said, her voice rising. 'And this cover-up you've been engaged in for whatever reason is frankly shocking and hardly in the Harlows' best interest.'

The publicist's eyes went wide. She grabbed Maines by the arm, spun her away from the cameras. 'You tipped her!' she hissed, while Bobbie blathered on, getting only half of her facts correct, a record high for her.

'I did not tip anyone,' Maines retorted hotly. 'But I *was* about to notify the FBI because I simply could not wait any longer for Mr. Morgan here to step up and do the right thing.'

'Ouch,' I said. 'In my defense, I spent last night chasing a mass murderer and praying until dawn while my best friend underwent spinal surgery after he was injured in the pier bombing.'

Maines blinked. 'Oh, I'm sorry, Jack, I–'

'It doesn't matter,' Sanders said, still furious. He glared at me. 'Help us get them out of here, now, Jack. I won't have them treated like freaks. They need to be seen by qualified medical personnel, and–'

'Who died and made *you* their guardian?' Maines challenged.

Sanders turned cold. 'No one has died, to my knowledge, Cynthia,' he snarled. 'But Thom and Jennifer have stipulated in writing that in the event of death or incapacitation I will serve as the children's trustee and guardian. I believe kidnapping fits the definition of incapacitation in anyone's dictionary.'

He and Camilla Bronson moved toward the children.

Justine said, 'I'll help you.'

Cruz, Mo-bot, and Sci followed.

Maines said, 'I'm coming with you.'

Sanders whirled around. 'No, Cynthia, you most definitely are *not*. As I remember, you are paid by Harlow-Quinn, which means Terry Graves can and will fire you. Expect a call momentarily.'

Coats were draped over the children's heads. Justine, Mobot, and Sci wheeled the three children past the cameras while Bobbie Newton prattled inanely that they looked 'zombified.' Sanders got behind them. So did Camilla Bronson.

When Bobbie Newton tried to join the entourage, I couldn't take it anymore. I got out a pocketknife, slid behind her cameramen, and cut the cables that connected the cameras to their battery packs.

'Dead,' one said.

'Me too,' the other said.

I was already moving around them onto the escalator.

'What!' Bobbie cried as I disappeared below

163

her. 'No, I...'

She must have seen the cut cables because she appeared over the railing, looking like a nut job when she said, 'Of course it was you: Murdering Jack Morgan. What's your involvement in this, Jack? That's what I want to know. What's Murdering Jack Morgan's involvement?'

I winked at her, pulled out my cell phone, and called the FBI.

Chapter 53

Eight hours later, after a long nap, a shower, and a change of clothes, Justine entered a large private suite directly across the street from the Beverly Center inside Cedars-Sinai Medical Center, where the Harlow children were being kept overnight for further tests and observation. Sanders, Camilla Bronson, and Terry Graves had arranged it all.

Justine had not known such suites existed, but here was a common room occupied by Jack, Sci, Chief Fescoe, and a half-dozen others: two doctors, a private nurse, and government technicians linking cables to computer screens. Before joining Private, Justine had worked for the city and courts of Los Angeles as a child psychologist who interviewed and counseled victims of crime. Even though her horizons had broadened into investigations, she still felt confident that there wasn't anyone on the West Coast better at this kind of thing.

Most of the people gathered in the common room evidently agreed with her assessment. Chief Fescoe had readily signed off on Justine's involvement. So had District Attorney Blaze and Christine Townsend, special agent in charge of the FBI's Los Angeles office. A tall redhead with a beaky nose, Townsend was familiar with Justine and openly valued her skills and judgment. The Harlow team had been the only ones to object. They had been summarily overruled.

'What's their current status?' Justine asked.

'They're up after a five-hour nap,' the nurse replied. 'And Ms. Bronson just delivered them a large order from In-N-Out Burger.'

'Their favorite,' the publicist sniffed.

'Okay,' Justine said. 'I need you to get me completely up to date on what we know before I go in there.'

She looked at Dr. Allen Parks, the pediatric specialist overseeing the Harlow children's care.

'No sign of sexual or physical mistreatment,' Parks said. 'They've been nourished, well hydrated, and generally well cared for, other than the fact that they lived in the same clothes for five days. Our blood work confirmed Dr. Kloppenberg's findings.'

'I heard scopolamine and Percocet,' Justine said, looking to Sci.

Kloppenberg nodded. 'A modern update on a nineteenth-century cocktail German doctors used to give women in labor. They called it twilight sleep. Don't be surprised if they don't remember much.'

'That's the point of the stuff, isn't it?' Townsend asked.

'Pretty much, Special Agent,' Parks replied. 'Beyond that, Miguel has several bruises on his knees and shins. Malia suffered a sprained wrist. Jin appears untouched. And all three had puncture wounds that indicate someone had run IVs into them.'

Justine looked at Jack and Fescoe. 'Beverly Center security tapes?'

Jack nodded. 'Lots there. Men wearing dark hoodies brought them in off San Vicente Boulevard in the wheelchairs at ten fifteen a.m. They used elevators to get the children to level six. A camera outside the Apple Store showed the children were left there no more than three minutes before we arrived. The iPhones in their laps were junk knockoffs. No prints on the wheelchairs or the phones. Sci collected epithelial samples from their clothes.'

'No hits yet,' Kloppenberg said.

Justine looked at Townsend, who said, 'Not surprisingly, the media is going insane over this. It's gone viral and global. They're giving it much more attention than the No Prisoners killings and the pier explosion.'

'What did you expect?' Camilla Bronson said snidely. 'I've done nothing but field calls since Bobbie Newton went live.'

Justine said, 'Those children just went from fishbowl life to circus life.'

'You'll have to prepare them for that,' Townsend said.

'They won't be exposed to any circus if I have

anything to do with it,' said Terry Graves hotly. 'I won't stand for it.'

'Neither will I,' Sanders said.

'Absolutely not,' the Harlows' publicist said.

Justine softened, said, 'Well, good. That's a start.'

Chapter 54

Malia lay in the bed on the right, Jin on the left, and Miguel in the middle. They were eating and watching a rerun of *Family Guy*. All three children glanced at Justine suspiciously when she entered. Small cameras had been set up, feeding the discussion out to the screens and recorders in the common room.

'I'm Justine,' she said, turned off the television, set her purse on the floor.

'You with the police?' Malia asked.

'Working for them. And for the FBI.'

'Where are Jennifer and Thom?' Jin asked.

Justine thought it odd that she referred to her parents by their first names. Then again, nearly everyone referred to the Harlows by their first names. But was that just Jin? Hadn't Miguel called out for his mommy?

'We don't know,' Justine admitted at last. 'I'm part of a team trying to find your parents. We hoped you could help us.'

Miguel set down the last of his burger and closed his eyes, hiding his mouth behind his hand, saying nothing.

'I don't remember anything,' Malia said.

'Me neither,' Jin said.

Miguel still said nothing.

'Smells awful good in here,' Justine said, settling into a chair. 'What did you get for dinner?'

'Bacon cheeseburger,' Malia mumbled.

'Not me. Jennifer says it's bad for you, bacon,' Jin announced.

'No, it isn't,' Malia said. 'Anita says it's the best. Makes you strong.'

'What does Anita know?'

'Everything,' Miguel said, eyes still shut.

'She's here, you know, Anita, in Los Angeles,' Justine said.

Her goal now was just to keep them talking, build trust. Miguel's eyes opened and his hand dropped. 'Where is she?'

'I don't know exactly,' Justine admitted. 'But she's here. I know she'd love to see you all at some point.'

Miguel's face fell. 'Oh.'

'Would you like to see her?' Justine asked.

Miguel blinked, nodded. So did his sisters.

'I'm sure we can arrange that,' Justine said. 'But in the meantime, there is someone here I think you might also be happy to see.'

She opened the door and their bulldog came rushing in, trailing a leash, wagging her butt wildly, snuffling, whining, and trying to jump up on the bed.

'Stella!' Miguel cried. The boy leaped out of his bed and held the bulldog tight while she barked and licked his face. Then, with great effort – the

168

dog weighed more than fifty pounds – he picked her up and set her down on his bed while his sisters crowded in around their brother and beloved dog.

'Stella Bella is such a pretty girl,' Malia soothed.

'Prettiest in the world,' Jin said. 'Best dog in the world.'

Miguel beamed and scratched Stella's belly. The dog flopped on her side so all the children could get in on the scratching. Her jowls hung open, making her look like an alien. But then, to Justine's delight and wonder, the bulldog began to purr, almost like a cat.

'Does she always do that?' Justine asked.

'Only when she's happy,' Jin said. 'Stella's a wonder dog.'

'I can see that,' Justine said. 'She was very upset when we found her up at the ranch. Any idea why Stella would be so upset?'

Malia and Jin shook their heads, but Miguel said, 'Because she missed us, I bet.'

Justine knew from a brief scan of the children's medical records that in addition to the cleft palate, Miguel had been diagnosed as 'on the spectrum,' not autistic, but very awkward socially. To her surprise, however, at least in the presence of the dog, he exhibited few if any signs of Asperger's syndrome.

'I'll bet that's what it was,' Justine agreed. 'Stella's a smart dog.'

Miguel grinned. The dog made him happy. The dog made them all happy, and more relaxed, open. Justine decided the dog could be her ally.

169

'If Stella could talk,' Justine began, 'what do you think *she* would remember from the day you all disappeared? Anything. Anything at all.'

Chapter 55

'What kind of question is that?' Camilla Bronson demanded out in the suite's common room, where Justine's questioning unfolded on-screen.

'A brilliant one,' I retorted. 'She's getting them to separate from whatever happened to them by forcing them to engage their imaginations and look at their memories through the dog's eyes. Stella's like her key into their minds.'

Indeed, over the next two hours, using Stella whenever she could to preface questions, Justine brought out snippets of information that together created a loose tapestry of the Harlow family's life on the day before their disappearance.

Stella remembered that she suffered from jet lag but felt happy to be out of Vietnam, with all those crazy scooters that almost ran her over. The bulldog recalled getting up early with Malia, who'd promised Jennifer she'd feed and water the horses. Jennifer liked to sleep in. The dog also remembered that Jin had worked on a watercolor painting instead of unpacking her room, which had annoyed her mother no end. Stella further recalled that Miguel had climbed a live oak tree he'd never climbed before, and Héctor, the care-taker and groundskeeper, got upset with him,

170

and had to fetch a ladder to get him down.

'How long have you known Héctor?' Justine asked.

'Forever,' Malia said. 'Héctor came with the ranch, Thom told me once.'

Their adoptive father had gotten up around nine the day after their arrival back at the ranch, got coffee, and disappeared to his editing room in the basement. The bulldog and all three children saw him go through the kitchen on his way there. Despite his promise that he'd spend time with the children, Thom had spent much of the day working. Jennifer rose later, around noon, complained of jet lag; but then she too went to her office and worked for much of the day.

They'd had dinner together around six. Miguel wanted to play soccer afterward, but Thom said he had too much work to do, took a plate of food, and returned to his editing room. Stella remembered this because Thom had dropped a cubed piece of chicken and she'd snagged it before he could.

'Thom told Stella she was like a shark,' Jin recalled softly.

As the group that was gathered in the common room watched the screen, the bulldog, on the bed next to Miguel, seemed to grow puzzled. Was that possible? Her eyebrows definitely rose. She clearly knew the kids were talking about her.

'When did Stella go out last?' Justine asked.

'Probably after we went to bed,' Jin said. 'Jennifer always took her out last, let her go pee and poop while she went for a run.'

'Did Jennifer go for a run that night?' Justine asked.

'Jennifer never misses her run, no matter what,' Malia said flatly. 'I heard the screen door slam when she went out that night. It's below my window.'

'What time did Jennifer come back?'

'I dunno,' Malia said with a heavy shrug. 'I was in my room when she left, but then my iPhone died, so I went to where we watch television, off the kitchen?'

Justine nodded. 'And?'

'That's the last thing I remember,' Malia said. 'I was on the couch, watching the CW, and then like nothing.'

'How about you?' Justine asked Jin.

Chapter 56

Jin shook her head.

'Miguel?'

The boy looked off into the distance. He'd covered his mouth again with his hand. Even so, you could see the memory of some traumatic event ripple across his face. Then he shook his head, said, 'No.'

'What were you thinking about just then?' Justine asked.

Miguel shrugged, said, 'It was like a dream. I don't think it was real.'

'What happened in your dream?' Justine asked softly. 'Was Stella there?'

'She was sleeping in my bed,' the boy said.

172

'How do you know that?'

'Because she farted when I got up to go to pee. It was horrible.'

Jin giggled, nodded. 'Stella's the smartest, prettiest girl, but she's got the worstest farts.'

The dog's eyebrows went up again.

Justine said, 'Okay, so Stella farts in your dream, Miguel, and then you go pee, and then what?'

The boy blinked, and the repressed memory passed across his face again. 'I heard noises,' he said. 'I didn't know what they were, but I knew they were bad.'

'How?'

He hesitated, hand worrying the bulldog's neck, said, 'I don't know. But I was scared. I started to run, and I fell and hurt my legs.' He pointed to the bruises on his knees and shins. 'And then I don't remember anything.'

'When you say "bad noises," do you mean screams or–'

'Crying,' Jin said suddenly, looking off somewhere herself. 'I remember a dream too. Someone was crying.'

'Where were you?' Justine asked. 'In your room? At home?'

Jin appeared puzzled but then said, 'No. I was in like a bunk bed, because I was lying on my back, and I could reach up and touch the bottom of the mattress. It wasn't very far.'

'You remember seeing that in your dream?' Justine asked.

'No, it was night. I could just, like ... feel it?'

'And the crying?' Justine pressed. 'Where was that? Who was that?'

173

'I don't...' Jin said before her voice trailed off.

Malia's mouth hung open. 'I had that same dream too. Someone *was* crying.'

'Where?'

'Outside of where I was,' Malia said, growing agitated, tears starting to dribble. 'Only I don't think it was a bunk bed. I was in a box. I felt walls all around me. I heard the crying through the walls.'

'Was it a man or a woman crying? Your mom or dad?'

The oldest Harlow girl shook her head. 'No. It sounded like a child crying. Not Jennifer.'

'Couldn't have been Thom?'

Malia blinked, thought, said, 'But I heard men talking and that stopped the crying, and then I heard loud noises like chains clanking, and something heavy hitting something metal. And then a sound like a jet, the way the engine sounds when it starts up?'

'I know that sound,' Justine said, paused. 'The men you heard talking in your dream. What were they saying?'

'I don't know. They were speaking Spanish.'

Chapter 57

Del Rio's face was puffy, bandaged. A carbon-fiber-and-canvas girdle wrapped and supported his torso. He was flat on his back, hitched to several machines and an IV, but breathing without a tube.

'I'm spending too much time in hospitals,' I said in weary greeting. It was past ten. Other than two twenty-minute catnaps, I hadn't slept in nearly forty-eight hours. I should have listened to Justine, gone home, slept hard. But I felt I had to be by Del Rio's side. It was my duty, and my honor.

Del Rio smiled, coughed, looked at me through a medicated haze. 'They say it will all heal.'

'You can't know how happy I was to hear that news, Rick,' I said, grabbed his hand and shook it. 'How happy all of us are.'

'Don't feel jack now, Jack,' Del Rio said. 'But they got me on all sorts of stuff supposed to reduce the swelling.' He paused. 'What-all happened? Nobody'll tell me anything.'

I gave it to him in broad strokes, the death of Bud Rankin, the chase at the pier after the explosion, the identity of the kite-boarders, the sheriff trying to say Private should take the fall for the whole fiasco.

'What did I tell you?' Del Rio rasped.

I raised my hands in surrender. 'I should have listened to you, but we had and have immunity. Anyway, FBI's involved now. In both cases.'

'Both?'

I summarized Justine and Cruz's trip to Mexico, the release of the Harlow children, and their spare and fuzzy recollections of their capture and captivity.

Del Rio closed his eyes. For a second I thought he'd lost consciousness, but then he said, 'Those sounds she heard, the Harlow girl. Sounds like loading coffins on an airplane, right?'

175

I thought about it, nodded. 'Could be, or something like it.'

'There'll be paperwork on that somewhere,' he said. 'You can't just go flying bodies around in coffins.'

'That true?'

'Well, you'd think.'

I couldn't argue with his logic, said, 'I'll have Mo-bot look into cargo flights to Mexico the night they disappeared. Guadalajara.'

Del Rio nodded, glanced at the clock. 'I don't remember you saying Fescoe or anyone else got another demand from No Prisoners.'

'Because there hasn't been one, at least to my knowledge.'

'More than twenty-four hours,' he said. 'No more killings either.'

He was right. What did that mean? Anything? Or was No Prisoners just trying to lull us into thinking–

'Where's it all going next?' Del Rio asked. 'Private's end of things?'

'Justine and Sci are returning to the Harlows' ranch in the morning along with a team of FBI techs, see if there's anything they missed,' I said.

'Justine done with the kids?' he grunted. 'Couple of hours of mind-flogging doesn't seem enough for her.'

I shrugged. 'She offered to go back in the morning. But Sanders wanted to give the children time to get settled into his house before they were talked to again. I have to admit, he seems very protective of them. They all do. Camilla Bronson and Graves. Justine's arguing that I should send people back to Mexico ASAP. But the FBI's already heard her story and they've got more clout.'

'No Prisoners?'

'I want No Prisoners because of what he did to you,' I said coldly. 'But I have no idea what Private's official role will be going forward.'

My cell phone rang loudly. 'Shit.' I wasn't supposed to have the damn thing on. I glanced at the caller ID and was taken aback.

I hesitated, clicked ANSWER. 'More slanderous accusations to throw my way?'

'Jack,' Bobbie Newton sighed. 'I just have to draw the line at someone disrupting my God-given First Amendment rights.'

'Uh-huh,' I said.

'How are they, the poor li'l darlings?'

I could tell she'd been drinking. Bobbie liked to drink, early and often, another winning aspect of her character.

'Who?' I said.

'Coy boy,' she said in a scolding tone.

I let the silence grow, knowing it would drive her crazy, personally and from a journalistic point of view. Bobbie had broken the story of the Harlow kidnapping and the release of the children. No doubt about that. But stories like the Harlows' disappearance required near-constant updates to feed the cable, Internet, and network news monsters.

'Give Camilla a call,' I said. 'I'm sure she'd love to talk.'

'Camilla Bronson carries grudges,' Bobbie said.

'And I don't?'

'C'mon, Jack. That's old news. Live and let live.'

I waited several beats, then said, 'Tit for tat, Bobbie?'

'What's the tit?' she demanded, and I heard ice cubes clink against glass.

'An update on their physical and mental condition, the little we know about the day of the kidnapping,' I said.

'Mmmmm, that is tempting,' Bobbie said. 'The tat?'

'Who tipped you off? Was it Maines?'

'A good journalist never reveals sources,' she protested. 'You know that.'

'Too bad, then. Gotta go, Bobbie.'

'Wait, wait!' she cried. 'Okay, okay. You go first.'

'Nope,' I said, and stayed silent. 'Offer's good for ten seconds.'

Five seconds went by. Then nine. I was about to end the call when she said, 'Terry Graves.'

That threw me. Why would...?

'I'm waiting for my tit, Jack,' Bobbie said.

'Sorry, Bobbie, your information came in a second after tit deadline.'

'What? You ... you lying son of a–'

I ended the call, feeling like balance had been restored in the universe. You can only take so much grief from one person before you give it back.

I looked at Del Rio, hoping to... He was sleeping.

There was a recliner in the room. I sat in it, shut off my cell, kicked back, shut my eyes, and drifted off to a place where there were no mass killers, no celebrities, and no conniving attorneys, not like my hometown at all.

Chapter 58

Justine suffered that night.

In her nightmares, she kept hearing the muffled sounds of someone crying, kept seeing the chewed lips of Leona Casa Madre, and kept reliving the knife fight with Carla. Twice she woke up shaking and in a cold sweat, unsure where she was. Twice she wondered about the brutal vividness of the nightmares, worse than the actual experience. Was she infected? Running a fever? Hallucinating?

She woke for a third time a few minutes before five, feeling Carla's fingers around her throat, seeing the woman's insane eyes and the shiv sticking out of her back. Justine lay there panting, trying to figure out why the nightmares would not quit.

And then she thought she knew. She recalled hearing about this kind of relentless cyclic dream from soldiers returning from Iraq and Afghanistan. Jack had had this very same sort of dream. The dreams were what had driven him to seek her out in the first place.

'I think I'm suffering from PTSD,' she said, as she sat up and turned on the light.

Post-traumatic stress disorder, rampant among vets, seen in cops and firefighters. And now her? Was that what was going on?

Justine pulled her legs up tight to her chest, realizing that the attack in the jail cell was the closest she'd ever come to dying, the closest she'd ever come to deadly violence. Once again she felt invaded, like a part of her, some basic innocence, had been ripped from her, leaving no visible wound other than the ones on her arm and upper chest.

The clinician in Justine clicked through the symptoms of PTSD that might affect her: recurring nightmares, hyper-vigilance, inability to sleep, inability to feel certain emotions, heavy drinking, heavy medicating, acting out sexually.

Her head ached. She was still tired but did not want to sleep again.

She got out of bed, got dressed for Crossfit, thought it would be good to go sweat the horrors away. She found a coffee shack open at five thirty, got a double-shot latte, and prayed that the work-out of the day didn't include running. She arrived at ten to six and parked across the street from the box, which, to her surprise, was already lit up. Usually Ronny, the trainer at the early class, arrived at the very last second. She went inside, finding Ronny talking excitedly on his cell. He hung up, looking shaken.

'You okay?' Justine asked.

'No,' the trainer said, puffing his lips. 'My sister, she just went into labor, and her boyfriend left her. I said I'd be there for her.'

'Well, go on, then,' she said.

'I'll have to cancel class,' he said.

'Go,' she said. 'Give me the key. I'll wait until ten past, tell whoever shows, lock the place up, and put the key back through the mail slot.'

Ronny hesitated but then ripped the key from a

chain and took off. Justine looked around, thinking, *Life goes on, doesn't it? Bud Rankin dies. A baby is born.*

Chapter 59

Justine knew she probably shouldn't use the equipment without a trainer present, but she'd been there long enough to feel she could at least do something, say, ten rounds of five pull-ups, ten push-ups, and fifteen sit-ups?

She was into round six, hanging off the bars, when she heard the front door open. It was that guy, Paul. His curly brown hair hung above his soft, nice eyes, which found her immediately.

'We the only ones?' he asked, coming in, looking up at the clock. It was five past six.

'No class this morning,' Justine said, and explained about Ronny.

'Oh,' Paul said. 'What happened?' He was pointing at the bandages on her forearm. The one on her chest was hidden beneath her shirt.

Justine looked at her arm, hesitated, then said, 'Fell Rollerblading.'

'I broke my wrist once doing that,' he said. 'Are you working out?'

She told him she was.

'Mind if I join in?' he asked.

Justine once more noticed how appealing he was.

'Sure,' she said. 'Just no weights or rowers.

Liability issues, I think.'

Paul grinned. He warmed up and stretched while Justine finished her last four rounds, which left her sweating and heaving for air. When she got to her feet, Paul was crossing toward her, carrying a heavy green rubber band about three feet long.

'Can you show me how this kipping thing works?' he asked. 'Ronny said I should use the bands to learn it.'

'Uh, sure,' she said, checking the clock. Six-twenty. No one else was coming.

She helped Paul set up the band, looping it over the bar at the top of a pull-up station. She showed him how to step into the band with one foot while holding on to the bars.

'Now fully drop down,' she said, recalling how she'd been taught to kip.

He did. The band stretched. His feet hung two inches above the floor.

'Okay,' Justine said, 'now you want to get your body rocking, as if you were pushing your stomach out and then snapping it in and back toward your spine. That momentum carries you into the pull-up.'

Paul tried. It was a pitiful attempt. He was throwing his knees forward, not his belly. 'Here,' she said. 'Can I put my hands on you?'

He smiled down at her, a nice smile, a very nice smile. 'If it will help.'

'It helped me,' Justine said.

'Okay, then.'

She smiled, nodded, moved around to his side, put one hand on his lower back and the other on his stomach. 'Jump up.'

Paul jumped up and caught the bar with both hands. Justine pressed against his back so his belly arched against the band; then she pushed backward quickly. He swung on the band and lifted.

'Feel it?' she asked.

'I did,' he said, then began to play with the motion. 'It's almost like what trapeze artists do.'

'Exactly.'

In less than ten tries, he had it and was using his body and the band to snap himself up into the air, six, then seven times in a row.

Justine clapped. 'You've got it!'

Paul slowed, stepped out of the band. He was grinning. They were very close. 'You're a natural, you know that? Teacher, I mean.'

Justine noticed how good he smelled, blushed, but did not look away or try to create space between them. 'I just did what—'

'No,' he said, taking her hand. 'I mean it, you … you're really wonderful. I'm sorry to be so forward, but ever since I met you, I've thought about you a lot.'

They stood there looking at each other for several beats. Justine's heart raced. She felt outside herself somehow. She heard her own voice as if from far off, like in a dream, saying, 'Did you ever just want to give in sometimes and do something totally crazy? Totally not you?'

Paul's gaze went lazy, and he nodded. 'All the time.'

Justine could not believe that she replied, 'We should lock the door, then. Turn out the lights.'

A moment of surprise, then Paul murmured, 'Perfect. No one will even know we're here.'

Chapter 60

At five minutes to eight that morning, Terry Graves entered his office in the Harlow-Quinn Productions bungalow on the Warner lot. He carried a grande Starbucks and was reading that morning's *Hollywood Reporter*. Dave Sanders was trailing him, chewing on a bagel, engrossed in the *Los Angeles Times*.

The office was surprisingly small and the furniture surprisingly understated given the success of the company. Except for the various framed movie posters, you would not have pegged the room as belonging to a Hollywood power player.

The producer was almost around the back of his desk before he noticed me sitting in his chair, looking at him. I was finishing an egg-and-bacon sandwich, one eye on the television, which showed a clip from Bobbie Newton's footage of the Harlow children.

'What the hell are you doing in here, Jack?' Graves demanded.

'How the hell did you get in here?' Sanders said.

'I'm resourceful, remember?' I said. 'That's why you hired me.'

'What's this all about?' Graves said, indignant now.

'Bobbie Newton's footage of the Harlow kids?' I said. 'I just heard it's the number one clip on YouTube, something like seven million hits since

184

yesterday. And it's the number one most-linked-to site on Facebook. There isn't a news channel or newspaper in the world that isn't carrying the story.'

'Does that surprise you?' Sanders demanded.

'The question is: Does it surprise *you?*'

'What?' The producer scowled. 'Of course it doesn't surprise us.'

'I didn't think so.'

The attorney caught the edge in my voice. 'What's that mean?'

'Bobbie Newton told me that Terry here is the one who tipped her about the kids. I suspect you were in on it too, Dave. And maybe even Camilla.'

'What the fuck are you talking about?' Terry Graves snapped.

'The coverage. The uproar. The publicity value of the Harlows disappearing, especially when they're making the movie of a lifetime. Makes me wonder what's really going on here.'

The producer's eyes flared. 'I have no, zero, *nada* interest in this kind of publicity. And what Bobbie told you? That's an out-and-out lie from a lunatic lush who will say anything to further her own ego-glorifying ends.'

I had to admit, Terry Graves knew the Bobbie Newton I knew.

Sanders became livid. 'And for thinking that we had anything to do with any of this, you're fired, Morgan. Vacate the premises. Invoice me for your time.'

I watched him, saying nothing.

'Get ... out ... of ... my ... chair,' Terry Graves said.

185

'I don't think that's in your best interests, gentlemen,' I said, not moving.

'Our best...?' the producer shouted. 'Should I call security?'

'I dunno, will that be how you handle the FBI?'

'What are you talking about?' Sanders demanded.

'You don't think they're coming here eventually, Dave?' I asked. 'For an attorney, you have no sense of how criminal investigations go forward. They'll be wanting to review the books, look at every file that Terry and you and Camilla Bronson have concerning the Harlows.'

Sanders stiffened. 'My files are protected under attorney-client privilege.'

'And mine are protected under the First Amendment to the Constitution,' Terry Graves said.

I shook my head. 'I don't think any of that will fly in a case this high-profile. You will not be able to control this story, gentlemen, no matter what you do. It's taken on a life of its own. Stand in its way? Get ready to be trampled.'

Sanders thought about that. His tone turned more businesslike. 'What are you suggesting?'

'I'm not *suggesting* anything,' I replied. 'I'm *telling* you that if you are as smart as I think you are, you'll allow me and my investigators access to all your files. We'll look for anything amiss and notify you. That way you'll have a heads-up before the FBI hands it to you with your head down.'

'You don't think I know what's in my files?' Terry Graves asked. 'I do. And I'll tell you, Morgan, I'm more than comfortable with what's in there.'

'How about you, Dave?' I asked.

The entertainment attorney grimaced. 'I'm fine too. And we're not interested in your proposition. I stand by my decision. You and Private are fired. We don't need your advice or services anymore.'

'Suit yourself,' I said, standing up finally and reaching out to shake Terry Graves's hand.

The producer looked at my hand with extreme distaste, did not take it. Neither did Sanders. I exited as gracefully as I could, thinking that the Harlow-Quinn team really did need my advice, and really did need Private's services. Take their security system, for example, especially the computer security system.

Like most people, Terry Graves was lazy when it came to things like passwords. I'd found his written down on a sticky note under a divider in the top drawer of his desk.

Leaving the bungalow and heading toward the gate and my car, parked just outside the Warner grounds, I kept my hands in my pants pockets and gripped the flash drives I'd used to copy everything I could find in the producer's computer regarding the Harlows and *Saigon Falls*.

Chapter 61

Two hours later, Justine sat in the passenger seat of the Suburban as Sci drove them north out of Thousand Oaks on the 101. Kloppenberg was monitoring up-to-the-minute radio coverage of the Harlow disappearance.

Justine barely listened. Her mind surged with battling thoughts and emotions about what she'd done so blithely earlier in the morning. How could she have done that? She barely knew Paul. And locked door or not, they'd taken such a chance, making love on the floor of the gym and up against the steel poles that supported the pull-up stations. But maybe the possibility of getting caught had only magnified the experience. Even now, hours afterward, Justine had to admit that the sex had been incredible, mind-blowing.

But that's not me, she thought in sudden desperation. *The Justine I know doesn't hook up with strangers and...* She alternated between wanting to call Paul, to tell him how amazing it all had been, and wanting to sob.

Was this the kind of random sexual acting out she had feared? She couldn't come to any other conclusion. The knife fight in the jail cell in Guadalajara had seriously affected her. For God's sake, she knew risky sexual behavior was a symptom of PTSD, and yet she'd just gone ahead, almost as if she were an adolescent again, unable to make rational choices.

'You okay?' Sci asked as they drove into Ojai and headed toward the Harlows' ranch.

'Huh?' she replied, feeling foggier than normal. 'I'm just tired, Sci. I haven't been getting much sleep lately.'

'Lot of that going around,' Kloppenberg offered. 'You see the text from Jack and Del Rio?'

Justine shook her head.

'Rick moved his right big toe about an hour ago. Jack saw it.'

She smiled. 'That's so good.'

'I know, right?' Sci said. 'There they are.'

Ahead on the winding road, Justine could see several satellite broadcast trucks set up across from the gate to the Harlows' ranch. With klieg lights and cameras trained on the Suburban, Sci pulled into the drive behind two vans emblazoned with the symbol of the FBI. A short, slight man, forties, buzz cut, FBI blue Windbreaker, already stood by the front gate.

'Good,' Sci said. 'That's Todd McCormick. We work peachy together.'

'You being sarcastic?'

'No, I mean it. He's first-rate. Little uptight. FBI, what do you want? But the man's completely on it when it comes to forensics.'

They got out. Sci introduced Justine to McCormick, who seemed Kloppenberg's exact opposite in almost every way. And yet Justine noticed immediately that the men appeared to have some kind of quiet bond, a shared expertise and curiosity that was remarkably free of ego or competition.

'I saw the tapes of the children,' McCormick said. 'Of course, I've heard of you, though I've never seen you in action. Impressive, Ms. Smith.'

'Thank you,' Justine said.

'You trained in forensics as well as child psychology?' McCormick asked.

Justine shook her head.

'Gotta admit, it's a little off from my perspective,' the crime tech said.

'What's that?' Sci asked.

'Townsend letting you both back on the crime

189

scene,' McCormick said.

Sci grinned coldly. 'Private's forensics teams and labs are fully accredited with every major law enforcement agency in the country, even yours, Todd. If you remember, I have lectured at the FBI Academy.'

'I remember, Sci,' McCormick said before gesturing toward Justine with his chin. 'No offense, but I was talking about her.'

Justine said, 'Look, I'm here because Jack Morgan thinks I have a good eye for things. Special Agent Townsend concurs. I certainly won't touch anything you consider evidence, Mr. McCormick. I'll notify you the moment I find anything that seems germane to the investigation.'

You could tell the FBI tech didn't like it, but he nodded. 'You have a key?'

'No,' said Sci. 'I thought you got it from Sanders.'

Justine sighed, stepped by them to a keypad. 'Don't worry, gentlemen, I have the entry code. I wrote it down the last time I was here.'

Chapter 62

'How the hell did you get access to these kinds of files?' FBI SAC Christine Townsend asked me. We were inside the lab at Private. Mo-bot was at her workbench, uploading the data onto our system.

'I copied them from Graves's computer at Harlow-Quinn,' I said.

'Stole them, you mean?' Townsend cried. 'Are you out of your mind? I won't be part of this. Whatever you might find in there is tainted now. None of it can be used in any court in–'

'Does it really matter?' I demanded. 'Look, with all due respect, I thought we were in the business of finding the Harlows. Shouldn't we keep that the number one priority?'

'I have a sworn duty to uphold the Constitution,' she shot back.

'As Chief Fescoe and others have pointed out to me recently, I don't operate under the same restraints,' I replied. 'Besides, I don't like being lied to or being manipulated, and Sanders and Graves are guilty of both.'

'What's their motive?' Townsend said skeptically. 'Why does this situation benefit them beyond what you said about publicity? You said the Harlows were almost bankrupt, that the film was on the verge of ruining them financially. You'd think they'd be more focused on that.'

'I never said the Harlows were almost bankrupt,' I corrected. 'That's what Sanders told me. As of last night, I doubt nearly everything he has said in this case, and Graves and Bronson too. Taking the files is my way of double-checking things.'

Townsend said, 'I still can't be part of this.' She headed toward the door.

'Don't you want to know what we find?' I called after her.

'I didn't say that,' the special agent replied, and went out the door.

Mo-bot called to me. 'Where do you want me to start? This is a lot of ground to cover with a one-woman show.'

Before I could answer, my cell rang. A number I did not recognize, but given all that had been going on, I answered. 'Jack Morgan.'

'It's your favorite bail bondsman,' Carmine Noccia purred. 'We should meet sooner rather than later.'

'Carmine, it is not a good time.'

'Wasn't a good time for me last year when the DEA found that truck.'

So there it was. Carmine either knew or openly suspected me. 'I suppose not,' I said. 'But what's that got to do with me?'

Carmine laughed. 'Cool as ever, Jack. But again, we should meet sooner rather than later. The three of us.'

'Three?'

'Yeah. You. Me. Your brother. Tommy and I have a proposition for you.'

'An offer I can't refuse?'

A pause, then a short laugh. 'You're a cool son of a bitch, Jack.'

'I try.'

'How about Tommy and I drop by your office?' Carmine said. 'Haven't seen the place in a while. Say, like, an hour?'

'Say, like, I'll be waiting.'

Chapter 63

Justine wandered into the Harlows' bedroom, noticed the mirrors, six in total, none alike, two floor-lengths on either side wall, two smaller framed mirrors, one on the doors to the closets, and a long thin one on the interior wall up high, right below the ceiling. It seemed to reflect nothing but the Italian plaster.

She heard a grunt, noticed McCormick waving an ultraviolet wand over the sheets on the Harlows' bed. Weren't they fresh? The sheets? What did he expect to find on them?

Justine headed into Jennifer Harlow's closet, finding the drawer of sex toys Mo-bot had first discovered, and then the Sybian machine sitting on the floor beneath a row of haute couture dresses.

Justine closed her eyes, tried to get inside Jennifer's head. The woman was obviously highly sexed. The actress seemed to have one of the best of everything in the self-pleasure toy category. But what did that mean? A lot of highly creative people were also highly sexed, Picasso, for instance, and Anaïs Nin, and a dozen other actors she could name right off the top of her head. It certainly didn't mean ... or did it?

Was it possible that Jennifer used all these toys because her husband did not satisfy her often enough, or at all anymore? Justine flashed on an image of her entanglement with Paul earlier in the morning and felt faint. *What in God's name was I thinking?* Was that how Jennifer Harlow was? Sexually impulsive?

Or maybe the toys were just that, toys, something to energize a marriage of twenty-plus years. She opened her eyes, looked down, thought, *But how do you explain the Sybian?* She got down on her knees, looked at it. According to Sci, the machine was the ultimate in erotic gizmos for women, a combination of the thundering power of riding a horse bareback coupled with...

Justine imagined herself on the thing and then shook her head violently. She was not going there. She was getting this all under control.

Her hand lashed out, sweeping aside several of the dresses. She saw something behind the Sybian machine, a crack in the closet wall she hadn't noticed before. She pushed back the dresses, smelling faint perfume. Jennifer's?

The crack was regular, rectangular, like the seam around a narrow panel or door, except she could see no handle. She knocked on it and was surprised to find it was made of some kind of metal. She felt along the seam counterclockwise, pressing, prodding. Nothing.

She was about to get up to see if McCormick might have better luck, when she noticed an aberration in the wood trim that ran along the carpet five inches below the bottom seam. It was a knot that had not been sanded smooth.

Justine pushed at it, felt no give. She got her finger alongside the knot and nudged it left. Nothing. She pushed right, felt it give and slide until she heard a hydraulic click and the metal pocket door slid back, revealing a steel ladder bolted into the wall two feet away.

Chapter 64

The passage to the panic room, Justine thought, leaning out to shine her Maglite into the shaft. About twenty feet below her she spotted a cement floor and a door. About eight feet above her, a faint light shone from another passage.

She thought of telling McCormick, the FBI tech, but knew that meant she would not be able to explore for herself. She ducked through the open pocket door, leaned across the space, and climbed the ladder until she was level with the second passage.

Unlike the one below, this passage had no door, just a narrow entry that doglegged left. Justine held the light between her teeth, stepped across the space, found footing inside. She took another step, met a wall, turned left, and found herself in a room about seven feet high, fifteen feet long, and twenty deep. There were bunk beds, a table with six chairs, and a small kitchen whose shelves were stocked with canned goods.

She saw a switch at the entry and tripped it. Another pocket door slid out, blocking the entrance.

Light fell into the panic room from a window placed flush at the top of the wall. It was about a foot wide and ran most of the length of the space.

Just above the window on the ceiling, Justine noticed metal brackets, a series of them, spaced at three-foot intervals, five in all.

She tried to orient herself based on her movements after she'd left Jennifer Harlow's closet, tried to figure out where the window faced.

'It's not a window, it's a two-way mirror,' she muttered to herself.

Again she looked up at the brackets: simple bent and drilled steel bars screwed into the ceiling. There were extra holes in the bars, and signs that something had been bolted to them at one time.

Except for electrical plugs in the wall and what looked like a socket for a cable connection, the place was empty. A cable connection?

Justine looked back at the brackets, imagining screens and cable lines hanging there. But why? And then she saw it. Not screens. Cameras. It made sense, didn't it? The Harlows were film-makers, after all.

Justine wanted to see what a camera might pick up from the window. She jumped, grabbed hold of two brackets, and pulled herself high enough to peer through the two-way mirror, which afforded her a complete and elevated view of the Harlows' bed and the FBI tech still working on it. She swung her attention around the room, spotting the other four mirrors. Were there brackets for cameras behind them?

She was going to find out. As she returned to the ladder, questions and hypotheses darted through her mind. What were the cameras for? In case they had to use the panic room and wanted to document intruders?

She supposed that was possible, but for some reason it didn't make total sense to her. She tripped the switch; the door slid open again. She left it open and climbed back down the ladder. She almost turned and stepped back through the open pocket door into Jennifer Harlow's closet but decided to go all the way down the ladder first.

As she neared the bottom, her flashlight beam picked up an alcove of sorts set opposite a steel door. There were three steel shelves set in the cement in the alcove. On the wall between each shelf were an electrical socket and another of those cable connections. She looked closely at the shelves and saw no dust. Which meant what? The shelves were cleaned regularly? Or had they been cleaned after something was removed from them?

Unable to answer, Justine turned toward the door, spotted a switch beside it. She flipped it up. Nothing happened. She shrugged, turned the dead bolt, and yanked open the door.

In the darkness she heard a crash and then a voice yelled out, 'Who's there? Identify yourself or I swear to God, I'll shoot!'

Chapter 65

'Brother dearest,' Tommy said as he entered my office, arm spread wide. He was wearing a five-thousand-dollar suit, no tie, and appeared to have hit the tanning salon earlier in the morning.

I remembered my brother winking at me in the

courtroom the day of his arraignment. Was this part of his plan? Figure out a way to get me to admit that I was at the scene when Clay Harris took a 9mm round to the chest? It was not beyond Tommy to go this route. I still suspected that Tommy had hired Clay to kill my ex-girlfriend in the first place. In order to frame me for the murder. Since that didn't work out, it only made sense that he'd try to frame me for *Clay's* murder instead. But I had no proof.

Carmine entered my office right behind Tommy, his skin an even deeper red against his starched white collar and yellow cashmere sweater. 'Jack,' the mobster said, as if we were long-lost golf buddies. 'How gracious of you to entertain us at such short notice.'

'Uh-huh,' I said. 'What's the proposition?'

'What, no business pleasantries?' Tommy said, taking a seat across the desk from me.

'I'm not feeling particularly pleasant, brother,' I replied.

Tommy beamed at me as if I'd said something of deep significance.

Carmine shut the door. He looked around my office, a space I intentionally keep devoid of personal effects. In my line of work, I've found that it pays to know more about other people than they do about me. Carmine gazed at me, popped his chin up. 'Place bugged?'

'Good idea, but no,' I said. 'You fellows wearing wires?'

Tommy cocked his head as if I'd gone paranoid, which I had.

'Nah,' Carmine said. 'I was never one for tap-ing myself.'

I said nothing. Tommy scowled but took off his jacket, unbuttoned his shirt, and showed me his chest and back. 'Satisfied, brother?'

'Carmine?' I said.

'Fuck you,' Carmine said, as Tommy tucked his shirt back in.

I sighed wearily. 'What's the proposition, then? I'm a busy man.'

'I heard that,' Tommy said, and laughed. 'Saw that too: the expression on your face when Bobbie Newton caught you with the Harlow children. It was worth the price of admission. You're a television star, brother, you really are.'

'Glad to have entertained you,' I shot back. 'By the way, I found it interesting that *you* designed the security system at the Harlows' estate, Tommy. The one that was so easily foiled.' I looked at Carmine. 'You two didn't have anything to do with their disappearance, did you?'

The mobster acted insulted. 'Do I look like I'm in the business of kidnapping celebs?'

Chapter 66

I smiled and said, 'You look like a man capable of anything, Carmine.'

Carmine smiled. 'I'll take *that* as a compliment.'

'Wasn't meant that way at all.'

That wiped the smirk off his face, which reset as hard and as cold as I'd ever seen it. He sat in a chair across the desk from me, crossed his legs, a man who felt like he was in control. 'You fucked me over big-time, Jack.'

'How's that?'

'Six million in oxy,' Tommy said.

'I can't control the DEA,' I said.

'But you can tip them off,' Carmine growled. 'It's the simplest explanation, and I've come to believe that the simplest explanation is the most likely explanation.'

'Could simply be that someone in your organization ratted you out, or someone stumbled into the load and reported it. Shit luck.'

Carmine shot me his patented shark smile. 'Doesn't matter in this case, now does it, Jack? It's what *I* believe happened, am I right?'

I said nothing.

Carmine said, 'You gotta pay, Jack. You gotta balance things.'

Tommy laughed, and I wondered if he'd been drinking. 'It's not like you're gonna find some horse head in your bed.'

'Miracle of miracles. How about a guy carrying piano wire in the backseat?'

Carmine pursed his lips. 'You're behind the times.'

'Nothing like that,' Tommy said.

'Nah,' Carmine said. 'Your brother gave me deep insight into your complicated psyche.'

'Imagine that,' I said.

'Right?' Carmine said, and then made a gesture with an index finger that encompassed the room. 'Tommy here says you love this place, Private, more than anything in life, like every day you're trying to make up for the fuckup your father turned out to be.'

'Deep, Tommy.'

Tommy grinned and turned his palms up. 'Truth's the truth.'

'So?'

'So you're selling Tommy this dump,' Carmine said.

'We're buying you out, Jack,' Tommy confirmed. 'Putting Private where it should have been in the first place: in my hands.'

'Private's not for sale and never will be.'

'There's a lot to be said for economies of scale, you know?' Carmine said as if he hadn't heard my reply. 'With Tommy's company holding the lion's share of the security system design business, it doesn't make sense to go to all the trouble to build up our own investigative business when your company, Private, is right there for the taking.'

'Harvard B School,' Tommy said, tapping his temple with one finger. 'Great mind, that Carmine.'

'Do your homework, doltish,' I snapped. 'Carmine never finished Harvard B School. He got tossed out for cheating on an accounting exam.'

Carmine's red skin turned livid, but he held his voice in check. 'That's a lie, but it doesn't matter, Jack. Instead of piano wire, we'll offer you three point two million, which is a hell of a lot more than the company's assets. And you get the fuck out of L.A.'

'If you'd actually finished Harvard Business School, you'd know a company like Private is not valued on assets as much as client base and reputation, Carmine,' I replied calmly. 'Private's value is ten times your quote at minimum, but it doesn't matter because, as I said, the company is not for sale.'

'Of course it is,' Carmine said agreeably, 'because you are about to put it up for sale, Jack, and be more than willing to take our preemptive bid.'

'Why in God's name would I ever do that?' I asked just as agreeably.

The mobster looked like a cat that had just polished off a nice plump rat. He rubbed his belly, said, 'Because if you don't you'll be looking at the inside of Folsom or Pelican Bay with a reservation for a chemical cocktail.'

I felt my stomach go queasy, a feeling that deepened toward nausea when Tommy said, 'If you don't sell, brother, I'll have to go with defense plan B, which calls for me putting you at the scene of Clay Harris's murder, gun in your hand, with a cold reason for vengeance for what that bastard did to you. It's a much more plausible story than my supposed motive, definitely enough to cast reasonable doubt, and that's all I really need to skate on this. You, however, will be in for a world of shit.'

'Unless you sign over the company, of course,' Carmine said, pulling a checkbook from his pants pocket. 'I'm prepared to put down good-faith money right here, right now. We'll let the attorneys take care of the rest, okay?'

Tommy was almost gloating at the corner he and Carmine had boxed me into. Either I sold them Private, or my brother implicated me in a murder where I was present at the scene, but not a participant. Not to mention the possibility of piano wire.

I studied each man in turn, examining the angles of their proposition in my mind. 'Can I ask what defense plan A is, Tommy?'

'Attorney-client privilege on that one, brother,' Tommy said. 'But don't worry, it's just as bomb-proof. A shocker, as they say on Court TV.'

My twin seemed more than confident about the power he held over me, and over the company our father had left to me and not him. Carmine, meanwhile, looked like he'd just had a second helping of rat.

The mobster said, 'Let's just get this over with, shall we? Ten percent good? Three hundred and twenty grand earnest money?'

Chapter 67

'Sci!' Justine yelled. 'Don't shoot!'

'Oh, my God,' she heard Kloppenberg grunt. Shaking, she stepped back and flipped the switch in the shaft, flooding Thom Harlow's basement editing room with light. Sci had his hand on the console, struggled to get to his feet. He looked at her, affecting dignity with his nose up; he pushed his glasses tight to his forehead, said, 'Well, you succeeded in scaring the living bejeezus out of me.'

Justine laughed and put her hand over her heart. 'It didn't do much for my blood pressure either.' She looked around. 'What were you doing down here?'

Kloppenberg brushed lint from his jacket sleeve, said, 'Going over it a second time. As a matter of fact, I was wondering what was behind that door when the lights went off and you jumped out.'

'I didn't *jump out*,' Justine said. 'You make me sound like the boogeyman.'

'I thought that's who you were, exactly,' Sci said. 'What's up there?'

Justine described where the shaft led and what she'd found.

'So all computers and *all cameras* were taken with the family,' Sci said.

'Anything in here?'

He shook his head. 'All the editing equipment is intact, but there's no hard drives, no film.'

She frowned. 'Nothing at all to do with *Saigon Falls?*'

'Nothing.'

Justine ran the facts as she knew them through her head. The shaft connected the Harlows' bedroom suite to the panic room and the editing room.

The children had said that their father had spent much of their first days home down here in the editing room, working on the film, which was what Thom had told Sanders he was going to do when they got back.

Was the film behind their disappearance? Had Thom's cameras happened upon something politically explosive while they were in Vietnam? Or something that implicated...

McCormick, the FBI forensics tech, entered the editing room, looked surprised to see Justine,

204

glanced at the open door to the shaft, frowned, but said, 'Thought you should know, Sci. Cadaver-sniffing dogs just hit. We're digging for a body.'

Chapter 68

I pointed a finger toward my office door. 'Private's not for sale and you two were just leaving.'

'Heh,' Tommy said. 'That's not how this is–'

'It's exactly how this is ending,' I said, then gazed over at the mobster. 'Carmine, I respect you, so I've got to level with you. I told a fib earlier.'

'Gee, that's a fucking surprise. Gonna come clean now? Tell me you did tip the Feds and you're sorry? Sorry, no–'

'This place *is* bugged,' I said, staring him right in the eye. 'Audio, video, multiple angles. I've got every bit of your little extortion scheme on record, including your admission that you sought contraband narcotics and participated in a conspiracy to rig my brother's trial with me as the fall guy.'

Carmine's rat seemed to be giving him sudden indigestion. 'That's bullshit. You show me.'

'No, I think I'll show FBI Special Agent in Charge Christine Townsend, a personal friend, and take my chances in court, where I will testify against my brother,' I said, and folded my hands across my chest, not looking at Tommy at all. 'Anything else to say? Or are we done?'

Carmine licked his lips, looked around the office, trying to spot the bugs. Then he smiled.

'You think you can outmaneuver me?'

'I just did.'

That pissed him off completely. He stared bullets at me, muttered, 'You fucked me. And Carmine Noccia is like an elephant when it comes to that sort of thing.'

'So you're having tusks implanted to go along with your phony Harvard MBA? Is that what you're telling me?' I asked.

'You're a dead man, Jack,' Carmine said, stood, nodded to Tommy.

'A pleasure, Carmine, Tommy,' I said. 'As always.'

I waited until they slammed the door behind them, then held off another minute before collapsing into my chair. Sweat pooled at my lower back. They'd had me and I'd bluffed my way out. There were no bugs in the room. No audio. No video.

But there sure as hell were going to be by the end of the day.

Chapter 69

Sci and McCormick used soft brushes to whisk away the last of the soil covering the corpse's face. The victim's chest and denim shirt were already exposed, revealing a bloom of dried blood and the exit hole of a bullet wound. He'd been shot through the heart from behind. He had been in the ground at least five days and the smell on the downwind side of the grave was worse than the odor in Leona Casa Madre's bathroom.

Justine crouched upwind, listening as the barking cadaver dogs were loaded back into a kennel truck and watching Kloppenberg and the FBI tech work, uncovering the dead man's bloated features. For reasons she did not fully grasp, these things only served to throw her mind back to the attack in the jail cell. She saw Carla coming for her with that knife, that shiv.

Justine's breath began to speed and so did her heart. Spots appeared before her eyes. Suddenly she wanted to be anywhere but by a grave.

Then she heard Sci say, 'It's Héctor, Héctor Ramón, the groundskeeper.'

The spots faded and she looked down at the grotesque mask the decomposition had crafted. 'How can you know that?'

Kloppenberg gestured to a silver bolo tie around the victim's neck. 'I saw a picture of him in his quarters. He was wearing it.'

'We'll run dental records to confirm,' McCormick said.

Much the way her mind had whirled back to the attack in the cell in Guadalajara, Justine's thoughts now flew to the timeline of events she'd been carrying around in her head. Based on the surviving security camera footage, Jennifer Harlow had last been seen leaving the house on her evening run around eight. Justine would bet that Héctor Ramón was killed at roughly the same time, or shortly thereafter in that two-hour gap that Del Rio had discovered. But why kill the groundskeeper? Why not others?

'Are the dogs still searching?' she asked.

'Dissecting the estate on a grid pattern,' Mc-Cormick said.

Justine blinked, nodded, felt indescribably tired. She looked at Sci. 'I'm not feeling that well, Seymour. Think I need to head back to L.A.'

'You okay?' he asked.

'Just a little light-headed,' she said. 'And there's not much more I can do here today anyway.'

Sci's elastic face turned concerned. 'I've never heard you trying to cut short your workday before, Justine. You want to see a doctor?'

'No, I just need to go home, get some sleep. I'll be better tomorrow.'

Chapter 70

Guin Scott-Evans wore a mask, a bikini made of iridescent feathers, and glittering high-heeled pumps. She held out her hand to me, said, 'Have you seen Tommy or Carmine anywhere? They're late for the ball, Jack, and I so wanted to dance.'

'Jack?' Mo-bot called, and rapped on my door-jamb.

I startled awake from a nap on the sofa in my office, sat up, looked around groggily, saw the wonder lady moving toward my desk, and groaned. 'Time is it?'

'Four in the afternoon,' she said. 'Sci just called. Cadaver dogs sniffed Héctor Ramón's body at the Harlow estate.'

That woke me up. 'Any other bodies?'

208

'They're looking.'

Mo-bot is by nature a mothering type. She also has a case of OCD when it comes to messiness, and rearranges my desk whenever she can. She started stacking folders, said, 'Found a few things in those files you brought me.'

'Tell me,' I said, sitting up, desperately wanting a cup of coffee *now*.

Maureen looked down at the hopelessness of my desktop, hesitated, sighed, said, 'It's better I show you.'

I followed her down the hall to Sci's lab, trying to figure out why I was so damn tired, then remembering that facing down a mobster and a conniving brother is a stressful thing, wrings you out. I stopped in the office break room, got a cup of coffee, and then went to sit beside Mo-bot at her workstation, looking at an array of screens that displayed scans of various legal and financial documents detailing the activities of Harlow-Quinn Productions and the making of *Saigon Falls*.

'This is dense stuff,' Mo-bot began. 'And some of the accounting practices at work here are as archaic as a film studio's. And forgive me, I haven't waded through half of it yet, but–'

'But you've found something,' I pressed. Much as I love her, Mo-bot has a tendency to qualify everything if I let her.

She nodded, annoyed. 'Until roughly twenty-four hours before they disappeared, the whole kit and caboodle *was* on the verge of insolvency. They were burning through cash at an astonishing rate, shooting in Vietnam.'

'That's what Sanders said,' I replied.

'He did,' Mo-bot replied. 'He also said that Thom predicted a white-knight investor, which is what he got.'

'When?'

'Day after they got back,' she said, and typed on her keyboard.

Up popped evidence of a ten-million-dollar deposit in the account of Harlow-Quinn Productions.

'Canceled check?' I asked.

'Ahead of you.'

A scan of the check appeared on the screen, made out to Harlow-Quinn. The check was drawn on a Panamanian bank and dated two days prior to the Harlows' disappearance. The account holder was identified as ESH Ltd.

'Who's ESH Ltd?'

'Don't know,' she admitted. 'Yet. But here's the really interesting thing.'

Mo-bot gave her computer another command, and records of four other payments from ESH Ltd to Harlow-Quinn appeared. One for two million. Three for five million each. All had been made within the last twenty-four months.

I looked at the total, said, 'Twenty-seven million. There's the deep, deep pockets. Whoever ESH Ltd is, they own a third of this film, maybe more.'

'Sounds about right,' Mo-bot agreed. 'Whoever they are, they've got lots of money in the Harlow-Quinn game.'

'And yet Terry Graves never mentioned getting a ten-million-dollar cash infusion,' I said.

'Hard to believe,' Mo-bot said.

Chapter 71

'Sir, you're not supposed to be here,' a voice complained, and I felt my feet rudely pushed out of the way. 'You need to sleep, go home, find a hotel room or something.'

In a chair in the corner of Del Rio's room in the medical center, I blinked awake to find a Filipina nurse named Angela glaring at me, hands on her hips. She could not have been more than five feet tall, but she was imposing and I sat up quickly, saying, 'I didn't know I was–'

'Don't listen to him, Angela,' Del Rio called from the bed. 'Jack's been a freeloader going way back. He'll sleep anywhere he can.'

I grinned. That sounded like the Del Rio I knew and loved. Then I looked back at the nurse, who was still royally ticked off. My face fell. She tapped her nurse's clog on the floor, arms crossed, said, 'I have to bathe this poor man. You want to watch?'

'I think I'll spare Rick that final indignity,' I said, stood, edged away from her, feeling like she might try to bite me if I wasn't careful.

Del Rio was laughing, so I went out the door with a major smile on my face. There were many things about my life at that point that were muddy, to say the least, but hearing my best friend laugh was not one of them. Hearing that laugh gave me hope that no matter what Tommy or Carmine or the team at Harlow-Quinn or No Prisoners might be plotting, an important part of my life was going to be all right.

That thought was enough to keep me in a positive state as I waited until six a.m. for the cafeteria line to open, then ordered up two bacon-and-eggs-over-easy breakfasts and carried them back to Del Rio's room, mulling over events prior to my coming to the hospital last night.

Sanders, Terry Graves, and Camilla Bronson hadn't returned my calls. But Special Agent Christine Townsend had, and after hearing what we'd found in the Harlow-Quinn files, she'd promised to have someone look into ESH Ltd. The rub was that she didn't know how long that would take.

On the way over to the hospital, Sci had given me a full oral report on what had been discovered and not discovered at the Harlows' estate, including the body of Héctor Ramón, the secret shaft, and the camera mounts in the panic room. He also said Justine wasn't feeling well and had asked him to take her home early. He said she'd been quiet the entire trip down from Ojai.

'Doesn't sound like her,' I'd said.

'No, it doesn't,' Sci had admitted.

I'd called Justine's house and cell phone several times, left messages, but had not heard back until shortly before I fell asleep in Del Rio's hospital room. Around midnight, she'd texted me that she was okay, but dead tired and crazy for sleep.

I knew the feeling and yawned as I entered Del Rio's room with breakfast, only to come up short when Angela blocked the way, looking at the food suspiciously.

'What's that?' she demanded.

'Bacon and eggs over easy, English muffin, black coffee,' I replied. 'His all-time favorite breakfast.'

She shook her head. 'Richard is on a special diet.'

'No worries,' I said, sweeping past her. 'I'll eat Richard's bacon.'

'Wait–' she sputtered angrily.

'Angela?' Del Rio called. 'C'mon, I can't take the stuff they bring around on the carts. There's nothing wrong with my swallow reflex. A speech pathologist lady checked yesterday. She said I was good for anything I wanted.'

'Humph,' Angela said, glancing at me as if I were public enemy number one. 'I'll look at the chart again. If it's not on the chart, he's getting out of here.'

Then she stormed out of the room. Del Rio said, 'She's kind of protective.'

'Noticed that,' I said, putting his tray on the table.

Del Rio's attention flickered past the food, past me, focused on the television hanging from the ceiling. 'Turn that up,' he said. 'It's the pier.'

Picking up the remote, I turned off the mute. A gratingly familiar voice filled the room, a report by none other than Bobbie Newton, who was standing near the entrance to the Huntington Beach Pier.

'As the pier opens for the first time since the bombing, police, local businesspeople, and residents are cautiously optimistic,' she intoned. 'It was a sentiment echoed early this morning by both Mayor Wills and Chief Fescoe.'

213

The screen cut to the mayor and chief hurrying into City Hall. Wills slowed, said, 'There hasn't been an attack by No Prisoners in nearly thirty-six hours, and no contact from him whatsoever. We cautiously hope things stay that way.'

The screen jumped to Fescoe, who said, 'We're still in full pursuit of this maniac, but it is possible he's come to his senses, realized we will catch him, and decided to end the random violence and this obscene extortion scheme before it goes any further.'

Chapter 72

In the garage in the City of Commerce, Cobb and the others were watching the same television coverage, listening to the same remarks by Mayor Wills and Chief Fescoe.

'Close enough,' Cobb said, clapping his hand against his thigh. 'No Prisoners is back in action. You're up, Mr. Johnson.'

The wiry African-American cranked his head around, cracking his neck. 'Have you developed a scene of opportunity, Mr. Cobb?'

'We have,' Cobb said. 'It will take nerves of steel to take full advantage of the situation.'

'Luckily I've got them,' Johnson said.

Cobb nodded. It was true. Johnson had been with him longer than any of the other men. He was not creative or impulsive like Hernandez. He wasn't clever with his hands like Nickerson, or a

214

tech genius like Watson, or a savvy Web guy like Kelleher. But Johnson did have nerves, no, balls of steel. The crazier the situation, the tighter he stuck to the plan, to the objective. Bullets could be flying. People could be dying all around him in the chaos of war, but Johnson just kept plowing forward.

'Noon,' Cobb told Johnson. 'Lunchtime.'

'That'll shake them up,' Hernandez said. 'Shock 'em out of the mundane.'

'Exactly, Mr. Hernandez,' Cobb said. 'And when they're good and shocked, we'll turn the tables on them one last time and take them for every penny we can get.'

'I like that idea, Mr. Cobb,' Hernandez said.

'Me too,' Johnson said. 'A lot. I'm thinking a place in Tahiti, you know?'

'Don't let yourself start dreaming of how you'll spend it all, gentlemen,' Cobb cautioned. 'We have to be totally focused until the deed is done. Then you may dream as big as you want.'

'Hoorah,' Johnson said softly. 'Hoo-fucking-rah.'

Cobb looked at Nickerson. 'You'll brief him?'

'My pleasure, Mr. Cobb,' Nickerson said, handing an iPad to Johnson. 'You'll see the floor plan, as well as photographs I shot in there yesterday. I've identified suggested entrances, exits. This should be a target-rich environment if there ever was one.'

Watson continued to coach Johnson through the particulars of his attack plan, but Cobb's mind was already pushing on. He looked at Watson, who was staring as he had been for hours at the screen of an iPad.

215

'Where are we, Mr. Watson?' Cobb asked. 'Will you be ready?'

Watson stroked his pale goat's beard, looked up, nodded. 'All they have to do is make the connection and it should be a short crawl back up the data stream to the open digital vault.'

'Traceability on their end?' Cobb asked.

'Virtually nil,' Watson said. 'They'd have to be looking for us to counterattack in the virtual world, and what's the chance of that?'

'None,' Cobb said happily. 'Their attention will be completely diverted. Outstanding.'

Watson beamed at this rare compliment. But Cobb noticed Kelleher tensing and looking up, worried now. 'We just lost Facebook. Shut us down. Too bad, we had more than three hundred and fifty thousand following the feed. I believe we'll lose YouTube next, but as of now, we have over fifteen million hits.'

Cobb thought about this. 'They'll try to track us through the accounts?'

'Affirmative,' Watson said. 'They won't get anywhere. Everything we fed them was done on stolen computers that are now in a landfill in Oxnard.'

'Suggestions, gentlemen,' Cobb said. 'Options.'

Kelleher said, 'We could go to Twitter.'

Cobb considered that for several seconds, said, 'No, I vote silence. Nothing unnerves people more than silence, especially people whose mundane lives are threatened. Every creak in the building, every sudden movement by a stranger, every loud noise gets reflected and amplified until every moment becomes tainted with fear and anguish. That's what we're after here, gentlemen.'

PART FOUR

NO EXIT

Chapter 73

An hour earlier, just as dawn was cracking, Justine sat in her car down the street from Crossfit, watching the regulars filing groggily into the box, wanting to join them but feeling as if she'd betrayed them, betrayed herself by using the place as ... well...

She'd hoped that a solid night's rest would help her see things more clearly, more rationally, but now all she felt was confusion. Who was this person growing inside her whom she simply did not recognize?

Then she saw Paul and her confusion deepened. He was jogging down the sidewalk from the east toward the gym, that endearing smile plastered across his face. Her overwhelming impulse was to leap from her car. Part of her wanted to stop him before he entered and bring him back home to her bed. Another part of her wanted to confront him, tell him it was a horrible mistake brought on by a horrible incident, and that it could never happen again. Or at least not without their getting to know each other better. But the better part of her wanted to rest her head on the steering wheel and cry.

For much of her life Justine had felt in control of her emotions and actions, anchored in a way that helped her help others deal with the aftermath of trauma. Now she felt weirdly unanchored, beyond adrift, as if she'd been caught in a slowly twisting whirlpool that threatened to drown the person she'd always believed herself to be.

Fighting for air, literally feeling the panic of drowning, she threw the car into gear and, without looking, pulled out onto the street. Tires screeched on cement. A yellow low-rider pickup truck nearly sideswiped her, veered into the opposite lane, almost had a head-on with an approaching bus, but then swerved back into the lane beside her.

Justine almost threw up from the adrenaline that flooded through her.

The sensation got worse when an irate home-boy in shades and a wife-beater shirt hung out the passenger window of the pickup, started screaming at her, 'Bitch, I should cap your ass for what you just did! There's two kids in this car. You coulda killed us all!'

Justine suddenly couldn't do anything but nod and start to cry. 'I'm sorry,' she sobbed back at him. 'I'm having a bad, bad day.'

The rage in the homeboy's face lessened. 'Hey, lady, pull over or something. Get a grip. You're gonna kill someone if you don't watch it.'

Justine did just that, wiping away tears, pulling off the street into a strip mall parking lot. She parked away from the cars near Starbucks, away from anyone else. Leaning her head on the steering wheel, she began to cry again, and let herself do it freely. The attack in the jailhouse had up-ended her in ways she just couldn't explain, couldn't control.

'I've got to see someone,' she decided, speaking out loud. 'I've got to treat this like what it is, the–'

Her cell phone rang. She hesitated at first to look at the caller ID, fearing Paul, or even Jack. But then she did, and saw a number she did not recognize.

She cleared her throat, answered, 'Hello.'

'Is Ms. Smith?' came a heavily accented woman's voice that sounded vaguely familiar.

'Yes, this is Justine Smith. Who is this?'

The woman's voice dropped to a whisper. 'Is Anita. Anita Fontana. I work for–'

'I know who you are, Ms. Fontana. I remember. What's wrong?'

A moment's hesitation before the Harlows' housekeeper said with increasing urgency, 'We see them on the news, but we hear nothing except the children are okay. Mr. Sanders and Ms. Bronson won't tell us what is happened, where the children are. They won't let us see them. They won't let us see Miguel or...' She wept. 'Please help us.'

Whatever fugue state had gripped Justine now left her as quickly as fog on a wind. She heard the housekeeper's anguish and from that found direction, strength. The people at Harlow-Quinn were way too controlling, she decided, way too Machiavellian, and it was about time she got to the bottom of why.

'Tell me where they're keeping you,' she said. 'I'll come there, tell you everything I know.'

Chapter 74

About eight thirty that morning, after showering, shaving, and changing in the washroom off my office, I entered the lab and found Mo-bot already at her workstation. She was gulping coffee, munching on a Krispy Kreme doughnut.

'Those'll give you a heart attack, Maureen,' I said.

Her brow rose archly. '*You* are parenting *me* now, Jack?'

'Okay, we're not going there,' I replied, hands up in instant surrender.

'No, we're not, and let me be the first to tell you, I still don't have squat on ESH Ltd. It's a shell company, of course, registered in the Caymans, but all I'm coming up with is a filing agent in George Town, and he's not answering his phone or returning my calls.'

I thought about Christine Townsend's promise to look into the company. How long would that take?

'We have anyone on retainer in the Caribbean?'

'I'd be glad to pop over to Grand Cayman in the jet.'

'You're too valuable here,' I said.

She pouted.

'What can I say? It's the downside of being supercompetent.'

Mo-bot bit viciously into the last of her Krispy

Kreme, gave her computer an order, scanned the screen, swallowed, said, 'Carlos San Cielo, Puerto Rico.'

'I remember him, good guy,' I said. 'Contact him. Have him fly in there, pay Mr. Registered Agent a visit in person, tell him he represents someone with deep pockets who wishes to form, say, a dozen companies there, but in return, we need a little bit of information about ESH Ltd.'

She looked at me as if she'd caught me with my hand in the Krispy Kreme bag. 'But *you* have no intention of forming companies in the Caymans.'

'Your point?' I asked.

Before Maureen could reply, Sci entered the lab, displayed a white iPhone in a plastic evidence sleeve, said, 'It's Malia Harlow's. Last night it occurred to me that it was the only device with a memory left inside the Harlow house except those doctored security tapes.'

'Okay?' I said.

'I got it going at home and had a look,' Kloppenberg said, rolling his eyes at Mo-bot. 'Some of the texts regarding Justin Bieber were a bit over the top.'

'Texts regarding Justin can never be over the top,' Mo-bot shot back. She had a picture of the teen crooner taped to the side of her computer along with a dozen other pop celebrities.

I frowned, checked my watch, and said, 'Did you find anything? If not, I'm out of here. I've got a conference call with Peter Knight in the London office. He's up to his waist in some sex scandal that's breaking in Parliament.'

'Nothing as tawdry as that on Malia's phone,'

Sci said. 'And nothing that answers any questions.'

'Too bad,' I said, heading toward the door.

'But I found something that raises questions,' he said, stopping me.

From his breast pocket, Kloppenberg removed a SIM card in a smaller evidence sleeve, donned latex gloves, got it out, and inserted it into a reader attached to one of the lab computers. A second later, a picture popped up on the screen. The photo was date-stamped September 24, roughly a month prior, and showed a group shot that must have been taken on a location set for *Saigon Falls*, with jungle vegetation and a muddy river visible in the background, perhaps the Mekong.

Thom Harlow was in the center of the picture, wearing Vietnam-era US Army fatigues, looking ruggedly handsome and yet sincere, sympathetic, and lovable – traits that had made him a bankable box-office star. Thom's arm was draped lazily around his wife's shoulder. Jennifer's dark hair was pulled back tight, revealing the remarkable bone structure of her face. She wore a white short-sleeved blouse, khaki shorts, and aviator sunglasses. A vintage Nikon camera hung off one shoulder. Her pose, her entire look, said smart, adventurous, and yet oozed mystery and sexuality, traits that had made her an even more bankable star than her husband.

The children sat at their feet, arms around their knees. Malia and Jin were smiling. Miguel was looking off to his right somewhere. Cynthia Maines was there too, standing slightly to the left of the family, carrying a clipboard. Camilla Bronson and Terry Graves were there as well. My attention, however, swung to and held on the only other person in the picture.

Crouched above and behind the children, below and in front of Thom and Jennifer, she was stunningly exotic, mesmerizing in her own way even in the shadow of Jennifer, a woman whom *People* magazine twice voted 'Sexiest Woman Alive.' Late teens, early twenties, she appeared to be at least partly Latina and partly Asian, with thick shiny dark hair pulled back in a long braid and skin the color of caramel. Her soft doe eyes seemed to speak of sadness or some hidden wound, making her look entirely vulnerable. But her cheekbones, teeth, and full lips were set hard, as if beneath whatever haunted her, she was built of iron or steel.

'Who is she?' I asked, gesturing at the photo.

'Exactly,' Sci said.

Chapter 75

Justine found the address Anita Fontana had given her around ten thirty that morning. It was a small pale-blue fifties-era bungalow on a sleepy side street off Lankershim Boulevard in Burbank.

She knocked at the door. A few moments later, a woman's voice called softly in Spanish, 'Who is there, please?'

'It's Justine Smith,' she replied. 'Anita called me.'

After a moment, she heard a dead bolt thrown. The door opened several inches on a security

225

chain. Maria Toro, the Harlows' plump cook, looked out. She asked in English, 'Are you alone?'

'Yes,' Justine said.

'We think someone watches us,' Maria whispered. 'Can you leave? Come back to alley? Anita finds you there.'

Justine was confused, wondered if their paranoia was justified or invented, but nodded. 'Give me five minutes.'

She returned to her car as if she'd gotten the wrong address, trying to spot whoever they suspected of watching them, but saw no one and no vehicle that stood out. She drove back to Lankershim, turned left, and then made an immediate left again into an alleyway that ran behind the bungalows.

Anita Fontana stood in the alley by an open gate. She pointed to an open garage door on the opposite side of the alley, and Justine pulled in and parked. When Justine exited, the Harlows' housekeeper pointed a remote control device at the garage and the door lowered.

Justine followed Anita through the gate into a yard that had seen better times. Untended orchid plants and a riot of cactus and vines crept onto the deck around a pool brimming with algae-green water.

'Who owns this place?' Justine asked as she followed the Harlows' housekeeper through an open screen door into a dim room furnished with 1960s furniture and a shag rug. A television blared in the corner, cable coverage of the hunt for the Harlows. Jacinta Feliz, the youngest of the Harlow staff, sat on the couch, arms folded, watching Justine as she entered.

'I don't know this for sure,' Anita said. 'How are the girls? And Miguel?'

The housekeeper asked this with a longing in her voice that impressed Justine with its intensity.

'You love them, don't you?' asked Justine. 'Miguel? The girls?'

Anita's eyes glistened and she clasped her hands. '*Sí*, I love Miguel ... all of them. How could I...?' She choked and began to cry.

Maria Toro, the cook, came up beside Anita, put her arm firmly around the housekeeper, looked fiercely at Justine. 'We all love the children. E-pecially Anita. She has no children of her own.'

At that, Anita began to sob and hold herself tight, as if pierced with inner pain. 'Sit down,' Justine soothed. 'It's okay, we'll figure out a way for you to see them, for all of you to see them. Okay?'

'Mr. Sanders, he say no,' Anita wailed. 'I ask him. He say no.'

The poor woman was beside herself now. Jacinta Feliz had gone to her side, put her arm around the older woman too.

'You will see those children,' Justine said firmly. 'Have you been contacted by the FBI?'

'No, no one,' the cook said. 'We come here that same day we see you at the ranch, when they are just gone. We here ever since. Someone brings us food. Ms. Bronson, Mr. Sanders, they say they want to protect us from reporters, say we stay here until these things calm down.'

Justine heard her smartphone chime, telling her she'd received a text. She ignored it, said, 'This is America, ladies. Mr. Sanders and Camilla Bron-

227

son can't make you do anything, do you understand? You all have green cards, yes?'

They shook their heads. 'We come on temporary visa, ten-month,' said Maria Toro.

'How long have you worked for the Harlows?' Justine asked, surprised.

'Twelve years,' Anita said.

'Eight,' said the cook.

'Four,' said the maid.

'And they never offered to sponsor you to try to get citizenship?' Justine was beginning to doubt the Harlows' public personas in a big way.

Anita began to cry again, shaking her head. 'No, they no do this for us.'

'Did you ask?'

They all nodded. 'But Mr. Thom say they already bring in the children, it is difficult to get more through *la Migra* with them as sponsors,' Maria Toro said.

'But he can get you the ten-month work visas?'

'This is not a problem, I think,' Jacinta said.

Justine didn't know what to make of all of this. On its face, the fact that the Harlows were willing to get the women work visas but not green cards seemed lame, and counter to the Harlows' reputation. But then again, she wasn't at all well versed in current US immigration laws, quotas and such.

Anita wiped at her eyes, said, 'You can help us?'

'Yes, of course,' Justine said. 'Anything–' Her phone chimed again. 'Hold on a second.'

She dug the phone from her purse and saw that she'd received a photo from Sci. She opened the file, looked at the group picture, read the text that accompanied it: 'Do you know who the

228

young woman front row center is?'

Justine frowned, zoomed in on the woman, a girl, really. Gorgeous. But no, she didn't recognize her at all. She was about to text back 'Negative' when she had a different idea.

'Do you know this girl with the Harlows?' she asked, turning the phone to show the three women.

Maria Toro reached out, took the phone, studied the picture, and shook her head. She handed it to Anita, who looked at the photo with great suspicion but then said, 'I no know her.'

'Jacinta?' Justine asked.

The young maid took the phone, glanced at it, hesitated, then shook her head. She walked it back to Justine, who said, 'For a second there, you thought you knew her?'

'No,' Jacinta said. 'I was just thinking that maybe it was the nanny they hire after we leave and before they go for Vietnam.'

Chapter 76

At eleven minutes to noon that day, Johnson Rollerbladed along Sunset Boulevard in West Hollywood. He wore white-framed, sequined sunglasses with a built-in fiber-optic camera, pink stretch pants, a platinum-blond wig cut a la Marilyn, and, over a heavily padded bra, a white T-shirt that read 'Blonde Ambition.' But for a backpack carrying two suppressed pistols, and four pink sweatbands on each forearm that hid spare clips, he could have been any old drag queen out for a skate on a fine October day.

'Location?' Cobb asked through the earbud Johnson wore.

'Coming onto Londonderry Place, turning north,' Johnson replied, adding a little butt shake to his skate as he passed the patrons sitting outdoors at the Mexican place on the corner, as if he were listening to some throbbing Latin beat, instead of plotting with his coconspirators to commit mass murder.

Londonderry Place climbs steeply north off the Sunset Strip. Johnson cut diagonally northwest across the narrow street to where the opposite sidewalk met a low chain-link fence. He straddle-vaulted it, landed in thick ground cover atop a retaining wall that had been turned into a planter for five palm trees.

Below him was a parking lot. Johnson took it in at a glance, seeing nine vehicles parked there in all, including one he wasn't expecting. He lowered himself four feet down the wall behind a blue Toyota sedan.

'LAPD cruiser in lot, empty,' Johnson said. He skated out from behind the car, knelt in the wide open, pretended to retie his skates, but took glances at the cruiser and the entry to Mel's Drive-In. 'Mr. Cobb?'

'Take them first,' Cobb said.

'If they're not outside?'

'Take them first.'

Johnson had been trained since the age of seventeen not only to follow orders, but also to adapt to evolving orders. He was what Mr. Cobb liked to call mission proficient. Johnson called it getting things done.

The diner's exterior almost exactly matched the one in the seventies movie *American Graffiti*. Mel's was a chain now, but a good one that attracted tourists and locals alike. The initial plan had Johnson getting the guns out at the far end of the parking lot and then skating around toward the front of the diner and its terrace, which faced the Sunset Strip. But he kept the weapons in the pack for now, skated toward Mel's, eyes everywhere as he went left at the dog-leg in the parking lot and back onto the sidewalk along Sunset heading west.

He took in everyone eating on Mel's terrace before skating on past Drybar into a second entry to the parking lot. He'd seen a Hispanic couple and their kid, three duffers wearing golf jackets, and two moms with teenage daughters having ice cream sundaes. But no cops.

Which meant they were inside. He glanced down at the Rollerblades, which he'd decided to use because they had originally conceived this as an exterior job – swoop in, execute, and leave.

A new strategy evolved in Johnson's brain almost instantly. He skated back past the people eating outside, and around into the entry to Mel's. A startled old woman wearing a green sweatshirt that featured a leaping trout and the words 'Thief River Falls Is Paradise' opened the door, carrying a pack of Marlboros. She gaped at him as he rolled past her into the diner, where he caught the full whiff of burgers frying, heard

231

Elvis crooning from the jukebox, came face to face with a cheery hostess, who said brightly, 'No blades inside, ma'am, uh, sir.'

Johnson had looked deeper into the diner, seen the two cops, male-female partners, sitting at the counter. A waitress had just served them cheeseburgers and fries.

'Ma'am?' the hostess said, a big grin.

'Oh, honey cheeks, I know,' Johnson said, turning to her and laying on a sweet effeminate accent. 'I'll take 'em off 'fore I eat, but this girl's gotta pee.'

Without waiting for an answer, Johnson darted by her toward the restrooms. 'Sir!' the hostess called after him. 'Ma'am?'

But Johnson paid her no mind as he pushed into the men's room and let the door shut behind him. Finding an empty stall, he entered, got the guns from the pack, and put it back on. He held the suppressed pistols reversed, butts facing the front, palm to the action, fingers cradling the trigger guards, barrels flush to his lower forearms, a carry that often fooled the best trained of men and women, even if only for an extra moment or two.

Stepping from the stall less than twenty-five seconds after he'd entered, Johnson said, 'Minute thirty, maybe less.'

'He's waiting,' Cobb said.

From that point forward, Johnson did not pause. He pulled open the door, skated past a family of five chatting with the hostess. Dodging around them, he passed between a waitress filling a coffeepot next to the stainless kitchen door and a mom with three Cub Scouts, never heard them giggling at him.

Rolling now across the gray-green floor, seeing the cops in tunnel vision, Johnson crossed his hands, popped the left gun into the air and let go of the right weapon. He grabbed the guns with opposite hands. Unfolding his arms, swinging the suppressed barrels inward, past each other, and forward, he found the triggers and aimed at point-blank range.

Chapter 77

Justine found Cynthia Maines just where she'd said she would be: in Burbank, in the cafeteria on the Warner Brothers lot. It was late afternoon and the place was quiet, just a few people having coffee. Justine had not seen the Harlows' personal assistant since the children were released. She remembered how Maines had been angry, defiant. Now she appeared overwhelmed, sick, almost defeated.

'What's happening?' Maines asked as if she couldn't take any more.

Justine had called Maines and requested the meeting. But she'd found over the years that understanding up front the state of mind of the person she was interviewing helped immensely during investigations. She said, 'Tell me what's going on with you first.'

Maines made a disgusted noise and gestured toward the cafeteria window. 'Evidently I don't have an office at Harlow-Quinn anymore. I was told to leave this morning.'

'By Terry Graves?'

Maines nodded bitterly 'Camilla and Dave were there too. My God, I've known them all for more than ten years. They just cut me off.'

'You tell this to the FBI?'

'Of course,' Maines said.

'And?'

'They said that's their prerogative, and then asked me all this stuff that was all BS.'

'Like?'

'I don't know,' Maines said, throwing her napkin on the table. 'About the studio, and whether Warner and the other investors were freaking out, wondering if all the money invested in *Saigon Falls* is gone. They said the studio execs hardly mentioned Thom or Jennifer, said it was just the money they were interested in, which is fucking depressing, you know?'

'That all?'

'No, they asked me the same kind of stuff you did. And about Terry and Camilla, and Sanders, and everyone who works at H-Q.'

Tears began again. 'It's like I've been shipwrecked or something, cut off.' She choked. 'I miss Jen and Thom. This is the only job I've ever had, and I...'

Maines wept. Justine sighed, and, wondering about all the hurt that seemed to be going around lately, she moved to the other side of the table to hold the woman.

Maines said, 'I feel helpless. I feel like people are blaming me.'

'Helpless is a horrible place to be,' Justine said, rubbing her back. 'Being blamed for things beyond your control is worse. Dealing with this sort of situation usually involves letting go and focusing on what you can control.'

Maines stilled, looked embarrassed, grabbed the napkin and wiped at her tears. 'I don't know what to do.'

'How about helping me find the Harlows?'

That seemed to offer Maines some hope to grasp because she said, 'Anything you want. Any time you want. Same as I told the FBI.'

'Okay,' Justine said, returning to her seat. 'Did you know about the secret passage off Jennifer's closet, the one that led down to Thom's editing room and also up to a panic room with a two-way mirror that overlooks their bedroom?'

Maines looked at Justine as if she'd been speaking Urdu. 'What?'

Justine described in detail what she'd found, including the empty camera brackets, the missing hard drives.

Maines shook her head.

'We're assuming some of the drives had all the footage from the location shoot,' Justine said. 'Is that a problem?'

'No. Everything having to do with *Saigon Falls* was backed up every day to a server here, and there's another backup somewhere in Minneapolis. From the ranch, from Vietnam, from here. It didn't matter. Constant backups.'

Justine thought about that, set *Saigon Falls* aside for the moment, dug in her purse for her phone, and showed Maines the picture Sci had sent her.

235

'Who is she?'

Maines appeared momentarily transfixed, looking at the photograph as if wrapped up in another time and place altogether. In a dazed tone, she said, 'I forgot her. In all this craziness I completely forgot Adelita.'

Chapter 78

The two police officers having lunch at Mel's Drive-In never knew what hit them, just kind of sagged when the suppressed bullets blew through their skulls and ricocheted off the counter. Officer Kate Rangel slumped forward into her French fries. Her partner, Officer Lance Barfield, drifted off his green stool onto the floor.

Bill Haley's 'Rock Around the Clock' was blasting from the jukebox, covering some of the noise, so Johnson was already ten feet beyond their corpses, looking for his next target – two down, five to go – when one of the Cub Scouts realized what had happened and began to scream.

Like an infection spreading, more screams echoed as others joined him.

'The tranny's got guns!' someone shouted.

'You bet he does, sugar!' Johnson yelled in that high squeaky voice before pulling the trigger of his right pistol twice, blowing side-by-side holes in the chest of a busboy unfortunate enough to have been clearing a booth in his path.

Pandemonium swept the diner, patrons and

staff all wailing, diving to the floor, ducking beneath tables. Johnson skated calmly through the place toward the exit facing the Strip. A steroidal punk came out low from behind a table, tried to knock Johnson off his blades.

Johnson shot him left-handed, double-tap to the crown of the skull. The man died and the chaos began anew. Johnson heard pleas for mercy, cries of 'No, Please, No!' and the sort of foolish shout-outs to God that their kind always make when people around them get to dying.

Johnson pushed open the glass door, stepped out onto the landing of the four-step stair that led down to the outdoor eating area. The people below him were on their feet, some running, others frozen, several crying now that they saw the pistols in his hands. He had to move now. Sirens would not be long in coming.

He jumped the stairs, landed in a rolling crouch, shot two of the duffers, hitting both men in the back as they tried to flee. Angling hard right now between tables, oblivious to the screaming, he was thinking, *Six down, one to go.*

Johnson got over the low railing and onto the sidewalk, aware of cars rushing in both directions up and down the Strip, oblivious to the bloody mayhem he was causing as they passed. His instinct was to kill whoever remained at the west end of the eating terrace, closest to Drybar. That would put him near the parking lot where Nickerson would be waiting with one of the vans.

As Johnson swung the guns west, he spotted the old lady who'd gaped at him when he entered the diner, the one wearing the sweatshirt promoting a trout paradise. She was squared off in a horse stance twelve feet away, both hands wrapped around a small-caliber pistol.

'You get down now!' she yelled at him in a hoarse voice. 'I have passed an NRA handgun self-defense course. I will shoot you!'

An NRA course? What was that? A weekend? Two? Johnson almost laughed. The truth was that unless you were deranged or enraged, it took a lot of training to be able to actually shoot someone in cold blood. Most first-timers just yanked the trigger and threw the shot wide.

Knowing that, Johnson took his chance. He grinned at her, said, 'Sure, Grandma,' dropped his right pistol, and whipped the left one up at her.

He was aware of the old woman blinking as the shot went off.

Her bullet hit Johnson's rib cage, passed below the heart, through the lung, where it expelled its energy before blowing out his back. The second pistol dropped. Johnson crumpled to the sidewalk after it, coughing up the blood already drowning him, dying in surging disbelief, utterly baffled by the fact that he had lived through so many days of full-on combat in his life with hardly a scratch to show for it, like he'd had some invisible shield around him; and yet here he was shot down in drag by some pistol-packing grandma she-bitch from Thief River Falls.

Chapter 79

I got the call from Chief Fescoe about the latest No Prisoners attack twelve minutes after it went down, almost as soon as he understood the scope of the massacre and the nature of the victims.

'I've got two of my own dead down there,' Fescoe said, sounding rattled. 'I'm on my way there with a forensics team, so is Townsend, but both our departments are spread thin. It won't be enough. We'd like a team of your techs if we can get them.'

'Right away,' I promised, and within nine minutes Sci, Mobot, the Kid, and three other techs were with me, driving as fast as we dared from our offices to the Sunset Strip.

The block between Londonderry Place and Sunset Plaza Drive was taped off. The full-on media carnival was yet to arrive, but the sideshow was already set up and running. As we moved gear inside the police lines from the east, Bobbie Newton was on air, having a best-friends-forever moment with June Wanta, the sixty-seven-year-old grandmother of ten who'd shot and killed the gunman who'd rampaged through Mel's.

'Where's your gun, June?' Bobbie Newton asked breathlessly.

'I gave it to the police, of course,' Wanta said, nervously lighting a Marlboro, puffing.

The smoke went in Bobbie Newton's face,

made her unhappy, but she moved upwind and gushed, 'You're a hero, June! How does it feel?'

'I'm no hero,' the old woman said, taking another puff. Her hands were trembling. 'I just defended myself from a crazy fool the way anyone who'd taken an NRA handgun course would.'

The crowd that had gathered broke into laughter and cheers. Bobbie Newton, however, looked at the grandmother as if she'd suddenly sprouted a set of horns. Then she peered into the camera, said, 'Yes. See there, friends, the value of education. It never ceases to amaze me.'

Turning back to the grandmother, Bobbie said, 'Now, I understand you came face to face with the shooter before he started, uh, shooting.'

'That's right,' Wanta said, took a drag off her cigarette.

'How are you sure it was him?'

The grandmother looked at Bobbie Newton like she was a ninny, said, 'Back home in Thief River you don't see too many black guys dressed up like Marilyn Monroe Does the Roller Derby.'

The crowd roared. Mrs. Wanta looked over, puffed, smiled, waved, and then said, 'Gotta go now, Bobbie. Police want to talk to me.'

She turned, walked away, smoke trailing her. The crowd cheered more loudly.

'There you go,' Bobbie Newton said, grinning inanely at the camera. 'A reluctant hero blows away the bad guy and saves who knows how many lives in the process. I have the feeling we're going to be hearing much more from Mrs. June Wanta. A star is born. Can we say movie deal?'

'Why does everything have to end up with a movie deal in L.A.?' Mo-bot snorted as we moved away into the crime scene.

'Company town,' I replied before spotting Fescoe and FBI Special Agent in Charge Christine Townsend emerging from Mel's Drive-In.

'It's carnage in there, Jack,' Fescoe said, clearly shocked. 'Son of a bitch supposedly skated through the place shooting anyone he pleased.'

'Until he got to Grandma,' I said.

'Wish there were more like her,' Townsend said, looking over at Mrs. Wanta, who was lighting another cigarette and listening to a detective's questions.

'We wanted Sci to process the shooter's body,' Fescoe said, gesturing toward the sidewalk and the corpse of the wiry cross-dresser. 'That's his specialty, right?'

'Among many others,' I replied, motioning Kloppenberg, Mo-bot, and the rest of their team toward the dead killer. 'You think he's No Prisoners?'

Fescoe shrugged. 'Haven't seen the calling card yet. But he did try to kill seven people.'

'Doesn't look anything like the guy at the CVS.'

Special Agent Townsend shrugged. 'Maybe he wore makeup in the CVS job and this is over.'

'No,' Fescoe said. 'Jack's right. This guy's got a different facial structure.'

'Then this isn't over,' I said. 'The dead guy, whoever he is, is just one of any number of people, at least two, who could be behind this entire–'

Fescoe's phone rang. The chief turned away, answered.

'Anything new on the Harlows?' I asked Townsend.

'Nothing hard,' she replied. 'You?'

'I've got a guy flying to Panama.'

'You have unlimited resources or something?'

'What can I say? They pissed me off.'

'That was the mayor,' Fescoe said, interrupting, sweating now. 'No Prisoners has made contact, demanding three million or eight more will die.'

Chapter 80

Inside the garage in the City of Commerce, Cobb and the other three remaining members of No Prisoners were glued to the coverage of the shootings at Mel's Drive-In. CNN's Anderson Cooper had been in L.A. already to report on the Harlow case and had rushed to the scene. So had affiliates from every major news network, all of them leading with footage of June Wanta smoking, listening to their questions skeptically, cracking jokes, and consistently downplaying any idea that she was a hero.

'You have no idea what kinda broad I am,' she said, rasping in laughter at Anderson Cooper, who didn't seem to know what to make of her.

Neither did Cobb, who felt like he wanted to pick something up and smash it. Johnson had been his best man, the one who'd been with him longest, the most loyal friend he'd ever had. It was Johnson who'd carried Cobb, seen to his

242

medical care after the explosion that turned his face into a spider's web.

'I don't get it,' Hernandez said. 'How does a chain-smoking grandma from Minnesota kill Johnson?'

Anderson Cooper asked virtually the same question onscreen.

The old lady didn't miss a beat. 'She pulls the trigger,' Mrs. Wanta said.

Cobb wanted to reach through the screen and throttle the bitch, who went on to reveal to Cooper that she was in Los Angeles 'seeing the sights alone because my damn fool of a husband, Barney, wouldn't get out of his–'

Cobb couldn't take her anymore and muted the screen.

Watson was gazing at him. 'We still good, Mr. Cobb?'

Cobb felt the others watching him, looking to him for leadership. 'You think we're jeopardized because they've got Johnson's body?'

The other three men shrugged or nodded.

'Fear not, gentlemen,' Cobb said. 'I believe we're still good to go for quite a while yet. I mean, we don't officially exist, do we? Isn't that what they did to us? Stripped us of everything, threw us to the hyenas?'

'They did, Mr. Cobb,' Kelleher said, anger flaring across his face. 'And thorough bastards they were about it.'

'So what exactly makes any of you think they can identify us, let alone locate and catch us before we're finished here, and long gone?'

Chapter 81

After nine that night, I returned to the office for a conference call with Mattie Engel in Private's Berlin office regarding an embezzlement case she'd been working on for nearly a month on behalf of Sherman Wilkerson, our client who lived above the beach where the first No Prisoners bodies were found.

I hung up believing that Engel had the situation well in hand and would be ready to file a full report to Sherman sometime the following–

A knock. I looked up, saw Justine, felt that little pang I always get in my chest when I haven't seen her in a while.

'Got a minute?' she asked.

'Absolutely,' I said. 'I was going to have a drink. Want one?'

'Oh, God, I'd love one,' she said, coming in and sitting down in an overstuffed chair by the couch.

As I reached into my lower desk drawer to get out a bottle of Midleton Very Rare Irish Whiskey, I was thinking again that something had changed about her recently, aged her in a way I'd never seen before.

I handed her a glass with two fingers of Midleton in it neat. She took a sip, closed her eyes, and said, 'That helps.'

'You saw that No Prisoners struck again?' I asked.

'Heard it on the radio. Some grandmother killed him?'

'We believe No Prisoners is several people acting in concert. The dead guy's just one of them.'

'ID yet?'

'Sci and Mo-bot are working with the FBI on that.'

Her eyebrows rose. 'So we're back on that case again?'

'Just the lab for now,' I said. 'But there's a twist in the demand No Prisoners made to the mayor that might bring us in deeper.'

'A twist you can't discuss?'

'For now,' I said.

She nodded absently.

'You wanted to tell me something?' I said. 'If not, I was going to head over to see Rick.'

Justine startled, confused, but then nodded. 'That picture Sci sent me? I know who the mystery girl is. Her name is Adelita. I'll tell you her last name later.'

Intrigued now, I sat in a chair across the coffee table from her, sipped the whiskey, and listened as she told me all she'd learned about Adelita from Cynthia Maines.

Six weeks before the Harlows were to fly to Saigon for filming, Maines was sent over to organize the family's living arrangements and to hire a staff in Vietnam. She was not there when Adelita came into the Harlows' life. Jennifer was always hiring and firing nannies, usually one a year, sometimes two. She'd fired her last nanny twelve days before the family was to fly to Vietnam, and no one she'd interviewed in the meantime suited her.

Enter Adelita. She'd only been in Los Angeles three days, here on a student visa from Mexico to study acting for six months. She had defied her parents on her eighteenth birthday and used a small inheritance from her grandmother to fund a plane ticket, a few months' rent, and the acting lessons.

Eight days before their flight to Vietnam, the Harlows were at their Westwood apartment, staging up before the big move overseas. Adelita ran into Jennifer Harlow, one of her acting idols, on the sidewalk outside a deli. Jennifer was harried, trying to deal with Miguel, who was throwing a fit, while she juggled a phone call regarding *Saigon Falls*.

Star-struck as she was, Adelita charmed Miguel into calming down. Impulsive, perceptive, Jennifer talked to Adelita, took her to lunch with the children, got her to admit she wanted to be an actress.

'Jennifer offered her the job as nanny,' Justine said, reaching to pour herself more whiskey. 'The idea was that she'd get to see the world and get to really understand the life of an actor.'

I said, 'Sounds like the offer of a lifetime, one of those fated meetings you used to hear took place at soda fountains where stars found their fortunes.'

'Right?' Justine said. 'Anyway, Maines said Adelita accepted, flew to Saigon with them a week later. She said Adelita was great with the kids, and the entire family seemed to love her. The nanny was evidently a pretty good actress as well. They gave her a minor role in the film. She

246

plays the daughter of an American diplomat fleeing Saigon as the Vietcong advance.'

'Where is she – Adelita?' I asked.

'I'm coming to that,' Justine said, taking another large draw on the whiskey, which surprised me because I'd never seen her drink like this before.

Maines said something happened to Adelita about halfway through the nine months in Vietnam. The girl who had been so enthralled by the Harlows' world, so excited to be given a part in their film, became infinitely more subdued. She worked just as hard, cared for the children just as well, but something was definitely off about her.

'Maines tried to get her to open up once, but Adelita forcefully shut her down,' Justine continued. 'In any case, before they returned from Vietnam, Adelita was offered the same vacation Cynthia was, three weeks off with a bonus of an additional three weeks' pay. She took them up on the deal and left Saigon two days before Maines and the Harlows.'

'Where'd Adelita go?' I asked.

'Home,' Justine said, closing her eyes. 'Mexico. Guadalajara, in fact.'

'Really,' I said, piecing some of it together. 'So what's her last name?'

'Gomez,' Justine said, eyes still closed, but wincing. 'Same last name as the Jalisco State Police captain who put Cruz and me in jail down there.'

Chapter 82

Before I could put that information into context, Sci knocked at my doorjamb, entered. He saw the Midleton bottle. 'That looks good.'

'You look like you could use a snort,' Justine said, turning in her seat.

'A snort?' I said.

'Well, I don't know,' she said, reaching for the bottle again. 'What else do you call it?'

'Snort will do,' Kloppenberg said, taking the bottle from her after she'd poured a fifth and sixth finger of the whiskey.

'Any luck on identifying the shooter?' I asked as Sci got a glass.

'No,' he said. 'Which is why I'm here.'

Yet another knock came at my door. Mo-bot entered, yawning, but looked at Sci pouring, said, 'Gimme one of those.'

'Another strikeout?' Sci asked, pouring her a glass.

'Total wall,' she said. 'Even dental records.'

'One of you want to tell me what you're talking about?' I asked.

Sci handed Mo-bot her drink and plopped down beside her on the couch, said, 'So we had beautiful fingerprints, all the DNA material anyone could need, dental pics, you name it, and nothing.'

'Well, something,' Mo-bot said. 'But what it is isn't exactly clear.'

'You sound like you've been drinking already,' Justine observed with a slight slur.

Mo-bot sipped her whiskey, sighed with pleasure, and then explained that when they'd run the fingerprints and dental records of the dead homicidal drag queen through various law enforcement databases around the world, they'd gotten a positive match.

'And?' I said.

'And nothing,' Sci said.

'Whaddya mean, nothing?' Justine asked.

'It's like the database freezes and doesn't let us go forward,' Mo-bot said.

'You're being blocked?' I asked.

'I wouldn't say blocked,' Sci said. 'More like frozen.'

Mo-bot nodded. 'It's like there's still an echo or a ghost of that guy's fingerprints in the system that's being recognized, but everything else about him has been scrubbed clean.'

'Is that possible?'

'Well, totally corrupted, at least,' Sci said.

'What database did you freeze in?' I asked.

Kloppenberg pursed his lips, said, 'US Department of Defense personnel records. Past ten years.'

I slapped my leg. 'I said this felt like military guys from the get-go.'

'But which military guys?' Justine asked loudly, the slur stronger. 'Bud Rankin was an ex-marine. He would have known how to figure it out. And, you know, why aren't we raising a toast to poor Bud Rankin?'

She'd had too much already. But I nodded,

said, 'To Bud. An old soul who will be missed.'

'Hear, hear,' they all muttered, and downed their drinks. 'When this is over we'll have a proper memorial for Bud,' I said.

Justine reached again for the bottle. I slid it away from her, said, 'Why don't I get you home for some much-needed rest?'

She raised her finger at me, trying to focus, trying to argue, but then licked her lips and nodded. I put the empty glass on my desk and turned back to her, seeing the amusement on Sci's and Mo-bot's faces.

Justine was out cold, already snoring.

Chapter 83

It was almost midnight before I reached UCLA Medical Center. I got past security by showing my Private ID. We've done pro bono work for the hospital in the past, which helps when we want access at odd hours.

I reached the floor of the ICU, my mind whirling with everything that had unfolded during the day, including several things Justine had said to me before I was able to get her back to her apartment, into her bed, under the covers, lights off with a bucket by the nightstand.

In my car on the way there, she'd roused from her stupor.

'Love you, Jack,' she mumbled. 'Thanks.'

'I love you, too, Justine, and no problem.'

She shook her head. 'Can't work, though. Us.'
'I know.'

Joy and Luck, her female Jack Russell terriers, kept jumping up on her bed and whining after I'd laid her in bed fully clothed.

Justine's eyes were glassy and roaming as she soothed the dogs into lying beside her. 'Sorry.'

'For what? You had a few too many. I was glad to bring you home.'

Her eyes closed. 'Not 'bout that,' she said.

'Go to sleep, Justine. I'll let the girls out, talk to you in the morning.'

'I had ... I had sex with this perfect ... no, not-perfect stranger, and ... I'm not perfect stranger, and...'

She passed out again, and I walked the dogs and headed for the hospital, feeling oddly hollowed out by her convoluted drunken confession. Justine having sex with not-perfect strangers? Getting drunker than I'd ever seen her?

What the hell was going on?

That question was still bouncing through my brain when I went through the ICU doors and saw Angela, Del Rio's Filipina guardian angel, glaring at me from inside the nursing station.

'He's sleeping,' she hissed. 'You can't go in there.'

I held up my fingers in a cross and hurried past her. I could hear her clogs clip-clopping after me all the way to Del Rio's room. Ducking inside, I found him sitting up, watching Anderson Cooper's interview with June Wanta.

'You see this?' he asked, laughing. 'Crazy old lady.'

251

I stopped at the foot of his bed, looked to my right, saw Angela coming, said, 'Speak of the devil.'

Del Rio laughed again and then said, 'Angela, it's okay. I couldn't sleep, and this guy's so boring to listen to he's better than pills or counting sheep.'

She thought about that, shot me another hostile glance, said, 'You cannot sleep here. UCLA Medical Center is no Super Eight.'

'I'll leave when he conks out,' I promised, and waited until she'd left before taking a chair. 'How are you?'

'Lift the sheets,' Del Rio said.

I did and was amazed to see him moving both of his feet ever so slightly.

I said, 'Keep this up, you'll be back dancing with the Bolshoi in no time.'

'The Bolshoi?'

'Twyla Tharp?'

'Better,' he said.

'Riverdance?'

'You better quit while you're ahead.'

The banter between us felt good. Everything in that room felt good, and I was grateful: despite all the strange and disturbing things I'd faced during the day, Del Rio was on the mend, and *my* best friend forever was in good enough spirits to crack wise with me.

'What do I need to know?' Del Rio asked. 'Get me up to speed.'

I told him everything that had happened during the course of the day from the time I'd left his hospital room until my return. Mo-bot's discovery of the bank account and shell company in the Caymans feeding millions to Harlow-Quinn Productions; Justine's chats with the maids and with Cynthia Maines about Adelita Gomez. I gave him all of it except for Justine's drunken admission that she loved me but couldn't be with me, and that she'd had sex with a not-perfect stranger, or something to that effect.

When I told Del Rio what Sci and Mo-bot had found when they tried to place the fingerprints of the shooter at Mel's Drive-In, he said, 'Sounds like someone's expunged the file.'

'Yeah, but why? FBI's getting nowhere with DOD on this either. They're saying there are no files. That the system is throwing false positives.'

Del Rio blinked, looked off into memory, said, 'There is someone who might be able to tell us if they're lying or not.'

'You know someone who'd know something like that?'

'You know him too, Jack, or did. Back in Kandahar?'

I thought about that, flashed on a face from our Afghanistan days before the helicopter crash, a big, doughy, cherub-faced man with cold, dark eyes, a fellow I'd once heard accurately described as having the look of an angel and the heart of an assassin.

'Guy Carpenter,' I said.

'The one and only.'

'That was ten years ago. I wouldn't begin to know where to find someone like him. He's an ultraspook, for God's sake.'

'Ultraspook or not,' Del Rio said, 'I got his

address *and* phone number.'

'What? How?' I asked, incredulous.

Del Rio shot me a look of pity. 'Guess you didn't make the assassin's list of friends and loved ones, Jack, but Carpenter sends yours truly a Christmas card each and every year.'

Chapter 84

Justine woke at a quarter past five the next morning with a colossal hangover dominated by a meat cleaver of a headache and a mouth that tasted of Very Rare Irish Whiskey and dried Elmer's Glue.

How in God's name did I get...?

She remembered being in Jack's office on an empty stomach, whiskey that tasted oh so incredibly good and made her feel even better; and then it all went whirly on her, and then dark. She reached out, felt the dogs. One of them licked her hand.

Why did I...? How did I...?

Justine flashed on Jack bringing her into the apartment in a fireman's carry and vaguely recalled saying something about...

'Oh, God,' she groaned into her pillow. 'Please don't let *that* be true.'

But was it? Had she confessed to Jack something about having perfect sex with a stranger, or something like that?

'Oh, God,' she groaned again. 'Why? What am I going to...?'

And then she knew. Hangover or not, world-class headache or not, she was getting up. She was going to Crossfit. She was confronting what she'd done, and what it meant, and she was doing it now, not later. This was the kind of thing the old Justine would have done without hesitation. But why did she feel like this could be worse than returning to that jail cell in Guadalajara?

Twenty minutes later, after chugging a quart of water and swallowing a banana walnut muffin, two shots of espresso, and an Aleve, she pulled up to the Crossfit box, still unable to answer that question. She absolutely did not want to go inside. She knew the workout might force her to her knees, make her retch her insides out. But in a way, that kind of suffering felt fitting, a penance for her shitty choices of late, whatever their root cause.

Justine got out of the car, feeling only slightly less queasy than she had upon waking. Her ears rang. Her eyes felt swollen. Was that possible?

She trudged into the box, glanced around, seeing most of the regulars, but no Paul. She tried to smile at the trainer, said, 'Did your sister have the baby, Ronny?'

'Girl,' he said, grinning. 'Elena. Six pounds eleven ounces. Thanks for taking care of the place for me, telling everyone there was no class that day.'

'Only a couple of people showed anyway,' she said.

'Yeah, Paul said you and he did a workout with a bunch of pull-ups and push-ups,' the trainer said. 'Too many, he said. He strained his back.'

'Oh,' Justine said, feeling her head pounding

255

again. 'That's too bad.'

'Ready for this?' Ronny asked.

Justine turned her head to look at the white-board, saw the workout of the day posted there, and shuddered at the simple name: 'Fran.'

Some Crossfit workouts had been given names, women's names because they were like hurricanes. Of all the hurricanes, nothing was worse than Fran, which involved racing the clock to complete twenty-one thrusters, a move where you had to hold a sixty-five-pound barbell at your collarbone, squat, then explode the weight up overhead. Then you had to do twenty-one pull-ups, then fifteen thrusters, then fifteen pull-ups, then nine thrusters, then nine pull-ups.

Okay, little sister, Justine thought miserably *You're about to suffer for your sins in a big, big way.*

Chapter 85

Justine finshed Fran in nine minutes forty seconds, a time that included two trips to the washroom to hurl the poisons from her system. But as she lay on the floor of the box, sweating like a horse, incapable of moving, her abs, hams, and shoulders on fire, she felt better for having suffered.

She had deserved to suffer.

'Know what I like about you, Justine?' Ronny said.

'What's that?' she croaked.

'You don't give up,' the trainer said, grinning. 'You come in hungover to the gills, visit with Mr. Pukey twice, and you still go the whole nine yards. I like that in a person. Call me crazy, but I like someone who finishes what they start, no matter what.'

She managed a soft grin. 'Thanks, Ronny. I think. I'll let you know when my body stops twitching.'

The sun was up by the time Justine walked stiffly from the box. Her brain felt slightly scalded, but her head no longer pounded. Her stomach was much better, and she'd sweated most of the booze out of her system. She sat in her car, drank another quart of water, tried to figure out what to do.

Sooner the better. Now, not later.

Those old maxims guided Justine more than her emotions as she put the car in gear and drove through the streets toward the Bonaventure Charter School in Clarkdale, about six miles away.

Bonaventure was housed in a retrofitted apartment building on Mentone Avenue that had been bequeathed to the school's founder by a wealthy aunt. Mission style and stucco finished, the school sat back from the road, fronted by a beautifully tended flower garden crisscrossed by brick walkways. It was still early, only seven fifteen, and the schoolyard stood empty.

Justine parallel parked across and down the street where she could see the walkways. She rolled down her window to get some air, hoping to spot Paul coming in before his students, hoping to right the course of her life somehow, or at least to find out exactly where the harsh winds of fate had

257

brought her.

The first student, eight or nine, an African-American girl dressed in a school uniform of gray plaid skirt and white collared shirt, came down the sidewalk with her mother ten minutes later. She gave her mother a hug before skipping toward the school.

The girl put Justine very much in mind of Malia, the Harlows' oldest daughter, and then of Jin and Miguel, and how they might be feeling more than a week into the disappearance of their parents, and four days into life under the control of Dave Sanders. Orphans to begin with, they had to be shocked and upended by finding themselves in that same wretched state again, alone at such a young age, trying to find an anchor, trying to cope, trying to survive a nightmare ordeal.

Seeing the children's faces in her mind, Justine couldn't help feeling admiration for the Harlows. Yes, there were things about Thom and Jennifer that she found troubling: not helping the women who worked for them to obtain citizenship; and those camera brackets in the roof of the panic room, aiming into their bedroom. But at the same time, when they really didn't have to, the Harlows had adopted three needy orphans and had started up a foundation for the benefit of parentless children the world over. Justine tapped her fingers on the steering wheel, wondering about the foundation, realizing it was the only aspect of Thom's and Jennifer's lives that they knew little about.

Justine had seen the commercials, and the pictures of one or both of the Harlows in some far-flung and impoverished land, invariably hold-

258

ing a malnourished but utterly adorable child. The Harlows built schools and dorms and improved water resources for–

Justine's attention wrenched to the street. Paul's blue Toyota Camry was pulling up to the curb in front of one of Bonaventure's walkways. He climbed out of the passenger side, grinning, looking tousle-haired and handsome as usual.

But Justine barely gave him a second glance. She was staring horrified at the pretty blond woman behind the steering wheel and the two young children sitting in car seats behind her. The mom blew a kiss to Paul, who caught it and then walked toward the school, his right hand massaging his lower back.

The Toyota pulled away and drove past Justine. The woman's window was down. She was looking in the rearview mirror at her children, a boy, a girl, neither more than three. They were all singing, 'The wheels on the bus go round and round, round and round, round and round.'

'Oh, my God,' Justine whispered, her eyes brimming with bitter tears, her cheeks burning with utter shame. 'What have I done?'

Chapter 86

'No Prisoners sent an e-mail that appears, like the others, untraceable for the time being,' Mayor Wills informed a conference room crowded with city, county, state, and federal law enforcement. 'They said they no longer wished to be paid in cash.'

Shortly after dawn, Mickey Fescoe had called to alert me to this meeting, waking me from a dead sleep in my own bedroom, a first since Del Rio had been injured. Fescoe briefed me on No Prisoners' demands. I'd suggested I bring Kloppenberg and Maureen Roth along to get their perspective, and he'd agreed.

The three of us were standing against the back wall of the room, strictly observers, possibly advisors.

'How do they want it, then?' Sheriff Cammarata demanded.

'Electronic transfer of funds,' the mayor said somberly. 'We'll be texted or e-mailed an account number and routing information, then have ten minutes to respond with payment. If we arrange to pay today, it's seven million dollars. If we don't arrange to pay by midnight, the fee jumps to ten million. If we don't arrange to pay by tomorrow midnight, eight will die.'

A grumble rolled through the room as people tried to get their heads around No Prisoners' demands, see angles to those demands that might be exploited. To my surprise, when the grumbling drifted toward silence, Mo-bot was the first to offer advice.

'Mayor, if I were you, I'd be willing to move ten million tomorrow,' she said quite loudly and forcefully.

That offended Sheriff Cammarata, who looked at me and asked, 'Does she toss around ten million dollars in public money all the time, Morgan?'

But the mayor seemed surprised and looked at Mo-bot with great interest. 'Why would I do that, Ms. Roth?'

Mo-bot shot the sheriff a belittling smile, said, 'Because by waiting until tomorrow you'll give us time to attach a digital bug to the transfer file, a bug that will follow that money wherever it goes, making the money retrievable.'

Even FBI Special Agent Christine Townsend seemed impressed. She looked at me. 'Private can do that? I don't even think we can do that.'

In all honesty, I didn't think so, but before I could reply, Sci said, 'Well, not Private, exactly, but friends of Maureen's, folks from Cal Poly that we keep on retainer. I imagine they could put something like that together lickety-split.'

Imagine? I thought. *Lickety-split?* I wondered if that was true. I mean, it was true that Private did have on retainer top scientists at Cal Poly, Stanford, and Berkeley. Whether they could devise a digital bug that would do what Mo-bot and Sci were suggesting, and overnight, was another story.

But I said, 'I think it's worth a fifteen-minute phone call on Maureen's part to make sure this is, indeed, possible.'

'Go ahead, Ms. Roth,' Mayor Wills said, and Mo-bot left the room.

'What about the money?' asked the FBI special agent in charge. 'Where are you going to get ten million dollars to transfer, even if you can get it back?'

Wills hesitated, then threw up her hands. 'I honestly don't know what I can do without opening myself up to a lawsuit, or worse, criminal charges should we fail to get the money back.'

'You could ask private citizens, Hollywood,' Chief Fescoe said. 'Give them some kind of guarantee on the loan of the funds.'

The mayor didn't like that either, and I didn't blame her. No Prisoners had killed twenty-one people, including two police officers. Going to private citizens for the money smacked of an inability to handle the situation, not a good thing for a politician with aspirations to higher office.

'You could call the governor,' said Bill Ikeda, who was representing the criminal division of the California Department of Justice. 'Under these circumstances he might be willing to authorize having the funds drawn from one of the general accounts. As long as the transfer carries this bug, I mean.'

'We don't know if this bug will work!' the sheriff complained. 'We're...'

Mo-bot reentered the room. She was sipping a cup of coffee, noticed all eyes on her, and stopped. 'What?'

'Can they make the bug?' the mayor asked.

'Oh,' she said, as if she'd been thinking of something else. 'Of course.'

'How much is this bug going to cost?' Townsend asked me.

'Nothing,' I replied. 'Private won't take a dime for this, and neither will the computer scientists. We want to catch these guys and make L.A. safe again as much as you do.'

Chapter 87

'I've got your back, but you're going to have to take the lead on this,' I told Mo-bot as we exited City Hall, heading for our cars around nine thirty that morning. 'How soon can the Cal Poly boys be here?'

'They're all women,' she shot back. 'And they're on their way already, working in their car, if I know them. The key, of course, is where the money is coming from, and the nature of the files and security codes that surround transfers from whatever fund they end up tapping.'

I said, 'I just want to know it will work.'

'It'll work,' Sci said. 'Think of it like a tick.'

'You mean as in dog tick?'

'Or deer tick, or in this case, digital file tick,' he replied. 'The program they'll devise will be tiny and will attach itself deep in the metadata of the transfer file. To any but the most sophisticated of coders, it will look simply like a string of numbers, an afterthought.'

Mo-bot nodded. 'The tick will also have the ability to replicate itself so one of its offspring will travel in the metadata of each subsequent transfer, on and on, kind of like a computer virus, but not.'

'So how do we get the money back?'

'The tick will be programmed to transmit a location back at each stop, each account,' Sci said.

'No matter how many times the money's transferred?'

'That's the idea,' Mo-bot said.

'Okay,' I said. 'I'm impressed. I didn't know we could do that sort of thing.'

'Learn something new about your company every day, Jack,' Sci said.

We'd reached the parking garage by then, and I told them I'd meet them back at the offices. I wanted to swing by Justine's. She'd called in sick and I wanted to see how bad her hangover had turned out.

As I climbed into the Touareg, my cell rang. I fired the ignition so the Bluetooth function on the stereo connected before answering. 'Morgan.'

'Is that you, Jack, my California friend?' came a male voice soaked in the Caribbean.

It had been a while, but I recognized it. I backed out of the parking space, heading for the exit. 'I believe I'm speaking with Carlos San Cielo?'

'Long time, Jack,' San Cielo replied. 'I'm calling from the Caymans.'

'Lucky you.'

'Beautiful day here,' he said. 'Thanks for the assignment.'

'Thought of you first. Hope you found something?'

The detective hesitated. 'I did. But it cost you a bit more than my ordinary retainer and daily fee.'

'How's that?' I asked.

'This shithead attorney down here, the filing agent,' San Cielo replied. 'He tells me he can't divulge the names of the owners of this ESH Ltd, even after I lie and tell him I represent Mr. Deep

Pockets, who wants to make many of these phony corporations.'

'Okay?' I said, driving out of the parking garage and heading toward the Harbor Freeway, Santa Monica, and Justine's house.

Another pause. 'I had to pay him five grand to get him to cough up what you wanted to know.'

'I'll pay it,' I said, weaving through traffic. 'Who's behind ESH?'

San Cielo whistled, said, 'I cannot believe it when he said it, so I asked to see the articles of incorporation for my own eyes.'

'Out with it, Carlos, I'm a busy man,' I said.

'Oh, yes, of course, Jack. It is just that I am not so used to... Thom and Jennifer Harlow and a David Sanders and a Terry Graves. They own this LTD called ESH.'

I left the freeway really confused. The Harlows and their attorney and head of production had moved money through an offshore corporation to their own company? Why? I supposed there had to be certain tax benefits. But then why had Sanders claimed that the Harlows were almost bankrupt, when they had access to millions offshore? And why had Sanders lied about it in the first place?

He'd told us that Thom Harlow claimed to have a new secret investor who was willing to front him enough money to finish *Saigon Falls*. And yet the financial records clearly showed that the twenty-seven million transferred to Harlow-Quinn Productions came from another Harlow-owned concern. Why? Was that how the investor wanted it? Was he or she offshore to begin with?

'Jack?'

265

'I'm here,' I said finally. 'Did you ask the attorney how much money the company had?'

'Of course,' San Cielo replied. 'The answer cost you another five grand.'

'Another?' I replied, turning a corner. 'How much did this conversation cost me altogether?'

A hesitation. 'Uh, twenty in all.'

'Twenty?' I said, my eyebrows rising. 'This had better be good information, Carlos, or I'll have to seriously reconsider our business relationship.'

'No, no, Jack, it is the best information money can buy about this ESH Ltd,' San Cielo assured me. 'The agent was very happy after all to show me and to make copies of records. Much money in ESH. More all the time.'

'From where? From who?'

'Many places and companies and peoples from all over the world,' he replied. 'There is currently another twenty-three million in account of ESH Ltd in Panama.'

Twenty-three million. 'That it?'

'Well, I scan and send all records to your office. You can see for yourself where money comes from.'

'Do that,' I replied, turning onto Justine's street. 'Send them to Maureen Roth.'

'The Mo-bot. Yes, of course, within two hours tops.'

'Carlos?'

'Yes, Jack?' he replied, sounding a tad defensive.

'Good job. Glad to do business with you.'

I could almost hear him smile from four thousand miles away. 'I look forward to representing Private's interests in the future.'

266

'I'll let you know,' I said, pulling into Justine's steep driveway.

I hung up, parked, set the brake, and sat there a moment, car still running, thinking that there could be another explanation for the money in ESH Ltd's accounts, and for its sources. The Harlows were international superstars. They made movies all over the world. Their movies were shown all over the world, generated income from all over the world. It probably made sense in a lot of ways to have a company with an account offshore, someplace tax neutral, or something like that.

I was still dwelling on that scenario as I started to climb out of the SUV, figuring I'd check on Justine at the door, be on my way, no need to even shut the motor off. So I was barely aware that another vehicle had stopped in the street behind me, and that a man in dark denim clothing was climbing from the car. But as I took that first step, turning to close the door, I caught a glimpse of something in the man's hand, and felt panic explode when he swung a suppressed pistol at me.

Chapter 88

'They decide it is better to pay ten million dollars than seven,' Cobb said quietly when Alice, the waitress who had taken their lunch order, walked away. 'Why?'

He and the rest of his men, Watson, Nickerson, Hernandez, and Kelleher, sat in a booth at the Robby Eden Café on Atlantic Avenue. The café offered burgers and interesting sandwiches. But more importantly, it was less than a mile from the garage where they'd been living the past two months.

In that time they'd become regulars at Robby Eden's, wearing olive-green work clothes that made them part of the crew at L.A. Standard Demolition, a fictional service devised to allow them to move about unnoticed.

Cobb looked out from behind the heavy make-up and the dark glasses he wore in addition to the uniform, peered around the table at his men, still waiting for an answer. Only a few minutes before, they'd seen the phrase 'Ten Tomorrow' appear on the city's website, notifying them of the mayor's decision.

'Ten million is a lot these days, no matter who you are, Mr. Cobb,' Kelleher offered. 'Probably take time for them to get the money together.'

'Sounds right to me,' Hernandez said.

'Who cares?' Nickerson said. 'It's ten million, right? Which is a lot better than seven million. Or am I missing something?'

'We're not after seven million, or ten million, Mr. Nickerson,' Cobb said.

'Yes, I know, Mr. Cobb,' Nickerson replied. 'But that might be all we get if they don't move the money out of some big government account.'

Cobb shook his head. 'That's where it will come from, and they'll try to trace the money.'

'You don't know–' Watson began.

'We *do* know, Mr. Watson, by deductive reasoning,' Cobb insisted. 'It only makes sense, which is why you're going to send that money off into oblivion, and while they're chasing that paltry ten million, you're going to have the account codes and passwords necessary to steal them blind, whatever is in the big account, however much we want.'

'What if there's nothing?' Hernandez demanded skeptically. 'Not a cent beyond ten million, Mr. Cobb?'

With no hesitation, Cobb said, 'Isn't it obvious, Mr. Hernandez? We'll call the scammers on trying to track the money, and Mr. Kelleher will step up to take No Prisoners out for a spin again.'

'Sounds like a plan,' Nickerson said, raised his hand, and called to the waitress, 'Say, Alice, can we get our check?'

Chapter 89

I did the only thing I could think of, ducked and threw myself back into the car, hearing the spit and ping of the suppressed round shattering the driver's-side window of the Touareg, then another, smacking the door as I yanked in my legs, adrenaline surging, trying to get to my gun.

But I couldn't reach it, and I could hear footsteps. Lying across the bucket seat and the central console, I saw the emergency brake lever, released it.

The door was still open as the heavy Touareg almost immediately began to drop back down the steep drive, slapping the side of the guy trying to kill me.

He swore in Russian, wild-eyed, trying to stop my vehicle and get a clean shot at me. I slammed the shift into reverse, kicked the gas pedal, pinned the shooter against the door, dragging him as we went flying backward into the street, hurling him from my sight when we crashed broadside into his car with a sound like a dump truck dropping its gate.

On impact I'd been slammed back against the seats, but I came up fast, dug for my pistol, kicked my way out through the door and up into a squared-off shooter's stance, sweeping the...

He was sprawled, grunting, on the road beside an older Pontiac Trans Am that was making coughing noises and backfiring. His gun lay eight feet from him. I kicked it farther away into the gutter, noticed that his right leg was grotesquely broken, and now bright blood bubbled at one corner of his lips. Behind me I could hear Joy and Luck, Justine's terriers, barking wildly inside her house.

'Why'd you try to kill me?' I asked.

'Fuck you,' he rasped.

I kicked him in the broken leg, barely aware of people coming out of their houses, happy to hear him scream, or at least try. 'Why?' I asked again. 'Or this time, I'll stomp on your leg.'

'There is no why,' he said in a thick Russian accent. 'I do job. Hired.'

'By who?' I demanded. 'Who wanted me...?'

270

The Russian got a look of disbelief on his face, coughed up a gout of that bright frothy blood, and died there in the back-streets of Santa Monica, right in front of Justine's house.

Chapter 90

An hour earlier, Justine was sitting in an over-stuffed chair in her bedroom, both dogs in her lap, still dressed in her workout clothes, wanting to cry again. She'd seduced a married man with a pretty wife and kids who rode in car seats and sang about the wheels on the bus. Pulling Joy and Luck close to her, she thought miserably, *I'm a home wrecker.*

The idea went against nearly everything Justine stood for, and yet there it was, hovering about like a ghost, trying to get her to break down, to succumb to the weight of what she'd done with Paul, and of the attack in Mexico.

She was suffering, but it didn't mitigate things, she thought fiercely. A diagnosis of PTSD would not change what she had done, who she was, what she had become.

Justine's next thought was that she had to right things somehow, atone for her sins. Should she go to Paul's wife and confess? But what good would that do? She'd scar the poor woman and destroy their marriage. The truth was, Justine had been the aggressor. She had encouraged the tension that had been building with Paul, knowing nearly nothing about the man, not even his last name. It

271

was true that he'd allowed himself to be seduced, and asked her out for coffee the day before, but...

It was all so confusing. She didn't know what to do. Then she did. She called up Ellen Hayes, a fellow psychologist she admired, got put through.

'Justine,' Hayes said. 'So good to hear from you.'

'It's been too long, Ellen,' Justine allowed. 'But I'm looking for a recommendation for a therapist who specializes in the aftermath of trauma.'

'That would be you, dear.'

'The referral *is* for me, Ellen.'

Silence, and then, 'Are you all right?'

'Physically, yes,' Justine said. 'The rest I'm trying to figure out.'

'Then you'll come see me,' Hayes insisted. 'I can fit you in ... how about tomorrow afternoon, four?'

'Perfect, and thanks,' Justine said, and hung up.

She went into the shower, stood there under the beating hot water, trying to take hope from the fact that she'd soon be able to talk to someone about what had been going on in her life. In the meantime, she told herself she had to have some purpose for the rest of her day, or she'd surely drive herself guilty, bitter, and quite possibly crazy.

Drying off, Justine forced herself to make a list of options.

She could return to Guadalajara, find Adelita Gomez, figure out her relationship to Captain Gomez, if any. But that idea made her almost breathless, and she realized she feared Captain Gomez almost as much as she did Carla, the big woman in the jail cell.

That left, for today, anyway, the Harlows' charity, Sharing Hands.

272

After drying her hair and dressing in yoga pants and a USC Trojans sweatshirt, Justine got her laptop, sat on the floor in her living room, and called up the Sharing Hands website. Tom and Jennifer Harlow dominated the charity's home page, heads touching, hands clasped, shooting the camera fetching looks, as if they'd been interrupted in a moment of deep intimacy but were still darn happy to see you.

Indeed, at first glance, Justine had trouble understanding that this was actually a website for an organization that benefited orphans. But then she saw that in the background of that photograph of the Harlows, there was a jungle landscape with a clearing and a bright-white school building.

Reading through the rest of the site, which showed orphanages being built and happy children gathering around one or both Harlows, Justine was struck by the scope of what they were trying to do, how many children they were trying to help, and the gentle, respectful request for money to fund that vision that appeared on every page: 'Help Our Hands Share.'

And a PayPal button. They made it that easy.

Justine decided to check the California attorney general's site for any complaints about the charity, and found none. She consulted several online charity watchdogs. Sharing Hands received exemplary reviews for transparency and innovation, as well as gushing praise for the actors' involvement. Several reviews also noted the Harlows' decision to keep back fifty percent of all raised money to build an endowment for the nonprofit, much the way universities do to ensure that scholarships and other good works continue far into the–

A tremendous crashing noise out in the street in front of her house tore her away from the computer.

Joy and Luck went nuts, racing across the living room and up onto the couch below the front window, howling and barking. Justine got up, looked out through the blinds, and saw Jack's Touareg smashed into the side of a black Trans Am.

Jack was holding a gun on a man who was obviously bleeding to death.

Chapter 91

My Irish luck that two of my favorite LAPD detectives were sent to investigate what had happened in front of Justine's house. Lieutenant Mitch Tandy and Detective Len Ziegler were the same duo who had attempted to railroad me for my old girlfriend's murder. I kept things professional, answered every question straight, told them I'd been with the mayor and Chief Fescoe that morning, that I'd driven to Justine's to check on her, and what had happened during the attack.

'He said he was hired?' asked Lieutenant Tandy, a tough little guy in love with tanning beds.

'He said it was a job,' I replied. 'I asked who hired him. He died.'

We were standing in Justine's driveway. She stood off to the side, holding Joy and Luck on leashes, taking in the swarm of crime scene investigators and patrol officers who'd taken over her neighborhood.

'Convenient, he croaks like that,' said Detective Ziegler, a former swimmer gone to pot, with big shoulders and a Milwaukee tumor where his waistline should have been. He looked more and more like a walrus every time I saw him.

'For who?' I asked, already knowing where this was leading.

'You,' said Ziegler, who also seemed to approach everything in life through the prism of conspiracy theories that crystallized out of his head in all sorts of illogical shapes and sizes.

'You know, Len, for once I agree with you,' I said. 'It was extremely convenient for me that he died and I didn't. Sorry if I don't apologize for that.'

Tandy gave a flick of his hand, calling off the conspiracy walrus. 'Any idea who'd want you dead, Jack?'

I was unnerved to come up with multiple possibilities, Carmine Noccia, No Prisoners, whoever took the Harlows, and my own brother among them. But what good would telling these guys do? I'd just be asking them to stick their nose in affairs I'd rather keep quiet.

'No,' I said at last. 'I've been doing nothing lately but spreading good cheer and doing good deeds. Ask anyone.'

'Right,' Ziegler said. 'You're a regular Thom Harlow.'

I ignored him, talked to Tandy. 'You'll tell me who he is?'

'I think you know who he is,' Ziegler said.

I did, actually. I'd searched the car and found a wallet and ID: Vladimir Karenoff, thirty-seven, resident alien currently living in Brighton Beach, New York. The car was registered in New York as well. I'd taken photos of all his documents and returned them before the police arrived.

Looking at Ziegler placidly, I said, 'And I think you know I know who he is.'

'What?' Ziegler said, confused.

'I'm walking away now,' I said. 'You're sworn to uphold the law, so go find whoever tried to kill me.'

I went toward Justine and the dogs. We hadn't had time to say much to each other since she'd called 911.

'Want some coffee?' she asked, looking anxious, sad, and wan in a way I'd never seen before.

'I'd love some.'

Inside the bungalow she had the blinds drawn, but the windows behind them were open and you could hear the vague rumor of the ongoing crime scene investigation. Every once in a while one or the other of the dogs would start growling at the noise, and Justine would hush her. My mind was clanging, and my hand was trembling at the memories of the attack. If I hadn't gotten my foot on the pedal, who knows?

Justine came over, poured me coffee. I studied her as a way to escape my own thoughts, and as she turned, it struck me that she was carrying some heavy burden. Her not-so-perfect lover?

'You all right?' I asked.

She nodded. 'Just a little green around the gills.

I'm not used to drinking that much on an empty stomach.'

I said nothing as she sat on the opposite side of the kitchen counter, stirring her coffee and finding it terribly interesting. 'How do you deal with it?' she asked at last.

'What are we talking about?'

'Violence,' she said. 'You seem at ease during times of violence.'

'I wouldn't say at ease,' I replied. 'I was just taught to be resourceful when things get chaotic.'

'You either have the capacity for it or you don't, I suppose,' she said.

'What's this all...?'

She shook her head. 'We've got more important things on our plate. I've been looking into Sharing Hands.'

I still wanted to know what was going on with her, but I could tell she was in no mood to go there. So I said, 'The orphans' charity?'

'Yes,' she said. 'It's quite a remarkable operation.'

Justine showed me the Sharing Hands website, summarized the reviews the organization had received from various philanthropy watchdogs that cited the Harlows' commitment and the charity's foresight in building an endowment.

'Makes them sound like saints,' I said.

'It does,' Justine said. 'Then again, how many family-values congressmen get caught with mistresses?'

'More than a few. Let's keep digging.'

We scrolled through a dozen or more references to Sharing Hands's good deeds before spotting an aberration in the comments section below an article about the charity that had run in the London *Times* two months before.

The comment was signed, 'A. Aboubacar.'

Mr. Aboubacar claimed to be from Nigeria.

'They promised us an orphanage and a school,' Aboubacar wrote. 'They say they have built several in my country. But ignore the Harlows' glamour. Come here and look for yourself. There are none that I can find.'

Justine said, 'He's probably just a kook, don't you think?'

The rest of the testimonials we'd looked at had been so uniformly full of praise that I was about to agree with her. But then I noticed something that had been staring us in the face all along.

Doors began to open in my mind, and through them I saw dimensions we'd never considered before when it came to Thom and Jennifer Harlow.

'What?' Justine said, seeing something in my expression. 'You believe him?'

'We have a bunch of things to check out before I'll say that,' I replied. 'And then we're going to have a face-to-face chat with the friendly crew over at Harlow-Quinn.'

Chapter 92

Dave Sanders lived in Brentwood in a sprawling Georgian manor surrounded by a high wall and a gate that faced North Carmelina Avenue. Driving one of the company Suburbans now that

278

my Touareg was totaled, I pulled up to the gate around seven thirty that night, about forty minutes after the Kid alerted us that Sanders had returned home and, surprise, was entertaining this evening. His guests? Camilla Bronson and Terry Graves.

I hit the buzzer by the gate, looked up at the camera. After several moments, Sanders answered gruffly, 'What do you want, Morgan?'

'I've got the Harlows' staff from the ranch with me,' I said. 'They'd like to see the children.'

'Impossible,' he snapped. 'What business do you—?'

'I've got a writ here,' I said, cutting him off and waving a piece of paper out the window. 'Signed by Judge Maxwell, ordering you to allow them to see the Harlow children. If you do not open this gate, I will call LAPD, and they will see the order carried out.'

For several seconds Sanders said nothing, then, 'I don't know what you're up to, Jack. But fair warning, I don't trust you.'

'Feeling's mutual, Dave,' I said brightly. 'Now open the gate.'

A pause, then a loud click and the steel gates swung back. We drove onto a lighted drive that split before a long narrow reflecting pool that finished in a fountain in front of the house.

'Wasn't this place in *The Beverly Hillbillies?*' I asked Justine as I took the right fork in the drive.

She looked at me quizzically. 'Sorry, that show was a bit before my time.'

'Mine too, but watch it sometime,' I replied. 'A classic. I really think this might be the place where Jethro and Miss Hathaway did their funny business.'

She looked at me like I was nuts, and then laughed. It was good to see her smile again. We parked out front where the cement drive gave way to a mosaic of inlaid stone. We got out, opened the back doors, released Anita Fontana, Maria Toro, and Jacinta Feliz, who turned nervous and submissive when Sanders opened the massive front door and came out under the portico, followed by Camilla Bronson and Terry Graves.

'Where's this writ?' Sanders demanded.

I handed it to him, winked at the publicist and the producer, said, 'Amazing how swiftly judges react when the FBI's special agent in charge requests something. And you'll see that Justine Smith is named as court-appointed supervisor of this and future visits.'

For once Camilla Bronson was at a loss for words. Terry Graves acted as if we were unpleasant bugs come to call.

Sanders read the writ closely, looking for loopholes, I suppose, but the document was ironclad. He handed it back to me, sniffed, 'You could have called and made an appointment.'

'And miss breaking bread with the Harlow-Quinn team?' I said. 'Not a chance. But first: the kids?'

The Harlows' attorney nodded stiffly toward the door. The housekeeper, the cook, and the maid went by him quickly into a large marble foyer with a sweeping staircase that rose to a second floor. I came in last, nodded, said, 'In the old *Beverly Hillbillies* show, didn't Jed Clampett live here, in

280

this house?'

Sanders looked insulted. 'He most certainly did not.'

'Striking resemblance.'

In a deepening huff, the attorney led us off the foyer to a screening room where the children were watching a movie about a tailless dolphin.

'Miguel!' Anita cried.

The boy looked over the seat at her, acted as if he'd expected never to see her again. 'Nita!' he yelled, and ran into her arms.

The Harlows' housekeeper fell to her knees and embraced the boy, tears streaming down her face as she kissed him and spoke to him in Spanish, calling him her little one and her best boy. Pressing her shiny cheeks to his, she looked radiant and complete in an unexpected way. As if the two were deep soul mates.

Malia and Jin were on their feet, hugging Maria Toro and Jacinta Feliz, who'd also broken into tears.

'Look how big you get,' the cook said to Malia, who towered over her.

'You good?' Jacinta asked Jin.

Jin glanced at Sanders, bit her lower lip, but nodded.

'They're being well cared for,' Camilla Bronson declared.

'Dave's hired round-the-clock help,' Terry Graves said.

'Cook. Maid. Tutors. Psychologists,' Sanders added. 'Even a physical-fitness instructor. And we got a Wii and a Nintendo installed. Isn't that right?'

Malia shrugged and then bobbed her head.

'But he won't let us go out, Nita,' Miguel complained to the housekeeper. 'He won't let us watch TV hardly ever. He won't tell us what happened to Thom and Jen. And he keeps Stella in a kennel all the time.'

Sanders gave a sickly smile to the boy, then to me and Justine, and said, 'The dog's been peeing everywhere.'

'And I advised that the children not be seen in public,' Camilla Bronson said.

'We're trying to protect them from the howling mob,' Terry Graves said.

'I'm sure you are,' I said. 'But who's here to protect them from you three?'

Sanders acted as if I'd slapped him, sputtered, 'How dare you insinuate that anything untoward has ever–'

'We're fine,' Malia said to Justine. 'No one's hurt us or anything.'

Jin nodded, but her brother's head was bowed.

Sanders's chin rose and he gazed at us in triumph.

'Jack,' the publicist said. 'You don't really need to be here, do you?'

I winked at her a second time. 'Why don't you go get the dog so the kids can play with her, and then the five of us will have a little chat.'

'About what?' Terry Graves asked icily.

'C'mon,' I said. 'You sound like someone who likes to know the end of a movie before you've even seen it.'

Chapter 93

After bringing Stella to the screening room, where the bulldog was greeted like Cleopatra returning to Luxor, Sanders reluctantly led us into his private library, a polished, meticulous man cave done up like an alpine lodge: oxford-red leather club chairs and couch; a poster-sized photograph of the attorney skiing at Aspen when he was younger; his framed degrees from USC and Boalt Hall; and a massive flat-screen television above the gas fireplace where the moose head should have been.

'What's this all about?' demanded Sanders, who was flanked by Camilla Bronson and Terry Graves, both of whom were regarding Justine and me as if we were ferrets or some other kind of blood-seeking weasel.

I took one of the club chairs while they remained standing, said, 'We think we've made a break in the Harlow case. Several, in fact.'

Their expressions mutated through a variety of emotions, surprise, skepticism, and wariness, all in a matter of two seconds.

'What–?' Camilla Bronson began before Sanders cut her off.

'You were fired, Jack.'

'Absolutely,' Terry Graves said. 'Whatever you've turned up, don't expect to be paid for it.'

'Wouldn't dream of that,' I said, marveling at the way the man's brain worked. 'But you should know that people who work at Private are suckers for lost causes. We also have a deep aversion for jobs left unfinished.'

The producer's eyes darted to Justine and back. 'What have you found?'

'That the three of you are colossal liars,' I said, speeding up before any of them could protest. 'We can't figure out exactly why yet.'

'But we're close,' Justine said.

'Get out,' Sanders said hotly. 'Take the help with you. Time's up.'

I didn't move, said as firmly as I would to one of Justine's terriers, 'Sit down. The three of you. Or I will make a call to the FBI that will turn your world so fucking far upside down and confining, it will take a Houdini act on your part to get any of it right again.'

They watched me for a long beat, trying to see if I was bluffing. Then, one by one, and more contritely, they took seats.

Camilla Bronson cleared her throat, said, 'What is it you think we've lied to you about?'

'All sorts of things,' Justine said.

Sanders scowled.

I said, 'But we'll limit the discussion at present to the Harlows' finances.'

That got their attention. 'What about them?'

'You told us, Dave, that they were on the verge of bankruptcy,' I said. 'Nothing could be further from the truth, isn't that right?'

'No, it's not right,' he snapped. 'They were spending far beyond their means, and they were in danger of personal bankruptcy, Chapter Seven.'

I saw the nuance. 'But not corporate bankruptcy, Chapter Eleven?'

He studied me. 'They were on more solid ground there.'

'Why?' I asked. 'Because Thom got the cash from the mystery investor you told us about?'

'That's right,' he said, sounding like he was on surer ground himself.

'Or should I say Harlow-Quinn got the money?' I said, looking at Terry Graves. 'Is that right?'

The producer hesitated but then nodded. 'Yes, it was ... a good thing.'

'No doubt,' Justine said agreeably. 'So who is Mr. Mysterious Deep Pockets?'

Sanders rolled his palms outward. 'As I'm sure you understand, this kind of investor prefers to remain anonymous, and we can't breach the attorney-client and fiduciary privileges.'

Terry Graves almost smiled. But Camilla Bronson was scratching her right forearm. It was the first unpolished thing I'd ever seen her do.

'Lying again,' I snapped. 'You three are pathological. What did that come from? A genetic defect? A rotten childhood? Or did you all study hard to be lying asses?'

As one, their faces reddened and twisted in anger. Sanders struggled to stand. The publicist did too, saying, 'I'm not listening to–'

Justine said, 'We know that ESH Ltd is the deep pockets.'

'Nicely done, by the way,' I said. 'The offshore company. The Panamanian bank. Just enough distance that you could claim the money came from a mysterious investor.'

Sanders's face had looked ready to explode, but

now he sank into his chair. Camilla Bronson followed, scratching at her forearm again.

Terry Graves had paled considerably. 'How could you know about ESH?'

'We're good,' I said. 'It's why you hired us. Breaking the registering agent's will only cost me twenty grand. Thom and Jennifer own ESH Ltd.'

Sanders said quickly, 'So what? We use ESH to receive and hold monies earned overseas. There's absolutely nothing illegal—'

'Then why lie?' Justine asked.

I made a *tsk-tsk* gesture with my finger. 'Let's just get it out on the table, shall we? No more beating about the whatever. ESH is indeed where the Harlows gather overseas money to be funneled into Harlow-Quinn Productions. But the money is not from foreign film proceeds. Or not so much, anyway.'

Not one of them responded.

I went on, enjoying myself, saying, 'That's what we thought ESH was all about when we first learned of its existence. But earlier today we figured out that ESH really stands for 'Endowment Sharing Hands,' the fund boasted about ad nauseam on the so-called charity's website.'

'So-called charity?' Camilla Bronson said fiercely. 'That foundation has saved hundreds, thousands of lives.'

'Probably,' Justine said. 'But think how many more kids could have been saved if the twenty-seven million the Harlows siphoned away to fund their for-profit movie business had actually been spent on orphans.'

'Siphoned?' Terry Graves cried. 'It's not like

that at all.'

'Sure it is,' I replied. 'Did you know that Private has done a lot of work with PayPal the last few years? Lots and lots of goodwill there.'

'PayPal?' the producer said, confused. 'So what?'

Justine said, 'You jiggered the PayPal account associated with Sharing Hands so that fifty per-cent of every dollar was diverted and deposited in ESH Ltd's Panamanian bank account.'

'Brilliantly conceived,' I said. 'A secret piggy bank that just keeps filling for little piggies like you, Dave. And you, Camilla and Terry.'

'Not to mention Thom and Jennifer,' Justine said.

'It's not like that at all,' Sanders protested. 'There are promissory notes, and detailed con-tracts, agreements. Those funds *were* an invest-ment for Sharing Hands. The charity stands to make back its money fivefold when *Saigon Falls* hits.'

Incredulous, I said, 'But you've got interlocking boards of directors between the charity, an off-shore legal entity, and a production company designed to make its owners multimillion-dollar profits? That's collusion any way you look at it, Counselor. And the way *I* look at it, when this comes to light, you will all be put in prison, punished, and publicly vilified for taking money from orphans to make a goddamned movie, no matter how brilliant it might be.'

Chapter 94

The Harlow-Quinn team sat there, looking at us in stunned silence. It was the kind of moment where someone might lose it and go for a weapon. My right hand moved slowly to my pistol.

But instead of running amok, Sanders gave a shudder and his shoulders trembled. His eyes watered. His face twisted in open despair as he choked, 'I tried to rein them in.'

Camilla Bronson panicked. 'Shut up, Dave.'

'Fuck you, Camilla,' said Terry Graves, then looked at me, trying to project earnestness. 'Dave and I both tried to keep Thom from chasing every grandiose dream that came into his unbe-fucking-lievably creative genius brain.' He threw up his hands to an invisible audience. 'I couldn't stand up to Thom when it came to spending.'

'You two are making a monstrous mistake,' the publicist warned.

The attorney ignored her. 'And I couldn't stop Jennifer from spending like a freak in their personal life, a fucking OCD spending freak!'

Terry Graves said, 'Thom would come in, all explosive energy, manic with it, and he'd make you see his visions. And then later, in the theater, he'd show you far beyond what he'd caused you to imagine in the first place, right up there thirty feet high on the screen, like he was some kind of supermagician, or god.

'The way he looked at life and his stories, they made you want to laugh, to cheer, and to cry, didn't they? Thom could make you endure deep tragedy and know the far reaches of love and humanity.' He shook his head, now gazing at Justine in bewilderment. 'How do you deal with someone who can do all that?'

I reappraised him but said nothing, leaving Justine to ask, 'What really happened to Thom and Jennifer Harlow?'

'We don't know,' Camilla Bronson said, tears forming in her eyes. 'We honestly don't. And all I can think is that it's a tragedy that the world might never see *Saigon Falls*, never see their final incredible vision.'

'Save that crap for a retrospective in *Entertainment Weekly*,' I said. 'Tell us about Adelita Gomez.'

'Adelita?' Sanders said.

Terry Graves blinked. 'What about her?'

'She's from Guadalajara,' Justine replied. 'Which is where a blogger was murdered recently after posting that Jennifer and Thom had been seen in that city after their disappearance, highly intoxicated, or on drugs.'

'I saw that,' the publicist said as if she'd chewed something bitter. '*National Enquirer* nonsense.'

'Maybe not,' I said. 'Again, tell us about Adelita.'

'She was the nanny,' the attorney said. 'She went to Vietnam with them, which is where I met her briefly twice during my trips over there.'

Terry Graves was studying his hands. 'They loved her. Thom and Jennifer gave her a small role in the film.'

'Why?' Camilla Bronson said. 'Where is Adelita?

What is she saying?'

'We have no idea where she is or what she's saying,' I replied. 'Cynthia Maines told us Adelita left Saigon two days before the Harlows, bound for Mexico on a vacation.'

'There you are, then,' Sanders said.

'Don't you think it's strange she hasn't contacted someone about the Harlows? It's international news.'

'I don't know what to tell you,' he said, and I believed him.

'Then tell us about the cameras in the panic room above the Harlows' bedroom,' Justine said.

All three of them squinted at her. 'What?' Terry Graves asked.

She told them what she'd found. They listened, openly confused.

'You didn't know they had a panic room?' I asked when she finished.

'I had only a vague idea they did,' Sanders said.

The producer said, 'I've never seen it, but Thom said it was installed when Sandy Shine owned the place. Maybe Sandy put those brackets there. He was a professional degenerate, you know.'

Sandy Shine was a hyper, mercurial actor who'd been nominated for an Oscar at sixteen, only to turn wild in his twenties: drugs, alcohol, and a long series of scandals, rehabs, and tawdry affairs that somehow transformed him into a comedic superstar with his own top-rated television show.

'We'll check it out,' I said, stood, and motioned to Justine that we were leaving.

'What are you going to do with all this information?' Camilla Bronson asked.

'We haven't decided yet,' I replied.

The attorney rubbed his hands together and said in a beseeching tone, 'What can we do? How can we help you?'

Terry Graves picked up on his angle, said, 'That's right. What can we change so this isn't made public?'

I thought about that. Justine beat me to it. 'How about you start by firing the cook and maid you hired and bringing in the Harlows' help in their place? The children love them. It will help stabilize them. It's what I would tell a court.'

'Of course,' Sanders said as if he were suddenly our fawning servant. The trio followed us out of the man cave down the hall toward the screening room. 'I should have thought of that before.'

'We should have thought about that,' echoed Terry Graves.

'But none of us ever had children, you know?' said Camilla Bronson.

Why didn't that surprise me?

In any case, I tuned out their blather, turned the corner, glanced into the screening room, and saw the Harlow children and the Harlow help. Miguel sat in Anita's lap. The others were on the floor, giving the bulldog a belly rub.

Justine gasped beside me. I startled, looked at her. She was staring into the screening room, watching them, her lips parted in wonder.

'What?' I asked.

Justine tore her attention away, looked at me, deeply puzzled, but then shook her head and said, 'Nothing. I just thought I saw something I hadn't ... but it's nothing, I'm sure.'

291

Chapter 95

Justine would not elaborate on what she'd been thinking back in Sanders's mansion as she looked at the Harlow children and their beloved servants. Indeed, she didn't seem to want to talk about anything at all on the ride back to her bungalow. She just stared out at L.A. blipping by as if it were some foreign country she was reluctantly visiting for the first time.

The crime scene investigators were gone when we reached her street, though the chalk mark that had surrounded the assassin's body was still there, along with the blood that darkened the pavement.

'Talk in the morning?' I asked when Justine reached for the door handle.

She nodded, hesitated, looked at me. 'Last night, when you brought me home and I was drunk...'

'I was completely honorable.'

'No, of course, nothing like... Did I say anything ... strange? Not me?'

My eyes never left hers as I shook my head. 'Justine, I don't remember anything strange or not you at all. You were tired. You drank a little too much. In our business it happens.'

She softened. 'You are a good person, Jack.'

'I try to be,' I said. 'Need me to walk you to the door?'

'No,' she said. 'The dogs are there. I'll be fine.'

I watched her until she'd opened her door, the Jack Russells jumping around her. She looked back at me and waved. Putting the Suburban in reverse, I was suddenly exhausted. I'd survived a murder attempt and helped uncover fraud on a massive scale. I deserved a good night's sleep.

As I drove home, I put in a call to Mo-bot, asked her how the coding party was coming along.

'The money's going to be transferred from the California general fund account,' she said. 'We just got word of that a few minutes ago, and we're making some last-minute changes so the tick hides deep in the file's metadata.'

'If you say so,' I replied. 'They're the best, right?'

'The fine ladies of Cal Poly?' Maureen said as if it were heresy to even question their qualifications. 'They've thought of a ridiculous number of things Sci and I missed.'

'Enough said. We'll talk in the morning. I'll explain what ESH Ltd is.'

'Look forward to it,' she said, hung up.

I reached my house. It was cool outside. The sea breeze was building. I went inside, turned on the gas fire. I sprawled on the couch, watching the flames. I thought of the last time I'd watched the fire. I thought of Guin Scott-Evans and wondered when the actress was returning from London.

Then Justine elbowed her way back into my thoughts.

Justine had always been the level head in the room. Or at least it had always seemed that way to me. And she'd always been the one to try to get me to open up. Now she seemed to be retreating into herself. Why?

I got a Sam Adams from the fridge, drank it while eating a bag of microwave popcorn, trying unsuccessfully to figure out what was beating her up so badly. I finally decided she'd tell me in her own time – if that was what she decided. If not, I'd give her the space to try and work it through.

After getting a second Sam, I turned on the television, tried to watch the Lakers-Bulls game. But it was preseason stuff and none of the plays looked crisp, and I quickly got bored. Passing on a perfect chance to catch up on *The Real House-wives of Beverly Hills,* I instead turned the TV off, listened to the silence of my house, and went back to watching the fake fire in my hearth.

Someone had tried to kill me. Someone had sent an assassin to take me out. Who? Why? Earlier in the day, I'd come up with several likely suspects, and lying there on the couch, I tried to go through them one by one.

Front and center: Carmine Noccia. He'd out-right accused me of tipping the DEA to the hi-jacked shipment of painkillers. I'd outbluffed him when he and Tommy had tried to extort me out of Private. No doubt about it, Carmine had cause.

Two: Tommy? I wanted desperately to say im-possible, but he was ruthless, and mean, and more than a little fucked up in too many ways to count. He might try to leverage me in ways I hadn't con-sidered. He'd pretend that he'd implicate me in murder. But would he? He'd certainly screw me over if he could, and had succeeded at that more than once. But in the end I was his brother, right? There was a line somewhere that he wouldn't cross, right? He wouldn't personally hire a Russian

294

assassin, would he? Or was I just a hopeless romantic when it came to what my brother might have been?

Three: No Prisoners? Possibly. But why would they key on me? I hadn't exactly been front and center on that case. LAPD and L.A. Sheriff's had helped me in that respect, putting their own people in front of the cameras.

Four: members of the Harlow-Quinn team? Had one of them threatened to blow the story on the orphans' fund? Or had the actors been ignorant of the way the money was being funneled to the *Saigon Falls* project, then discovered it, and had they been preparing to go to the authorities?

Five: whoever took the Harlows, excluding the Harlow-Quinn team.

I supposed that was possible. Maybe we were close and someone had decided to take me out?

Then again, for the most part, Justine had taken the lead in that investigation. Had she been the assassin's real target, with me a lucky opportunity?

It was suddenly all too much to think about. My head ached and I closed my eyes. I honestly don't remember falling asleep.

Chapter 96

My cell phone rang and I jerked alert on my couch, head groggy. What time was it? Three thirty a.m.? I'd been sleeping five hours?

Yawning, I picked up the cell, saw a number I

didn't recognize, answered, 'This better be good.'

'Didn't want to come tell me in person that someone tried to kill you, huh?'

I hung my head, feeling guilty for having forgotten to visit Del Rio, or at least call him. 'It was a crazy day, Rick,' I began.

'I'm sure it was,' he said. 'Make up for it. Get over here ASAP.'

'It's three thirty in the morning.'

'There's someone here wants to see you, misses you deeply.'

I flashed on Angela, the Filipina nurse. 'It's three thirty in the morning.'

'Which is why you better get your ass over here, Jack,' Del Rio said firmly. 'Ghosts like the one standing in front of me need to be gone and well hidden in spooky spook land long before sunrise.'

Chapter 97

I hadn't seen him in more than a decade, but he had not aged a bit and still looked like an overgrown choirboy, with pale pinkish skin, a pleasant pie-shaped face, and a riot of curly orange hair. But the eyes gave the lie to everything else, hard and dark as sapphires even if his lips were smiling.

'Guy Carpenter,' I said when I saw him in the chair usually reserved for me in Del Rio's hospital room.

Carpenter was dressed in boat shoes, khakis, a white polo shirt, and a blue Windbreaker sporting the logo of a country club in Chevy Chase, Maryland. With the Titleist ball cap on his head, he looked ready for thirty-six holes. I knew better. He'd never been in a country club in his life, unless it was one constructed especially for bad-asses, which he most definitely was.

'Jack Morgan,' Carpenter said, getting to his feet, shooting me a winning smile, and shaking my hand while those hard sapphire eyes danced over me, making me feel oddly expendable. 'Been following your career since the 'Stan.'

'Can't say the same about you.'

'Yeah, well, I was always better suited to the shadows than you were. How long *did* you last at the company?'

'Two years,' I said. 'Difference of philosophy.'

'I figured that,' he replied, then laughed and shook his head. 'Isn't it strange the way life unfolds? The unexpected turns and twists?'

Del Rio spoke up from the bed. 'You come here to tell us something, Guy, or get all touchy-feely about life unfolding in its grand arc?'

'He hasn't changed,' Carpenter said to me, throwing a thumb Del Rio's way. 'Even with a broken back he hasn't changed.'

'Not a bit,' I replied.

Carpenter's smiling face fell then, and I saw the darkness I'd glimpsed several times in Afghanistan when Del Rio and I were charged with moving him about the country on missions we never fully understood.

He went to the door and shut it, then jammed a chair under the doorknob. 'That nurse is a real pain,' he said. 'I figured she might try to interrupt our business just to get her jollies.'

'You were always a quick study,' I said.

'Dartmouth will do that for you,' Carpenter replied before looking at Del Rio. 'Those fingerprints you sent me?'

'Yes?'

'They don't exist.'

'And that's why you flew three thousand miles to see me?' Del Rio asked.

'I heard your back was broken.'

'Bullshit,' Del Rio said.

'Whatever,' Carpenter replied, his face hardening. 'Those fingerprints belong to no one, and because the three of us go way back, I thought you'd want to hear me say that in person. Take it as a warning if you want, but don't try to find someone who doesn't exist.'

'Wait,' I said. 'Warning from who?'

'People with far more reach than I've got,' Carpenter said. 'Spooky, spooky spook people.'

'Did Rick tell you where the fingerprints came from?' I asked.

'As a matter of fact, no,' he replied. 'But it doesn't matter.'

'Oh, but it does,' I said.

I told him everything, described seeing the four dead bodies on Malibu Beach, the killings in the CVS, and the explosion on the Huntington Beach Pier. Then I described how a drag-queen shooter playing Marilyn Monroe on skates killed six at Mel's Drive-In before a granny who would have been the seventh shot him dead.

'This is our first serious clue as to who is behind No Prisoners,' I said. 'We need your help or eight will die tomorrow.'

Through all of it, Carpenter had listened impassively, as if he were hearing the plot of a new action movie and not the gruesome details of an actual mass-murder spree.

When I was done, he blinked several times, rubbed his fair cheeks, and pursed his lips. 'I read about some of this,' he said. 'No Prisoners?'

'That's the handle,' Del Rio said. 'You recognize it?'

Carpenter shook his head.

'But you know those fingerprints,' I said. 'Otherwise, I don't see you coming here at all, as compassionate a man as you are. And I don't think that warning was coming from any triple-spooky people. I think it's coming from you.'

Carpenter thought that was funny but said, 'No one ever said you were a dummy, Jack. But from me or whoever, take it as fair warning.'

Del Rio said, 'There are twenty-one people dead. Innocent people. Eight more may die. Women. Children. Doesn't that kind of thing get through to you? Or are you so jaded by your life in the shadows that nothing gets through anymore?'

To my surprise, Carpenter's face cracked and the hard bravado fled, and he honestly seemed to age right in front of me, his eyes hollowing and his cheeks sagging. He said in a weary voice, 'These kinds of things get to me more than you could ever imagine, Rick. The things I've seen? The stuff I know? I haven't slept right in years.'

'High time to get some of it off your chest,' I replied. 'Either that or the twenty-one people dead here in L.A. are going to become a perman-

299

ent part of your nightmares and obsessions.'

Carpenter's shoulders hunched and he gazed at me as if I were Jacob Marley's ghost, showing him the length and weight of an invisible chain that threatened to hang from him for all eternity.

'I don't want that,' he said quietly.

'Then tell us what you know,' Del Rio said. 'Help us stop these killings.'

Chapter 98

Carpenter looked at the floor for a long time, as if seeing something on the antiseptic film that coated the hospital tiles.

'Okay,' he said at last. 'But none of this can become public. And none of this can ever be traced to me. If you attribute the information to me, well...'

'We get it,' I replied. 'Far as I'm concerned, you were some mirage I once hallucinated in Afghanistan.'

Del Rio nodded. 'You've got our word.'

Carpenter sighed, slouched in the recliner, and for the next hour and a half, and on past sunrise, told us a story that we never would have believed if Del Rio and I hadn't been in Afghanistan ourselves during the crazy times after the invasion, after Bin Laden's escape from the Tora Bora cave system, during the beginnings of the neo-Taliban counterinsurgency, long before the surge.

Carpenter said the fingerprints belonged to

300

Clive Johnson, Master Sergeant Clive Johnson, who'd served in the Rangers and then with several Joint Special Operations Command teams, which drew elite warriors from all four branches of the military.

'It was early 2003, and the forces we'd committed to Afghanistan were being drawn down, sent to stage up in Kuwait before the invasion of Iraq,' Carpenter said. 'There was a lot of dissension in the ranks, especially among spec ops who'd been in country since November 2001, right from the beginning.'

I remembered. 'They felt they were being undercut, forgotten.'

Carpenter nodded. 'They were being given all sorts of conflicting signals regarding the rules of engagement, when you could shoot, who you could shoot, that kind of thing.'

Del Rio nodded. 'All sorts of good men died because of that. Hell, that was still going on two years later when SEAL Team Ten turned into the lone survivor because they wouldn't kill the kid who betrayed them to the Taliban.'

Carpenter nodded. 'That was just the worst of it.'

But back in 2003, frustration among the special forces hit another, earlier high point. These elite soldiers were asking themselves whether they were in Afghanistan to fight and beat the Taliban, or merely to offer Al Qaeda easy access to walking, talking American targets. Indeed, those questions echoed high into the US chain of command in Kabul.

'An army general who shall remain nameless

decided that enough was enough,' Carpenter said. 'He decided on his own to detach a new secret JSOC team out of Kandahar. Their job was simple: to disrupt the trade in raw opium and black tar heroin that was funding the Taliban insurgency in the mountains along the Pakistani border. By any means necessary.'

'Johnson was a member of that JSOC team?' Del Rio asked.

'Handpicked by the marine recon commander the general chose to lead the secret team.'

Carpenter got a tablet computer from a backpack I hadn't noticed and called up a grainy snapshot of a man in his early forties. The left side of his face was covered in scars, and he gave off the distinct impression that he could eat broken glass and like it.

'Meet Lee Cobb, one bad dude,' Carpenter said, looking old again. 'He got the scars in the first Gulf War. Land mine. Shook it off, healed up, went right back at it. Remember when you took me on that night drop-off, spring of oh-four?'

'Snowstorm?' I asked. 'Zabul province?'

'That's the one,' Carpenter said. 'West of Qalat.'

I remembered it. Brutal terrain. Hard-core Taliban country.

Thinking back on how stranger than normal Carpenter had seemed that night, I said, 'You were going to meet up with Cobb and his team?'

'More like try to stop them before they committed any more atrocities,' Carpenter said in a hollow voice.

Chapter 99

From early March 2003 through April 2006, while the world's attention was largely focused on the invasion of Iraq, the chaotic aftermath of the overthrow of Saddam Hussein, and the rise of the radical Shiite cleric Muqtada al-Sadr, Cobb's team ran ad hoc missions in some of the most dangerous country in Afghanistan.

'At first, Cobb and his men stuck to the general's playbook,' Carpenter said. 'They worked to break up networks developing between poppy growers and Taliban fighters demanding tribute from the heroin manufacturers. In return for security, the growers paid the Taliban, who used the cash to fund their war.'

'At first?' Del Rio said.

'At first,' Carpenter replied. 'Spring of 2004, things slipped off the rails while Cobb and his men were on a mission northwest of Tarin Kot. The general had a heart attack and died, having destroyed virtually all records regarding the secret JSOC team. They were, shall we say, left to their own devices.'

'I don't follow,' I said.

'They became a ghost team,' Carpenter said. 'They didn't exist. So they were never extracted. Left out there, in country.'

'Until you went in after them?' Del Rio asked.

'I was the third to try to bring them in,' Carpenter said.

He said that in the summer of 2004, US Defense intelligence began getting reports of a rogue unit operating in the rugged massif north of Kandahar. Cobb and his men were said to be turning the tables on the Taliban, demanding their own tribute from the poppy growers and executing anyone or anything suspected of supporting Al Qaeda and the insurgency.

'Men, women, children, dogs, horses,' Carpenter said quietly. 'You name it, they killed it if their demands weren't met.'

'So Cobb kind of went Colonel Kurtz?' I asked.

'You could say he found his own way to the heart of darkness,' Carpenter agreed. 'You could also say that he led a thirteen-month reign of terror that quite frankly worked.'

'How so?' Del Rio asked.

'The Taliban lost ground or died out everywhere Cobb's team went,' Carpenter replied. 'Poppy growers paid up or died too. And there was ample evidence that Cobb and his men amassed a small fortune in gold and black tar heroin that they managed to stash across the border in Pakistan.'

By late fall of 2004, the evidence of a secret JSOC team was overwhelming. Two senior CIA Special Activities Division, or SAD, operators were sent in to convince Cobb to come out of the hills and report his activities.

'We lost contact with both men, and they were and are presumed dead,' Carpenter said. 'You two flew me into their area when the snow started thawing in the spring of oh-five.'

That sounded right, and I nodded.

Carpenter said it took him two weeks to find Cobb's team, but he did, living in a box canyon deep in the mountains. He delivered an ultimatum. Cobb and his men could continue their lawless activities, be branded renegades, hunted, captured, court-martialed, and sent to Leavenworth for execution.

'Or?' Del Rio asked.

'Or they could leave the mountains with me, quietly, without anyone knowing,' Carpenter said.

'And in return?'

Carpenter cleared his throat. 'They got immunity for their actions.'

'They took the deal?' Del Rio asked.

Carpenter nodded. 'You two had crashed in the meantime, so you weren't the ones to extract us. I brought Cobb's team back to Kabul, where they were debriefed about their activities. The intelligence officers were horrified by what they learned. But Cobb and his men had immunity and no legal action could be taken. Illegal action was something else again.'

'What do you mean?' I asked.

Carpenter pinched the bridge of his nose. 'The way I heard it, secretly and at the highest levels of the US military and intelligence apparatus, a decision was made to punish Cobb's team, to turn them into pariahs.'

'How?'

'By making them what they had become in Afghanistan, a team of savages that no longer existed,' Carpenter said. 'Literally over the course of two days, the records of all six men were permanently expunged from all government databases.

305

Their money was seized, their bank accounts erased. Their pensions were nullified and evaporated. All credit lines vanished as well. Their next of kin were notified of their deaths in combat, given generous bulk death payments and weighted coffins to bury.

'Then Cobb and his men were flown back into the mountains north of Kandahar and dumped, weaponless, deep inside Taliban-controlled country. Until you sent that set of fingerprints to me, Cobb, Johnson, and the others had not been heard from since. Everyone had assumed they were long dead.'

PART FIVE

IN COUNTRY

Chapter 100

'Are we ready, Mr. Watson?' Cobb asked. He was dressed in the olive-green uniform of the L.A. Standard Demolition Company.

'We are ready, Mr. Cobb.'

Watson sat hunched over the wireless keyboard, signed into an anonymous e-mail site based in Peshawar, Pakistan. On the right-hand side of the screen, a thin rectangular box overlaid the e-mail site. Six dozen codes were stacked in the box. Watson knew every one of them by heart.

Cobb believed he was about to witness a virtuoso performance on Watson's part, the result of almost two years of work, two years of hacking his way into dozens of federal and state computer systems, learning how their digital security worked. For two years Watson had planned the route the ten million would take out into the financial ether, breaking into pieces, moving through bank accounts and on again, splitting and transferring a total of six dozen times.

Cobb allowed himself a rare smile, knowing that while the feeble law enforcement people chased the ten million they'd demanded, Watson would be going the other way on the digital stream, after a whole lot more.

He looked around at Nickerson, Hernandez, Kelleher, men who'd walked with him out of a war zone unarmed, men who'd killed with their bare hands, men who were disciplined enough to think long term and long range.

'Ready, gentlemen?'

They nodded. He glanced at the clock: 9:40 a.m.

'Our time is now,' Cobb said. 'Send it, Mr. Watson.'

Chapter 101

'And we're supposed to believe the secondhand word of one man, some CIA spook we can't interrogate for ourselves?' cried Sheriff Cammarata after I explained to the mayor, Chief Fescoe, and Special Agent Christine Townsend who was behind the No Prisoners murder and extortion scheme.

'*You* can believe what *you* want,' I snapped. 'But those prints belong to Johnson. And I believe Cobb and the rest of his team are going to be on the receiving end of ten million dollars in about ten minutes or so, whenever you get the text, Your Honor.'

'Show them the picture,' Mo-bot urged.

Mo-bot stood in the background with several middle-aged women who, by their attire, looked more prepared for a yoga retreat than an extortion payoff.

I nodded, smiled at the ladies from Cal Poly, as Mo-bot had been referring to them, and then typed in a command on a laptop.

On the screen at the end of the conference room, up popped a grainy picture shot on a foggy spring day in the Afghan highlands. A group of battle-hardened men stood in the melting snow.

'That's them,' I said. 'Cobb's far left, then Clive Johnson, Peter Kelleher, Jesus Hernandez, Denton Nickerson, and Albert Watson, who our source says is something of a genius when it comes to weapons and computers.'

Everyone in the room studied the picture. Cobb and his men looked either stoic or harshly amused. You'd never know they'd committed atrocities and enriched themselves in the months before Carpenter took the photograph.

'This is what time frame?' Mayor Wills asked.

'April 2005, Your Honor,' I said. 'They'll look quite a bit older now.'

'But what do we do with this?' Cammarata demanded. 'Can we put it out there when we have no way of corroborating that this is real, that these men are the ones doing the killing?'

'I see what you're saying, Sheriff,' I said. 'But we're not getting any other files on these men. Other than burial records in their hometowns, they're gone.'

'How did they survive?' Fescoe asked. 'How did they get here?'

'We talked about that,' I said. 'Our source's theory is that they walked out of Afghanistan along the same trails the Taliban used to bring in supplies from Pakistan. Somehow they got to their stash of gold and black tar heroin, made their way to Peshawar or some other lawless place, and bought the necessary documents. Beyond that, we

311

have no clue.'

The mayor's cell phone buzzed. She stiffened, looked at it, breathed hard, said, 'We've got ten minutes, an account number, password, and routing code.'

'Okay, ladies,' Mo-bot said. 'You're up.'

Chapter 102

Drs. Esther Goldburg, Lauren Hollings, and Katherine Clarkson – the ladies of Cal Poly – were all cutting-edge computer scientists. They went quickly to their laptops, gave them instructions, and within seconds the photograph of Cobb's team disappeared and the screen split into thirds.

The center third showed a secure website inside the California State Treasurer's Office. The right third displayed the Google Earth macrosatellite view of the globe. The left third of the screen featured a live feed of the face of Carlton Watts, the current treasurer of the State of California.

'Are we ready?' Watts asked.

'We are, Carlton,' Mayor Wills said, handing Esther Goldberg her cell phone so she could read the codes and routing instructions.

Goldberg quickly entered the information into the secure website, hit ENTER.

A moment later, Watts nodded. 'Request is here.' He hesitated, appearing worried. 'You're sure this tracking thingamajob will attach on the way out?'

'As sure as I am that Einstein discovered the

photoelectric effect,' Goldberg said coolly.

'You tell 'em, girl,' Mo-bot muttered.

'On your say, then,' Watts said. 'I'm entering my password and the transfer authorization codes.'

We heard the clacking of his keyboard, then the snap of a return.

The center screen hesitated, jumped. Below the California State emblem, and along with an icon that looked like a slender green tube, the figure $10,000,000 appeared. The tube began to drain of green, and in less than three seconds it was gone. On the screen to the right, Google Earth zoomed in on California, showed a line from Sacramento to Los Angeles.

'Got it,' said Lauren Hollings, staring at her screen. 'File and metadata are moving through our tracking software. Ticks embedding. Almost ready to transfer onto that bank account.'

'I've already got a jump on that, tracked it through the bank identification code on the SWIFT network,' said Katherine Clarkson. 'The money's heading to Banco Delta Asia Ltd in Macau.'

'And there she goes,' said Goldberg.

Up on the screen, Google Earth had retreated, showed the Pacific Rim, and another line speeding toward Macau. It was there in less than four seconds.

Mayor Wills said, 'Can we contact this bank?'

'It's not staying there,' said Goldberg. 'They're not that stupid.'

Sure enough, fifteen seconds after the ten million arrived in Macau, two lines burst on the Google Earth map and began to arc away from each other.

'Five million, five million,' Hollings said.

The first five million landed in a bank in India; the second I couldn't tell, but it looked near England.

'The first is in the Bank of Rajasthan, New Delhi,' Clarkson announced. 'Second in Conister Bank, Wigan, Isle of Man.'

'I'll be a son of a bitch,' said Sheriff Cammarata. 'It's working.'

'What did you expect?' Mo-bot asked with a slight sneer.

Before Cammarata could reply, four lines burst from those locations, each heading out in one of the four cardinal directions. But when they had traveled only a short distance on Google Earth, they hesitated, stopped, blinked, and then disappeared.

Chapter 103

There were gasps from the various law enforcement officials present.

'Where'd it go?' Mayor Wills asked.

'I don't...' Goldberg began.

'I knew it,' said Sheriff Cammarata, spitting the words like they were tobacco juice.

People began to argue among themselves. State Treasurer Watts cried, 'What's going on down there?'

'Your money's gone bye-bye, Carlton!' the sheriff shouted.

'It is not bye-bye!' Goldberg shouted emphatically. 'They're not stupid, they found the tick and stripped it.'

'What?' Chief Fescoe said. 'I thought–'

'But the ladies from Cal Poly are smarter,' Mo-bot said. 'Or actually, Dr. Hollings is smarter.'

The youngest of the computer scientists beamed.

'What are you talking about?' Cammarata demanded.

'She thought of putting an easy-to-spot tick on the transfer, and another virtually impossible to spot,' Goldberg said with great satisfaction.

Mo-bot poked me in the ribs with her index finger, whispered, 'Told you they were good.'

Hollings, meanwhile, had given her computer more instructions, and almost instantly the lines on the Google Earth screen ran on, dividing and moving, dividing and moving, until within no more than a minute the satellite view of Earth looked loosely strung in almost every direction. I was focusing on the dizzying complexity of the transfers, barely aware that the center third of the screen, the one still linked to the account within the California State Treasurer's Office, was now blinking.

'We're out to sixty-four different accounts,' Goldberg announced. 'And they appear to have stopped. We know where every dollar–'

She stopped, stared up from her laptop screen toward the large one on the wall, her mouth gaping. 'What's going on?'

The center screen showed one of those green

tubes, then three, then ten. Beside each was the figure $15,000,000. They began to drain.

'What's happening?' I demanded.

Mo-bot had lost all color. 'Someone's looting that account.'

'What?' State Treasurer Watts yelled. On the live feed, he was frantically typing on his keyboard. 'No. Goddammit! It won't stop! What the fuck!'

The tubes emptied. The screen blinked. The numbers went to zero.

'Holy shit,' Goldberg said, her hands across her face.

Watts looked like he'd been hit with a left hook.

'How much did they get?' Mayor Wills asked in shock.

Chapter 104

'A hundred and fifty million!' Watson crowed, and slapped the table inside the garage in the City of Commerce.

Cobb threw his hands in the air, then hugged Watson. Nickerson, Kelleher, and Hernandez were celebrating too, throwing high fives, doing little jigs of victory.

'You are a goddamned genius, Mr. Watson!' Kelleher cried.

'Thirty million apiece,' Nickerson laughed. 'Thirty million untraceable.'

'I'm seeing Venezuelan women on a beach,' Hernandez said, eyes closed, doing a slow dance.

Watson beamed. 'I'll e-mail you the various accounts where your money will land.'

'Gentlemen,' Cobb said. 'Once again, I have to tell you what an honor it is to have served with you.'

'Hoorah,' Nickerson said. 'Hoo-fuckin'-rah.'

Hernandez opened his eyes, stopped dancing, and said, 'That mean we're cool to go now?'

'We still need to strip this place down, pack up,' Kelleher said.

'We're in no hurry,' Cobb said. 'That money is far, far from here and they have absolutely no idea where we are, or who we are. We can be gone by eight, nine at the latest. In the meantime, anyone interested in lunch? I'm starving.'

'I could go for a burger,' Hernandez admitted. 'Though what I'd really like is a prime New York steak.'

'No big spending in the next few weeks,' Cobb cautioned.

'I'll pass on the burger, start getting my gear together,' Nickerson said.

'Double cheese with bacon with a large order of onion rings sounds like the right thing before packing up,' Kelleher said.

'You three go ahead,' Watson said. 'I want to get the account numbers to you as quickly as possible. Look for them on your phone. I'll be along right after.'

Cobb gazed at him for a long moment, then nodded. 'We'll save you a seat,' he said. 'Outstanding job, Mr. Watson. Absolutely outstanding.'

Chapter 105

'The Governor is going to fire me for gross incompetence,' moaned the state treasury secretary. 'A hundred and sixty million? Are you kidding? That money was just transferred in here from the Franchise Tax Board!'

Mo-bot was white as a sheet. 'How did they do that?'

The ladies from Cal Poly looked at each other as if communicating telepathically. Then Goldberg said, 'The only thing we can come up with is the rest of the metadata on the file. The stuff that came from the state to us.'

'Translate, ladies,' I said, feeling more and more eyes on me. Private had assured them the ten million would be recoverable, which it still was. But a hundred and fifty million had been taken from the state with no tick attached. They were looking for a scapegoat. I was looking very good for the role.

Hollings said, 'The passwords and access codes must have been referenced in the metadata that went along with the original transfer. Someone bright had to have recognized it, copied it, and then used it to go back into the account while it was sitting there, in effect, open.'

'I'm fucked,' Watts said, growing red. 'Fucked!'

He began to slam his fist on his desk. 'They used *my* password. Fucked!'

'Any chance it went through our software?' I asked.

Clarkson shook her head. 'Bypassed us.'

'Are you saying this is the perfect crime?' the sheriff demanded. 'There's no way to track it at all?'

'No, I–' Goldberg began.

'Wait a second,' Hollings called out. 'The ten million. The first ten million. It's moving again.'

You couldn't tell up on the Google Earth map until the computer scientist gave her machine an order and new colored lines appeared. They all looked like they were heading back to the United States, to Southern California. But not quite. The lines converged south of the Mexican border.

'Banco Santander Mexico,' Goldberg said. 'Ensenada.'

'Call that bank,' I said. 'Find out who owns *that* account.'

Special Agent Townsend said, 'I know someone at the consulate here.'

Ten minutes later, she hung up her cell phone. She was grinning.

'The account holder is Edward Gonzalez. Mexican national. Claims to live in Tijuana, but does virtually all of his banking online.'

'They have records of his user name, password, and IP address?' Hollings demanded.

'They did,' Townsend said, handing her a sheet of paper.

The ladies from Cal Poly were joined by Mobot, all of them feeding the information through various tracking systems too esoteric for me to grasp.

Five minutes later, however, Mo-bot threw up her fist and said, 'We've got them! They're in the City of Commerce. That computer is live and on-line from a light-industrial complex east of South Atlantic Boulevard. The place is leased to a company doing business as L.A. Standard Demolition.'

Chapter 106

And suddenly there was not much Private could do.

FBI, LAPD, and L.A. Sheriff's SWAT commanders took control of the situation. If Cobb and his men were as dangerous as Carpenter had described, it was going to take a whole lot of firepower to corral and subdue them.

By eleven that morning, teams were secretly staging in the Hobart Railyard a mile west of the address Mo-bot and the ladies from Cal Poly had given us. FBI snipers had already moved into the area around the building that housed the demolition company. They'd used infrared scopes on the exterior roll-up door and had seen evidence of two men inside.

Were there others? Or had this been a three-man show that with the death of the drag-queen skater was now reduced to two?

Had they flown? Or were they just out somewhere?

Special Agent Townsend, in consultation with

her hostage rescue leader, decided to wait to see if more conspirators returned to the garage, a confined space where they could be surrounded and taken without civilian injury.

It made sense. From the high ground the FBI snipers had already taken up on the roofs, Cobb and his men would be sitting ducks if they tried to resist. It was a waiting game now.

I yawned, realized I'd been up since three thirty. My stomach began to growl. I'd eaten nothing since the beer and popcorn the evening before. Well, if you didn't count five cups of coffee and the stale doughnut I'd salvaged from a plate in the mayor's office. In any case, I was ravenous. Townsend said there was food on the way, but that it would be at least another half hour. She added that I was good to take off in search of a quick meal. Unless something drastic happened, her teams were unlikely to assault the garage in the next couple of hours. She said she'd text me if the situation changed.

I hesitated but then nodded, got the Suburban, and drove toward the east entrance to the railyard, listening to my phone messages. There were several from our overseas offices. Mattie Engel had nailed the embezzler in Berlin, caught him red-handed on tape. *Good news*, I thought as I cut across Telegraph Road onto Atlantic Boulevard and drove north. The light-industrial area was to my immediate west now. A few blocks away, members of No Prisoners were being hunted, and there wasn't a thing I could do to help.

The next phone message was from Peter Knight in London. He'd managed to extricate a very important client from the sex scandal sweeping through Parliament. Our client had nothing to do with it, only a tangential link at best. But she was young and a royal of some note. While the British tabloids are notoriously carnivorous when it comes to political sex scandals, even the whiff of a *royal* political sex scandal would have provoked a feeding frenzy that would likely have tainted her reputation for life.

'Well done, Peter,' I said, leaving a message on his phone at work. Knight was also the man who'd stopped the maniac who'd stalked the summer Olympics in London last year.

I crossed Whittier Boulevard thinking that Knight deserved another pay raise, and so did Mattie Engel. I also wondered if I might be able to convince Knight to transfer to our New York or Los Angeles offices. The widowed father of two was carrying on a long-distance relationship with Hunter Pierce, the American doctor and diver who'd so dramatically won the ten-meter platform gold medal at the...

I passed the Robby Eden Café, the first decent restaurant I'd seen since leaving the railyard. I'd eaten there several times and fondly remembered the 'Bobby's Best' sandwich, a hot pastrami and melted provolone cheese on toasted pumpernickel rye that came with a side order of perfectly crisp onion rings. My stomach growled loudly in approval of a repeat visit, and I parallel parked a block to the north of the strip mall that Bobby's called home.

It was pushing noon by that point, and not surprisingly the café's booths were jammed. But

I spotted an open stool at the counter, and the hostess said by all means. I took a seat, my eyes burning and my ears buzzing from fatigue.

A waitress named Alice came over, and I gave her my order along with a request for a bottom-less cup of coffee. She said it all would be right up and walked away.

I yawned again, pulled out my phone, checked for text messages, found one from Justine alert-ing me to the fact she had a doctor's appoint-ment and would be unavailable between four and five that afternoon. At first I was annoyed. Why did I need to know...?

Wait, was Justine sick? Was that why she'd been acting so strange lately?

A handful of horrible diagnoses tumbled through my brain, and the hunger gnawing in my stomach disappeared, replaced by a sickening feeling. What could she have...?

'Thanks, Alice,' a man said somewhere behind me and well to my left. His voice was hoarse and hinted at a midwestern accent.

'You be in tomorrow, boys?' the waitress asked.

'Nope,' the man said. 'Got a job in Phoenix to take care of.'

For some reason, I glanced across the counter at the mirror on the wall facing me. Three men in green work clothes were paying up in the second-farthest booth by the window. Two of them I could see only from behind, a burly Hispanic fellow and a taller Caucasian with wild red hair.

The third man was quartering to my position, however, offering me a look at the right side of his face and chest. Gaunt, with iron-gray hair, he was busy putting cash on the table and laughing at something the other men had said. I almost looked away, but then one of them, the Latino, began to hum that old Doors tune 'Peace Frog.'

The guy sitting opposite him swung his attention away from the table, looking directly to his right, looking for the waitress, who'd gone into the kitchen.

There was something wrong with the left side of his face. Unnatural. As if he were wearing a skin prosthesis or heavy makeup, or both. I stared into the mirror at the patch on the chest of the green jacket he was wearing: 'N-O-I-T-I-L-O-M-E-D.'

I flipped the letters in my mind. DEMO-LITION.

Chapter 107

My heart began to slam in my chest.

Cobb and two of his cold-blooded killers, whom I now recognized as Hernandez and Kelleher, were not twenty feet from me, eating at the restaurant closest to the garage. Wearing urban camouflage. Hiding in the wide, wide open.

I looked away. For a moment I was unsure what to do. Robby Eden's was crowded and they had to be armed. Any shooting in here could easily kill an innocent bystander, like the young mom and two kids sitting in the booth right behind the killers.

I'd have to wait until they left, call Townsend to warn—

The decision was made for me.

Cobb began to slide from the booth. Hernandez beat him to it, getting to his feet, blocking my view of Cobb for a second and then stepping left to allow Kelleher to exit.

When he did, I could see Cobb clearly. He was staring in the mirror, locked on *my* reflection, and then broke his attention away fast and in alarm. He'd recognized me somehow.

It all went instinctual at that point, no choice of action but one.

I went for the Glock in my shoulder holster, got it in one motion, spinning on the counter stool toward the No Prisoners conspirators, meaning to shout and threaten the killers onto the floor, fingers laced behind their heads.

But Hernandez and Kelleher must have seen the warning in Cobb's eyes. They ducked and twisted toward me, hands clawing for weapons.

My first shot caught Kelleher in the side of the neck, blew him back onto the table. My second shot glanced off Hernandez's rising gun, severed the tritium bead, and entered his skull through the right eye socket.

Ignoring their bodies falling, ignoring the jerky movements of chaos rising all around me, the screams of panic and the muzzle blast ringing in my ears, I felt as if my gun sought Cobb of its own accord, as if I were nothing but a part of the weapon and not its controller at all.

Cobb stood facing me next to the last booth in the restaurant before a hallway. A terrified young family cowered in the booth beside him. He grinned at me. A thin metal ring and post hung from his teeth.

He held grenades.

Two of them.

'Drop the gun, Mr. Morgan,' he said, around the pin that locked the flip trigger on the explosive. 'Or many, many people will die.'

Chapter 108

At a glance I could tell the grenades were not US made, but Russian, old Soviet F1s, the kind the Taliban used to lob at patrols in the high country north of Kandahar when they were really hard up for weapons.

I knew this because fellow pilots liked to talk, and we'd hear from the patrols we were ferrying in and out of enemy terrain. The F1 is distinctive, with a long stainless spoon and a pin safety system exactly like the one dangling from Cobb's teeth. The F1 is also obsolete, no longer manufactured, even back then, which meant that Cobb's explosives were old, probably thirty, maybe forty years old. Another thing I'd learned about F1s in Afghanistan? The older they got, the higher the chance of a malfunction. That was why the Taliban hated using them. They much preferred the M10s we gave them back in the eighties when the Taliban was called the Mujahideen.

So I put the laser sight right in the middle of his

forehead. Cobb spat out the pin, said, 'You shoot me, you take out Mommy here and the two kids and forty other people. So put it down, chopper boy.'

'Not a chance, atrocity boy,' I said.

'These little lemons throw shrapnel for two hundred meters,' Cobb said, yanking the second pin with his teeth, spitting it out. 'Know how I know that?'

'Because you've got the scars to prove it,' I said.

'I do,' Cobb said. 'So I'm not afraid to go this way. I've been here before.'

Cobb looked beyond me. He roared at the terrified patrons and waitstaff. 'Anyone makes a move for their cell phone, and I will lob this right into your lap.'

He began to back up, and I realized there was an emergency exit in the hall behind him. I took a step for every one of his, moving past the dead bodies of his men, oblivious to the crying and terror all around me, intent on keeping the red dot of the laser sight slightly above and between his eyes.

'How do you know who I am?' Cobb asked as he moved fully into the hallway. 'They erased me. They erased all of us.'

'A ghost named Carpenter told us who you were, what you did.'

He recognized that name, turned bitter. 'How'd you find us?'

I stepped into the hall after him, released one hand from the pistol and waved it behind me, telling the patrons to get the hell out of the restaurant. The whole time I kept talking: 'One of your men got greedy, transferred the ten million we were tracking into his personal account in Mexico. We were able to track that account to a computer with an IPO address in the garage where you set up the phony demolition company.'

Cobb's face tightened. 'Fucking Watson. Fucking greedy little—'

'He's dead,' I lied. 'Both your men at the garage are dead. Your two men here are dead. And Johnson's on ice in a morgue locker. You're the sole survivor, Captain Cobb.'

Cobb's back was to the emergency exit now. Behind me I could hear people gathering courage and fleeing. 'Give it up,' I said, wanting his undivided attention. 'You go out that door, you're dying like Butch Cassidy and the Sundance Kid.'

'How's that?' Cobb asked.

'FBI, LAPD, Sheriff's snipers are waiting for you to step outside.'

He hesitated and then grinned at me the way recon scouts used to aboard my helicopter as I landed them in a fire zone, smirking in the face of death.

'I think you're full of shit,' Cobb said. 'There's no one out there. If there was, it wouldn't have been you they sent inside.'

He pressed his butt against the lever. The door clicked, opened two inches. Light poured in. Cobb shifted his head to look outside, opened the door farther. His face was silhouetted now. The laser sight trembled on his temple.

Chapter 109

My finger tightened on the trigger as my mind whirled with thoughts, options, and dire consequences.

If I shot Cobb just as he was going out the door and I was lucky, he'd pitch forward and drop the grenades. What was outside? An alley? A parking lot? I had no idea.

In any case, it had to be better than the bombs going off in here. If I was really lucky, the door would shut behind Cobb before they blew. If I was unlucky, he'd crumple backward at the shot and drop the grenades, and I'd be shredded.

If they went off.

Cobb made the decision for me. He swiveled his head back at me and then made a quick jerking motion with his right hand, suggesting that he was going to throw the grenade at me. He sold the pump fake as well any NFL quarterback. I couldn't help it. I cringed, shrank, just for a moment. But it was enough for the laser sight to slide off his head and for him to shoulder open the door and dart outside.

I fired at the last of him. The round struck the steel door right behind his back. The door started to swing shut. Without thinking, I took four big leaps, heard a clanking noise, and kicked open the door.

The second I saw the Dumpster directly across

the alley from me I knew what Cobb had done and I threw myself sideways and down. The grenade defied time and blew with extraordinary force. I felt it like a giant hand slapping me, boxing my ears, deafening me, and dazing me.

But I wasn't cut. The grenade had landed in the near-empty Dumpster. The heavy-gauge steel walls had contained the explosion, forced the shrapnel upward like a deadly geyser. Knowing that what goes up must eventually come down, I threw my arms over my head and struggled to my feet.

By the time I got oriented and turned, Cobb had exited the alley and was running diagonally across East Sixth Street. He disappeared from view. I felt slightly off-balance as I tried to sprint after him.

Where was Cobb going? Anywhere but here? Or to a car?

I got my answer when I reached the end of the alley and saw him running into a used-car lot on the north side of Sixth. I tried to aim but had no clear shot.

I ran out into traffic. I still couldn't hear much, but then caught over the din in my ears the honking of horns and the screeching of tires as cars tried to avoid hitting me. Were those sirens?

My eyes were scanning back and forth from Cobb to the area around him. I reached the sidewalk just as he vaulted a fence and landed in a second used-car dealership. I crouched and scurried over to Atlantic, hearing shouts as I turned north, really hurrying now.

Ahead of me half a block a cement mixer was

parked, turning, while three laborers who'd been laying new sidewalk were looking toward the car lot. I popped up, saw Cobb pulling a guy from a silver Chrysler convertible with a yellow balloon attached to its antenna. He jumped in and the car started moving.

At first I was sure Cobb was heading for the rear exit back into the alley. But he suddenly turned hard right, heading toward Atlantic.

I ran, screaming at the guys working the cement, 'Get down! He's got a grenade!'

Either they saw my gun or they understood and dove into the wet cement. The others were slower to understand and were still standing there puzzled when I ran past, gun up, just as Cobb nosed the car across the existing sidewalk, looking to pull out onto Atlantic.

I couldn't have been more than ten feet from him when I yelled, 'Cobb!'

He glanced at me, showed little surprise, and side-armed the second grenade at me.

Chapter 110

Time seemed to slow as the grenade bounced and rattled down the sidewalk toward me. Cobb stomped on the gas, shot out onto Atlantic, and sideswiped a commercial van.

But I was focused on that bouncing grenade. An F1 has roughly a four-second fuse. I caught it right-handed at two seconds, twisted, saw my target, and threw it at three seconds.

Once upon a time all I wanted to do was to play football. For years, I'd throw footballs through a tire my father hung from a tree in our backyard, keeping at it for hours on end. Practice more than talent got me onto my college team.

That day practice saved my life.

The grenade dropped into the cement hopper on top of the mixer, dropped into the huge barrel of the mixer itself, and blew with a muffled thud. Wet cement erupted from the hopper and discharge chute and rained down on me as I leaped out into the street.

The van Cobb had sideswiped had crashed into a parked car on the other side of Atlantic. Cobb's convertible was picking up speed, heading back toward Sixth. I went singular again, raised the pistol, and took one shot at his head. I missed and hit the back of the driver's seat.

The convertible went out of control and crashed into a fire hydrant. When I got to the car, LAPD cruisers were coming at me from three directions.

Cobb sat slumped against the driver's-side door. His breathing was labored, he was coughing out a fine pink mist. I couldn't hear anything but the sirens now but knew Cobb was probably making a gurgling sound, sign of a sucking chest wound, a sound that would have ordinarily sent me spinning back to Afghanistan, in country, where anything deadly was possible.

But not that day. I was cold and utterly rooted in reality when I stepped up, gun trained on Cobb's scarred face. As more frothy blood began

332

to appear at his nostrils and lips, he gazed at me with utter bewilderment.

'Chopper pilot?' he whispered. 'How did I...? How did you...?'

He couldn't finish, but I understood. He knew who I was. He knew some of my background. He considered me a stark inferior.

'Everyone gets lucky once in a while,' I said as the patrol cars skidded to a stop. 'Why did you do it, Cobb?'

His expression mutated into derision, as if I were an idiot not to understand why he and his men had killed twenty-one people, blown up the Huntington Beach Pier, extorted the City of Los Angeles, and looted a state revenue account for a hundred and fifty million.

'We needed the money,' he rasped, laughed, hiccupped, and then shuddered when blood poured from his mouth in a torrent, washing away the makeup and exposing that spider's web of scars.

I heard someone shout, 'Drop your weapon!'

I did, still watching Cobb.

He looked at me as he bled out.

I can honestly say there was not a lick of self-pity in his eyes as they lost their light and went dead, dull, and gone.

Chapter 111

Ellen Hayes ran her therapy practice out of an office on a side street near Century City. Justine parked, looked at the building and then the sky, thanking God that Jack had survived his encounter with the No Prisoners conspirators. The news was all over the radio stations. Somehow he'd walked away relatively unscathed. That was what the news reader had said, but a big part of her wondered if that was true, if it could be true.

Mo-bot had called to fill her in on what they weren't reporting yet on the radio. The final two members of the No Prisoners conspiracy had been taken without shots fired, surrounded on all sides by snipers when they tried to flee after learning about the firefight at Robby Eden's Café. Albert Watson and Denton Nickerson were in federal custody. So was Jack, while law enforcement sought to establish exactly what had happened inside the restaurant.

Justine checked her watch. Five minutes to four. For a moment she tried to convince herself to call Ellen Hayes, to tell her about the shoot-out, and that she needed to be with Jack for the moment. They could reschedule.

But the old Justine pushed her out of the car. She couldn't be a friend to Jack or to anybody while she was walking around like this, feeling like this.

Hayes was waiting for her. 'I've been worried since you called yesterday,' the therapist said, leading Justine into her office. 'What's going on?'

Justine sat in a chair, sighed, and said, 'I have this friend, Jack.'

Hayes rolled her eyes as she took another chair. 'We're not doing the friend thing, are we? You said on the phone this was about you.'

'This *is* about me,' Justine said. 'But I wanted to tell you about this friend of mine, Jack, my boss, actually. I told him recently I couldn't understand him because he seems to grow calmer in chaotic situations, unfazed by violence unfolding right in front of him.'

Hayes frowned. 'Okay?'

Justine paused a beat, swallowing against the emotion rising in her throat. 'I found out something about myself recently, Ellen. In many ways I am Jack's opposite. I am unnerved in chaotic situations. I am ... terrified of ... violence ... haunted by it in a way that...'

Hayes sat forward sympathetically. 'Tell me what's haunting you.'

It spilled out of Justine over the next forty minutes: Mexico, her anxiety, her casual liaison with a married man.

'You've described the attack,' Hayes said when she'd finished. 'But not how it made you feel.'

Raw emotion welled up inside Justine. 'I don't know,' she choked. 'I guess I saw how random and violent life becomes in an instant. It almost makes you afraid of the next moment. You know?'

'If you let it,' Hayes said. 'We are the sum of our thoughts. What *you* choose to dwell on will dictate *your* emotions.'

'I know all this.'

'Even experts need to hear it every once in a while,' the therapist replied. 'Let's start by dwelling on the fact that you're alive. A good thing.'

'Yes, but even that carries scars...' Justine stopped, stared into her lap, her shoulders quivering.

'Justine?'

'This has changed me into someone I despise,' Justine sobbed. 'I have to own what I've done. There's no excuse for what I did with Paul.'

Chapter 112

The therapist sat quietly for a moment, then nodded, said, 'You do have to own what you've done, Justine. You also have to own the fact that you went through an extremely traumatic experience and because of that experience acted on a romantic impulse when you didn't have all the facts. Isn't that right?'

'He's married,' Justine said.

'Yes,' Ellen said. 'And *he* has to own that. He wasn't wearing a wedding ring. He asked you out for coffee. He didn't try to stop you in the gym.'

'I was the aggressor.'

'You're saying you were more powerful than Paul was, able to bend his free will so easily?'

Justine blew her nose, tried to smile. 'I am stronger than he is. I can do more pull-ups than he

336

can, anyway.'

'But can you control his will?'

Justine thought about that, then shook her head.

'Good,' the therapist said. 'Now, I don't want you to minimize what happened with Paul. But at the same time, I don't want you to minimize his free will in failing to tell you he was married, and a father.'

Justine said nothing for a moment, but then sniffed and nodded.

'Okay,' Hayes said. 'I think we've made more than a little progress. But our time's up. I have another client coming. Shall we schedule another appointment?'

'But what am I going to do about–'

'What you're going to do about Paul is a subject for our next session. It's enough for today for you to have gotten it off your chest.'

Justine wanted to argue, but sighed, 'You're the therapist.'

Outside, she could hear the din of rush-hour traffic – it was five o'clock. She got to her car, feeling a little less confused, a little lighter, more... Her cell phone rang. She answered.

'Justine?'

'Cynthia?' Justine said, recognizing the voice of the Harlows' personal assistant.

'Can you come to the Warner lot?' Maines asked, agitated. 'Right now?'

'What's wrong?' Justine demanded.

'It's worse,' Maines choked. 'Much worse than you could ever imagine.'

Chapter 113

Cynthia Maines was waiting in a golf cart at the main gate of the Warner lot in the last light of Halloween. Justine hadn't remembered the date until she'd seen the kids dressed in costumes running from house to house.

The Harlows' personal assistant looked shell-shocked. She'd obviously been crying.

'What's happened?' Justine asked, climbing into the passenger seat.

Maines drove on, her shoulders hunched forward as she said, 'I've learned that my life is not what I thought it was. I've learned that my beliefs are suspect. And that my instincts are worthless.' She glanced over at Justine, looking lost. 'How is that possible? How is it possible to spend years of your life with people and not see them?'

'Tell me,' Justine said.

Maines shook her head in disgust. 'It's something that has to be seen.'

They drove past the turn to the Harlow-Quinn bungalow, past the soundstages, and parked not far from the cafeteria. They walked into a nondescript building with a central hallway.

'I got a friend of mine to let me use the screening room,' Maines said, putting a key into a lock and opening a door for Justine.

There were six theater seats inside and a good-sized screen. Justine had no idea what was going

338

on when Maines scooped up an iPad and gave it orders.

Maines's hands were shaking. She seemed to be having trouble picking out the commands.

'I got worried after you left the other day,' Maines said hoarsely. 'About the computers missing at the ranch, and whether the files for *Saigon Falls* had actually been backed up.'

'Okay?' Justine said.

'I couldn't get into Harlow-Quinn to take a look,' Maines said. 'So I contacted the repository in Minneapolis where all the digital files were supposed to be sent. I had to talk to them a couple of times when we were setting this all up before the move to Vietnam, so they knew me. They had no idea I'd been fired and gave me a temporary password that allowed me to review the logs.'

'Was *Saigon Falls* backed up?'

Maines's eyes were glistening with tears. 'That's what makes this all so awful. It was there, backed up around six the day Thom and Jen disappeared. It was a rough edit, but you can already see the genius of it. The story line. The acting. The cinematography. I'd love to show it to you, but it seems so...'

'Seems so what?' Justine said, wondering where this was going.

Maines looked lost again before saying, 'There was another backup made from the ranch the night they disappeared, some sort of emergency thing. Maybe triggered by the power going off and the generator taking over? I don't know. But about a hundred files were sent to the data bank that had never been there before.'

'What were they?'

Maines replied, 'How is it possible that the artists who created *Saigon Falls* also created this?'

She hit RETURN on the smart tablet. The huge LED screen lit, showing the Harlows' master bedroom at the ranch in Ojai.

Chapter 114

A naked woman knelt on the bed, feet and butt facing the hidden cameras. She was whimpering in pain as Thom Harlow crouched over her, naked too, sodomizing her while Jennifer shoved a dildo into her vagina and smacked her ass with her open palm.

'You came back early because you love this,' Jen Harlow said in a taunting tone. 'Admit it, you little bitch whore.'

The woman just kept making soft, painful noises, like a rabbit Justine had once seen with a broken leg.

'Admit it!' Thom roared.

'Turn it off,' Justine said, feeling sickened.

'Wait,' Maines said bitterly. 'It's important.'

Justine tuned out the increasingly lewd and degrading things Jennifer and Thom Harlow were saying to the woman, watched from her peripheral vision until Maines said, 'There.'

Thom Harlow had come off his knees, rolled onto his right side, and pulled the woman down after him, so that the cameras caught the front of her body.

Adelita Gomez winced with every one of Thom's thrusts, but she was not broken. She was looking defiantly at Jennifer, as if she would not allow herself to display any sign of humiliation or submission.

Justine looked away toward Maines, who said in a numb, flat tone, 'I found other films like this with Adelita starring. When they were in Vietnam, they got her drunk. She cried like a baby the first time they took her.'

'Turn it off,' Justine said again, repulsed and filled with sympathy for the nanny. What was she, eighteen?

'Not yet,' Maines said in a dull voice. 'It gets worse.'

'I don't think I–'

'There he is,' said the Harlows' personal assistant before her hand flew to her mouth. She whined, 'Oh, God, the poor little guy.'

In the lowest part of the screen Miguel Harlow had wandered into the room. For a moment he was frozen, watching his adopted parents defile his nanny. Then he turned and ran out of the picture. His parents seemed not to notice him at all.

'This had to have been shot the night the Harlows disappeared,' Justine said, watching Maines. 'Miguel didn't just hear strange noises, he saw this, he got scared, he ran, he tripped and fell, bruised his shins, and–'

'Get off her or I fucking kill you!'

Up on the screen, four men dressed in black and wearing black balaclavas had burst into the Harlows' bedroom, shotguns and pistols trained

341

on the trio.

Thom Harlow stopped his frantic thrusting and squirmed away from Adelita, trying to cover himself, while Jennifer screamed, jumped off the bed, and reached for a robe. One man grabbed the actress's hair and hurled her against the wall. 'You going nowhere you're gonna need that, bitch.'

He picked up the robe, looked away from Adelita, tossed it to her.

'What do you want?' Thom Harlow demanded, now over his initial shock and trying to sound like one of the action heroes he'd played over the years.

The men said nothing.

Adelita Gomez, in Jennifer's robe now, glared at Thom and spat bitterly at him: 'I want justice.'

Chapter 115

'That's really what she said?' Mo-bot asked, appreciation starting to show on her face. '"I want justice"?'

Justine nodded, then shook her head when Sci offered her the bottle of Midleton Very Rare Irish Whiskey. Almost everyone from the L.A. office was in Del Rio's hospital room, called there by me to celebrate the fact that that afternoon, while I was battling No Prisoners, Rick had shown movement in both knees, and feeling as high as his hips.

Sci offered me the bottle. I wanted it, but the nurse who'd examined me earlier in the evening said I'd probably suffered a mild concussion and should lay off the booze for a week or two.

Meanwhile, Emilio Cruz was saying, 'So someone, maybe that son of a bitch Captain Gomez, sent those men to snatch the Harlows?'

'Or maybe Adelita recruited the gunmen,' I offered. 'I mean, she had to be the one who got them past the security. She had to have been the one who cast that shadow we saw behind Jennifer when she was returning from her jog the night they disappeared.'

'How would she know how to disable security at the ranch?' Del Rio asked. 'She'd never been there, right?'

'Not to my knowledge,' Justine agreed. 'But maybe she snooped around in their computers and found a diagram of it. Who knows? But I watched those guys in the black hoods shoot up the Harlows with hypodermic needles and carry them out of the bedroom. The cameras seemed to be feeding directly to the data bank in Minneapolis until someone tore out the cameras and presumably took all the computers in the house.'

'So you think they made a hundred of these films?' Sci said, pouring himself a little whiskey. 'That's seriously twisted. Going back how long?'

Justine looked even more disgusted, said, 'Cynthia made me watch one more of them. It was worse, openly sadistic.' She paused. 'I recognized the victim almost immediately.'

'Who?' I asked.

Justine shook her head as if she couldn't believe it. 'I suspected something the other night at Sanders's, but I couldn't have known the deeper, terrible secret.'

'What are you talking about, Justine?' Mo-bot pressed.

'*Who* are we talking about?' Del Rio asked.

'Anita Fontana,' Justine said. 'The Harlows' housekeeper.'

'No way,' I said, flabbergasted. 'She's been with them, what? Twelve years? Why would she stay? She could have left them, refused to come back when she went home on vacations.'

'I think she had a reason she couldn't stay away,' Justine said, her face a mix of compassion and ruefulness.

'What?' Mo-bot asked.

'Miguel,' Justine said. 'Last night when we were leaving Sanders's house, I happened to be at the perfect angle, watching her hold him in her lap, both of them in profile, the left side of his face, the side not affected by the cleft palate and all the operations he's had.'

'You trying to say she's his mother?' Mo-bot cried in confusion.

'I'm willing to bet on it,' Justine said. 'I just can't bear to confront the poor woman with it. Not tonight.'

'Wait a second,' I said. 'Why would she give her baby to the Harlows?'

'I'm guessing,' Justine allowed. 'But it's not hard to imagine Anita wanting the best possible medical care for her baby, especially when he was born with such a dramatic abnormality, one that required so many operations. You could also imagine Anita, nanny to little Malia and baby Jin, sexual slave to the Harlows, being submissive to their rights and demands.'

'Wait,' Cruz said. 'What rights and demands?'

'Paternal,' Justine said coldly. 'I think Miguel is Thom Harlow's son.'

There was dead silence in the hospital room.

I could see it. Thom Harlow fathers a deformed child while acting out his and Jennifer's perverse desires. The Harlows, with their pristine public image, don't want any of that coming out. It absolutely will not do.

So they offer to 'adopt' Miguel, making it seem to the world as if they're even more saintly than everybody thought. And Anita? She's allowed to work in the house, no longer nanny, no longer sexual slave, but forced to live a lie for the sake of her son.

'Amazing job,' I told Justine, and meant it and more. 'There's only one thing left for us to do now.'

'What's that?' Justine asked with some trepidation in her voice.

'Go back to Guadalajara.'

Chapter 116

Two nights later, around eleven in the evening on November second, Mo-bot pulled a tan Ford van over and parked down the street from La Fuente, a five-star cantina on Pino Suárez about a block from the Ministry of Justice in central Guadalajara.

In the rear of the van, I checked the action of a

Smith & Wesson .45. Pablo Cordova, the big Mexican in the long black duster sitting in the front seat, had provided the weapons as well as the van. Cordova was once a top investigator with the Mexican federal police. Now he runs our Mexico City office and is one of those guys who operate on the right side of the law.

For the most part. When it suits his purposes.

Cordova had met us at the Manzanillo airport about five hours from Guadalajara earlier on the second Day of the Dead, an annual celebration that involves everyone's ancestors and lots of tequila. The streets were filled with revelers wearing skeleton masks.

'Sci?' I said into a Bluetooth device in my ear.

A blare from a mariachi band before Sci replied from inside the cantina. 'They're paying up now.'

'How drunk are they?' Justine asked. She was cradling a Remington pump-action combat shotgun with a halo sight.

'I saw them drink seven rounds with *cerveza* chasers,' Sci said. 'But they probably had one more before I got in here because they're not looking too steady on their feet.'

'Perfect,' I said.

In the front seat, Cordova nodded, said, 'I'm up, Jack?'

'Seems time,' I replied.

Cordova tugged a skeleton mask down over his face, climbed from the van, shut the door, and started down the sidewalk toward the cantina just as Commandant Raoúl Gomez of the Jalisco State Police stumbled from the bar, followed by his drinking companion, Chief Arturo Fox of the

346

Guadalajara Police Department.

'This could get ugly and has big downsides,' I said. 'Last chance to bail.'

'Here we go,' Justine said, tugging down her own skeleton mask.

Mo-bot and I did the same, despite the fact that our plan could backfire and get us thrown into a Mexican prison for a significant stretch of our lives.

'Okay, Cruz,' I said. 'They're heading toward Independence.'

Mo-bot threw the van into gear, came parallel and then abreast of our targets and Pablo Cordova, who was quickly closing on them. Cruz, wearing a skeleton mask and a long black duster like Cordova's, appeared in front of the drunken cops. The right sleeve of the coat was empty. Cruz's right hand lifted, parting the coat, revealing a sawed-off double-barreled shotgun, which he aimed point-blank at the stomachs of Chief Fox and Commandant Gomez. We eased to a stop, blocking any bystanders' view of what was happening. I slid back the door.

'Get in!' Cruz ordered. 'Or die.'

Chapter 117

For an instant I felt sure that the police officers were going to go for their weapons, but then Cordova prodded them from behind with his sawed-off shotgun and growled, 'You want to join your ancestors on the Day of the Dead, *señores?*'

Chief Fox broke first, turning and lurching into the van.

'You're making a big mistake,' Commandant Gomez snarled as he followed his colleague unsteadily inside the van.

'On your stomachs,' Justine said, making her voice hoarse and pointing her gun at them from the shadows.

Cruz climbed in after them, took their weapons, and emptied them of bullets as I slid the door shut. Cordova jumped into the front seat. Mo-bot started driving again.

'Nice easy pace,' Cordova said.

Cruz and I meanwhile threw zip-tie restraints around the men's wrists and ankles. They reeked of tequila and sweat but showed surprisingly little fear when we sat them up.

'You'll spend many years behind bars for this,' said Commandant Gomez in an angry, drunken tone. 'If you're lucky and I don't kill you first.'

Cruz gagged them. I blindfolded them.

No one spoke during the drive. South of Guadalajara, near the town of El Zapote, Mo-bot turned off onto a two-track dirt road and bumped up it for several hundred yards next to a condemned building that we'd scouted earlier in the day. Sci pulled up in a second panel van.

Still wearing the skeleton masks, we got the two men from the van and took them inside what had once been a tool and die operation, using red-lensed flashlights to lead them through the debris that had been left behind. In a high-ceilinged space deep inside the structure, we sat the two

348

men in chairs.

Cordova said, 'We cut off the wristbands. But if you move, we will shoot you with your own guns, *señores*. Nod if you understand.'

Both men bobbed their heads. Cruz used a pocketknife to slit the ties. Sci set glasses of water in front of them as they undid their gags. The second the gags were off, Mo-bot threw a switch and high-intensity spotlights glared down on them.

Chapter 118

'What is this?' Chief Fox demanded, holding up an arm to block the light glaring into his bleary red eyes. 'Who are you? What do you want?'

The state police commandant squinted into the light and demanded angrily, 'Do you have any idea who the fuck we are?'

'*Sí*,' Cruz said. 'We know who you are.'

'No,' Gomez insisted. 'Do you really know *who* we are? And what will happen to you if you don't release us?'

'His brother-in-law is a very powerful man,' Chief Fox said. 'Listen to him, my friends. You don't want to do this. We pay our dues. We are protected.'

'By who?' Cruz asked.

'De la Vega,' Fox said, almost boasting. 'Antonio de la Vega.'

I felt a hand on my forearm, looked over at Cordova. We were behind the spotlights, still wearing our skeleton masks.

He whispered in my ear, 'De la Vega drug cartel. One bad *hombre*. Reclusive. Doesn't like attention.'

'Even better,' I said, leaned over, repeated to Justine what Cordova had just told me, and finished with: 'Have at them.'

Justine brought a chair with her. She sat opposite the men, pulled off her mask.

Commandant Gomez recognized her, first incredulous but then filled with drunken rancor. 'You will never leave Mexico alive.'

'What is your relationship to Adelita Gomez, Commandant?' she asked.

The state police commandant's head retreated toward his shoulders several inches, like a turtle drawing into its shell or a snake about to strike. 'I don't know no one by that name.'

'You don't know Adelita?' Justine said, looking at him with great skepticism. 'The Harlows' nanny? From Guadalajara?'

'No,' Gomez said. 'Never heard of this girl.'

Fox shook his head. 'Guadalajara is a big place.'

I took that as my cue, turned and made a cutting motion across my throat, and saw a red light blink back in the shadows. Cordova took the commandant's pistol from Cruz and ran the mechanism as he stepped out into the light, still wearing the long duster and the skeleton mask.

'Get a better memory, *señores,* or I shoot you,' he said in English. 'Not to kill, but to wound.'

They looked uncertain, but then Gomez started to say, 'I don't–'

Cordova aimed at the front of the commandant's

left boot and fired. Gomez screamed, tried to get up, and fell to the floor, writhing in pain, grabbing at his boot, and screeching in Spanish.

'You're next, Chief,' Cordova promised Fox above Gomez's agony. 'But I think I'll aim higher with you. What do you want? The shin? Or the kneecap?'

The police chief had started to perspire. The sweat ran in rivulets down his face. *'Por favor,'* he began.

'Tell us something about Adelita,' Justine said.

Cordova ran the muzzle of the gun up the police chief's right shin, across his kneecap and thigh, aimed it at his groin.

'You would not do such a thing!' Fox cried in horror.

'Try me,' Cordova said.

Fox looked down at Commandant Gomez, still writhing on the floor, his screams reduced to moans. Fox looked back to Justine. 'I'll tell you what I know.'

Cordova tucked the gun inside the duster. I threw a thumbs-up into the darkness, seeing that red light blink again.

'Tell me about Adelita,' Justine said.

'Adelita,' Chief Fox said. 'She is Raoúl's niece.'

'You son of a fucking pig!' Gomez yelled at him. 'Where is she?'

'Keep your mouth shut or you will die horribly, Arturo,' Gomez grunted.

'What makes you think you're both not going to die horribly?' Cordova said. 'Where is she?'

Commandant Gomez struggled up to his chair. 'Take me to a doctor, maybe I tell you.'

'Where is Adelita Gomez?' Justine demanded again.

Chief Fox glanced at the blood seeping from his friend's boot, said, 'Recovering, I think.'

'From what?' Justine asked.

'Plastic surgery,' Commandant Gomez hissed, his face screwing up in rage. 'After what the Harlows did to her, our beautiful Adelita could not stand the sight of her own beautiful face anymore.'

Chapter 119

'I've seen the films,' Justine said softly. 'A terrible thing to happen to someone you love, Commandant. Where is your niece?'

'I don't know,' Gomez said sullenly.

'I think you do,' Justine pressed. 'I think she is with your brother-in-law. Antonio de la Vega masterminded the abduction of the Harlows. He's the one who had Leona Casa Madre killed.'

The state police commandant said nothing.

'Where are the Harlows?'

'Some things are better *not* known.'

'Where is your brother-in-law, then?' Cordova demanded.

'I have not seen Antonio in ten years,' Gomez said. 'This is the truth.'

'But you can get word to him,' Cordova said. 'I mean, he is your brother-in-law. Your wife and her sister must talk.'

'I need to see a doctor,' Gomez complained.

I removed my mask and stepped into the light, saying, 'We'll take you to one. But then you are getting a message to your brother-in-law. We want the Harlows. We aren't leaving Mexico without them.'

Gomez snorted as if I were mad. 'You think you gringos can just come to Mexico and order a man like Antonio around?'

'Actually, yes, we do,' I said, and then nodded at the darkness beyond the spotlights.

More lights came on, revealing Sci and Mo-bot in their masks, aiming video cameras at Gomez and Fox.

Chapter 120

'What is this?' Chief Fox asked, bewildered.

'Shut up, you idiot!' Commandant Gomez shouted, and then looked angrily at us. 'You can't use anything we just said.'

'Of course we can,' Justine said. 'The Harlow disappearance is the story of the century. Or the decade, anyway. There will be all sorts of people interested in your confession.'

'The footage has already been sent to a safe place in the USA,' I said. 'Which means you are going to go to your brother-in-law, and you are going to get us what we want.'

Gomez looked at us as if we were insane. 'My life does not matter to Antonio. Your life does not matter to Antonio. If he thinks I am to be exposed, he will kill me so I do not talk about him. Eventually he will kill all of you.'

'No, he won't,' Justine said. 'If he kills you, if he kills any of us, the repercussions will be the same. People the world over will know of Antonio de la Vega's role in the Harlow abduction.'

'So what does he care?' Gomez said.

'*Si*,' Chief Fox said. 'Antonio is afraid of nothing.'

'Bullshit, Antonio's a cockroach,' Cordova said. 'And cockroaches don't like light. They need the darkness to thrive.'

'The Harlows are like royalty,' I explained. 'If their hundreds of millions of fans find out Antonio was behind the disappearance, the political pressure will become enormous, the law enforcement pressure will become enormous, beyond anything in your brother-in-law's wildest dreams. No amount of bribery will keep him safe. His cartel, his life, will be over. So will Adelita's.'

'They'll both be torn limb from limb,' Justine said. 'And you along with them, Commandant.'

Gomez said nothing.

'Here's how it's going to work,' I said. 'We will be at the Hilton, waiting. If we don't hear from you in twenty-four hours, the footage of your confession will be uploaded to YouTube and the feeding frenzy will begin for you, for your niece, but especially for Antonio. If you or Antonio or anybody tries to kill us, the same thing will happen. There won't be a dark hole anywhere in the world that any of you can retreat to.'

'And if he complies?' Chief Fox asked.

'His role remains a mystery,' I said. 'And your

354

role remains a mystery. We're only interested in bringing the Harlows to safety.'

The commandant grumbled, 'What makes you think they're alive?'

'If they're not, we want the bodies,' I said.

Chapter 121

Before grabbing Commandant Gomez and Chief Fox, we'd checked into a suite at the Hilton. Mobot and Sci rigged a fiber-optic camera at the suite door and linked it to a secure website that we monitored from sixteen blocks away in a shabby house surrounded by a high wall topped with glass shards.

Cordova had rented the house from an old woman who asked no questions when he told her he'd pay five times the going rate if she left us alone.

In shifts we watched the website. For nearly twenty hours after we dropped Gomez and Chief Fox at a hospital, no one entered the Hilton suite except a maid around eleven a.m. on November third.

She looked around, realized no one had used the place, and left.

'You okay?' Justine asked around eight that evening.

I'd been staring obsessively at the screen while everyone ate burritos Cordova had brought in. 'I wish you and the others would take my offer.'

355

'We're not going to leave you here to deal with de la Vega alone, Jack,' she said. 'Just not happening.'

'This was my idea,' I reminded her. 'And I'm beginning to think it was a bad one, that de la Vega might go Scarface somehow, and that I may have put us all in his crosshairs unnecessarily.'

Justine laid her hand on my shoulder. 'We're all in this together, Jack. We're seeing this through together.'

But with every passing minute I was becoming more and more on edge. Time gives an opponent a chance to come up with a countermove. Had I given them too much time?

'Shit,' Mo-bot said.

'Double shit,' Sci said.

I glanced away from the screen. Sci and Mo-bot looked like they were each about to birth a cow. Mo-bot was gesturing wildly at her computer, where bright-orange numbers were blinking – 2, 3, and 4 – alerting us to the tripping of motion detectors we'd placed inside the wall that surrounded the house and yard.

Someone had found us.

Make that three, maybe four people had found us.

And they had no interest in knocking.

Chapter 122

The drapes were drawn, but Cordova flipped off the lights.

'Get low, spread out,' Jack whispered.

In the dim light shining from the computers Justine saw Cruz, Cordova, and Sci fan in different directions. It seemed surreal to see Kloppenberg carrying one of the sawed-off shotguns. It felt even stranger to be holding the combat shotgun, her finger on the safety.

Justine flashed on the image of Carla and had a moment of uncertainty until Jack eased up beside her, whispered, 'Some people will tell you that the best thing you can do when you're outgunned is to give up and negotiate for your safety. Nothing is further from the truth. If someone attacks you, fight and keep fighting with whatever you've got, especially when you're dealing with people who have probably killed before.'

'Like assassins sent by a drug lord?'

'Exactly,' Jack said, looked at Mo-bot. 'First shot, you upload that video.'

Mo-bot nodded, but Justine could tell she was shaking.

For several minutes there was just the sound of their breathing. Then Justine heard a soft *ding* from Mo-bot's computer. Two new numbers were flashing – 8 and 9, the rear bedroom and the bathroom windows.

They'd already been breached and no one had heard a sound.

Chapter 123

I gestured to Cruz to cover the front door and to Justine to cover the windows in the main room. Then Cordova and I slipped off our shoes, turned on the red flashlights, held them beneath the barrels of our weapons, went back to back, moved sideways over rough wood floors into the hallway, guns and lights aimed in the direction of the doors to the bathroom and the rear bedroom.

As we listened for any sound, any movement, any reason to open fire, I wondered whether this was it, after everything I'd been through, my family's disintegration and disgrace, the helicopter crash, my tortured relationship with my brother. Was I going to die in a squalid house in Guadalajara? Were Justine and the others going to follow me to the grave?

We reached the end of the hallway and split. Cordova stood to the doorknob side of the bedroom door. I did the same with the bathroom door. It took everything in me to stay calm, control my breath and my heart so I could hear.

A shuffle. Right there on the other side of the door.

Sometimes the best defense is surprise. Without thinking I twisted the knob, hurled the door inward, felt it hit something soft and crunchy. I heard a grunt and jumped around into the doorway, trying to get square to shoot.

But I came up short at a trembling sleek black pistol aimed by a street urchin who could not have been more than fourteen. He kept moving his right leg and cringing.

'Get back or I'll kill you,' the kid snarled. 'No matter what my orders are, I'll kill you if you make one more move.'

Chapter 124

At ten past ten that evening, we drove past the wall that surrounded El Panteón de Belén cemetery in Guadalajara.

'Park here,' the boy said, rubbing at his knee where the door had hit him. He said his name was Roberto. He sat in the passenger seat of one of the panel vans, his pistol in his lap, lazily aimed at my waist as I drove.

We'd come to something of a Mexican standoff back there in the house and had negotiated a truce that allowed me to keep my weapon and my life in return for going with him and his two friends. Justine came along too. The others had been forced to remain behind, which didn't sit well with Cordova or Cruz. But that was the deal if we wanted to find out what had happened to the Harlows.

'Where are we going?' I asked.

'Inside,' Roberto said.

'What's in there?' I asked.

'What do you usually find in cemeteries?' he said. 'Get out.'

'Who sent you?' Justine asked from the back, where two other armed teenage street urchins watched her.

'That's right, we're not getting out until you tell us who sent you, Roberto,' I said. 'De la Vega? Gomez? Fox?'

'I do not know these men,' he said, opening his door. 'And I don't know who you are. And I don't care. This is a business transaction. Understand?'

Chapter 125

Justine walked with Jack toward the entrance to the dark cemetery with the armed kids walking behind them. For reasons she wasn't quite sure she could identify, she felt none of the terror she'd endured during the attack inside the jail. Indeed, she felt strangely calm as they passed through an arched wrought-iron gate and she smelled the faint odors of incense and Jack.

What do you usually find in cemeteries?

Roberto clicked on a flashlight and aimed it ahead of them. There were gravestones, monuments, and tombs everywhere. Many were coated in red wax, which Justine guessed came from candles that had burned in the cemetery during the two Days of the Dead.

'This cemetery is haunted,' the boy said.

'By who?' Justine asked.

'Vampire,' Roberto replied. 'He hunted the citizens of Guadalajara two hundred years ago. It started with small animals, dogs and cats, found all over the city drained completely of their blood. Later, human babies were found dead and exsanguinated as well.'

'Exsanguinated?' Jack said.

'That's what I said,' the boy replied.

'Where'd you learn to speak English so well?' Justine asked.

'Arizona,' Roberto said. 'Lived there until my parents died two years ago. Then I came back here. Take a right there onto that path.'

Very smart kid, Justine thought. *How did he come to this?*

Roberto, meanwhile, was going on with his story about the vampire. 'Everyone lived in fear. They stayed indoors after dark and prayed for their lives. A group of citizens who were tired of living in constant terror decided to end the daily nightmare and track down the vampire. They eventually found him and when they did, they drove a wooden stake through his heart.'

'I like it when that happens,' Jack said. 'Reassuring.'

'But this was not over,' the boy replied. 'The morning after they kill the vampire, the townspeople bring his body here. They bring many rocks too and bury the body beneath them, hoping he will never return from the dead.

'You see this big tree here?' Roberto asked, shining his light through a wrought-iron fence that surrounded a massive live oak tree. 'They say the vampire is buried under this tree. They say that if the tree is ever cut down, he will rise from the dead and hunt again.'

Chapter 126

Okay, I admit it, walking in front of an armed hypersmart fourteen-year-old kid through a graveyard haunted by vampires had me more than a little unnerved. I could see scores of ways this could turn out wrong, and more than half of them had me and Justine never going back to Los Angeles again.

'All right, then,' Roberto said. 'Go left.'

I did as he said, walking past mausoleums, aware of the traffic noise and snatches of music coming over the cemetery wall, and something else. Was that crying? Then I lost the sound to a backfiring bus that accelerated away in the neighborhood adjacent to the cemetery.

'Are they here?' Justine asked. 'The Harlows?'

Roberto and the other boys said nothing, and I looked all around at the dark outlines of the crypts, wondering again if the Harlows were dead. A sense of futility swept over me then. What had it all been for? Had we exposed the skeletons in the Harlows' closet only to find where their corpses lay?

Then there they were. Before the flashlight

went out I caught a glimpse of fresh graves in front of me, three of them, two mounded over, one yawning.

'Stop,' Roberto said. 'Do not move.'

Was this it? Would guns be pressed to the backs of our heads, and then a brilliant flash of light and nothing more but a hole in the ground?

'They deserved it,' a woman's voice said. 'They deserved to die.'

My head twisted about, eyes peering into the shadows in the cemetery, and then spotting her on top of a mausoleum about fifteen feet to our left. She wore a black dress and a hood of some kind.

'Adelita?' Justine said.

'Adelita no longer exists,' she replied bitterly 'She has decided to enter a convent, become someone else, try to find some way to believe in God again.'

'By becoming the Harlows' killer?' Justine asked.

Chapter 127

Justine felt sick to her stomach, waiting for Adelita Gomez to reply. She too had seen the graves before the light had gone out.

After all the work, all the risk, the Harlows were dead, killed by the nanny they had defiled. No matter how she felt about the actors' many secret lives, she was shocked by the fact that they were

363

gone. The Harlows were part of so many lives, including Justine's; she'd seen virtually every movie they'd ever made. And now they were gone. Everything about this case suddenly felt cursed somehow.

How would she tell the Harlows' children? What would become of them? Would they be manipulated and led by people like Dave Sanders, Camilla Bronson, and Terry Graves their whole lives? Justine felt overwhelmingly sad at the thought.

Adelita coughed hoarsely. 'I said the Harlows deserved to die. I didn't say they got what they deserved.'

'Wait, they're alive?' Jack said.

'There's only one reason they aren't a meal for pigs,' Adelita said. 'Cynthia Maines sent an e-mail to my old box. She said copies of the tapes had gotten backed up somewhere in Minnesota. She said she would turn them over to the police if I wanted. Or return them to me. And I realized that given what's happened here in Mexico, maybe living would become worse than dying for Jennifer and Thom.'

'Where are they?' Justine asked.

'Tell Cynthia I do not want the tapes made public and I do not want them,' Adelita said flatly. 'I will not come forward to testify against the Harlows in any way. And if you or the Harlows or anyone tries to come after me, my uncle will hunt Jennifer and Thom down like dogs.'

And then Justine heard it, the muffled sound of people crying, and she turned her head away from Adelita, trying to locate its source.

'Listen,' Adelita said. 'They sound like me now.'

'They're in the open grave,' Jack said, moving toward the sound.

Justine made to go after him but glanced back at the top of the mausoleum. Adelita was gone. Justine whipped her head around, realizing that Roberto and the other boys were gone too. She'd never heard any of them move.

In seconds she and Jack were shining their Maglites into the hole. The man and the woman sitting at the bottom of the grave were naked, filthy, and blindfolded, their wrists and hands tied together with rope. Even through the grime Justine saw the festering sores on their skin where they'd been burned repeatedly with what would turn out to be a small, round branding iron.

The woman had four such weeping burns on her face, which was so swollen that for a moment Justine did not recognize her as the most glamorous and famous actress in the world.

Jennifer Harlow cringed from the light, whimpered, and clung to her husband, whose face looked worse than his wife's.

'Mr. and Mrs. Harlow,' Justine said, trying to calm down. 'You're safe now. My name is Justine Smith.'

'We're with Private Investigations Worldwide,' Jack said, jumping down into the hole, taking off his jacket and putting it over Jennifer before he set about removing their blindfolds and untying their bonds. 'We've come to take you home.'

The actors both collapsed into sobbing.

Justine dialed Cordova's number on her cell phone, asked him to order their pilot to fly Private's jet from Manzanillo to Guadalajara, and to hire a discreet doctor willing to fly with them to Los Angeles. She also told Mo-bot to alert Cynthia Maines, David Sanders, Camilla Bronson, and Terry Graves.

'Do people know we're gone?' Jennifer asked weakly when they'd gotten the Harlows out of the grave. 'The fans?'

'It's been international news, Mrs. Harlow,' Jack said.

Jennifer stared off into space at the wonder of that. Thom said, 'What will people think of us now, when they see what's been done to us?'

'I honestly don't know, Mr. Harlow,' Justine replied. 'I'm afraid that's something you and your wife will have to discover for yourselves.'

EPILOGUE

THE SHOW MUST GO ON

Chapter 128

Late on the afternoon of November fifteenth, Justine and I sat in a dive bar not far from the Warner lot in Burbank, sipping beer and watching Bobbie Newton gush some total fabrication crafted by Camilla Bronson about the Harlows' 'daring escape' from the clutches of 'their biggest fan,' an insane obsessed man who'd held them in a doomsday preppers' bunker in the Sonoran desert somewhere south of Tucson.

'There you have it, the most up-to-date scoop on the entire sordid affair,' she said. 'Though we've yet to see Jennifer and Thom appear in public, the FBI and Mexican authorities assure us that they are hunting for the as-yet unnamed madman. Until my next status update, this is your best friend forever, saying follow me on Twitter, #BFFBOBBIENEWTON. I'll be tweeting all updates in the Harlow case as they unfold, round the clock.'

'No mention of Private at all,' Justine said, finishing her beer.

'Just the way we like it,' I said, getting off the stool and laying down a generous tip. 'L.A.'s finest ninjas.'

'What do you think they want to talk to us about?'

'I'd imagine they'll have an entire agenda,' I said.

We drove Justine's car to the Warner gate, where Cynthia Maines was waiting for us. We'd spoken several times since our return from Mexico, but this was the first time we'd seen her in person.

'Have you spoken with them?' Justine asked.

'Not a peep,' the actors' former assistant said. 'I just got a summons from Dave Sanders, just like you.'

We walked to the Harlow-Quinn bungalow, where we found Camilla Bronson waiting for us out front. 'Thank you for coming.'

'Wouldn't have missed this for the world,' I said.

The publicist went stony, barely gave a nod to Cynthia Maines, turned and walked inside. She led the way into Terry Graves's office. Dave Sanders stood by the window. Jennifer and Thom Harlow sat at a conference table. Their faces were still heavily bandaged from the emergency plastic surgery that had taken place immediately upon their arrival in Los Angeles, but their famous eyes inspected us one by one.

'Hello, Cynthia,' Jennifer began in a mumbling voice.

Her former personal assistant shot back, 'If it wasn't for Adelita's wishes, I'd be turning over those tapes right now.'

'Don't even think about that,' Sanders growled. 'Those tapes were and are private property, recordings of activities among legal, consenting adults.'

'Consenting?' Cynthia cried.

Terry Graves shut the door, said, 'Shall we all calm down here? Discuss our differences? Figure

370

out a way to win-win?'

I really wanted to punch the producer right then but kept my cool, said, 'What did you have in mind, Terry?'

Chapter 129

The head of Harlow-Quinn Productions went into full-on schmooze mode.

'Jack, Justine,' Terry Graves said, exuding the deepest sincerity. 'Jennifer and Thom would be saying these things themselves, but they've been advised by their surgeons to speak as little as possible.'

Justine glanced over at the actors, whose eyes locked with hers a second. She saw every shade of pain in them, and fear, but it did not change her opinion of the Harlows. Not one bit.

Terry Graves went on, saying, 'We, all of us at Harlow-Quinn, Jen and Thom, are eternally grateful to you two and to Private for the courageous acts that saved the Harlows and brought them home to us and to their children.'

Justine had to bite her tongue. For the first four hours after their rescue, long into the flight back to Los Angeles, neither Thom nor Jennifer Harlow had mentioned their children. Granted, they'd been doped up on painkillers.

But not once?

Dave Sanders picked up the pitch from the producer. 'We're all grateful for your discretion, as well, in keeping your promise of client privilege regarding what really happened in Mexico.'

'And why,' Camilla Bronson said, glancing nervously at Thom and Jennifer, who'd taken to inspecting the wood grain on the table.

'Yes, well,' Terry Graves said, and coughed. 'But the important thing is that the Harlows are home, and soon they'll finish their masterpiece. And they, we, wanted to thank you.'

Graves reached over and handed Jack an envelope. Jack took it, opened it, looked inside, and then showed it to Justine. A check for five million dollars.

'We trust that's enough for you to ensure bonuses for all the good people at Private who were involved in the rescue,' Sanders said.

'Sure would be,' Jack agreed. 'But Private's not in the business of taking money from starving orphans to save degenerates from a just reward.'

Chapter 130

A silence so complete took the room that I swore I could hear the pounding heartbeats of Jennifer and Thom Harlow.

'What's that supposed to mean?' Camilla Bronson said in an uncharacteristically high-pitched voice.

'It means that this is not going to be the typical Hollywood scandal complete with requisite cover-up,' I said. 'For once, this is going to unwind with justice being served.'

Sanders's face turned almost purple. 'You and Private have a legal obligation to–'

'No, Dave, we don't,' I said calmly. 'That obligation went south the day you fired Private. What we did in Mexico, we did on our own. So we'll be the ones who decide just compensation and penalty.'

'You – you'll get nothing if you expose them,' Camilla Bronson sputtered.

'Everything will be ruined,' Terry Graves said. 'Their careers. Their children. The orphans. Countless others.'

'We see that,' Justine replied.

'And we know justice isn't always just,' I said.

A garbled voice said, 'What's that s'posed to mean?' It was the first thing Thom Harlow had said since we'd arrived.

'It means, Mr. Harlow, that we're not going to tell the police or the FBI about your secret lives and transgressions,' Justine said.

There was a collective sigh.

'But in return, we have specific demands,' I said. 'These are nonnegotiable terms.'

'And these terms are?' Jennifer Harlow said.

Cynthia Maines said, 'Number one: the Harlows will never seek to retaliate against Adelita Gomez in any way.'

'Deal,' Thom Harlow said.

'Number two: the Harlows and Harlow-Quinn Productions will sign over sixty percent of all gross proceeds from *Saigon Falls* to Sharing Hands,' I said.

'Sixty percent of the gross!' Sanders cried. 'Are

373

you mad?'

Jennifer Harlow made a wheezing sound. Her husband started to shake his head, but then Justine said, 'Perfectly sane. In return for our not revealing the extent of your fraudulent use of nonprofit funds for personal and corporate gain, you are going to increase that orphans' endowment tenfold.'

'But the Harlows put their life savings into the film,' Terry Graves protested.

'Tell that to someone who gives a shit, Terry,' I said. 'That's term two. Accept it or suffer the consequences.'

Chapter 131

No one said a thing for a moment, until Camilla Bronson chimed in: 'It could be to your benefit, Jen, Thom. We announce the profit-sharing deal a month before *Saigon Falls* debuts and the public will think you're saints.'

First Jennifer and then Thom Harlow nodded.

'Smart move,' I said. 'Term three: financial control of Sharing Hands, including the endowment fund, will be turned over to an independent and impartial trustee, who will manage it the way it is supposed to be managed. In this case, that trustee will be Cynthia Maines.'

All eyes turned to the Harlows' former personal assistant, who said, 'I feel like I have a lot to make up for.'

Sanders looked ready to argue but said, 'We agree. Anything else?'

'Yes, one last term,' Justine said before staring at Thom Harlow. 'The Harlows will sponsor Anita Fontana, Maria Toro, and Jacinta Feliz for US citizenship. The Harlows will also pay Ms. Fontana a sum of three million–'

'What!' Sanders thundered.

'Three million dollars,' Justine insisted, 'and guarantee that Ms. Fontana will be given un-restricted access to her son, Miguel, and to Malia and Jin. The cook and the maid will receive a million apiece.'

This last exchange caught the Harlow-Quinn team completely off-guard.

'Wait a second,' Camilla Bronson said. 'Miguel's Anita's–?'

'Deal,' Jennifer Harlow said.

'Excellent doing business with you,' I said, standing up and pocketing the check Terry Graves had given me. 'Once Ms. Maines assures me that all the money you siphoned from the orphans' fund has been repaid in full, I'll cash this, use it to fund pro bono work.'

Chapter 132

'That went better than expected,' Justine said when we'd gotten back to her car and were head-ing to the office.

'It did, didn't it?' I said, feeling like we'd

375

actually righted wrongs.

'Karma will still find them, you know,' Justine said. 'The Harlows. What goes around comes around.'

'Let's hope they avoid it for a little while longer,' I replied, then glanced over at her. 'You look happy.'

'Do I?' Justine said. 'Well, I suppose I am.'

'For a while there, I thought you were sick or something.'

I caught a hesitation before Justine said, 'Maybe I was. I'm getting over it.'

She didn't say another word, and I figured that was the way she wanted it. I looked out the window the rest of the drive back, past Disney and Universal and up over Barham Boulevard to Mulholland Drive and down into Hollywood, thinking that there was no real truth in L.A., only the clever stories people choose to tell themselves and to believe.

'Want to go somewhere, get another drink?' I asked Justine when we pulled up in front of Private's offices.

'Doctor's appointment,' Justine said.

I peered at her. 'You okay?'

'Getting close,' she replied.

'You ever want to talk–'

'I know,' she said.

I got out, watched Justine drive away, and suddenly felt exhausted and in need of a vacation.

'Jack Morgan?'

'Yes,' I said, turning to see a stocky bald guy walking toward me, hand reaching inside his jacket.

My mind screamed, *Gun! Carmine's hired someone else to–*

'Consider yourself served and subpoenaed,' the bald guy said, slapping a sheaf of court papers against my chest.

I took them, opened them as he walked away, found that the subpoena had been filed by Shank, Rossi, and Petard – one of the premier criminal-defense firms in the country – in the case of *California v. Thomas Morgan, Jr.*

Chapter 133

Tommy was wasting no time in bringing me into an airing of his dirty stories. The trial date was at least four months away, but he and his high-dollar lawyers – courtesy, no doubt, of one Carmine Noccia – were letting me know in no uncertain terms that they planned to put me on the stand.

I almost went inside. But it was all so depressing that I just started walking. I didn't want to think about my brother, or Carmine, or whoever might have hired the hit man who'd tried to kill me at Justine's. I didn't want to rethink the Harlows and how we'd played them. I didn't even want to think about Del Rio and the fact that he'd be leaving for a more aggressive rehab unit in the morning.

I just wanted to walk until I had a clear mind, and then maybe go look for a little fun, a little peace, a little time away from me. I set off down Sunset Boulevard, a man without a car, a freakish thing in L.A., moving with no particular place to go, hoping for serendipity to–

My phone rang. I stopped, closed my eyes, and prayed it wasn't someone like Sherman Wilkerson, my client who'd discovered the first bodies in the No Prisoners case, telling me about some emergency I had to attend to, clean up.

But it was a number I didn't recognize.

I answered, 'Jack Morgan.'

'I was thinking again that we've had enough dress rehearsals, Jack,' crooned Guin Scott-Evans.

I smiled. 'Were you really?'

'I was,' she said. 'I am.'

'Where are you?'

'My place,' she said. 'I got home yesterday.'

'You have plans tonight?'

'That's why I called. I was hoping *you* might have a plan, Jack.'

My smile broadened. I crammed the subpoena into one of my pockets, feeling serendipity swirling my way, and said, 'Meet me at my place in an hour. I'll be showered, changed, and ready. I'll take you out for a first-class meal, an excellent bottle of wine, and ... well.'

'A grand opening night?' she teased.

'I was thinking *Masterpiece Theatre*.'

'Oooh, I want front-row seats for that performance.'

Chapter 134

Justine drove north on the Pacific Coast Highway. The sun had set. She'd just left her fifth session with her therapist, Ellen Hayes, since returning from Mexico. Things were better. Not perfect. But better. She'd gotten perspective on what had happened to her in the jail cell in Guadalajara, and on the Harlows, especially now that she and Jack had put the screws to them.

But Justine remained unsure of how and where to talk to Paul, and what she should say to him. She hadn't gone to Crossfit once since coming back for fear of running into him. Her therapist had recommended the direct approach in a quiet, neutral venue, like a Starbucks.

Was that the way to go?

I need a man's perspective, Justine thought, and it became clear to her that she had to go to Jack's. And then she realized that subconsciously she'd already been on her way there.

I'll tell him, she decided. *Everything. I'll ask his advice.*

A few minutes later, Justine almost pulled into his driveway but saw two cars she didn't recognize. That wasn't unusual. One of Jack's few vices, besides Midleton Very Rare Irish Whiskey, was a love of high-performance cars.

He bought and traded them all the time.

Justine parked up the street, thought about

379

calling ahead but figured Jack wouldn't be upset if she just knocked on his door. *He said any time I wanted to talk, didn't he?*

Jack's house was set slightly down the bank. A high hedge helped block it from the highway bustle. Justine was almost to the end of that hedge, almost to his driveway, when she heard a door open, footsteps, and a woman laughing.

Jack joined her, saying, 'I swear to God!'

The woman said, 'I like you, Jack Morgan. You are a funny guy.'

Justine knew that voice, that accent, didn't she? Australian?

'And I don't think I know a smarter, funnier, or more beautiful woman,' Jack replied.

Unable to help herself now, Justine peered through the hedge and saw Guin Scott-Evans climbing into the passenger side of a black Mercedes sports car. She looked absolutely stunning.

Justine's stomach fell a long, long way, and she was suddenly hyperaware that she was horribly alone in life. Jack was dating Guin Scott-Evans? When had that started? The memory of what Justine had once had with Jack seemed almost suffocating right then.

'Not sexy?' Guin said, and shut the door of the Mercedes.

'Oh, you've got that sexy thing in spades and aces,' Jack said, climbing into the driver's side, shutting the door, and starting the engine.

For a second there, as Jack was getting into that Mercedes, Justine saw him clearly in the light. He looked genuinely happy, the kind of happy you didn't see often. It was that rare a thing.

Justine spun around and hurried away up the sidewalk as the Mercedes backed out and drove off, heading south. She stood by her car, watched them leave. Jack's taillights blurred into every other taillight in Los Angeles and disappeared.

For a long moment, Justine just stood there, staring off at the point where she'd lost them, telling herself it was good that Jack had someone new and exciting in his life, even though it made her realize she had feelings for Jack that she just couldn't ignore. She couldn't stop herself from hoping that maybe one day, they would make it work. *You've done a lot of things tougher than this, little sister.*

Wiping away a few tears, Justine already felt stronger, as if she'd shouldered the weight and was ready to do the heavy lifting in her life again.

The publishers hope that this book has given you enjoyable reading. Large Print Books are especially designed to be as easy to see and hold as possible. If you wish a complete list of our books please ask at your local library or write directly to:

Magna Large Print Books
Magna House, Long Preston,
Skipton, North Yorkshire.
BD23 4ND

This Large Print Book for the partially sighted, who cannot read normal print, is published under the auspices of

THE ULVERSCROFT FOUNDATION